D0276910

Aberdeenshire Library and Information Service
www.aberdeenshire.gov.uk/libraries
Renewals Hotline 01224 661511

1 5 MAR 20

– 5 APR 2007

1 3 OCT 2014

– 7 JAN 2015

1 8 JUL 2019

1 8 OCT 2019

2 4 AUG 2015

2 1 JAN 2016

HEADQUARTERS

2 8 JAN 2009

3 – MAR 2009

2 9 SEP 2016

2 5 OCT 2011

0 9 AUG 2017

0 8 MAR 2018

HEADQUARTERS

1 4 NOV 2013

1 5 DEC 2018   0 4 APR 2018

2 8 MAY 2019

1 7 JUL 2014

WOLSTENCROFT, David

Contact Zero

A L I S
1710225

Contact Zero

Also by David Wolstencroft

Good News, Bad News

David Wolstencroft

Contact Zero

HODDER &
STOUGHTON

Copyright © 2006 by David Wolstencroft

First published in Great Britain in 2006 by Hodder and Stoughton
A division of Hodder Headline

The right of David Wolstencroft to be identified as the Author
of the Work has been asserted by him in accordance with the
Copyright, Designs and Patents Act 1988.

A Hodder & Stoughton Book

1

All rights reserved. No part of this publication may be reproduced, stored
in a retrieval system, or transmitted, in any form or by any means without
the prior written permission of the publisher, nor be otherwise circulated in
any form of binding or cover other than that in which it is published and
without a similar condition being imposed on the subsequent purchaser.

All characters in this publication are fictitious
or are used fictitiously and are not to be construed
as real. Any other resemblance to real persons, living
or dead, is purely coincidental.

A CIP catalogue record for this title
is available from the British Library

Hardback ISBN 0 340 89558 6
Trade Paperback ISBN 0 340 83165 0

Typeset in FairfieldLH Light by Hewer Text UK Ltd, Edinburgh
Printed and bound by Clays Ltd, St Ives plc

Hodder Headline's policy is to use papers that are natural, renewable
and recyclable products and made from wood grown in sustainable
forests. The logging and manufacturing processes are expected to
conform to the environmental regulations of the country of origin.

Hodder and Stoughton Ltd
A division of Hodder Headline
338 Euston Road
London NW1 3BH

ABERDEENSHIRE LIBRARY AND	
INFORMATION SERVICES	
1710225	
CAW	387739
FT	£10.00
AD	KINP

To the memory of my grandparents

The greatest derangement of the mind is to believe in something because one wishes it to be so.

—Louis Pasteur

Notice

This is a work of fiction. It does, however, balance itself on a platform of fact. Given the potentially sensitive content of some of these 'real' elements, readers should note that the United Kingdom Defence Press and Broadcasting Committee reserves the right to review all content prior to publication.

This is done in the interests of national and/or operational security.

This volume may therefore contain obscured or redacted elements within the body text, in order to conceal any information that breaches their guidelines.

Such editing is beyond the control of the author.

Foreword

The operational information that enabled me to write this book was sourced at great length through an eclectic range of channels. The vast majority came through interviews I conducted with men and women of the Secret Intelligence Service (M16), both current and retired. Those who spoke to me about what has become known as the 'Contact Zero' network did so only on condition of complete anonymity. In the interests of security, these interviews took place in person and were not recorded. Remarkably, a small minority of interviewees displayed a deeply humbling intestinal fortitude and requested that they themselves be named, if only to give credence and legitimacy to a concept that has of late descended into the realm of myth and legend. For personal reasons, as well as for the continuing security and safety of these brave individuals and their families, I have decided not to document their identities here.

At the time of writing, no documents relating to the Contact Zero network or its infrastructure have been declassified. There are no references to its global reach or its extraordinary history. The only available record, until now, has been confined to the world of anecdote. And of course, over the years, it has evolved, quite simply, into a kind of espionage parable – an illustrative fairy tale that amuses SIS analysts and other intelligence personnel when the nights draw in and the rain lashes down on the triple glazing of their offices at Vauxhall Cross.

However, travel up a few floors to the management level of the intelligence apparatus and the rumours persist. Like a vapour, many reach these higher altitudes and condense. Once invisible and airborne, they now take an earthly form, an unsettling reality. When operations fail spectacularly, when the blowback from a botched recruitment strikes hard and careers are jeopardized . . . when calamities such as these occur, the fingers begin to point and the tongues begin to wag. The need to siphon off blame to a third party can be all-consuming. There are many options open to an astute politician. Increasingly, a sprinkling of the Contact Zero myth has become as convenient a scapegoat as any. Entire governments have pointed at shadows in the dark or knives in the attic. An intelligence service that considers itself a city-state by other means has no qualms about doing the same. No one has proved Contact Zero exists, of course. But then, no one has proved it does not. Because as Tacitus tells us in the *Agricola*: 'Rumour is not always wrong.'

D.W.
April 2005

Beginnings

How sweet it is to be alive.

Dripping from the river, he was reborn. A crude mechanical, some might say, a needless contrivance. But the immersion was necessary, vital . . . to take these new steps, a new man must be made. No matter that the old vessel had not yet departed. These were dangerous times when men were moved to extremes. The discussions were ended. Only actions remained. What must be done, must be done. He heaved himself up on to the dockside, the dark night embracing him.

Sweet shall be my name, *he thought.*

Sludge from the boots, mud from the ears, the casting-off of a chrysalis. A shudder held his chest suddenly – partly the cold and filthy water freezing his bones, partly sunburst and flutter, the anticipation in his heart.

This liberation. This second chance to serve.

Behold, here: a modern-day Lazarus.

There were still many miles to go, many steps, many traps and unpickings to test the will. The reinvention was only beginning. But even here, on the cold stone, he felt his heart thunder in his breast and smiled.

To live in freedom. To fight anew.

How sweet it was, how sweet.

Zero

Yes, *these are my breasts.*

Claire hated this street. She hated the crowds, she hated the dirt, the heat, the smell, the oh-so-subtle stares of every human male within a sixty-foot radius. This was Sukhumvit 4, a notoriously chaotic shopping precinct: it was on her way home, it chopped at least twenty minutes off her commute if she jumped off the bus early and cut through . . . but how she loathed running the gauntlet. If anything, the place was getting more crowded. Faces loomed out at her from street stalls, doorways. Yes. Correct. Breasts. They belong to me, Claire Elizabeth Williams, they're here, I've had them for twenty-six years and they're mine. As in: not yours. Now please bugger off and leave me alone. I've had a hard day.

Harder than you could possibly know.

The flight from Chiang Mai had been unsettlingly bumpy. She'd tried to sleep but as usual she'd woken herself up at the start of their descent and helped to land the plane. She never understood quite why she did this, as if by sitting in her window seat and turning her full mental attention to the wings she might somehow lend the pilot a bit of cosmic assistance. She would laugh about it afterwards, of course. But she could never bring herself to turn away from the

5

task. Somewhere inside, she felt the pilot was counting on her.

Once out of the airport, she squeezed on to a local bus, stopped at the office to drop off her notes and was on her way home, looking forward to the peaceful hum of her antiquated air conditioning. But right now, here on the street, the city was infernal. The air rippled up in a heat haze from the pavement, thick with the smell of fried chillies, sewage, molten asphalt. Her auburn hair normally cascaded down over her shoulders, but today Claire had pulled it back tight into a ponytail, in the vain hope it might cool her neck a little. Most days Claire's top looked as if she'd been wearing it in the shower. This, plus the daily eyeballing, was the reason that despite Bangkok's dehumanizing temperatures, Claire always wore her dark denim jacket. The sweat was better than the scrutiny. Claire despised being looked at. Perhaps that was why she'd joined up for this lark in the first place.

Claire walked on.

The crowds, the stares, the heat.

The hissing sound that passed for wolf whistles.

On edge now.

A Mercedes with blacked-out windows had passed her. Force of habit had made her look at the numberplate and she was sure it was the same one that had passed her a week before. Perhaps a seventh sense. Perhaps honest-to-God paranoia. Whatever it was, Claire clicked it up a gear.

Breaking out across the main drag, Claire hopped, skipped and jumped around the gridlock, dodged past a grumbling flotilla of tuk-tuks and lunged into the welcoming gloom of her doorway.

Peace. Quiet. Exhale.

Now, the stairs.

She trod heavily, taking them two at a time, as she ran back the mental videotape of her day. A constructive one, all told. She had spent the last few days up in the north of the country, making acquaintances with people who might one day become something more. She already had a handle on their likes and dislikes, strengths and weaknesses. This was simply groundwork for a more fulfilling friendship. As she neared her landing on the second floor, she allowed herself a tired smile and hoped her footfalls worked out to an even number. For some reason, in Claire's universe, an even number of stairs meant that all would be good with the world. Claire's uncle, a psychiatrist, would have called this an 'overvalued idea'. At the top of her climb, one step was left over. She tried to brush the disappointment from her mind.

As she unlocked the door, she glanced at the fragment of hair she had placed on the doorjamb before she had departed on her trip north two days before. It was in exactly the same position as she had left it.

Good.

The familiar space embraced her. She locked the door behind her. Next, she flung her jacket on the chair, whacked on the air conditioner and, punching the answerphone, made a beeline for the fridge. On the door, a yellow Post-It note proclaimed: *Charge Your Mobile*. She saw it and cringed. She'd forgotten.

Again. Never mind.

Thought that counts.

From the answerphone, a message stuttered into being.

Hi, Greg here – checking you got in all right . . .

The freezer door disgorged a merciful mist of cooling air. Claire closed her eyes and breathed deeply. Goosebumps shivered across her forearms.

Hey, it's Scriphathan, from the mag – you said to call if I bumped into my friend again . . . well, I did . . . just letting you know.

But it wasn't the phone message or the fridge. Something else was making her skin flush, her eyelids snap open. A thought. She closed the fridge quietly and scanned the room. Three windows, sealed carefully from the narrow balcony outside. She checked the talcum powder around the sills. She had sprinkled it as carefully as she could, a uniform layer. Not a single particle had been disturbed.

Hello, love, Mum here. I sent you a birthday package yesterday, but don't open it when it comes. I want you to wait, until the day, so you've got something to open on the actual morning. Hope you're fine . . .

The floorboards creaked in protest as she strode to the desk in the corner. Every drawer, the same status quo – her security measures were all as perfect as the day she'd left them.

And that's what was starting to scare her.

Because this was Thailand – nothing stayed the same. Drops of moisture left footprints in the window dust. Mould grew in bone-dry closets. Cockroaches the size of beagles roamed with impunity. In the space of forty-eight hours the heat and humidity would have started to lift the shards of sellotape from the jambs, the drawer joints . . . The very structure itself moved and listed with the wind, the traffic, the phases of the moon . . .

As her mother's voice burbled on from the answering machine, Claire checked the landing outside her door again. The hair was absolutely fixed in place, to the millimetre. She glanced down the empty hallways and closed the door, locking it with the two deadbolts she'd purchased on her first day in the city. Her eyes darting now to surfaces, furnishings, checking her countermeasures across the room. As she looked, she tugged the blinds down, the thought buzzing in her mind.

Nothing had changed.

Everything was exactly as she'd left it.

Exactly.

Claire moved to the phone, grabbed the portable handset from its dock and moved to the bedroom. *My security has been compromised*. Time to act. She punched the talk button and heard the dial tone purr. She got as far as pressing zero when the dark arms enfolded her.

She felt his warm hair and skin and stale sweat across her neck even as she felt her larynx *crack* . . .

The Red Sea
Fifty miles north of Port Sudan

The ocean surface was shimmering somewhere above him in a vast canopy of white. Shafts of light crept down to his left, visible through gaps in the rusted metal. Chris Dunlop knew his air would not last long. He was at a depth of fifty feet and already there was not enough to last the ascent. He was also bleeding, disorientated and without his mask, the wound in his stomach billowing clouds of red into the water. The vast looming blackness directly above him was a small part of the wreck of the *Blue Belt*, a large cargo ship that had sunk one clear December morning in 1977.

Theoretically Chris should have known better than to explore a site like this. But then his host and diving partner was an avid Jacques Cousteau freak – a man who had visited nearly every wreck in the vicinity. It made sense to get on his good side.

They'd descended quickly to fifty feet, entered the hull

through the gaping holes all along its western flank and explored the cargo bays. The sheer grotesque beauty of rusting vehicles, stacked like fallen dominoes, briefly transported Chris away from his focus.

A moment was all it took.

Under his ribs, a sharp pain made him turn – but by the time he realized he was bleeding, it was too late to move. Three cars descended from above and wedged him against the steel handrails of a catwalk on the hull. His neck was compressed and his head forced down towards his chest by the weight. His mask floated somewhere nearby, torn off by the impact. He flipped backwards over the rails but the cars followed too quickly and his legs became hooked over the edge.

For some strange reason, as his shins slowly scraped away and disintegrated under the jagged weight of metal, Chris began to think of his friends. He wondered whether Claire had ever managed to remember to recharge her mobile. What the hell the Mexicans had made of Lucy. If Jamie was injuring anyone on the Odessa dance floors with those bony elbows of his. He even thought of Ben. They all phased in and out of his mind's eye, car windows winking in the sun.

His last breath, a bubble the size of a football, ascended through a hole in the hull. It caught the attention of a passing sea turtle and stayed intact until breaking with a sigh on the surface.

Mexico City

Lucy woke in a dark space.

There was the smell of oil and sweat. The air shuddering from her in vast, animalistic breaths. Lucy had seen this survival instinct herself once before, close up, as a teenager. She'd been walking up the steep hill behind her mother's house when she heard the squeal of brakes. Looking up, she'd seen a man falling from his bicycle. Over the handlebars, headfirst, slamming on to the road. He'd lain there, unconscious. Almost immediately, his lungs had kicked in, inflating like a balloon, devouring the air and hissing it out with startling ferocity. It was almost beautiful. And here she was now, in this moment for herself, sucking in, out. Her head sparkled with pain. She tried to shout out but her throat was like ground glass. She could hardly manage a whisper.

A deafening noise from below, wind whistling above.

She was in the trunk of a car.

She became aware of her hands behind her. A sharp pain in her shoulder explained why they felt strange. She was tied up. The car she was in was travelling at high speed along a road. The surface was smooth, probably tarmac.

It was unclear how long they'd been travelling but from the pool of sweat she could feel sloshing under the small of her back it was probably in the region of an hour. The last thing Lucy Matthews could remember was drinking in La Conchita, a boisterous tequila bar around the corner from her apartment. She thought of Juan – could he have something to do with this? It was possible. Everything was possible. Just one thing was clear. *Either someone spiked my drink or this is the worst hangover in the history of humanity.*

The car made a few sickening turns and was soon lurching over bumpy ground – a side road now, Lucy estimated. They had left the highway.

Ten minutes or so later by her reckoning, the car stopped. Lucy decided now was a good time to protest. She had her brain back and there was nothing like pain to focus the mind.

Her ankles were tied together but unattached to anything else. Rolling painfully on to her side she aimed a kick at the roof of the trunk. Not even a dent. The thing was solid. She tried again.

All she got for her efforts was pain, more pain.

Outside, a noise. Two car doors opened but only one slammed shut. Footsteps rounded on the back. She braced herself but only the quietest of voices filtered in, muffled. Lucy tried to form an image of the outside in her mind. She thought she heard the rustle of palm trees in the breeze. Her head was full of greens and yellows, the russet brown of the mud.

Then, slowly, the voices trailed off and disappeared.

Silence.

Nothing but the sound of her heart in her head, in her mouth. The shuddering was gone. She was simply hyperventilating now – with the effort, with the terror of the dark. She wondered how much air she had left.

Twenty minutes, she thought. Maybe less.

She tried to control her breathing. Gradually, her lungs calmed down. She gritted her teeth and brought her heart rate back under 160 beats a minute. *Relax, idiot girl. Relax or die.*

Then another noise. The sound of those palms, fronds, foliage, something organic at any rate, as it strafed the sides of the vehicle. The car was moving again.

Yet the engine made no sound.

It took Lucy a moment to work out that someone must have let off the handbrake. This was gravity doing its work. The car was gaining speed. The car was sliding down a hill.

Which meant – *shit shit shit shit* . . .

She aimed both heels at the trunk roof and lashed out. The metal was unforgiving. Again, again, again. The noise deafening her, her agonized screams pinching in her swollen throat, all other sound drowned by the echoes of metal. She ground her teeth and cried with effort. The trunk was not moving.

Again.

A crack of sunlight. Crimson, like the sunset outside. The car was old. The lock began to give. *Yes*. Lucy's heart soared. Still the car accelerated, down, down. Another brutal kick. The crack widened. *Come on!* Her bound legs became a pile-driver of force and ferocity. A blur of effort, sweat, pain. The lip edged open.

A moment of elation.

It was working. The car was slowing down. Levelling. And as it slowed, Lucy heard the sound of water.

Softly at first, then gaining in volume.

Seconds later a torrent of brackish liquid spewed into the trunk void. It came in through the space Lucy had hammered open, through the join by the back seat, through the rusted holes in the spare tyre housing. It only took a few seconds for the trunk to fill with water. Lucy found her voice at last and screamed out loud, kicking again, sucking up the last of the air as the tears rolled down her cheeks.

Peace for a moment.

Then the car began to sink.

As it descended, as Lucy struggled inside, the heavier engine began gently pitching forward, dragging the rest of the car down with it. A graceful arc that swiftly became a somersault. Lucy felt the blood rushing to her head and knew then that the car was upside down.

By the time Lucy had ripped her bloodied hands from their bonds and shoved her head through the tiny opening of the trunk all she could see was a murky expanse of mud and rock coming to meet her.

MEMORANDUM

TO: ALL GRECO ASSOCIATES
FROM: DIRECTOR, GRECO
DIRECT LINE: 0207 233 █████████
SUBJECT: STAGE ONE

SECRET AND STRICTLY PERSONAL – GRECO EYES ONLY

NOTE THIS SECTION IS NOW LIVE. AMEND YOUR
ENCRYPTION CODES ACCORDINGLY. THE FOLLOWING
INDIVIDUALS ARE NOW WITHIN GRECO JURISDICTION:

DE SANTOS, ANDREW
DUNLOP, CHRISTOPHER
FREEMAN, DANIEL
GALLAGHER, JAMES
KENNEDY, JANE
MATTHEWS, LUCY
MUNRO, ALEXANDRA
SINCLAIR, BENJAMIN
TURNER, NATHAN
WILLIAMS, CLAIRE

LEDGER DISTRIBUTION STRICTLY LIMITED. DO NOT
COPY OR CIRCULATE THIS MEMORANDUM UNLESS
AUTHORIZED TO DO SO BY THE DIRECTOR. WITH YOUR
HELP, AND THAT OF YOUR COLLEAGUES, WE CAN
ENSURE A SMOOTH AND SUCCESSFUL PROSECUTION
OF THE OPERATION.

WITH ALL BEST WISHES, YOURS ETC.
KB

14

One

Lima, Peru

They were punching him in the face and all he could think of was Jon Bon Jovi.

As the cartilage of his nose dissolved under a shitstorm of brass knuckle blows, Ben found it impossible to rid his mind of the chorus to 'Livin' on a Prayer'. They were going to kill him and it occurred to him suddenly that, if they succeeded, this was the last song he would ever hear. It made him more determined than ever to keep his heart beating.

Bon Jovi had, of course, not just appeared randomly. His arrival in Ben's life was the culmination of what had been in the first instance, a day like any other.

Woken at six o'clock by the daily domestic dispute from upstairs, Ben had savoured his palindromic breakfast (cigarette, triple espresso, cigarette) and stared himself awake in the bathroom mirror.

Staring back at him was a serious man in his mid-twenties. Laughter lines spread with grim irony at the edge of his eyes. The eyes were blue today. Occasionally, they could be green or even grey. His mother had always said it depended on the weather. Ben was tall, lean and olive-skinned. Together with his thick black hair Ben could have been Argentinian or even Italian perhaps, from the colder corners of the boot. The one thing he did not look was English, which he was, 100 per cent straight down the middle. Not only English, in fact, but *the salt, pepper and mustard of the earth*, as his dad used to have it. Ben had been the first of his family to go to university, or indeed regularly read a broadsheet newspaper. He had been briefly concerned that he didn't look very much like anyone in his family, as both of his parents were blond, squat and fair-skinned. There were endless family gags about Spanish milkmen, which morphed after a while into another nickname – Prince Harry – that his mother found quietly hilarious but his father refused to use for patriotic reasons.

He peered closer into the mirror, clamped a grey hair between his fingernails and drew it gently out from his temple. Unsure what to do with the offending strand, he stuck it on the chin of the garden gnome whose smiling face adorned his toothbrush holder. Vanity was not the reason Ben did this, however. It was simply something Steven Locke would do.

Ben knew Steven very well by now.

He picked up his razor. His stubble was starting to show beard-like pretensions and for a while he actually considered shaving. But the sheer effort of the act turned him off.

Instead, Ben showered to a blast of Radio Panamericana, which seemed to play the same four hectic salsa tracks on a continuous loop. He sang tunelessly along to a familiar Celia Cruz song and only stopped when he could feel the downstairs neighbours hammering on their ceiling with a broom handle.

He pulled on a sweatshirt and sauntered out of the front entrance of La Paz Apartments, his home for the last five months.

On the way to work he stopped off at a house on Avenida Saycuzca. As usual, it was full of the smell of Ernesto's cooking – a trainee chef at a small local eatery around the corner from

16

Ben's offices, Ernesto had a predilection for taking his work home with him that Ben could never understand. His wife Maria came to Ben's office building each morning in the early hours to clean. Since this was often Ben's preferred time to catch up on paperwork, the two quickly became friends. When he was working round the clock, as he often did, or when he was out of town on business – as again he often was – Ben would entrust her with the keys to his own apartment. She would clean for him, water his plants and collect his mail. In return, Maria's wage packet each week would normally include a solid collection of US dollars in amongst the handful of nuevo soles she earned in her day job.

Politely declining their offer of breakfast, Ben left an envelope for Maria to cover the week that he'd be gone. As usual, Maria walked with him to the door and kissed him on the cheek as he left.

Ben reached his office at eight. Avoiding the instant coffee available in the kitchen area, he resolved to subsist on nicotine and adrenaline until lunchtime. He checked the cubicles around his quadrant of the office and was pleased to see only one other early bird – Ana, the young and angular picture editor. Ana and Ben occasionally shared Ben's joints when they worked late. Much of their friendship was based on this quiet enjoyment. She was sharp as a sushi knife and considered working at the magazine to be akin to winning the lottery. Ben knew otherwise, of course, but could never bring himself to enlighten her.

'A very good morning,' said Ben, summoning a smile and remembering how nice she looked in polo necks.

'I suppose you're right,' she smirked back. 'But let's not jump to any conclusions.' Ben's mental filing cabinet alerted him once again to the fact that he hadn't followed up and asked her out yet. In truth, he was still enjoying what amounted to a low-speed chase. In any case, he felt sympathy for her. He didn't want to inflict his dysfunctional relationship skills on her just yet. An ex-girlfriend had once told him: 'The problem with you, Ben? No traction.'

They had lunch at Café Haiti but didn't really talk. Ana quietly admired his scruffy detachment from behind her paper as she finished her *guanábana* juice. She approved of his quiet physicality, his aloofness. In private moments, when he thought no one was watching, his eyes blazed with private dilemmas, hidden conflicts. As she paid the bill, she wondered if she'd ever work out what was going on inside this man – who she had known from the beginning as 'Steven'.

The last thing on Ben's mind, in truth, was clapping eyes on Jon Bon Jovi at Jorge Chavez International Airport. But, four hours later, that's exactly what was happening.

He'd misjudged the traffic and arrived early. He'd been sipping an Inca Cola at the balcony bar when a colossal wave of shrieking echoed up from the concourse below.

Peering over the side, he could see a small man in jeans below, striding with great urgency across the central expanse of the terminal. He was surrounded by a group of minders, pushing his baggage cart towards the VIP area. Two seconds later, from the other side of the building, hundreds of screaming teenagers surged across Ben's field of view, a human tidal wave. Two security guards stepped in front of the crowds like sandbags and somehow managed to prevent a full-square impact, and the wave of teens gradually dissipated into a swirling mass of baseball caps and T-shirts. It occurred to Ben that nearly all of these fans had probably bought bootleg versions of the man's music or just downloaded them illegally.

18

If anything, thought Ben, Bon Jovi should have been running at *them*.

Ben drained the last of the yellow fizz from the soft drink bottle and slung his backpack over his shoulder. His flight to London would board in a couple of hours.

He joined the line that snaked into the international departures area, towards the gates and security check. He was genuinely looking forward to the flight. His mum's fiftieth birthday would be another opportunity to be grilled by relatives, it was true, but a promise was a promise. And anyway, since Dad had left them both last year – thank you, cancer, thank you *very fucking much* – it was more important than ever to make the trip.

At security, he smiled at the officer and watched his carry-on rucksack slide mournfully into the X-ray machine. The red light flashed on.

A guard on the other side beckoned him through. Ben obliged. The machine beeped abruptly at him.

'*Levante sus manos,*' said the officer.

Ben lifted his arms and glanced back. The conveyor belt had stopped and the red light was still on. He wondered why his bag was taking so long. The man in charge of the belt was staring at his computer screen. He inched the belt forward, then backed it up again.

Forward, back. Forward, back.

Come along, thought Ben.

Two male guards were talking now, nodding towards a partition nearby. Ben watched as a female guard stepped out and made a call on her mobile phone. Impatient travellers, spotting the snag in the work flow, began choosing more fluid lines on the other side of the security screen, like supermarket shoppers evaluating queues at the checkout.

Forward, back.

More discussion.

Ben tried to appear nonchalant but from all his years of travelling he could sense trouble before he saw it. He willed himself not to lick his lips. He always licked his lips when he was nervous and he hated himself for doing it.

'Stand over there,' said the guard.

Ben obeyed. The woman with the phone had now been joined by a very different kind of armed guard. Ben wondered if he was with the customs team. But he'd seen the customs gang on the way in. And this gentleman had none of their charm and good looks. Charm School, as Ben now decided to call him, glanced in his direction. He gestured at Ben: *you*, it went, *come here*.

Ben licked his lips.

Somewhere inside his head, Bon Jovi started singing. Ben tried to banish the man from his mind and followed Charm School towards a plain beige door set beside a series of one-way mirrors in the wall.

In the reflection, Ben saw two things that gave him no reassurance. One, his backpack, being carried by a guard towards another door entirely; and, two, a spiralling argument between the customs officers and the new arrivals. The entire exchange had the air of rank-pulling, the Spanish as quiet as it was furious. What Ben managed to excavate was no comfort. *Under whose authority?* spat one guard. *Enough to get you fired*, rejoined the woman with the phone.

Charm School guided Ben through the door. He heard it slam behind him and glanced at his watch. Seven o'clock. The flight left in two hours. A long corridor beckoned. Fluorescent lights buzzed and flickered on a low-slung series of ceiling panels. There were plain offices on either side with the blinds

20

completely drawn. Ben knew he had no reason to be scared. He'd been briefed about these situations, and in these situations, he was sure, he had a safety net. Yet . . . his shirt clung to his back. A lead weight growing in his gut. It was something Charm School had said. Or rather, how he'd said it. On the surface, there was friendliness –

'It's just in here, please.'

But what Ben heard was this:

The spoken word was for Ben a melody – sometimes hidden and in counterpoint; sometimes overt, spot-lit, isolated and beautiful. There were staccatos and drones, arpeggios and diminuendos. And within that music, patterns could appear. In these spoken words Ben could detect the melodies of untruth concealed within a song of sincerity. There were lies inside this music – a final upward glissando, a lilted crescendo that signified false hope. His stomach churned at the thought.

Ben stepped into the room.

It took him a few seconds to realize the bag sitting on top of his open rucksack was almost certainly a wrap of heroin.

Two

Bangkok, Thailand
Two minutes later

C laire was not strong, she knew that. She wasn't tall and
she wasn't heavy. But even as she felt the arms enclosing
her, even as her throat began to bruise and crumple under the
pressure of his grip, she was already tucking in her chin to
preserve airflow and stamping with explosive fury at a place
directly behind her.

She was quick. And it saved her life.

A satisfying crunch travelled up through her leg, the echoes
of an instep splintering under her heel. Sensing the ebb of
muscle twitch in his arm, she at once bit hard into the hairy
forearm and pirouetted on her other foot.

Her leading elbow whipped around and connected with
jawbone. A muted cry from behind and a second later she had
wriggled free. Her attacker was more surprised than hurt but
his shattered instep gave Claire a head start.

She made it to the front door. To her horror, she recalled
she'd already locked herself up for the night. As she fumbled
with the warm metal, the phone started to ring. She heard him
breathing hard across the room behind her as her hands
trembled. But the lock wasn't moving, her fingers weren't
doing what her brain was telling them, and the phone, the

bloody phone . . . she could scream for help, but to answer would be suicide. The spike of anger and adrenaline was pumping around her body so hard she couldn't finesse a simple fucking lock – bolt – latch –

On the stairs now. Keeping it together, eyes on the steps. She wasn't looking back, though she had a strong desire to see his face. She could identify him from a line-up simply by smell if need be. She would never forget that smell as long as she lived.

A procession of schoolchildren yelled and shrieked as Claire burst out on to the main drag, scattering like chickens, those endless probing eyes immediately on her, mouths jabbering at that crazy *farang* woman pushing her way through the crowds to the road. She heard the door moments later, the unsteady footsteps in hot pursuit.

She would cut back through the shopping precinct, she thought. Even with the stares – yes, in fact, the stares would help, the stares would protect her. An address flashed in her mind, one she'd committed to memory just for this kind of moment. She'd cut through there and ring the bell and find a friend.

That was right, wasn't it?

Moving forward. Ignore the pain. Only forward.

She ran across the road and despite herself, despite her training and her focus on procedure, she allowed herself a glance back at her pursuer. A hulking shape, undulating with the injury. She turned back to see the bus driver's screaming face and the sound of the horn.

Another sound soon followed, that of her hip breaking, she thought, cracking clean through, a sharp *snap* as the impact tossed her forward twenty yards, depositing her at the bare feet of a young boy selling lighters. He had a black toenail, she noticed. It was ingrowing.

She was still fully conscious as the crowds gathered. Into the gawping semicircle of faces he came, the shape of a man, a clean black shadow phasing in and out of the sun. He shouted at the others to get back, he was a doctor, he explained, and they should go about their business and give the girl some air.

Claire knew he meant to kill her, right here.

She tried to scramble back, to jump up and run, but her limbs hung uselessly, her spine shattered in three places. She tried to scream, to call out to the numbly staring boy with the lighters to stay, please stay, but her voice box was gone, torn and shredded by the arms that now pressed hard on her windpipe, two fingers taking a pulse, two more and a thumb squeezing what was left of her life from her as he casually looked at his watch as if he were counting the heartbeats inside her.

Which he was, in a way.

The last images imprinted on her brain were all the eyes, still staring, cruel and cold in the shimmering heat. As her eyes rolled back and his arms lifted her up and away, she wondered who'd been trying to call her.

Three

The room had no air conditioning. The walls and ceiling were sweating. Charm School regarded Ben's UK passport as if it were the menu in a Chinese restaurant.

'Mister Steven Locke,' he'd said in a grunting accent that placed him full square in the barrios just outside Lima. *A rough bloke from a rough place*, thought Ben. *Tread carefully*.

'*Sí, señor*,' Ben had smiled. 'Yes, that's my name.'

'From Coventry UK,' continued Charm School.

'Again, that is absolutely correct,' said Ben patiently. 'I was born in Coventry.' The expression on Charm School's face suggested that this was insufficient information. Ben cleared his throat and tried again. 'That's . . . *Coventry*.'

In fact, although Ben, as Steven Locke, could wax eloquent about the Midlands town, he had never actually been there himself. Ben's true home was Bristol, a city of old stone, parks, bridges. The Sinclairs had moved there from London when Ben's father had been laid off from the car plant in Dagenham. They found themselves in a mouldering semi-detached house on the Hartcliffe council estate. This was not the Bristol of the travel brochures. Taxi drivers would not take or pick up passengers within half a mile of the place. Forbidding Eastern

25

Bloc towers rose from a maze-like network of cul-de-sacs, alleyways and overgrown flowerbeds scattered with beer cans and broken glass. Nonetheless, Ben knew no different and made the best he could of it. It was where he climbed his first tree (to impress a girl), drank his first pint (to impress his friends) and lost his virginity (to the sound of Massive Attack, before they were famous). It was where he passed from boyhood to manhood. It was where he saw his older brother murdered, some three feet in front of him.

So overcome was Ben by these memories of home, he barely registered that Charm School had started punching him in the face.

It only took a couple of minutes of this to leave Ben exhaling through his only operational nostril, sniffing out a cherry-red bubble. His nose was pitched at a painful angle, churning out the blood that covered his face, his shirt, the floor.

'I need to speak to my embassy,' said Ben, when Charm School took another breather. 'Please call the Operations Desk. Ask for Jake and quote this reference number: ████████████████████ – I can write it down if you like. Call him and tell him, and he will tell you you are making a mistake.'

Charm School just stared, chest heaving. Ben wondered what the chances were that he would keel over from a coronary before he finished him off.

'I am a UK citizen and have rights; you will be held accountable,' added Ben, his voice now hollowed out with a new nasal quality. It made him sound faintly ridiculous.

Charm School punched him in the temple and his skull chimed like a wineglass. Ben gritted his teeth and tried his hardest to maintain his concentration. He bit his tongue to make the pain go away and a rivulet of blood trickled down his throat. He gagged, coughed, spat and forced a smile.

'I mean,' said Ben, 'why even interrogate me when you've got the evidence you wanted to find just sitting there in a bag? I mean, you put it there for crying out loud—'

Another man now stood in the doorway. He wore his suit as if he had been born inside it and it had expanded, over time, to fit his portly frame. He looked a bit like a Russian doll, the ones that contained seven replicas inside. Charm School approached him nervously. Ben named the new man 'Babushka'. He closed the door and stepped past Ben. His accent wasn't Peruvian. It had a languid, almost drunken tempo to it that suggested he'd spent a good deal of time in Bolivia. He spat at Charm School in guttural Spanish: *'Remember where we are.'* Babushka looked up and caught Ben's flash of linguistic recognition. He turned away and continued to talk in a sinister whisper. This was conspiracy in a minor key.

Bad, thought Ben.

He glanced down to the roll of money he had conspicuously dropped near Charm School – the large denominations were clearly visible and yet also left untouched. Bribery was normally a guaranteed get-out-of-jail-free token. But not here, or now, it would seem.

Very very bad.

Babushka approached him and smiled with his teeth. His eyes, however, remained frozen in contempt. 'We have to transfer you to another location,' he said tonelessly.

'No,' said Ben, shaking his head. 'Before you do anything else, you will call my embassy. I've already tried to explain that to your learned colleague here . . .'

'We will call them,' said Babushka, 'from the other location. Please. I must insist. This way.'

Babushka opened a second door on the other side of the interrogation room. There would be no more negotiation. Ben breathed deep and in this moment of decision he knew his life would change forever. He'd heard about these kinds of situations, where the normal rules — such as they were — simply did not apply. Gone was the appeal to a higher power, to see the manager, to write a letter of complaint, to threaten from a position of superiority. All that was left were the wits, the body and time. At some point very soon he would have to face a choice. To either live or die. Charm School began to escort him to the doorway.

Ben glanced back at the heroin.

Choose Life, he thought.

Four

London, England
Two minutes later

Tremayne moved his mouse three inches to the right, double-clicked, then moved it three inches back towards his work station. He made sure the straight edges of the mouse were parallel with the sides of his keyboard, which in turn followed perfectly the leading edge of his desk. The arrangement gave him much satisfaction.

He stared at the clock and willed the seconds to pass. If anything, the hands began to slow down. Tremayne absorbed this as some form of cosmic judgement and resigned himself to waiting. It was 4 a.m. and another night shift was coming to an end. The air conditioning had been playing up since midnight and now the entire floor smelled faintly of cabbage.

The call finally came and released him from his desk. Tremayne had kept almost entirely under the radar during his inauspicious career as a junior surveillance analyst for the Secret Intelligence Service. Normally, his daily grind was nothing more than the statistical equivalent of ensuring his mouse was parallel with his keyboard.

Intelligence work involved data. There were patterns in data. Simply put, his job was to be sensitive to small changes within those patterns. In his mind it was a little like being a fisherman's friend. Watching the still waters for the smallest signs of a trout.

He had been working on the Greco project for a week now and already the place was a veritable fish farm.

Before this point, Tremayne hadn't really been sure if he even *had* a curiosity gland. But now he knew he did.

What's more, it had been *piqued*.

What was so interesting to him was the fact that after an initial period of grave-like silence from the nascent Peruvian network he'd been assigned to monitor, the floodgates had suddenly opened.

And now this memo from the director of Greco.

He shrugged on the heavy topcoat he was starting to hate and sneezed uncontrollably as the loitering dust rose in a swirl around his face. He smoothed down what remained of his hair, inadvertently brushing flecks of dandruff on to his collar. Outside, the dawn air had a sneer to it and Tremayne winced behind his glasses. His early-onset-pattern baldness felt cool, small beads of sweat now evaporating in the chill. Across the river, he noticed the Houses of Parliament were floodlit still, halogen-white, silhouetted in negative against a dark and indifferent sky. The Daimler glided towards him and near blinded him with full beams. Despite his relatively junior position he'd been allowed to use his family money to fund at least the semblance of an executive perk. He didn't care what anyone else thought. No Tremayne was ever seen dead on public transport. Not even his grandfather, and *he'd* owned a bus company.

Settling in the back seat, he began to ruminate on the lonely afternoon to come. He wondered whether the housekeeper would have left the lights on all night again. He hated returning to emptiness. The afternoon was a void all to itself, particularly in Highgate. It made him miserable and when he was miserable, he ate. Since his father had passed on, there was no one to shout at him when he raided the larder. He needed to lose weight. Loneliness was fattening.

The driver knew better than to engage him in conversation. He'd driven his father before him. The Tremaynes were a family that spent most of its time staring thoughtfully out of windows.

Tremayne rubbed his eyes with his fists and thought about the memo again. 'I wonder,' he said aloud and rapped on the partition, circling his finger. The driver nodded and the Daimler swung around in a lazy U-turn, descending once again through the anonymous gate and into the subterranean parking lot just south of Vauxhall Cross.

Five minutes later Tremayne was back at his desk.

Five

The car was already hitting seventy kilometres per hour, nothing special of course; in Lima it was practically the school run speed for the blond middle-class *Petucho* mothers in their 4Runners, but considering this was a small Datsun Sunny, rusting at every corner, stuck together with spit and sellotape and prayer . . . considering its genetics, it was a major achievement they were moving at all.

Still, Ben needed more, how you say, *velocidad*.

He pressed his foot down a little harder.

Eighty-five. Ninety. The chassis was rattling, protesting in its mother tongue. *Dios mio*, it shouted. *Hijo de puta y tu mama tambien . . .*

Ben's hands were slick on the wheel.

The car was still behind him in the rear-view.

Ben's brain was still frantically piecing together the last few minutes of his life, and it was like trying to catch butterflies with his bare hands. He remembered being frogmarched from the interrogation room, through maintenance passageways and out into a car. He'd been driven half a mile from the airport entrance and pushed out as they rolled to a stop. He must have been knocked out, because, when he came round, there were two vehicles penning him in. Perhaps they thought he was dead. But when Charm School had been foolish enough to take a lazy kick at him, Ben's frenzied attack had taken him by surprise. More surprised was Ben, who until that point had been unaware of how truly brutal he could be when cornered. He presumed Charm School was still bleeding on the tarmac where he'd left him.

The speedometer hit 100.

Ben had reasoned at the time that they meant to kill him. He'd not been able to work out the lineage at all, though. They weren't airport workers, that was clear. They had probably leveraged contacts within the security apparatus to plant the drugs and siphon him off from the main interrogation stream in order to rough him up. Quite why they would bother doing him over on airport premises before taking him out to finish him off was confusing, however.

He let the thought rest. He was travelling at 106 kilometres per hour and had other things to think about.

That rapidly approaching corner, for instance.

Ben threw the vehicle into a handbrake turn.

Babushka, in the pursuing car, followed suit, momentarily amazed at this highly manoeuvrable pile of junk ahead of him. His car ploughed unceremoniously into a stall selling bootleg CDs, then kept its line and came screaming after Ben.

Ben had never believed in fortune or fate. His brother's death had left him with the simple conclusion that there was no design to the chaos, only your choice to roll with it or not. But breaking away from two men in a car park, he'd mouthed a silent prayer when he'd spotted this car, this poor old wreck, alone and unattended on the street. Even for a blood-caked, half-fit, one-nostriled sceptic, he'd been thanking every god in the multiverse for the blessing.

They were going to kill me, he kept repeating to himself.
I had no choice.

110. 120.

Ben found the main Miraflores road. A stretch of motorway with a comforting lack of bends. A recent landslide had left a trail of boulders and small rocks in the oncoming lane. Ben swerved at the last minute to provide his pursuer an unwelcome surprise as he rocketed up behind him. Babushka swerved with him. But his car was longer, broader, newer. Lower. The rock stuck in the broad front axle and, as Ben hit top speed, above the rattling of his own engine he heard what sounded like a rapid-fire staccato of timpani – and, glancing into the mirror, he caught a flash of flame as the pursuing car skirled off the highway and disappeared from view.

Ben ditched the car down a slip road on the next bend and scrambled up the rocky slope from the highway. Several times his handhold slipped, and jagged rocks scraped small channels of skin from his forearms. His breathing was fast, shallow. He realized he'd been working with one nostril ever since Charm School had started his onslaught. Without thought to pain or consequences, Ben grimly *cracked* the cartilage back into place. He reached the top of the slope and his legs crumpled from under him. He lay there for a moment, holding his head in the searing white agony, blinking tears. He could hear sirens approaching.

Rising to his knees, he saw the gloomy maze of a barrio spread before him, a random dilapidation of adobe shacks and houses on the inner-city edge of Lima. The rooftops a patchwork of corrugated iron and gaping tiles.

He shook the dizziness from his brain and walked on.

This was a dangerous move into a dangerous neighbourhood,

he knew, but the blood on his face and the fire in his eyes deflected any unwanted attention. What he needed now more than anything was somewhere to stop and think.

Before that, however, came business.

Ben ran through what he knew about emergency procedures. Escape and evasion. He realized he didn't know much – only what the protocols demanded, what training had taught him. But at that moment Ben knew the chasm between the theory and the hot seat, between the comfort of a Vauxhall Cross seminar room and the cold dark Peruvian dirt underneath his feet.

There were basics, of course. He recalled those, at least.

He needed to speak to Mum.

But not here. He found his strength and began to run. Shacks gave way to apartment buildings, streetlights, neon. His bones ached and his right ankle was swelling badly. He kept to the shadows and eventually located a solitary phone booth that was still vaguely operational.

He punched an international freephone number from memory.

The phone rang – a single, double-handed UK tone.

The voice on the other end was female, warm, reassuring. Motherly.

'Hello?'

'Mum, sorry to call you so early.'

'Don't worry about it, dear, I was just making some tea.'

The prelude over, a new sound appeared – an automated voice that rattled off another number. A randomly selected configuration. Ben listened, memorized and hung up. The phone rang again and Ben punched the same eleven figures in a blur. A pause on the line – an electronic lock turning in an electronic key. Finally the warm voice was back.

'What's the matter?'

'My friends don't love me any more.'

The voice tutted. 'What makes you think that?'

'I'm bleeding. It's their fault.'

'Who was it?'

Ben knew this meant – *where are you?* 'It was a friend of William,' he said. This meant *Lima, Peru*.

And Mum, in the voice that all training suggested was truly the only voice to restart the human heart, a voice suffused with reason and love and security, a voice that told any officer, anywhere, that everything would be all right, cleared her throat and said: 'This is all your fucking fault.'

Ben swallowed. His tonsils were sandpaper. He was seriously dehydrated, he realized.

'Sorry – what?'

'You get yourself into that kind of trouble, you reap the whirlwind. We can't protect you from crimes you choose to commit on your own time. You're a bloody idiot.'

'Now – just – wait a minute here—'

'You're looking at two years in El Sexto prison on a concrete floor before the legal system even deigns to glance at your case. You'd probably die of food poisoning before then anyway. You could try the embassy. I'm sure they might try and do their best. Where are you now, exactly?'

The last words hung in the air. The final syllables a little too solicitous for true concern. This was not the enquiry into his problem. It was a need for confirmation. The itch at the back of Ben's brain was too acute to ignore.

Go, it said. *Hang up.*

He hung up and started to run.

Six

Mexico City

Lucy's wrists were bleeding. She had jammed them in the join between the lip of the trunk and the worn rubber lining to prevent the mechanism closing her up for good as the car approached the bottom. She knew there would still be an air bubble somewhere to the back of the car, but that there was no chance of her getting to it.

From what she could see in the murky blur of her vision, the canal itself was on a camber, sloping away to one side. Lucy summoned her last reserves of energy and threw herself frantically from side to side, calculating correctly that the movement would destabilize the vehicle before it hit the mud. As the car impacted, it was enough to tip the car over – and enough to allow Lucy to use her own body as a shoehorn, forcing the trunk open to torso width.

Her air had run out and she had taken a few monstrous lungfuls of water, but still she pushed her head through the join. Her torso followed after, scraping painfully on the worn lip of the trunk, her legs thrashing and powering her out of the trunk and up towards the surface. She clung to the nettles and weeds at the edge of the canal and vomited until she tasted blood. Certain there was no one watching, she hauled herself fully on to dry land, scanning frantically for a log, a rock, something solid. She found a cinder block. She draped herself gratefully over it, face down; then, making a fist and positioning it just above her navel, she pressed herself down hard over the rough edge of the block, and, with her last ounce of strength, thrust her fists back into her stomach and then up towards her throat, a self-inflicted Heimlich manoeuvre. She tried a second time. A stream of filthy water spewed up the slope and trickled back down towards her feet. Lucy rolled off the block and on to the mud, sucking air into her lungs, suppressing a need to cry her name out in screeching defiance – *I'm still here, you fuckers. I'm still here!*

But there were more important things to conserve her energy for. She staunched her bleeding wrists and ensured only skin, and not vein, had been punctured. Running across the road to raid a washing line, she was nearly impaled on the grille of a pickup truck. She stared into the eyes of the driver. The shock must have saved her – he swerved and drove on without sounding his horn.

Such was life, she mused as she changed into what turned out to be quite a fetching stolen outfit. A memory clicked back into place as she sheltered in a doorway while the strength seeped back into her limbs. Back in La Conchita, in the bar, by the door. Two men talking to Yossi, the barman. He'd been pointing her out. Yossi, to whom she had never confided her real name.

But those men knew. She was sure of it.

It took her two hours to reach her apartment.

She ransacked the place as quickly as she could, changing clothes and patching up the wounds on her arms. She grabbed her backpack and stuffed as much as she could inside – more clothes, a leather jacket, a passport of someone called Alison Owens and, most importantly for now, a small pair of high-powered binoculars.

Seven

Lima, Peru
Miraflores district

As he ran, a memory crept into Ben's mind. He tried to run faster, to shake it off. But the faster he went, the stronger the vision became.

A grey Sunday afternoon at the end of summer. Ben was barely twelve years old and his brother John, aged nineteen, had been working the first shift at the Mercer's Arms, a pub near the leafy city centre. John was getting some money together at the weekends before beginning a two-year commission in the Navy. School was starting again in a week and John had called from the pub and asked Ben to meet him in town. It was their mother's birthday, and John needed Ben's advice on what gift to buy. John often needed Ben's advice. Ben enjoyed his brother's need of him. It was a mutually helpful arrangement.

John had been late, but apologetic. Ben had suggested a nearby department store and struggled briefly to keep up with his brother's powerful strides. John always seemed to be in a hurry, even when he was sitting down.

It only took a second. The two men emerged from a doorway like an avenging shadow and pulled John to the ground. Ben had screamed and seen the serrated edge of a hunting knife.

Before he could draw breath to cry again, the men were gone and John was lying on his side, moaning softly, his stomach torn apart.

He looked like he'd been ripped open by a wild animal.

Ben had tried to run, to scream for help, but he couldn't will himself to leave his brother's side. It was as if he were tied to him by elastic, running to the corner to yell for help but being pulled back to his brother's rag-doll body on the ground. Ben held his brother's head as he died, as John's eyes looked up in complete bafflement that here, on this pavement, in this moment, was the end.

The police were also baffled. There was no connection, no possible reason or motive for the killing. The area was not covered by closed circuit security cameras. There were no witnesses.

In the end, it was put down to a case of mistaken identity, a plausible yet banal truth that proved no comfort to his parents. They had changed that day they buried him, a quantum shift as they tried their best for Ben, but their laughter never sounded the same, their eyes far away, John's grinning face smiling down from the mantelpiece above the electric fire of their hire purchase living room a constant reminder that theirs was a family tainted by tragedy. Some families seemed to glide through happy decades bothered by nothing more than chipped paint on the bannisters, snotty noses, middle-age spread. The Sinclairs felt themselves ambushed and exploited. Life had betrayed their trust through the random violence of the city and nothing would ever be the same again.

From that day on, Ben felt himself draw *in*.

The trick, he discovered, was control. Small decisions, baby steps. The lump in the throat could be dissolved. The tremble of the lip smothered and smoothed, like an experienced gymnast absorbing sudden impact through shock-absorber knees. By controlling his feelings in this way, he felt in charge. Random acts could not touch him again. No matter what life threw in his path, it was his own ability to pilot himself, to tune himself out of pain like an old radio, that kept him safe from harm.

As he grew older, he maintained and improved on this skill to the point where he no longer knew what he truly felt about anything. He could fully remove himself from any situation. He became, in these moments, a mere spectator. Women found him to be the ultimate puzzle. Ben had no answers for them. Over time he realized that many women were drawn to him simply for this potential energy, for the chance of being the first to coax the inner Ben blinking into the open. And, over time, Ben learned to say just enough to give them that impression. To himself, he remained a blank canvas.

Ben slowed down and noticed he'd been so consumed with these thoughts that he'd not paid attention to where he was running. His legs had instinctively taken him towards his apartment block. But fear teased itself into his gut as the familiar building edged closer. This was not a good idea. If the embassy wonks were happy for him to be picked up by the local authorities, they might well have felt cruel enough to leak his details to the police despatch. He remembered the sirens. They'd been coming from the airport. His instinct told him to turn around. But perhaps Mum was wrong. She was based in London in any case. Lima Station would understand.

Ben decided on a temperature reading. He found another phone and fumbled for change. It rang and rang. Ben was about to hang up when an American man answered, shouting above what sounded like live salsa music.

'Lockhart.'

Chase Lockhart was Lima Station's CIA liaison. As well as being a party animal, he was also fabulously indiscreet. Since the centralized bureaucracy wasn't giving him any clues, Ben thought Chase might tip the balance of information in his favour. Chase was so leaky, the joke went around, *you could wash lettuce in him.*

'Chase, it's Steven. Can we meet?'

Although Chase and the British officers he drank with shared many things, Steven Locke's real name was not one of them.

'You got a ten-foot pole?'

'What's going on? What have you heard?'

'Enough,' said Chase.

And the line went dead.

Ben doubled back on himself at a dead run, flicking through his mental address book. Sod the embassy. He decided to listen to his instinct after all. *A safe house*, it said, *is safer*.

There are two kinds of safe houses. Those that are operationally mundane, employed to host a variety of potential agents, sources, informers in a supportive environment. An office, in fact, by another name. Granted it was an office that had been dry-cleaned every day of its existence, placed two or three steps removed from even the vague whiff of the intelligence officer's true identity or business.

Then there are the other kind of safe houses.

The RV houses.

Where the first kind are passive resting places, RV houses are stepping stones across a very dangerous pond. Their express purpose is to give security. Their very existence known only to the officer in place and any superiors in the line of fire.

There were RV houses at regular intervals north, south, east and west of most embassy stations. Here in South America, the rendezvous 'pipe' (as it was known) was really a trumped-up treasure hunt of temporary sanctuaries, all within half a day's drive of each other. One pipe headed north, one south to Chile, and one east, towards Bolivia. Ben knew of three RV houses in Lima that could theoretically support him for a night or two. But that was all. Still, it would be enough. If properly used, they could transport any number of fugitives out of cities, across countries, through borders and, eventually, to safety. Oleg Gordievski, the KGB double agent spirited back to England by MI6, used just such a method as he crossed from Moscow to Finland in 1985. His case officers had been alerted to a series of tip-offs from Russian moles in Washington, Aldrich Ames being the most prominently known source. The Russians had been suspicious about him for months and had recalled him to Moscow. Acting on the confirmation from their sources, they were now preparing to move in and end the embarrassment. Rather than let their man download and die, two SIS officers accompanied him from safe house to safe house until they delivered him to a run-down farmhouse in Suffolk for debriefing. More recently, the same extraction procedure had been used on ███████████. Ben knew all of this because he had studied it in his probation year at MI6. He had been to lectures that outlined some of the most extraordinary feats of espionage through the centuries. The irony usually struck him that, unlike other history lessons, the greatest heroes in these tales generally had the fewest column inches – if indeed they appeared at all.

Most of all, Ben knew that no amount of classroom theory could ever prepare him for what he faced now.

The RV house was halfway down a nearby street. The structure itself, an old laundromat, was accessed from both the road and from the narrow alleyway at the back. Both approaches were potholed and barely lit. Ben skirted the building in ever narrowing circles, never taking his eyes away from the first-floor windows, unshuttered but dark. Unshuttered was good. Unshuttered was: no one's home.

Wasn't it?

He crept into the garage area below. In a shakily constructed carport, several trash cans were overflowing against a wall and a colony of monstrous ants were busying themselves with the contents.

Ben moved one of the garbage cans away from the wall and placed it gently on the concrete.

From somewhere behind him, a noise – controlled breathing. A faint whistle from the nostril. Instinct took over and Ben powered himself to the ground. As the garbage can tumbled over in front of him, Ben heard the explosion of a gunshot. The can helped deflect the round away from Ben's heart and into the cracked concrete floor. Ben craned his neck around and only saw a shadow, to his right – but in that millisecond Ben was already diving left. The second shot scudded against the wall inches from his ankle. Whether they were simply bad shots or the gun had jammed, no more bullets came in Ben's direction. He seized the upper hand and ran into the street, diving over an adjoining wall and tucking shoulder first into a roll as he hit the dirt. The incline was steep over the other side, however, and the fall was heavy and painful. He rolled downhill, losing control of the fall and hitting a tree some thirty feet from a festering canal. Glancing back behind him, Ben heard voices but no more shots. Dogs were barking nearby and as he pulled himself unsteadily to his feet he had to stop himself from throwing up.

He headed northeast, losing himself in more familiar territory. A cooling *garúa* had settled over the city, a light mist that coated his body with tiny dewdrops. The backstreets gave way to broader avenues, late-night revellers, palm trees. Around him soared high-rise apartment blocks, glass and steel, vintage streetlights. Only now did he slow down, relaxing into a confident stroll. This was the only neighbourhood in Lima where a gringo could appear even vaguely nonchalant at night. Tourists were common here and Ben felt the gazes pass over him. Just another drunken traveller after too many pisco sours.

Thoughts foamed through him like a waterfall.

His heart rate eased.

His brain, in return, began to work a little more clearly.

Mum had been pretty adamant about his chances of sanctuary at the embassy. Even Chase Lockhart had dropped him like a rancid tamale. Perhaps both reactions had been a bluff to help smooth things over with the Peruvian authorities. But Ben wasn't going to test those odds right now.

His cover had been burned. That was obvious. And from the looks of things everyone in town knew exactly what he was: Ben Sinclair. Twenty-six. An intelligence officer on his maiden posting for MI6. His job had been simple. Make friends. Follow up on rumours, like the one about a cache of SA-7s, rocket launchers, near the Colombian border. Get closer to the people involved. Ben was, as far as they were all concerned, a drunken travel journalist who liked hanging out with locals and indulging in gossip. It was a bread-and-butter freshman project – legwork, really, establishing contact and creating rapport. But now that legend was incinerated, his contacts, presumably, flapping to each other about how best to eliminate him from their lives. It seemed inconceivable to Ben that he was worth pursuing, but clearly word had spread that he was someone of enough gravity to kill.

Most probationers were seconded to the embassy as low-level secretaries, diplomatic attachés. But Ben was not a conventional part of the SIS apparatus. His was a 'natural cover', Steven Locke esquire. The embassy were aware of him, he even had friends there. But the contact was minimal and very discreet. Yet even Chase Lockhart was running very fast in the opposite direction. *Why?*

Another analysis of his position floated through Ben's mind as he walked.

Because I'm deniable, he thought.

Eight

Vauxhall Cross, London
Five minutes later

Tremayne had been searching the database for names.

Since the inception of the Greco project, the director had insisted on separation. The analysts only worked with the director. And they kept pretty much to themselves, simply getting the info dump of material from the signals centre at GCHQ and sifting through it with their own particular brand of rainbow-tinted spectacles.

Most of the team had done the decent thing and left for the night. But Tremayne had reasoned that some time zones would necessitate unsociable hours.

He located a colleague working on a group in Thailand and knocked on her cubicle door. She looked up at him shyly from under a pair of enormous tinted glasses. Her name was Sara Turnbull, she said with a smile. 'but no "H".' She was indeed responsible for monitoring a group in Thailand, much the same as Tremayne's charge was Peru.

But she, like Tremayne, was concerned. There had been a huge spike in communications in the past week that seemed completely out of character. She was convinced it was a blip. Only, it didn't seem to be going away.

Tremayne thanked her and headed for home.

But he couldn't sleep. He hadn't felt so much excitement since he'd first spotted an original Intercity 125 at Kemble Station in Gloucestershire. Until this moment he'd been worried that the upswing in surveillance traffic had been an anomaly, an error. GCHQ, the UK's monitoring centre, had a history of those, and it made sense to be aware. But Sara's corroboration meant one thing – whatever it was, this was real.

Nine

Lima, Peru
Miraflores district

The office buildings were dark from the street side. But creeping round the back, Ben scaled a drainpipe to the adjacent building and found a clear sightline into the office windows. From here a cluster of streetlights cast a sulphurous glow across an area of floor. He could see two grand doors at the back of the building that opened out on to the haphazard fire escape – it was there that he and Ana had often shared their night-time spliffs. It didn't take him long to find her from his vantage point. She was on the floor.

He recognized the skirt. And the shoes. The hair. She was prone, head twisted at an impossible angle, legs in a perverse running motion that made her look like the classic dead body's chalk outline they used in old detective movies. As Ben's eyes adjusted, he could make out a little more.

It was definitely Ana.

Head back, eyes wide, throat cut.

Ben felt himself step aside from the moment and observe her. He saw there was sadness here, regret. The shape she described on the carpet. The feelings quickly disappeared and as Ben stepped back into the centre of things he remembered there were four other regular employees. Ben had to presume

49

they too had been followed, targeted and killed. If they'd been in the offices, it was too late to warn anyone. And he couldn't risk visiting their apartments in person.

Ben knew he was rapidly running out of options. There was another possibility, of course. But he immediately discounted it. For one, he had no idea where to start. Two, he wasn't that desperate or that mad. Not yet, anyway.

He still had one place left to try.

The Watch Team at the embassy were due to finish work at eleven, but Jake decided to knock off early. It hadn't exactly been an auspicious shift; truth be known it had been a wet fart of a work day, the worst he'd endured in years in fact, and as he shrugged on his overcoat he longed for a hard, cold drink.

His apartment still smelled of burnt eggs, his only meal that day. The corporate digs in San Isidro retained no charm, only odours. He dumped his briefcase, hung up his coat and sought out the bathroom. As usual Jake was too tired to floss his teeth. Checking his watch, he reasoned there was no time for anything but sleep.

He kept the light off, choosing to disrobe ungracefully in the darkness and clamber heavily between the sheets. He breathed a long sigh that stopped abruptly as he saw the shadow of a man standing by the window.

'Hi, Jake.'

Jake shot bolt upright – and stared –

'Who's there?'

The man stepped forward from the corner but was still concealed in shadow. Jake peered into the gloom. It looked a little like Ben Sinclair, but . . .

'Ben?'

Instinctively, Jake leaned over to the bedside table . . .

'Leave the light off.'

Jake, who was used to being snapped at in the office, slowly withdrew and sat up.

'Lights stay off, phone stays where it is,' said Ben. His voice sounded nervous, even to him. His heart was pounding in his mouth. 'All right? It's an emergency.'

Jake nodded, rubbing his face, straining his eyes to see the figure now addressing him. Ben knew Jake from his telephone contacts with the Lima Station, the SIS portion of the embassy building. He saw in Jake one of the few station associates he felt he could trust. Despite this, of course, he soon found out where he lived, just in case he needed a quiet word.

As was the case right now.

That was the one good thing about growing up on the Hartcliffe estate, thought Ben. *You knew how to get into places, if you really needed to.*

Jake cleared his throat. 'Ben. Quick question. What the fuck are you doing?'

'Just tell me what's going on.'

Jake's moral outrage was simmering in the silence.

Ben felt a burning rock in his stomach. The open window blew a breeze that wafted the curtain towards his arm. He pushed it aside. He knew what this quiet semibreve normally meant in conversations.

Scorn rose in Jake as he reached for the phone. 'You're a filthy fucking smuggler,' he rasped. 'You get what you deserve.'

Ben waited for Jake to discover for himself the phone was dead. Jake didn't look at him, but instead threw the covers in the air and made for the door. Ben intercepted him and shoved him back towards the bed. Jake sat on the edge, staring at a spot on the floor. Ben took a step into the light.

A tiny smile crept across Jake's face, as if he was suddenly enjoying the power of knowledge he had over his one-time colleague. 'Don't think you can solve anything by running home. From what I've seen, it will not be pleasant, I promise. Your mum's job's in local government now, right? Supplementing her pension?'

Ben's eyes were stone in the darkness. He knew what this threat meant. And he knew they would have no hesitation in making his mother's life hell if they were feeling vindictive enough. He moved to the closet door and located a silk tie. He gestured to Jake, who knew what was coming next. He raised his arms above him and sighed impassively as Ben tied a double knot around his wrists, attaching him to the iron bedframe.

Ben located Jake's jacket on the back of a chair and removed his mobile phone. Jake rolled his eyes. 'Where will you go?'

Ben shrugged. 'Vegas.'

'Nice,' said Jake, forcing a smile. 'I'll be sure to pass that on. Stay away from roulette. Worst odds.'

Jake lay back on the bed as he heard the jangle of his keys and the front door slam. He'd liked Ben a lot, the few times they'd spoken. It was always a shock when people showed their true colours. As far as he'd been briefed, he was lucky to be alive. He resolved that moment to put in for a transfer back to London.

In the stairwell outside, Ben flew down the emergency stairs three at a time.

His last option had just disappeared.

Ben borrowed a push-bike and covered the two miles between Jake's apartment and Avenida Saycuzca in three minutes.

He knocked once, then twice, then once again. Ernesto arrived at the back window of the house to let him in. In the darkness and humidity of the night, Ben rested against the wall in their bathroom. The future felt blank and unknown. Minutes later, Ernesto came in with essentials: water, bandage, aspirin. Ben nodded in thanks and began patching himself up.

His head swam. He thought of Lucy, up there in Mexico. He had the strangest desire to hear her voice, despite everything that had happened between them, despite everything he knew she would say. She knew how training changed people. She knew the pressures first hand. And truth be told, she was the closest anyone had come to knowing who he was in a very long time.

Ben jolted as Maria knocked sharply on the door and presented him with a shoebox. Ben had asked her to store it behind her sink for a small fee and she'd been happy not to ask any questions. Ben asked her to stay and watch as he opened it. Inside, a solid strongbox. Ben checked the seal – Maria had kept her word, the box had not been touched. Ben removed his only key from a chain around his neck and opened it. Inside, underneath the false bottom, lay a stack of $100 bills. Maria's eyes flashed briefly at the riches. This was a couple of years' wages, staring right at her. Ben broke the news to her that he didn't want her to clean his offices any more. In fact, he didn't want her going anywhere near the place and he wanted her to find another place to live as soon as possible.

He watched the shock and anguish in her eyes for a few seconds – why, he didn't know – before giving her a reassuring smile. He then offered her half of the money. Maria stared at him for a moment and then burst out laughing. But Ben's eyes were cold and serious.

'This is for us?'

'It's yours. I mean it.'

Maria's eyes began to well up. With this money, they could even get a house. Start a family . . . She nodded an emphatic *yes*. Ben smiled, and as he handed it over to her, added the vital caveat:

'But you two also have to do something for me.'

Ten

L ucy had been running on empty for three hours now. She'd run out of water. Worse, she was running out of options.

Her hands were trembling from excess adrenaline as well as her injuries but the binoculars still gave her enough of a view to confirm her suspicions. She framed the upstairs window perfectly in the viewfinder. The woman on the left unclipping her bra was Teresa Gallegos, that pendulum-breasted cocktail waitress at the Hyatt. The man on the right with the back hair and his tongue firmly planted down her throat was Juan Marquez, Lucy's erstwhile boyfriend.

Despite the strange feeling she had churning in her stomach as she watched them, it was the best news she'd had all night. It meant he wasn't at home.

A call to 'Mum' had been less than comforting. An attempt on her life, she'd explained. Almost certain compromise of her cover.

You're in trouble, Mum had said.

I know, she'd replied. But the implication was more wide-ranging than she'd imagined. She decided to let the matter drop and ask what her next move should be.

Go to the embassy, Mum told her.

And she very nearly did.

But Lucy was more of a sceptic than a believer. As well as a practitioner of espionage, she was a student of its history. And she knew full well that natural cover agents were the easiest to drop when the going got knotty. On the way to the embassy buildings on Rio Lerma she noticed a marked increase in local police traffic. Instead of rounding Cuauhtémoc Circle and heading up Paseo de la Reforma on her moped, she kept going on Villalongin and traced a careful route around the corner to avoid the building's security cameras. There were four police cars parked at the front of the building. Considering the local law enforcement officials hated the consular and embassy workers more than their wives, this was not a good sign.

She took a chance and placed a call on her cellphone to a direct line in the cultural attaché's office. She told the man who she was and that she was arriving by taxi at the front gate.

She hung up and waited. Almost immediately she could hear a radio blaring and several police officers running to their cars. A solitary taxi, unfortunate enough to be driving past at that moment, was suddenly broadsided by three cars and penned in. A trap, and a clumsy one at that. Weaving in and out of traffic, Lucy flew back down through the Zona Rosa, tears pricking her eyes.

Thank God for Juan, the cheating bastard, she thought.

Juan's house was in a small gated development. The security at the back was appalling and Lucy had sneaked in and out of there enough times to know how long the man took a leak. He was doing that right now. Lucy used her leather jacket to insure herself against the pointed railings and heaved herself over the barrier. She stepped softly on the parched grass as she found her way to the back door.

His mahogany and leather office was illuminated by the screensaver on his computer monitor, showing Juan himself grinning proudly beside a giant bluefin marlin. Lucy padded towards the filing cabinet in the corner, and as her eyes adjusted to the darkness, she felt a slight twinge of panic. She unlocked the bottom drawer and was relieved to find the key she'd taped there when she first started spending the night on a regular basis. It was a vast leap of trust to keep her stash of money here. But she figured there were so many containers of cash littered around, one more anonymous strongbox wouldn't necessarily look out of place.

Five minutes later, the cash was in her moneybelt and Lucy was driving into the night. Tears came to her once more as she swerved around the green taxis sitting gridlocked even at this late hour. Diesel fumes choked her, horns blared. Despite it all, she had loved this country, adored working here and felt she was truly finding her feet. But she'd tried every escape route she knew, tried everywhere she could call the favours in. No one was helping. This was true exile, the end of everything. She was falling and there was no one here to catch her.

No one except herself. *Unless* . . .

She held the thought and charged the throttle.

Eleven

Urubamba province, Peru

The car pulled away, headlights off, brake lights smashed out, the grumble of tyre on the dirt road Ben's only reference point. Ernesto hadn't waved goodbye, even acknowledged his departure. He'd simply stopped, opened up the trunk and waited until Ben had climbed out.

After twenty-two hours inside, it was a miracle he could still stand. Now, he shivered in the absolute darkness. The Peruvian night was pinpricked with starlight, the ground underneath all shadow and silence.

The air was dangerously thin, impossibly cold. Ice crystals hung in the air, unsure whether to freeze or fall. Gradually, he began to make out the slope of rock beside him. Ben turned and started to climb. He hugged the woollen poncho around him, a parting gift from Maria. He reasoned it might save his life if he found himself too exhausted to keep moving.

A rough path hugged the mountain, spiralling up, past ancient Inca rocks and ruins that the tour guides tended to ignore. He emerged on the crest of a ridge as first light began to glow. A layer of clouds seemed to have been poured into the valley below. Here, above them, the sky was clear and blue-black.

Below lay ruins, spread out in terraces and plateaus.

Rough-hewn rock and smooth stone. Grassy planes, a patch-work of grey and green burned silver by the early light.

This was Machu Picchu. A place of such stupefying beauty and wonder that even the invading Spanish hordes, had they ever reached this prominence, would have dropped their halberds in apology and fled. For all the pillaging that Pizarro and his cronies had unleashed throughout the Inca kingdoms, the Urubamba Valley and beyond, their reach never got here.

For a man looking for a symbolic last-chance saloon, this was a pretty apt choice. During the day, they came from the town of Aguas Calientes to the south, herded on to coaches in their hundreds and thousands, delivered up the crazy hairpins of the access road by blithely irresponsible drivers and disgorged into the theme park entrance that the ancient site had become. Ben had taken this bus once, on his first week in Peru, when a sprained ankle prevented him from walking down alone.

Sitting on the coach, about to leave, he'd noticed a small Peruvian child limbering up nearby. The boy sported the feathery garb of ancient Inca nobility – although he'd gone to town a bit and it was more a Hallowe'en costume than a piece of authentic fashion history. The crowds of blue-rinsed tourists on the bus began to notice him too, especially when the bus moved off and the little man shot over the edge of the precipice ahead of them.

Necks craned to see where he'd gone but it was only as the bus rounded the next terraced turn below that Ben worked it out. A steep and narrow set of stairs cut a gruelling path straight up the mountain. Next to it, a barely visible dirt track. The boy was sprinting down this at speed to meet the coach each time it passed. He was shouting and waving. The tourists strained to hear him. Ben was way ahead of them.

'Is that an Inca word he's saying?' prodded the man in the

University of Alaska Southeast sweatshirt. '*Gubay?* That a blessing of some kind?'

'Goodbye,' said Ben, not looking at him. 'He's saying goodbye.'

When the bus stopped at the bottom of the hill, Ben was the only one to give the boy a tip. It wasn't an entirely philanthropic gesture. Two days later, when Ben returned, the boy had been happy to show him the best place in the Machu Picchu archaeological site to hide a small metal box.

Cigarette smoke and aromatic coffee thermals clogged the air of a cramped internet café in Cuzco, a long and narrow hole in the wall near the Plaza de Armas. Next door they sold cheaply made ponchos and alpaca dolls, hand-woven and hand-stuffed by silent Quechua women in the back room. On the other side, a tour company offered overpriced packages to the Nazca Lines, the ruins of the Sacred Valley and Colca Canyon.

Ben had already purchased a small knapsack from the market, his first stop after catching the single-gauge train back from Aguas Calientes. Locked inside the café's only toilet, he opened the metal box and removed from it a bland and anonymous overcoat. Sewn into the lining at different points were three fresh passports (Canada, Ireland, New Zealand) with accompanying receipts, bank cards and driving licences; a small Swiss army knife with USB memory stick; and six thousand dollars in assorted currencies.

Every spy had a get-out-of-jail-free card somewhere. Ben had always vowed his secret stash would itself have backup. And where better to hide it than the last outpost of the Incas?

He folded the overcoat carefully and placed it inside the knapsack. The metal box he drowned in the cistern.

Returning to a quiet corner seat, he took temporary refuge amongst the muted tip-tap of keys and murmur of conversation. Computer monitors fought for space with ashtrays on the tables.

Ben could feel his lungs settling down after the strains of the previous twenty-four hours, and allowed himself to drink up the Marlboro fumes. The passive nicotine sharpened his wits even as it killed his cells inside. For now, he was happy with the trade-off.

He logged on to his web mail. There was a God. Lucy had left a message for him. Ben said a silent agnostic prayer and checked around him again. The café had broadband, it seemed, but the computers were late Jurassic. It was a little like trying to play Grand Theft Auto on a Texas Instruments calculator. With tortuous languor, the screen managed to refresh itself.

The message was in Lucy's trademark permanent capitals. It was simple and to the point:

BENJYBOY
LOST MY CREDIT CARD. WOULD YOU BELIEVE IT? I
WANT TO GO HOME.
– LXXX

For the uninitiated, a very pedestrian email, one of millions sent from backpacker internet kiosks the world over. For Ben – indeed for anyone from his year's intake at the UK's Secret Intelligence Service – this was something far more imperative, far more serious.

This was an SOS.

He replied with a blank email of his own. As he waited impatiently, he noted a tiny URL at the bottom of Lucy's original message. It was simply a web address, a link to another location on the World Wide Web. Ben clicked on it. It took him to a daily newswire service page that slowly loaded in front of his eyes.

THAI NEWS DAILY 1041 GMT. Hua Hin Province. BACKPACKER/REPORTER BODY FOUND. Hua Hin police are looking for answers after farm workers found a dead body Monday afternoon. According to authorities, workers on a road improvement project saw a woman floating in reeds as they drained marshland in Hat Wanakon National Park, 22 km south of Prachuap Khiri Khan. The woman was identified later as Sandra Mitchell, 26, of Preston, United Kingdom. Homicide investigators are working to determine exactly what happened to the victim. An autopsy is scheduled Tuesday by the Chief Medical Examiner.

Ben stared at the screen for a few seconds, trying to work out why Lucy would send him this piece of information.

He was about to log off when he saw another missive from Lucy in his inbox. A reply.

She was online right now.

His neighbour had been reading over his shoulder. He had dreadlocks and a multicoloured pair of pyjamas as trousers. Ben turned to him and stared unsettlingly. The neighbour raised a bushy eyebrow and returned his gaze to the *Sydney Morning Echo* website. Ben kept one eye on him as he returned to his web mail in front of him.

Ben checked the new email.

It was short and to the point.

MAKE LOVE TO ME, it said.

Ben tapped 5 *MINS* and signed off. He had to find another console. His nosy neighbour was making him nervous. He swiftly relocated to a computer with no one in snooping range and signed on.

The World Wide Web offers many nooks and crannies where anonymous encounters are the norm. An adults only chatroom is the perfect environment for consenting adults to interact in any way they like. For the recent graduates of the Secret Intelligence Service Probation Programme, it was a place to discuss matters of high security and espionage case-work in a forum known as 'Pacific Northwest GangBang'. Ben logged on under his pre-agreed screen-name of CuriousGuy. Every so often, Ben knew, the likes of Lucy, Chris, Jamie and others would meet here at midnight GMT for a catch-up and gossip. Sometimes, Ben would join in, although these days only Jamie seemed to want to chat. Now Lucy was back on stream. The whole exchange had the feeling of an illicit affair about to go wrong. And there she was, waiting for him, as 'miniskirt'.

There were a few other people in the virtual chatroom. One of them, Marilyn123, and another, JHolmes007, were legiti-mate punters, engaged in a furious and clearly humourless bout of cyber sex.

YOU SEEM NICE, typed Ben.

LET'S GO, replied the virtual Lucy.

SIT ON MY BIG FAT CLOCK, blurted JHolmes007, clearly too overcome by carnal desire to spellcheck. But by that time Lucy and Ben were in a private chatroom space – and the pretence was quickly dropped.

R U OK? typed Ben.

NO I'M NOT, came the reply. Then: *DID YOU READ WHAT I SENT YOU?*

DIDN'T UNDERSTAND IT, typed Ben.

The screen was blank for a moment.

DID YOU READ THE F^&KING ARTICLE OR NOT?

Ben was getting impatient now. Lucy often did this, took about an hour to get around to the point she could have communicated in a quick sentence. Or, as in this case, simply ignored everyone else's agendas apart from her own. She was clearly bee in the bonnet about this. He hammered on the keys. She'd be sorry when she found out what had happened to him.

YES. I READ IT. SO WHAT?

He watched the screen intently as a reply scrolled almost immediately: *I FOUND IT ON THE NEWSWIRES WAITING FOR SOMEONE TO TURN UP.*

GOOD FOR YOU, typed Ben.

He almost heard the computer sigh as another riposte flashed up: *LOOK AT THE NAME.*

Ben clicked back to his web mail and re-read the piece. The dial-up connection was excruciatingly slow. Just when the screen began to scroll down, it tried to refresh itself. Ben gritted his teeth and breathed deep. *The woman was identified later as Sandra Mitchell, 26, of Preston, United Kingdom.* He didn't know anyone called Sandra Mitchell from Preston. Or Thailand, for that matter. Actually, not entirely true. The only person he knew in Thailand was –

The truth hit him like a sledgehammer.

He remembered a rainy night in a pub in South London. Their first assignments pending, the ten classmates had retired to the bare floorboards and strip lighting to recover from the previous weekend's training exercise. In the middle of the mayhem, more out of defiance towards each other than in a spirit of sharing, they had all drunkenly revealed their legends, the cover stories they were using to set up their stalls abroad. These were only preliminary identities, the travel documents, the initial base camps for their own highly secret operations. Claire had cosied up to him by the fruit machine and whispered her codename to him. Her breath had smelled of pineapple juice. Afterwards, she had laughed. Like Ben she'd just been through the chaos of the selection weekend. The laughter was more from post-traumatic mania than any real sense of joy.

Claire Williams's legend was Sandra Mitchell.

Which meant . . .

IT'S CLAIRE.

Ben was still processing the ugly, brutal reality of this sentence when another message popped up from Lucy: *I WAS CLOSE TO BEING A HEADLINE MYSELF TONIGHT.*

Ben rocked on his chair and checked no one was eavesdropping this time. His typing was a blur now. *WHAT HAPPENED?*

LONG STORY, replied Lucy.

Ben sighed and typed: *SAME HERE.*

A small pause. Then: *DO NOT FUCK ABOUT ON THIS BENJY I AM SERIOUS.*

SO AM I, he wrote back, irritated.

A pause. *DID YOU TRY GOING HOME?* She meant the embassy.

YES. I WAS MADE TO FEEL VERY UNWELCOME.

The cursor paused and then flourished again: *WE HAVE TO MEET.*

YOU'RE MILES AWAY, wrote Ben.

The cursor froze and for a minute Ben thought that Lucy was gone for good. But just as he began to lose faith, the words unfurled awkwardly across the screen.

COME FIND ME. I'LL LEAVE WORD. USUAL PLACE.

Ben licked his lips as he typed: *TOO RISKY. WHY NOT WAIT?*

Again the reply took a moment to appear on the screen. But when it arrived, it was emphatic.

BECAUSE THE SKY IS FALLING.

Twelve

Cuzco, Peru

The head of security had called them all 'lilywhites'. The branding had stuck. Some of those lilywhites he'd got to know well. Some he'd wished urinary tract infections upon. All of them were indelibly etched on his mind, runes on a stone. Even after a poisonous end to their year, it was their own special bond. Friends or enemies, they all shared the same watermark.

How strange memory was. Here, in this small internet café off the Plaza de Armas, Ben was assaulted by recollections of a night's drinking in London. The younger crowd traditionally headed north, over the bridge and met up with friends from Westminster at the Red Lion. But Ben's year was different. They were barflies of a different breed who relished the ratty boozers this side of town. The Green Man was a smoke-darkened strip-lit watering hole that smelt continually of damp carpet and chips. That night, it fitted their sombre, hard-edged mood perfectly.

Yet no one had very much to say to anyone. The events of the final assessment weekend a few days previously had forced everyone into themselves. The atmosphere had been heavy with sadness, a simmering and bitter rage from nearly everyone involved, travelling between them like bursts of static from a Van de Graaff generator.

It was a miracle anyone was there at all, but, Ben thought ruefully at the time, they didn't really have anywhere else to go and blow off steam before the enquiry. At least, there was no one else who'd really understand. He'd nodded to Andy de Santos but Andy was already drunk and horny, trying to get an even drunker and solipsistic Claire to kiss him by the jukebox.

Ben walked through to the pool playing area. A ziggurat of ten pence pieces had been stacked precariously on the side of the table. 'In for the night?' he'd said as he laid the pints out on a corner table. Jamie and Chris were mid-game.

Jamie had shrugged. 'Depends how quickly he loses,' he said, and smiled politely at Chris as he aimed a shot on the beer-stained baize.

They were an odd pairing – Chris was small and stocky, like a miniature prop forward. Jamie was impossibly tall and thin, all bones and sinew, and with the cue in his hand he looked a little as if he'd been constructed from Meccano, thin steel girders, nuts and bolts, as if Stephenson might have used him as an early prototype for the steam engine. Ball after ball clacked into the pockets. It was hard to believe that inside this gangly man beat the heart of an extreme athlete. Jamie Gallagher was the archetypal upper-crust action hero – climber, fell runner, skier. Off piste once near Verbier, he had blundered into a snowstorm and ploughed headfirst into a badly damaged snow fence. The top three feet of a broken fence-post had pierced him just below the shoulder. As the snowstorm intensified, he'd calculated that his chances of surviving the night were negligible without medical attention and, after somehow scrambling back to his feet, he skied through a mogul field down to the nearest village, the offending pole still wedged between flesh and bone, protruding like a handle from his torso. Jamie often recounted this story as someone else might recount the time they forgot their bag of shopping on the bus.

Ben watched Jamie line up another shot on the baize. Nat Turner was passing through the room on his way back from the toilets. 'It's a sitter,' he quipped to no one in particular in his best snooker-commentator growl, 'surely he can't miss.'

Ben eyed Nat quietly. He regarded his mussed-up hair that had been adjusted very precisely in the bathroom mirror. The shades perched permanently back on his head. Then there was the orange tracksuit top. It was open to show the T-shirt underneath – it had the words 'The Man', together with an arrow pointing up to his face, and 'The Legend', with an arrow pointing down towards his crotch.

In earlier weeks, Ben would have shared a silent look with the others, a moment of male telepathy that denoted they were all thinking the same thing. But here and now, Jamie flashed Nat a grim smile as he swaggered back through to the main bar. As Nat returned it, Ben tried to work out how things had ever come to this.

Ben pushed his chair back and tried to massage away a searing headache. Claire was dead. Murdered.

Then there was Lucy. *I WAS CLOSE TO BEING A HEADLINE MYSELF TONIGHT.*

Well, *join the club*.

Ben's Adam's apple still ached from where the sole of Charm School's shoe had connected with it. Time-zone issues aside, these attacks had all taken place at nearly the same time.

The curiosity gnawed at Ben, taunting him.

But time was pressing. Too long in one place, too long online . . . Ben's survival instinct kicked in. Lucy would have done the same thing he did. They needed to talk, face to face. Sitting here was doing no one any good.

He looked up and saw a police car whine past the street outside. Ben had one more website to visit. A newsgroup, in fact: *rec.travel.budget.backpack*. A recent poster Curably Liz, had advertised budget accommodation in Durban, South Africa. The poster had recommended a small out-of-the-way guesthouse in the beach town of Durban. But if anyone had decided to travel there, they would have had problems. Because the guesthouse didn't exist in South Africa. It did, however, exist in Brazil. The reason Ben knew this was because Curably Liz, of course, was an anagram.

Three minutes later Ben was buying a change of clothes in a market stall. He had cash, he had false papers and, now, a collaborator. He might have wished for someone else, but, given the circumstances, it could be worse. Despite the debacle of their final months of training, at least Lucy had been courteous enough to acknowledge his presence in the corridors of Vauxhall Cross. The likes of Nat Turner had gone out of their way to ignore him, to drop him like Mum, like Chase, Jake, the embassy and presumably, by inference, the rest of the human race by now. Ben shook what he presumed was bitterness clean away. It was idiotic to dwell on this. He focused back on Lucy. The past thirty-six hours had burdened them both with a dead weight of questions. Together, at least, they had a fighting chance of finding some answers.

Next stop: Lucy, Brazil.

Thirteen

Vauxhall Cross, London SE1
0530 GMT

KB watched the sun rise through the arc of triple glazing of the MI6 atrium. He could see his reflection in the glass, in triplicate of course. Even though he had worked through the night, his huge grey eyes were alive and glittered in their sockets. His ears seemed to flare outwards slightly at the tips, giving him a faint and unsettling resemblance to a bat. Lithe and thin-boned, the rest of him had a darting, bird-like energy, humanized and smoothed out by well-tailored suits and a hearty, inclusive laugh. He was proud of his vocal chords. His voice was five fathoms deep, rich, confident beyond all measure of doubt. Whatever he said appeared to be the final word on the matter.

Once, in East Berlin, he had persuaded one of the Stasi's most notorious and violent drunks to spare a barmaid who had spilled a full glass of beer over his crotch. The man had sworn blind he would make her pay once her shift was finished and had bullied KB into waiting for her outside in the cold. But when the time came to act, KB's voice had commanded such exquisite and fundamental authority that the very idea of following through seemed perverse in the extreme. The Cold War had given many gifts to KB, one of which was knowledge.

It had taught him the unerring value of confidence. With confidence came certainty. And with certainty, everything was possible.

He took another slug of peppermint tea and relished his good mood. So very different from sixteen months ago.

Back then, KB had found himself in a cesspit of a problem. He'd been in his office, much like now, staring not at the window but at the spreadsheet on his computer. The screen displayed his departmental budget for the year. And there's nothing like black and white figures to tell you that you're in trouble.

The problem was money.

In years gone by his entire raison d'être had been to pursue and destroy the enemies of M16 (and, mostly, the State) across the Soviet wastes, over the Berlin Wall, down to Saudi and back again.

In the seventies, he'd been obsessed with the Russians. In the eighties, with the IRA. But for KB, the nineties and beyond were all about so-called 'dual-use' technology. He'd been one of the first officers to identify the dangers of technological (specifically, nuclear) progress – the world was full of nations and networks who desired nuclear technology. The world was also full of equipment and expertise that, although not specifically designed to be put in a nuclear bomb, certainly could be. Such 'dual-use' science had continually demonstrated to him that breakthroughs could come in the strangest places. Any country unwilling to invest the billions and decades in developing a nuclear weapon from scratch (say, 100 per cent of them) might instead accept that existing, mostly innocent technologies – the vacuum pump in a piece of medical imaging equipment for example – would do just as nicely, thank you.

KB had lobbied the deputy chief for a budget and got one – he then travelled the world, posing as one of a hundred innocent businessmen, creating shell corporations and striking deals with thousands of well-meaning and patriotic individuals bent on procuring precious technology for their covert nuclear programmes. KB would then sell them faulty dual-use technology wired with GPS transmitters. The purchaser would thus help identify just exactly who and where was interested in nuclear technology. Unless they truly were a bona fide medical company. In which case, they got their money back. Hardly James Bond, but he was saving the world.

Such work had previously been a passion – if that was indeed possible – but it had now, over time, become relegated to a kind of laborious curiosity.

Then the world had exploded on September 11, 2001.

Suddenly, his budgets began to expand. And it wasn't for want of trying, but these days he simply couldn't spend it fast enough. There was no polite way to really say it: the post-9/11 world was *flush*. At least, it was if you worked in the intelligence services. Espionage, counterespionage, counterterror, electronic surveillance, these were once again the new growth industries in the world.

KB's problem was indeed money.

Too much of the bloody stuff.

Obviously, he could just be honest about it.

But losing his budget, he knew, would be a severe dent to the ego and a deflation of political mojo he could well do without. He could do the job just as well with half the amount he received. But that was not the point. Retirement was five years away (KB was fifty years old) and clout and ego were of the utmost importance. He had his legacy to think about. And he knew, staring at a spreadsheet stuffed with zeros, that it wasn't going to be easy.

I could gold-plate every field agent's shoes, he found himself musing in the bathroom. *Issue compulsory Armani undershorts to every analyst . . .* But try as he might, a believable strategy just wasn't coming to him. He *could* pay some agents a performance-related bonus, of course, but that would be ridiculous. It would stand out a mile.

No conventional options were open. No legitimate operations were plausible. But unless he found a creative way to disburse those funds in a defensible manner, it wouldn't be there next year. And maybe neither would he.

It had been a rainy night and streaks of water were running down the window. KB had regarded his reflection in the glow of a computer monitor. His skin was unnaturally taut around his cheekbones, as if someone were permanently holding him by the back of the neck and tugging. Wet pebble eyes darted around their sockets. While the cogs of his brain turned around and around, his expression always faded to neutral, his eyes the only part of his face that kept moving.

Unable to find a plausible cover story to scoop the funds himself, he'd begun another game of internet chess to calm his nerves. Before he made his first move, however, a thought held him fast.

And with that thought came the idea that would become Greco. A plan that wasn't just a justifiable and, as far as he was concerned, genius-level use of Department funds, it was also, he smiled to himself, the very definition of 'dual-use'.

The symmetry of it all tickled him very much.

KB consulted the calendar and was relieved to see that the

new intake of recruits had only just completed their induction week. They had at least eleven months to go.

Now, sixteen months later, as the sun rose over the Thames, all of that preparation was about to come to fruition. The second phase of Greco was under way. And the consequences would not only aid the United Kingdom in its ongoing fight against Ghastly Awfulness around the world.

It might just help its architect enjoy a good night's sleep for the first time in his adult life.

Fourteen

10,000 feet above Brazil
Five minutes later

B en held on to the back seat of the Cessna 172-R Skyhawk as it crested the darkening abyss of the Amazon Basin. He'd spent most of the flight staring out at the pulsating lights on the wings and the solid depths of darkness beyond.

He'd thought about using his contacts on the ecotourism routes to get him over to Brazil but he reasoned they too might have been touched by his bad luck. He didn't want to risk anyone else's life if he could possibly help it.

Through the headphones, he could hear the captain talking to the suited Malaysian man beside him, presumably the logging company executive. This was a routine business flight. He'd spent enough money to convince them he wasn't another Greenpeace activist on a sabotage mission. Nevertheless, the conversation he overheard made him feel even worse than he had before he boarded the plane.

Blinking lights formed on the horizon. Slowly they resolved themselves into an airstrip near Itacoatiara, a port city and trade nexus some 120 miles east of the region's capital, Manaus. The Cessna landed awkwardly on the mud. The pilot took the balance of his kickback without making eye contact and Ben's cash reserves were a thousand dollars lighter. The logging road was exactly where the pilot had said it was, and after an hour Ben paid his way west on a hefty truck with full beams. They powered on through the night, passing mile after mile of ransacked wilderness. The corpses of birds and mammals were occasionally illuminated by the headlights.

As the sun reached its zenith, Ben found himself in Manaus, a bustling, grimy place of chaos. It suited his mood perfectly, but this was not his final destination. A change of passports and tourist clothes later and Ben was queuing up at the airport with other hardy Amazonian travelling types who found themselves in the city at the end of their river adventure. He bought a ticket to Recife, some fifteen hundred miles away on the Atlantic coast, in cash. With no paper trail, multiple identities, a zigzagging route and no official record of his entry into Brazil, he was safe – for the moment. Of course, he had no tourist visa on his new fake passport. But that was the least of his problems right now. He preferred to presume no one knew he was here and deal with the problems of staying around later. He had no plans to stay for long.

The flight took him over the same rich green canopy of Amazonia, across the more arid scrubland that approaches the northeastern provinces, and deposited him four hours later in the cut and thrust of Recife, a vast and hectic port town. The crowds and anonymity would have suited Ben here, too, but again he wanted to keep moving. He was heading south. From the back of a local bus, Ben watched as the urban sprawl receded, mercifully, into low-rise resorts and fishing villages. The stretch of coastline in the Pernambuco region of Brazil was a vast necklace of sand, fishing communities and tourist commerce. Strung out at intervals down Highway 060 were countless guesthouses, *pousadas*, bars and cafés, interspersed with real lives – extended families and their livelihoods, all bewildered perhaps at the never-ending influx of tourism that the beauty of their neighbourhood had generated. But it was not that surprising. The weather was perfect, the sea warm (for the Atlantic, at least) and the welcome laid-back and friendly. Unlike the chaos of Rio a thousand miles to the south, there was no hard sell, no pestering, no invasions of personal space – well, hardly any.

This was a place a person could settle into and mostly coexist with others calmly, without anyone ever asking your name. For fugitives and tourists alike, this was paradise.

Five hours later, he watched as the bus disappeared over the horizon and, as the grumble of the diesel engine faded, the sound of the surf filtered in. He started to walk. Curably Liz's directions had been perfect. The Happy Times guesthouse was here. The structure had been added on to so many times it looked like a drunk person's conversation. Ben wandered into the reception with an air of mild curiosity and seemed to decide there and then, on a whim, to take a room for a couple of days. He paid in cash, in advance and slept all afternoon, despite his best intentions to keep alert. On waking, he ambled across the street to the only café in view, installed himself in a corner and acted as if it was all he had to do that day.

An hour went by. Then another.

He wondered what Lima Station in the embassy was up to. He figured they had issued a warrant for his arrest. Since he'd spurned their help and they were clearly keen to deny him any form of diplomatic protection, he reckoned his face would be on several regional police computers across Peru. It was doubtful the matter would spread to other countries, particularly Brazil. The thought calmed him a little. But it did not remove the knot in his gut – the vision of Ana, her throat ripped out, the others from the magazine office presumably surprised at home . . . He was the only one who deserved exposure. It didn't take a rocket scientist to work out he'd been the only one asking questions, talking to the jungle guides he knew were also helping babysit arms caches in the jungle, straying into the wrong areas with a 'sorry, I got lost' . . . Steve Locke was the innocent adventurer. Everyone else was an innocent bystander. And yet everyone he touched was tainted. A hex.

Perhaps he deserved to stay down here, in exile from everything he had ever known. Thoughts of home pricked him, the uncertainty of the future, his mind adrift with what he presumed was sadness as the minutes ticked by.

Ben located more cigarettes and began to smoke his way through them. Anything to burn a hole in the paranoia. He was starting to attract attention, this lone man with nothing to do but sit and smoke. Finally, as the sun began its descent over the hill, Ben squinted to see a figure rounding the corner that marked the end of the street. There was a slight incline to the road, so she looked to Ben as if she were rising slowly up from the tarmac.

She had her hair pulled chaotically back on her head, held in place by a yellow pencil. A charcoal-grey sweatshirt, designed to look lived in but probably designer. Below that, what Ben would have called an 'ethnic wrap', a sapphire-black sarong around her waist, trimmed with gold and silver threading. Sandals on her bare feet. The tattoo of a Celtic ring on her ankle, a remnant – she once told him – of a wild night in Dublin. She sashayed casually towards him, never once meeting his eye or acknowledging his presence. An untrained eye would have called it shyness. But Ben knew differently. Even here, he realized, she was trying to be cool. When she'd been a lilywhite probationer, he recalled, she'd made friends easily and quickly. She seemed at first to him to be a genuinely pleasant person, often warm, thoughtful. She had an open, honest, inquisitive face. Her eyes were pleased to see you. Her laugh was genuine and never forced. But if truth be known she also had an edge to her that kept itself hidden. She was not good with bad news. If you were forced to share sadness or tragedy with her, she would empathize ('Oh, God, poor you') but then step infinitesimally away, as if somehow it was catching.

It made you wonder what else she was thinking.

With time, of course, things had changed. With her, with him. With everyone. That was what probation did to people. It opened them up, inside out, for all to see, before closing them back up for good. Despite his exhaustion, his nerves, his isolation – she was here. A familiar and, mostly, friendly face. Her very presence reassured him. Ben began to smile.

And then he saw she was not alone.

Several yards behind her, a man was scuttling up the incline to catch up with her. Lucy's legs covered the ground with ease. This man was being forced into a semi-trot that seemed the polar opposite of her understated cool. Next to Lucy's monochrome chic he looked like a packet of fruit pastilles that had exploded. He wore a blue Hawaiian shirt and a golf visor that moulded his unruly hair into the shape of a mushroom. His wraparound shades were orange and his short stubby legs, the final protrusions of a short stubby body, stuck out the bottom of a pair of waxy yellow football shorts. The legs themselves were severely sunburned and pumped furiously over the ground in pursuit of Lucy's perfect size eights. Ben recognized him immediately and began to feel what he presumed to be his nerves tingling.

The man. The legend.

Nat Turner.

Ben eyed him as he approached. At least he wasn't wearing

that T-shirt. *Small mercies*, thought Ben. *Be grateful*. Nat saw the recognition behind Ben's eyes and, with a grim smile of shared tragedy, threw his flabby arms out wide. 'Benjy,' he barked. 'What a bloody business.'

Ben nodded in cursory greeting, then turned to Lucy, who had still failed to register that she knew Ben was there at all. Finally, she blessed him with a look and smiled.

'You never said he was with you,' Ben whispered to Lucy as they embraced in greeting.

Lucy pulled a nonplussed face from her mental dressing-up box. 'Didn't you get my text?'

Ben glared at her.

'I ditched my phone. You should too.'

'I did,' she said. 'Just after I texted you.'

He knew she was lying. She knew that he knew. It somehow made absolutely no difference.

'This seat taken?' said Nat. Ben summoned a genial smile that was more of a squint. Nat pulled a third chair to the table for two Ben was sitting at. The chair creaked heavily as Nat leaned back. He raised his feet and rested them on the table. The table legs were not strong and the pressure caused Ben's drink to teeter over the edge. Ben grabbed it before it hit the deck, soaking his hands, rescuing some of the contents. Lucy approached the bar and ordered two coffees.

Ben stared at Nat, who didn't seem to register his wrongdoing. His feet remained on the table, and the table remained on an incline. Ben quietly finished the rescued dregs of his Coke. Lucy normally responded best to nonverbal communications of annoyance. If you vocalized it, chances were she would walk on by – or worse: smile, empathize and forget all about it.

'Nat emailed me after I finished talking to you,' she said as the coffees arrived.

'Is that right?' said Ben.

'As a matter of fact, yes.'

'So how do we—'

'Newsflash, *compadres*,' blurted Nat, either not hearing Ben or choosing to speak over him. 'We are well and truly buggered to hell.'

'That's your analysis, is it?' asked Ben innocently.

'Oh, I don't know. Someone tries to run me off the road and into a ditch using automatic weapons just outside Havana. I get back home and find my flat's on fire. When I call in to activate a safe house someone has clearly already been informed about who I really am and there's the secret police ready and waiting for me. Embassy won't touch me because someone's told them I've been smuggling light arms into the country and it's only through the sheer quality and volume of my grey matter that I get through it in one piece and not strung up and framed up and shot at, although I was shot at, in fact, in copious amounts. That sort of thing, Ben. That's the sort of thing I'm talking about.'

Nat eyed him like a stand-up comedian who had delivered his punch line and sipped his coffee.

'How did you know to come here,' asked Ben, 'when I spent—'

'Same way you did, sunshine,' snapped Nat, with a nod to Lucy. Ben absorbed this new interruption quietly, as he always did. Nat pushed his shades back on his head and shaded his eyes from the sun. He had panda eyes from wearing sunglasses for too long. 'So they serve pancakes here or what?'

Ben watched Lucy carefully as they ordered food. She seemed on edge, but Ben couldn't work out why. Apart from the obvious. But he'd seen Lucy get bad news before and she'd never been like this.

'Have you heard from anyone else?' he asked.

The awkward silence was broken when Nat snorted so loudly he had to stop coffee from rerouting out of his nose.

'Well . . .' said Nat, *'no.'*

Ben's surprise showed on his face and the more it showed, the wider Nat's eyes became. Ben felt his cheeks flush with anger as a sadistic smile curled around Nat's lip. Even here, even now, Nat was relishing the upper hand.

'Oh, my God,' said Nat, wiping his face with a tissue. 'He doesn't know, Luce. He doesn't bloody know . . .'

Fifteen

Vauxhall Cross, SE1

It was the closest thing to a double-take Tremayne could
ever remember seeing in Vauxhall Cross.

'You're Bill's son?'

'Yes.'

'Good God. We used to work together, you know.'

'He didn't talk about work,' said Tremayne flatly.

Tremayne had appeared without warning on the fifth floor
and asked for him by name. Such brazen confidence, KB
reasoned, was the result of breeding. Walking up here to see
the director of his current project without an appointment . . .
that could only come from a blue-blooded old boy. Someone
with family connections to the Service. The air of entitlement,
suffused with arrogance, was a trademark of the upper classes
who still predominated in the corridors of Vauxhall Cross. In
this case, considering his lineage, it wasn't surprising the man
had such chutzpah.

His father had had it in spades.

KB smiled warmly and regarded his visitor for a moment.
Tremayne smoothed down a hair that was standing to attention
on his head. A memory seemed to cloud KB briefly. But it only
took him a second to snap back to business.

'GCHQ—' he said, referring to the UK's signalling interception centre. 'I presume it was they who . . .' He trailed off, allowing the man with the glasses a chance to continue.

'I was assigned the analyst position by them, yes. I believe you'd tasked them to assign one analyst per geographical area. I replaced Bernard Foulks, whose mother was ill, just before the operation began.'

KB nodded. He was right. He'd been told of the replacement. He just hadn't asked for the name.

Was God trying to punish him for something?

Bill Tremayne's son, of all people?

Tremayne noticed that KB had gone slightly pale.

'Is everything all right?'

KB nodded, suddenly returning to his old avuncular self. 'Of course, dear boy, of course. How can I help?'

'Well, I was looking at the data last night. My data, I mean. There seems to have been an extraordinary confluence of traffic peaks. A lot of people are suddenly talking at the same time.'

'That's splendid. I expect you'll be able to start constructing a hub diagram almost immediately?'

Tremayne had already begun, in fact. The target network in Peru had been going crazy for almost thirty-six hours. Phone calls, emails – there was genuine panic amongst them and it was incredibly easy for Tremayne to keep track of the call frequency. A pattern was emerging, he could see. A hub diagram was simply a map of who was calling whom. It was done for new networks, groups that had yet to show their power structures. It was the difference between a phonebook and a corporate contact list. It helped to know who was the cleaner and who was the chairman. In a hub diagram, person B might call person A, but person B would never call person C. Since C would get most of the calls, according to experience, C would start to emerge as the central figure, a hub. Tremayne had already started plotting these links down on a large sheet of graph paper stapled to a whiteboard in his office.

And there was something else. The content.

These people weren't just calling to chat about the weather. They were calling and emailing in large quantities about specific things. A good deal of the chatter he heard was variations on a theme of betrayal.

He smiled at KB. 'I just wanted to clarify that there wasn't an error. A reporting error, I mean. From GCHQ.'

'Their data has always been first-rate.'

'Good. That's what I thought.' An idea struck him. 'Were you expecting this volume of traffic? So soon?'

KB smiled back at him. 'Let's just say, we've hired the right people for the job.'

Sixteen

E ach sheet was a printout from a slowly dying inkjet printer. With each successive turn of the page, streaked lines began to appear, the ink slowly drying and fading. He had to strain to see the type. Lucy and Nat sat a respectful distance from Ben as he read. They'd had a little more time to come to terms with this.

The papers were all local news reports that Lucy had sourced on the internet. They all conformed to the same, bizarrely detached tone as the one Ben had read on screen about Claire. The first instinct of the brain must surely be to push such thoughts away. But as Ben looked down at the report in his hand, the comfort of denial was dissolving fast.

PORT SUDAN, EAST AFRICA. English visitor dies in scuba accident. An investigation is under way after a 25-year-old man died following a fatal diving expedition from a platform 50 miles north of the Port, say coastguard authorities this morning. The accident happened on Saturday morning at the Blue Belt dive . . . The victim, ALASTAIR FORBES of Norwich, Norfolk, UK, an experienced diver with more than 300 diving hours, was treated at the scene, but he later died at Port Sudan General Hospital . . .

That night in the pub, Chris had told him about his plans for 'Alastair Forbes'. 'My legend shall be a legend,' he smirked over his pint. 'An outlet for my shadow self.' Ben turned the page, dismissing the memory from his mind. He turned to another newswire printout, this one pitched at an odd angle down the face of the sheet.

GF NEWSWIRE 1442 GMT. Scots traveller dies on Moscow subway. A young Scottish woman has been killed jumping on to an electrified rail track. Helen Lyndhurst, twenty-four, died in Moscow early on Friday after a witness reported her erratic behaviour near the platform edge. The charity worker was waiting for a train just before 2 a.m. when she allegedly attempted to change platforms and brushed the 650-volt rail . . .

Alexandra, Ben knew, had chosen the name 'Helen' after much soul-searching. It was her mother's name and she'd died the previous year. Normally such close proximity to family names was frowned upon, but an exception had been made in her case.

Reading the pages sapped Ben's energy. His stomach knotted at every turn as faces, voices assailed him as he read. He tried to maintain his focus on the words as they came, each report bleeding into the next: *UK TRAVELLER DIES IN MALAYSIA . . . TWO DEAD IN EGYPT CAR CRASH . . . head-on collision on the main trucking route . . . THE VICTIM HAD BEEN SURPRISED BY A BURGLAR, SAID POLICE . . . the motorbike running off the road near KAFR EL-DAWAR . . . falling some 800 feet from the penthouse level to the Manila street below . . .* The final page nearly broke him. Jamie's posting to Odessa had been a plum job, a coveted position. As he put it himself, 'Nothing says international intrigue like that fleshpot city on the Black Sea.' His skills were clear to everyone, but even so he still seemed to resent the plaudit. Ben eventually found out why. His alias. It had been chosen for him by his handler, an irritating killjoy with a cruel sense of humour. All attempts to change this name had been doused, with the explanation that all paperwork and backstop receipts were already on their way to the printers. The article in front of Ben raised a faint smile even now. The man had been a friend, once. Even with the bitterness Ben still felt, he had to admit that. The ink had almost run out by this stage. Even the news report of his death was a ghost.

BACKPACKER DIES IN PLUNGE FROM HOTEL.

Odessa. Trevor Wilson, 25, was found dead at 4 a.m. yesterday morning by a street cleaner on the pavement outside his hotel, where he had fallen from or jumped from the balcony seven floors above . . .

Ben was still staring at the word 'jumped' when Lucy's hand clasped his shoulder.

'They're dead, Ben. All of them.'

Seventeen

B en had walked to the beach to watch the sunset. He stood there, frozen, staring at the horizon, bathed in orange and crimson. Lucy had seen him and knew to leave him alone for a few minutes.

Lucy left Nat to take a shower and followed Ben's footsteps to the shoreline. Billows of cigarette smoke were taken by the wind. Ben didn't turn round as she approached.

The sun disappeared below the horizon without a fanfare. Lucy had once been told that in the tropics the sun turns briefly green just before it dips below sight.

'No green flash tonight,' said Lucy.

'Guess not.'

'I think you only see them from boats.'

The onshore wind was strengthening now and she moved a strand of hair from her face.

Ben kept his eyes on the horizon as he spoke. 'It's weird, you know. I know it's your voice, I know it's you and yet – I can't believe you're here.'

Lucy smiled in accord. 'Are you okay?'

'It is what it is,' said Ben, finishing off his cigarette.

'What does that mean?'

'It means, like it or not, we're in this together.'

Lucy absorbed this for a moment and shivered slightly in the breeze. 'So, which is it?'

'I don't understand.'

'Do you like or do you not like?'

Ben turned to look at her in the weakening afterglow of the sunset. Her nose had become slightly freckled in the sunshine. Her eyes were more oval than he remembered. He sighed and shook his head. 'I know it's hard to believe, but it's almost good to see you.'

Lucy nodded. 'The disappearing man.'

Nat was scuttling over unsteadily across the beach. Ben glanced back at the little legs slipping on the sand and his eyes darkened. He looked as if he was about to say something to Lucy, but if he was tempted, he kept it inside.

Nat arrived out of breath, his hair dripping wet and slicked back in a wholly unattractive way.

'Sweet nothings?'

'Our friends are dead, Nat. We're deniable and disposable and may never see our families again. What could be sweeter?' Ben pushed past Nat and headed off down the beach.

Nat wheeled around to give chase but Lucy held his shoulder.

'I'm just as freaked out as he is—'

'He'll be all right in a minute, I promise.'

Nat eyed her for a moment and nodded. As they walked back towards the lights of the Happy Times Guesthouse, he was whistling something. A tune loud enough so Lucy could hear it. It took a few minutes for Lucy to realize it was a cheesy old song from the eighties. She tried to remember the name. Was it Whitney Houston? Elaine Page? Then it hit her. It was from a musical, *Chess*. The song was called 'I Know Him So Well'.

Lucy had already spread out a large map of the region and plotted out a string of *pousadas* that combined a location well off the beaten path with a relaxed attitude to guests – these, she surmised, would provide them with a de facto and un-official RV route north.

'Our covers are blown, so there's no way we'll be able to use the normal safe-house networks. The Service seems to think we're not worth saving either.'

'A little stronger than that, I think,' said Nat. 'They want rid of us permanently.'

'Why?'

'Only way we can find out is by staying alive,' said Ben. 'So why don't we focus on that?'

Nat and Lucy stared at him, but they knew he was right. 'Okay,' said Lucy. 'We have to presume the Service has distributed our details to anyone who'll listen.'

'Wouldn't take much to push it out to every foreign station on the list,' said Nat. 'It's like an electronic "Wanted" poster.'

'So what do you suggest we do?' ventured Ben. He knew Lucy liked to take charge, and when she did it was usually better to step back and let her get on with it.

'We improvise,' she announced. 'We think while we drink. Three friends backpacking our way through South America. And somewhere in the midst of all this fun, we try and work out what the hell just happened.'

Ben coughed. 'You said, "three friends".'

'I'd say we're better off sticking together. Wouldn't you? Nat's a better linguist than we are, you're a better operator and I'm a better thinker. I'd say it works much better this way. Wouldn't you say?'

Nat stared at Ben, and Ben stared right back.

'Is it likely that three people like us would go travelling together?' asked Ben.

'A couple and their friend,' said Nat. 'It could work.'

'Fine,' said Lucy. 'So, Ben and I were travelling and met you on the way.'

A flash of hurt passed across Nat's face. 'Yeah. Or you and me, you know. Either way.'

An awkward silence seeped between them.

Nat felt the need to break it. The silence was worse than getting to the nub of it. 'What's wrong with that?'

'Just—' Lucy tried not to look at him. Nat stared accusingly at Ben, as if he had something to do with it.

'It's fine,' said Ben, sensing another argument and not having the energy to engage with it.

Nat's eyes began to burn.

'Oh,' he said. 'I get it.'

'It's just a first-impression thingy,' said Lucy.

'Yep,' continued Nat, 'what we're talking about is *leagues*. The league system.'

It was true. While physically Ben and Lucy were a believable couple, Lucy and Nat were not.

'What you're saying is she's the European Championship,' said Nat, pointing at Lucy, 'and I'm . . . the Vauxhall Conference. Okay. Well. That's a frank and honest exchange of views.'

Lucy shook her head and stretched like a cat. Her top rode up and Ben noticed that she'd had her navel pierced since he'd last been privy to that area of her body. A hint of stomach muscle twitched as she yawned. She knew he was looking and avoided his gaze. 'Let's talk about this after we've all had some sleep. Maybe there's a plan B after all.'

Ben could also see the scars she'd suffered through her escape from the car. She pulled her sleeves back down over her palms.

'Come on. There is no plan B. This is all we've got.' Nat's

voice was wavering a little between North London upper-middle class (his natural accent) and a working-class affectation that revealed, Ben had always thought, a deep-seated insecurity. Ben thought it ironic that the majority of young aristocrats tried to affect the manners of the working classes; and those of humble origins sometimes spent their lives attempting to ape the airs and graces, if not the plummy accents, of the highborn. It was just another mask to wear.

They paid in advance for two nights, then quietly climbed out of their bedroom window with their belongings and on to the storage shed behind the structure. If anyone came looking for them here, it would delay them at least a while. The three then took a taxi down the coast a few miles to the town of Porto de Galinhas. It was a larger, more energized community and it felt good to be part of a crowd. The manager of the Pousada Galinhas was a short tubby man with light brown freckles and John Lennon glasses. The bizarre threesome in front of him had just made him very happy. Three new guests at this time of night were a good business omen, even if they were staying in a beach bungalow made for two. Lucy did her best impression of a laid-back traveller who didn't care what he thought and grinned.

But no one could sleep.

With such shadows looming over them, they resolved to talk through their options over a late supper.

They ate in silence at a beachside café with yellow plastic tables, washing their food down with warm beer. Nat was still sulking, while a brooding sense of menace gave Ben indigestion. Eventually, they began to talk, the dark ocean foaming before them.

Ben explained his narrow escape from the Peruvian authorities. For once, both Lucy and Nat listened in silence. Nat didn't even see fit to interrupt. After he'd finished, Nat's brow furrowed. He spoke quietly, barely audible above the sound of the surf.

'Sounds like you were lucky,' he said.

Ben said, 'I was.'

'I suppose we all are,' sighed Lucy, gulping a long mouthful of beer. 'And we can keep being lucky if we're clever about it. We can move every day. We can keep clear of trouble. But one day our papers will be checked; one day our luck will run out. So in advance of that, I hate to say it, but . . . what are we going to do? Really?'

Ben glanced at Nat, who was sighing overloudly.

'We can't run forever,' said Ben.

'Who says we can't?' said Nat, without looking at him.

'Common sense says,' said Ben with a shrug. 'Past history says. I says.'

'Well, *I says*: Bahia. Open a guesthouse down there.'

'Has it not occurred to you that the people who trained us seem very happy for us to die with our socks on?'

'Yes, Lucy, actually it has. It's occurred to me about every second since I got out of Cuba. The difference between you and me is, I am already *over it*. We've got cash to get started and enough savvy to keep our noses out of trouble. So I say: Bahia. You ever seen it down that way? It's insane.'

Lucy glared at him. 'We're not doing that.'

'Venezuela then. Cartagena, Colombia. Anywhere with a beach.'

'And never see our families again.'

'They can't get on a plane?'

Ben shook his head and sighed. 'Good idea. Perhaps they could fly from Heathrow in bright-yellow windcheaters, so they're easier to follow. Maybe they could hold up an umbrella too. Just in case anyone has a bit of trouble keeping up. Those fast-track countersurveillance classes weren't wasted on you, I'm relieved to see.'

'They're a government, Ben, not a big old conspiracy theory.'

'They'll keep tabs. Believe me.'

'Believe you? Sorry. Tried that once. Didn't work.'

Ben was quiet for a moment. Lucy saw it coming, a flash of memory. Ben was mostly a man of few words, until they all came at once. He turned and faced down Nat across the table.

'If this is going to work, we're going to have to have an agreement,' said Ben, eyes aflame, leaning over the table and nearly unbalancing Lucy's long-necked bottle of beer.

Nat and Lucy stared at him as he spoke.

'I will do my best to look out for you. I will pull my weight and I will share my cash, my energy, my blood, whatever it takes. In return, you will do the same for me and we will not talk about the past *any more*.'

'Come on—'

'What happened between all of us is irrelevant now.'

'Do me a favour.' Nat was almost laughing now.

'You have no idea what it was like for me,' said Ben.

'You forget, *muchacho*, I was right there in the middle of it with you—'

'I don't care what you think of me, Nat, although it's pretty clear. But since we're on the subject, I'm pretty clear about you too. Unfortunately, I have to believe that we all stand a better chance of getting through this if we all look out for each other. We move forward into the future, together, from here. No more looking back. Agreed?'

Lucy nodded grimly. 'Agreed.'

Nat pinched off a headache and softened. 'Fine. And I'll tell you what else. I'll just stop suggesting things for a bit and let you two brainboxes sort everything out. Let me know what you decide.'

Silence fell between the three of them.

'We have to start thinking about realities,' Ben said eventually. 'The fact is, we may never get home.'

Lucy shook her head. 'Don't say things like that.'

'You know what happens to officers in the field when they're no longer useful.'

'I do,' said Lucy. 'But never get home? I'm not so sure.'

'What makes you so confident?'

She was still staring off into space, half present.

'Don't bite my head off, but . . .' She appeared to take a very considered breath before continuing. She let it out slowly, changing the pace of the conversation. The ball was back in her court and she lowered her voice, glancing at the other tables. Eavesdropping distance.

'Anyone fancy a walk?'

A soft onshore breeze wafted Lucy's hair over her face and she secured it back behind her head with a clip. Three sets of footprints meandered back to the lights of the café. No one had spoken since Lucy's suggestion of a stroll. Both Nat and Ben knew this meant she was building up to something. They were right.

'Did you ever do the archivist rotation?'

Nat and Ben nodded. They'd all been through it at one time or another. All diplomatic traffic was filtered through the Archive, a now-computerized library, effectively, of all communications between MI6 headquarters and its stations throughout the world. Every new intake had to do a stint in the Archive. It was considered a form of punishment, a badge of honour in some ways, but Ben recalled the peace and quiet of the stuffy basement room with some fondness. 'It was the first thing I ever did at Vauxhall. I got assigned to a supervisor called Neville. He looked a bit like a werewolf.'

Nat nodded in memory. 'Neck hair. Elbow patches.'

'The very same,' said Lucy. 'I was helping him digitize old embassy cables from the 1930s. Some were falling apart, apparently. I read them all of course, even though I wasn't supposed to . . .'

'No surprises there,' said Ben.

'We've all done it so there's no point in getting on your high horse.'

'No horses,' said Ben flatly. 'There are no horses here.'

Nat looked momentarily confused, as did Lucy – a faraway look in her eyes.

Nat cleared his throat. 'Had to be there, I guess.'

'You were reading the cables,' said Ben.

Lucy pursed her lips for a moment and located a cigarette. 'Yes. And in the middle of it all I hit a seam that dealt with deaths in the field. Officers whose bodies were not recovered, missing in action. That sort of thing. Anyway . . .' She lit up and quietly blew rings above her as she spoke. 'A few of the messages were handwritten, but all of them were high-level communiqués. There's thousands of them, as you can imagine.'

Lucy paused again to take a drag. She could see she had both men's attention now and was taking her time to enjoy it. Ben's eyes twinkled a little with recognition. She decided he probably knew what she was going to say next and so carried on before he could ask a question.

'In the Second World War, with the Special Operations Executive, a lot of spies got burned. People were compromised, missions were blown apart, entire networks disappeared.'

'Careless talk costing lives,' said Ben.

'Quite literally, yes,' continued Lucy. 'But that was war, people became useful and then quickly lost their usefulness. Brutal times. So one minute you could be an agent in place, working for Her Majesty's War Effort; next minute you're a discarded asset. Useful to no one. Worthless to everyone. It broke my heart to read some of them. Neville saw I was getting into it and told me some of the history.'

'With a view to perhaps getting into your pants,' interrupted Nat with a suggestive leer.

Lucy ignored him.

'Around the time of these disappearances, Neville told me, a rumour started circulating in MI6. It was this: where did these errant spies get to? I mean, some bodies washed up. Some were reported, locations of the bodies and so on. But by no means everyone was found. And of these missing men and women, there was no record of them turning traitor and collaborating. They were too highly trained to fall prey to local forces. They just sort of . . . disappeared.'

Ben cleared his throat. 'And people started speculating they were still alive.'

'Yes,' said Lucy. 'And helping others in the same position to join them.'

A heavy silence fell between them all.

'You're talking about Contact Zero,' said Ben.

Eighteen

They had all heard about the concept, of course. No one who passed through the SIS training programme could avoid at least hearing the whispered rumours. Enough drink, enough secrecy and collusion and you'd hear more. The more senior members of management pooh-poohed the idea when asked, naturally, and dismissed it out of hand. Conspiracy nonsense, they would say. But of course, the more they denied, the more those who believed were convinced.

The most secret secret society on the planet.

Of course it was. It was run by spies.

They had paused for a moment and gazed over the rippled surface of the sea, white horses foaming over the reef in the distance. The moon was in its first quarter and away from the lights of the café it was becoming quite dark.

Lucy held Ben's eyes and nodded. This only confirmed Ben's doubts. She had truly lost her mind. But Nat was first to strike. 'That's your big idea? Lucy. Come on. There's no one called Contact Zero. It's the spy equivalent of the Wizard of Oz, for God's sake.'

'No one knows what it is,' snapped Lucy, sensing both men's antagonism.

'They know it's not true,' said Nat, interrupting.

Lucy wasn't listening. 'A person, a place, a network . . . no one knows.'

'Lucy. Come on. It's a fairy story,' said Ben.

'I'm telling you, it exists,' said Lucy.

Nat lowered the register of his voice to one of great portent, like a pirate discussing a vast and ancient treasure. 'An old spies' tale. 'Tis all.' He waited for a laugh. None came.

Lucy turned away from Nat. 'Tell that to the ones who got burned.'

Nat removed a bottle of beer from his pocket and drained it. His eyes were dark in their sockets, cold. 'We may as well hope for the Tooth Fairy or the bloody Thunderbirds to come and look out for us. At least they might have some weaponry.'

'Let me prove you both wrong,' said Lucy quietly.

Ben loved that about Lucy. The angrier she got, the quieter she became. You truly knew you were in deep shit when all you got was radio silence. She was close to it now.

'Be my guest,' smiled Nat. 'But for the record? This is a waste of bloody time.'

The breeze had ebbed to a whisper as Lucy spoke. 'Every SIS agent that goes missing has a "black box" file . . . a final record of their communications up to the point they disappear. Nearly all of these involve an SOS, a cry for help. Ignoring security and encryption procedures because, presumably, there's no time to mess around with anything but the basics.'

'I'm not surprised by that,' said Nat.

'Neither was I. But I was by something else. The final message, in a lot of these cases of disappearance at least, tends to have the same content. The location would change, of course, the place they sent the messages from, but certain key words within the content of the message always stay the same. It was as if they were hoping for it to be heard by as many people as possible. My theory is this: it's a call sign.'

'The Bat Signal,' murmured Nat.

'Whatever you want to call it. That's what signals to the Contact Zero network. The same message. Transmitted by generations of field officers. Most of whom are never heard from again.'

Nat's irritation boiled over as his face flushed crimson. 'Yeah. And you know why? Because they're all *dead*. Just like Claire is *dead*. Just like Jamie and Andy and every single one of the other poor bastards who signed up with us.' He glanced at Ben as he wheezed in another breath and coughed it out again. 'Maybe there's something about our year that the Grim Reaper's really taken a shine to, I dunno. But what I do know is they are all no more. Just like we will be if we waste any more time talking about this.'

'Lucy,' said Ben, counterpointing Nat softly. 'I've met Neville too. And do you know why he only works in the Archive? Because he's such a conspiracy nut and fantasist he's not allowed to mess around with current operations in case some-one gets hurt. Come on. Think about it.'

Lucy turned her gaze on him. 'Tomlinson used them when he left.'

Nat raised an eyebrow. Even Ben took a moment. Richard Tomlinson had been a renegade MI6 agent, or had certainly been touted as such, and spent years on the run after serving a year in prison. It was not an edifying period in either party's career.

'Well, great,' said Nat eventually, ''cos I really want to have *his* life. His life must be really *top notch* right now.'

'You ever see his file?' asked Lucy.

'Of course.'

'His email records?'

'Maybe. Can't remember. It's not something I thought was particularly pressing in my life.'

'I did. And I think he tried to go for Contact Zero . . . but they didn't want him.'

Ben was pacing now. 'How do you know that?'

'It's all in the Archive, if you can be arsed to look. Neville showed me one of the last emails the guy ever sent. It was to an anonymous departmental address at Vauxhall Cross. There's loads of them in reserve – info@sis.gov.uk – that kind of thing. Routine embassy traffic goes there, as do all public enquiries routed through the Foreign Office recruiting centre. So, my question is: why would someone in dire straits send an email to such a generic place? He'd been firing off emails to just about everyone else, he knew their addresses, he wasn't scattergunning at all. He was very precise. But, then, the last thing he ever did was to send a very innocent but specific email to a very generic address.'

'Define innocent,' said Ben.

'How's the weather. Having a lovely time. That kind of thing. Why would someone like him do that?'

'No idea,' said Ben.

'Insanity,' said Nat. 'A brain made of cheese.'

'Because,' continued Lucy quietly, 'he *knew* the email would be scanned. Just like the other final messages were scanned. I think someone *inside* SIS or GCHQ helps pick up on those embedded code words and knows what those words mean. This tells us two things: there is someone inside UK intelligence who passes on recommendations for Contact Zero; and, if we send an email with those key words in, we might just find ourselves recommended too.'

Ben shook his head and smiled.

'Your imagination,' he said, 'is something else.'

'I say we try it.'

'Nat?'

Nat was a little surprised to be spoken to by Ben. He recovered well and thought for a moment.

'What are the other options? We can't go back. Not right now. I spoke to my handler. He's a family friend, you know. Even he told me they're busy trying to pin the blame on me for my failed operation.'

'So none of us can go home,' said Lucy. 'None of us wants to run alone.'

Nat rubbed his eyes. 'We'll need to get lawyers, get a case together, get protection eventually. If we want to fight this officially, I mean. Shit, man. We'll need everything. Kitchen bloody sink. Throw this all back at the bastards.'

Lucy shook her head. 'They all cost, Nat. Time and money. We have neither at the moment. Not where extradition lawyers are concerned at least.'

'All right,' said Ben. 'For the sake of argument. How do we do this? It's not like we can put a postcard up in the supermarket. Three fugitive spies seek sanctuary: must be cat lovers—'

'Oh, come on, there's no point—' Nat had cut Ben off again. 'And anyway – you said those messages all had the same phrase structure. Same words. It's not as if you committed them to memory, is it, Luce?'

Lucy walked on a few paces and felt the two men's stares on her back. She heard Nat's footsteps hurry to keep up with her over the sand. And at that moment she knew she had them. Nat broke the silence.

'You remember? Lucy?'

She turned and smiled. 'Wouldn't *you* like to know?'

Nineteen

The guesthouse had two computers for guest use in a quiet corner of the reception area. Lucy located the manager, paid in advance and logged on.

Without a word, Nat nudged Lucy aside and began typing. Ben was about to step in but Lucy shook her head. They watched his podgy fingers hunt and peck the keyboard, registering for another email account. 'Any screen-name ideas?' he said after a while. 'We'll have to set up a new anonymous account.'

'Suit yourself,' said Ben.

Nat stared at him oddly, then brightened.

'Good choice,' he said and dutifully typed 'SUIT YOURSELF 2006' into the form. Thirty seconds later, they were ready to go.

Lucy now nudged Nat aside and began to type a message. Nat and Ben watched in silence as one sentence became three, and a small paragraph was born. It said simply:

'That's it?' said Ben after she was finished.

'Far as I can tell.'

'This is ridiculous,' chuckled Nat.

'Shut up and give me your finger.' Without waiting for a response, Lucy grabbed Nat's hand in hers and held it over the mouse. She then pulled Ben's hand to the same place.

'We send this together or not at all. Agreed?'

Ben and Nat nodded.

And on the count of three, they double-clicked.

They stared at the screen as it refreshed itself. A message said simply: 'SENT.'

'What now?' asked Nat.

'We wait.'

The hours refused to pass. The three had agreed to check for replies every ten minutes at first; then every thirty; eventually, every hour on the hour. With each passing moment, their mood began to descend.

Where Lucy clung vocally on to hope, Ben suffered in silence. Nat dismissed the very idea of waiting. 'There is no point in waiting for a bus,' he explained, 'in the Stone Ages. Because there are no buses. That is what we are doing here. We are standing in the middle of the Palaeolithic Era waiting for the number 12 to Piccadilly Circus. We are chasing a shadow.'

The next day, there was a message waiting.

The return address seemed oddly random.

Lucy clicked on it.

The message was simple and to the point. It said:

ENLARGE YOUR PENIS NATURALLY – NO PILLZ

Although they knew they should keep moving, something about the spam message punctured all of them in the same way. To move to another town was just to delay the inevitable. Still, training niggled at them and they packed their bags once again. Just before setting off, Lucy caved in and checked her mail again.

Nothing, bar the same spam message she'd left undeleted in

the inbox. A thought struck her as she stared. She clicked on the link.

'I don't know how to break this to you, Luce,' said Nat, 'but I'm not sure that product is aimed at you.'

The link sent them to a blank page.

The URL had a Swiss suffix, Nat noticed, and appeared to be cached on a backwater page of a local library near Bern.

'If the Swiss are selling penis enlargement pills via spam,' said Nat, 'I think the end of the world is just around the corner.'

'Why send us here? To a blank page?'

Nat leaned over Lucy, his forearm briefly brushing her bare shoulder, and pressed 'select all' on the keyboard.

'What are you doing?' snapped Lucy.

'Investigating a theory.'

Nat's keystroke had highlighted a small box of text at the bottom of the screen. Unseen by the casual visitor to the site, it was written in a tiny white font. Considering the page was also white, the thing was otherwise completely hidden.

The three of them squinted at it.

It said simply, 'REMAIN IN PLACE'.

Four days later, they were still there. Message or not, they were on edge. Staying in one place made them sitting ducks. The three of them agreed a rotation of sleep and keeping watch, without drawing too much attention to themselves.

But as time passed, resolve weakened.

Lucy began to release her hold on the hope she'd clung to so strongly. Perhaps this was all Contact Zero could offer, false hope, the promise of a stranger.

On their fifth night she succumbed to the stress and lost herself in margaritas. Nursing a hangover the next morning, she had made her mind up. It was time to move on. Message or no message, it was too dangerous to stay here. Her mind had been seduced by the sunshine, but was back and focused on the practicalities at hand. Where they would run to next. Where their money would come from when their current resources ran out, as they surely would, and sooner than they suspected.

That night, they had another meal by the beach, crunching *caranguejo mole* – crabs with edible shells – washed down with the ubiquitous sugar-cane drink, *caldo de cana*. Despite the spice, the sugar, enough to give anyone vital signs, the three simply kept their thoughts to themselves.

After dinner, they walked back in silence, spread out along the road, still lost in their own private ruminations. Had they not been so tired, so defeated, they would have been more aware of the world around them. If they'd focused on their surroundings and not their frustration, or perhaps if they'd concentrated a little harder in class, they would have realized that, for the last two and a half hours, they were being followed.

Twenty

Tremayne had been about to go home when he caught the newswire. A British national called Steven Locke had been held on suspicion of heroin smuggling but had over-powered customs officials during interrogation. One officer had been killed in the chase.

He found no mention of an outstanding arrest warrant, but presumed this was a typographical oversight. Most importantly and of much greater interest to Tremayne was that Mr Locke was also a natural cover agent assigned to gather preliminary data on the very same young networks Tremayne had been posted to cover.

He was part of Greco.

His real name was Ben Sinclair.

In a separate report, Tremayne noted the deaths of several young office workers in a building in downtown Lima. A burglar had been surprised, the report explained, by workers on a magazine's late shift. Tremayne diligently wrote down the name of the office building, cross-referenced it with the names he saw in the report and concluded that not only was the natural cover agent Steven Locke blown, but his cover station was too. Innocent people were dead.

The spike in conversations, the rash panic in voices, it all suddenly made sense. Feathers were flying because they had realized a simple fact: a spy was in their midst.

And now, that spy was on the run.

It was, Tremayne felt, a good thing he had come to this when he did – KB's concerns for timing were clearly well founded.

Tremayne was tired and felt awkward as he returned to KB's office. He was surprised to find he was still there.

'There's a natural cover agent working in the area I'm surveying,' Tremayne said finally.

'Sinclair,' said KB.

'Yes. Steven Locke. He's missing. So is another one from the Greco list, in Thailand.'

'This is very serious.'

'It certainly is.'

'You know, I remember my first posting,' smiled KB ruefully. 'I very nearly came a cropper myself.'

'Do you think they messed up?'

'I have no idea *what's* happened to those individuals. All I can assure you of is that there is a tried and tested network of safe houses and that all communications channels have been authorized to accept Greco SOS messages. In the meantime, the groups that you and Sara are researching must surely be in panic mode.'

'Well, yes. They're fighting like a pack of dogs.'

KB considered this new information as if he was conflicted about it. 'It might seem a little expedient, brutal even, but it makes sense to stay on top of the job at hand despite these personal tragedies playing out. We can only hope and pray for their safety,' said KB, fixing on him with a smile of sincerity.

Something about it made Tremayne very nervous indeed.

Twenty-One

B en was asleep, but his body was telling his brain something quite urgent. It was this: he couldn't breathe.

As he reached full consciousness he saw Nat's accusing eyes staring into his. He was three inches from his face. Reaching up, he felt Nat's hand pressing tightly over his mouth. He was being smothered.

It was still dark. Nat's fingers smelled of sweat, an overpowering musk. Ben scrabbled for a hold but Nat's hands were strong and he was leaning with all his weight. Ben flicked his legs above him and was about to throttle Nat with a ju-jitsu move when Nat whacked him on the head and put his finger to his lips. Ben turned his head and saw Lucy at the door. She was listening intently.

Slowly, Ben began to understand.

All three of them had fought against sleep. But it had found them sure enough. Nat had claimed the bed as his own, so, as a punishment, Lucy placed him on first watch and promptly clambered on the mattress herself. Ben remembered how he'd sat on the floor and offered to stay awake with Nat. But Nat refused, offended by the implication. Ben was on the floor and asleep before his head hit his backpack.

Ben refocused on the present.

He exhaled in a groan, hissing the air quietly back in as quietly as he could. He had to shut up. Had to. Ben tried to control his panicked breaths. It took two or three vast, meas-ured lungfuls to do so. His chest quivered in pain – he wanted nothing more than to gulp the air in, to pant.

Nat made a small gesture – 'fingers walking' – with his free hand. Ben nodded and Nat removed his hand. Ben listened intently. He signed to Lucy in some of the rudimentary sign language they'd acquired in training – *I can't hear anything*.

She signed back: *five minutes ago*.

Nat pointed to the door and Ben moved with him to join Lucy. On a silent count of three, she yanked the door open.

All was darkness, cicadas, the crash of the waves.

No one was there. 'Will o' the wisp,' smiled Ben.

'There were footsteps. Ten minutes ago.'

'You told me five.'

'I heard them too,' said Nat.

Nat stayed by the door as Lucy stepped outside on to the verandah with Ben. No figures could be seen outside. It was as if the person had vanished into the night air or drained quietly into the ground. As they turned back to Nat, they saw a look of bemused fascination on his face. Following his gaze, they could see why: the door.

A length of plain white cloth had been tied to the handle, on the exterior side. The remaining length had been wound tightly into a loop. Nat held part of that loop in his hand. He began to remove it gently from the handle.

'Where'd that come from?' asked Lucy.

Nat shot her a look and took it back into the room.

Ben crouched low to the ground and examined the dirt and sand around their doorway. He could see no evidence of footprints, any disturbance at all. It lent this bizarre gift some form of credence – if it had been a practical joke or a piece of drunken art, there would have been tracks of some description. The complete absence of them started Ben's heart racing.

He came back inside the beach bungalow and flicked the light on. Nat began to slowly unravel the cloth on the bed. His palms a little damp with anticipation, Ben thought the bizarre object looked like a long, porous bandage. It rolled out across the bed and back on to the floor. It appeared to be blank.

'What the hell is it?' asked Nat

Lucy held it in her hands. Unfurled completely, it was over four and a half feet long. 'I'm not sure,' she said, in a tone of voice that suggested she thought she knew exactly what it was, but wasn't saying – yet.

'Looks like a bandage,' said Nat. 'Maybe someone's sprained ankle was miraculously healed by the waters and they hung it there in a moment of liberation.'

Lucy stared at a space just past his right shoulder for a moment, her brow furrowed in concentration. Ben knew the look well and it confirmed what he had earlier suspected – she had an opinion and she knew she was right. It was unbearably sexy, compounded by the fact that it was one of the few expressions she pulled that was entirely natural.

'I think this was meant for us, specifically.'

Ben nodded. 'Can't see any evidence of an approach or retreat – unless they came over the roof to slip it on our door. They knew what they were doing, and they were doing it with a countersurveillance mindset.'

'Except,' said Nat, 'for the footsteps. That was a little bloody obvious.'

'Possibly a ruse to ensure we found the message before anyone else took it,' said Lucy.

'What message?'

She was holding it up to the light now. Sniffing it.

'I must say, I'm impressed.'

'What message? What is this?' Nat took it away from Lucy and did exactly the same as her, screwing up his nose as he smelled it.

'It's a scytale.'

'A what?'

Lucy flared her nostrils as if to say: *surely even YOU know what a scytale is . . .?* Nat's helpless look made her raise her eyes to the ceiling. 'Ben, at least tell me you know what I'm talking about.'

Ben licked his lips as he gazed from Lucy and back to the bandage. It gave him enough time to think without looking as if he was struggling. Abruptly he clicked his fingers and smiled. 'The Romans,' he said.

'Strictly speaking, the Spartans and Greeks as well.'

'My God. Low tech.'

'No kidding.'

'Hello? Anyone?' Nat ventured.

Ben pulled Nat over to the length of cloth. 'One of the earliest forms of cipher. The Romans used it all the time to communicate between legions . . .' He trailed off and suddenly looked panicked. He turned back to Lucy for reassurance. 'If memory serves.'

Lucy nodded. 'It does. As I said, it was the Greeks and Spartans who first used it but the Romans applied it wholesale. It's a primitive transposition cipher. You wind this cloth around a cylinder-shaped object, like a baton, spear, something like that. Then you write your message and transfer it in this form to someone else who also has the same kind of cylindrical decoder.'

'You mean you just wrap it round something again and read it?' said Nat.

'Precisely.'

'But how do you *know* that? I mean, from just looking at it?'

'Well, I don't *know*. I'm only *guessing*.'

'That's what I thought. I don't normally reply to emails with lengths of bandage.'

'Quite.'

'Although it might be quite a fun thing to do if you had enough time on your hands.'

'Look, there's one way to know for sure. Do you have a lighter?'

Nat rummaged in his pockets but Ben was there first, handing over a silver Zippo. Lucy charged it and held the flame six inches underneath the cloth.

'Many messages were written in urine,' Lucy said as she brought the flame a little closer. 'I think this was probably lemon juice. But then again I hate the smell of lemons too, so I'm easy either way.'

By now the flame was only a few inches from the cloth. Gradually, a transformation occurred in the weave. Letters and numbers began to appear, written in a solid, steady hand. Ben tilted his head and squinted at the message. It wasn't very enlightening.

JEI8OST1IAA3NMN9TAS0HR71

Nat mouthed the letters and numbers silently to himself as Lucy shook her head with disbelief.

'Shit a bloody brick,' said Nat.

Twenty-Two

They had tried to take their discussion outside, but their conversations were travelling too far in the night air and so they retreated back into the bungalow.

Theories and explanations swung back and forth between them. Nat explained that anyone with enough training in computer forensics and a good line in police impersonation could track them to the guesthouse computers via the 'return path' to a static IP address. That was the big fallacy of web-based email, he explained. It gave the illusion of anonymity without any of the benefits. The spam was a clever touch. By clicking on the link, they only helped to confirm their location.

'Well, why didn't you say that at the time?' asked Ben.

Nat scratched his head. 'I'm confused, mate. I thought we wanted to find them.'

'We have the message but not the cipher,' said Lucy. 'We don't even know what to wrap this around in order to read it.'

Nat rubbed his eyes and looked at the list of letters again. 'A cylinder, you said.'

'Not just any cylinder. The same size of cylinder. The one they used to write it.'

'We could just do a substitution matrix ourselves.'

'Numbers, Nat,' said Lucy, 'It might be a progressive substitution. We'd have no way of knowing whether the numbers were right, even if the letters made sense.'

114

'Well, how are we supposed to know what that is?'

'This town is pretty small. It could have been written close by. Maybe we can find the thing it was composed on in the first place.'

They agreed to a search.

The place was asleep, bar a few amorous couples rolling in the bushes. As it turned out, there were a number of potential candidates that immediately caught their eye. A flagpole protruded from a bar, the yellow, blue and green of Brazil fluttering limply in the shelter of the building. Ben shook his head as Nat attempted to remove it quietly – but it was stuck fast. The axles of cars, the crossbars of bikes, table legs, roadsign poles, the lamps still standing in darkened bars, the branches and trunks of every tree they could see. They gently wrapped the scytale around each one. But no sense came, no meaning.

Gradually, the candidates dwindled to nothing. It was farcical. Three people rooting around in the shadows for the correctly shaped cylinder.

The futility swept over all three of them at the same time. Perhaps we'll find out later, Ben told her, perhaps we're not meant to read the message yet. But Lucy was not convinced. It was a test, she had decided. A first hurdle in a long line of hurdles. And they had failed.

The moon was brighter than before, despite its first quarter. The sand was cold and fine like flour. Without too much moonlight, the stars were allowed to come into their own. A merciless infinity of other worlds, thought Ben. They would shine on future species and no doubt entrance them in turn. The reasons would never come.

Reason never did.

Reason had no place in this universe.

Just ask John Sinclair.

Ben was so busy gazing at the sky, he was the last to see the boat. A small fishing craft, recently abandoned, judging from the footprints heading away into the brush and the drag marks still visible in the wet sand.

One oar rested inside the vessel, peeking over the side. The second oar was standing vertically next to the prow, half plunged, like a royal standard, into the sand. A piece of white cloth was attached to the centre of the length, billowing like a flag in the onshore breeze.

Lucy was the first to reach it.

She lowered the oar carefully to the sand. Nat bent down to help her unwind the cloth. Ben caught up with both of them and produced his lighter. He cupped his hands as the flame blazed. The wind was too strong, and so the three of them moved around the boat to gain shelter from the portside. Ben charged the lighter again. Together they passed the cloth over the flame. But nothing happened.

'Intriguing,' said Lucy.

She held the lighter closer to the cloth. It began to catch fire. Swearing, she plunged it into the sand.

'Yes, intriguing,' muttered Nat. 'This "flame" burns "cloth". Perhaps there's an industrial use for that?'

Lucy pushed him aside and pulled the oar on to her lap. Then she began slowly wrapping the scytale cloth around the length of the oar. 'I think that was a signal and not a message,' she said as she worked. 'The cloth identified the oar as the key we needed. Only a student of espionage would know to test it as a scytale.'

'You know,' said Nat, 'seeing this boat, this beach . . . it all just brings back so many memories . . .'

Ben rounded on him, eyes blazing. 'We had an agreement,' he said. 'Only forward.'

116

'Quiet,' said Lucy.

Nat kept watch by the prow, but there was no activity up or down the beach. He shivered slightly in the wind. Two minutes later, Lucy's work was done. Ben prodded Nat gently with the end of the oar, making him jump. He scrambled back over the sand and sat with the others as they strained their eyes in the half-light of the coming dawn. Ben's Zippo struggled to shed a little more light. The cloth, wound tightly around the cylinder, now showed rows of six letters and numbers at a time.

JOINTH

ESAMAR

As Lucy turned the oar slowly, the two other lines appeared underneath:

ITANS7

813901

Ben stared at it for a moment and then grinned.

'It says, JOIN THE SAMARITANS,' he said.

Nat looked at him blankly, then returned his eyes to the oar. It took him another few moments to register this was indeed true. Nat had never been the brightest light in cryptography seminars and he showed his true colours again now. 'What about the rest of it? Bank account details? Safe deposit key-code?'

'Looks like a phone number if you ask me,' said Lucy.

Ben smiled. Lucy laughed. Nat just shook his head.

'Whoever they are,' said Ben, 'I like their style.'

Contact Five

Twenty-Three

There were many reasons why calling the number was the most sensible thing to do. There were other equally valid reasons why it was reckless in the extreme.

Nat had made the point that the path of least resistance was often the most dangerous. Lucy countered with the road least travelled being probably just the wrong road – the pattern of numbers, the manner of the contact, it was all pointing towards the telephone.

Ben sat back and let the argument resolve itself.

Why that message had been left, whatever the intentions – it was worth at least finding out who had sent it. At least, admitted Nat, to applaud them on their originality.

It was the only way to be sure, in any case.

Ben quietly made the point that so long as the phone call was the correct move, it would also help prove that Contact Zero, whatever it was, was more than just some mythical possibility. It was something plausible, tangible, a goal that could be achieved. Loyalty for Ben, like belief, was something that died unless it was tested. Together with his father he had experienced this on a weekly basis as a supporter of Bristol City Football Club.

By testing this myth, they might just prove it.

They waited for dawn and caught a local bus north, reasoning more crowds would mean more unscrutinized public phones. They'd agreed a local phone number was the most likely choice for the numbers on the message and in any case it was the easiest to test.

It took Ben an hour to convince Nat that the payphone they would choose would be secure enough for their needs. No payphone is truly secure, of course, but the ability of any intelligence agency to locate a person accurately based on their payphone use is shaky at best. It's the province of television cop shows, rather than real life.

The three of them wandered the streets together in their search, no one willing to let the others out of their sight. Ben wondered if it was tradecraft, trust or simple paranoia that did it. In the end he realized that they were all a little bit more nervous than they were letting on. There was safety, after all, in numbers. That's why they were sticking together. Wasn't it?

They located a payphone in a quieter road off the main strip of bars and hostels that had sprung up outside this once sleepy fishing village. The day was emerging blearily from the night before. Fishermen worked the waters off the coast and several passed as they walked to the local restaurants to hawk the morning's catch. A German couple emerged from a bar, apparently still enjoying their previous night.

To help mask their location, they used an international phonecard. Lucy held the handset as Ben dialled. Nat was fidgeting beside them, drumming his fingers on the metal box that enclosed the phone itself. When Lucy pressed the final digit, however, he stopped. The three of them held a collective breath.

A voice answered after three long tones. It was male, well-spoken and friendly. It was also untraceably neutral in accent.

'How can I help?'

Lucy was momentarily tongue-tied.

'Hello,' she said, closing her eyes in embarrassment. She gathered herself quickly and assumed a more formal tone. 'I was given this number by a friend. I'm looking for the Samaritans.'

The receiver seemed to click a couple of times, as if suddenly muted, then faded until the only noise Lucy could hear on the line was static. Lucy was about to speak again when:

'Are you calling about the tour?' said the voice.

'Yes.'

'Space is limited.'

'There's three of us.'

Another long silence. Music started blaring out of a nearby bar, a soundtrack for the cleaners. Ben stared at them as they set about their work. They were dancing as they mopped. Not a care in the universe. Lucy plugged a finger in her ear and listened as the man spoke again:

'Go to Recife, to the Terminal Integrado de Passageiros. Take the first northbound bus tomorrow morning. Direction will be Fortaleza. Ride for fifty kilometres . . .'

Lucy's brain struggled to keep up. The man was talking at a hundred miles an hour.

'. . . then get out. Fifty kilometres exactly. You will then follow further instructions.'

'How?'

'A brush past will occur during this time.'

'What time should I—'

But the phone went dead. Lucy sighed and replaced the receiver. Ben looked at her.

'What time should *we* . . .' he said.

She checked her watch impatiently. Already doing time and motion in her head.

'Yeah, well. My mistake,' said Lucy. 'Let's keep moving.'

They flagged down a decrepit combi, a cramped people-carrying minibus that was pulling out of the main drag. It was a commuter service, packed full of locals travelling up the coast to the bigger resorts. It bounced along towards the tarmac of the highway and headed north.

Ben thought about the phone call as the suspension shuddered over potholes and rocks. The directions were standard-issue rendezvous format. 'According to Winthrop' was an early lesson in SIS training. The Winthrop System stated that any set of physical instructions – be they to a dead drop, brush past or other contact – should be described in exactly four stages. Hence, the bus station, the northbound route, the fifty kilometres, the remain in place for further instructions. The next stage, Ben reasoned, would have the same parameters. It was somehow comforting. Whatever this was, whoever these people really were, they used the same familiar tools.

There was one other traveller with them in the combi. He'd sprinted after the thing from the sand just as they'd left, lugging his backpack with him as he ran. Settling himself into the back seat with an endless stream of excuse mes and pardons, he caught sight of the three other backpackers in the car and nodded. His tan was the colour of teak, curly black hair spilling down over a chiselled face. He would not have looked out of place on the beaches of Bahia.

'Love these fellas,' said the man, patting the combi like it was a dog. He turned out to be a chirpy Australian who introduced himself as Roger. This was precisely the opposite of what all three of them needed at that moment, but Lucy stepped into the breach with her freshest, most interested face as he spoke.

'You lot going far?'

'Dunno yet. Where are you headed?' smiled Lucy.

'Probably back down to Rio eventually. Want to make it for Carnival. Though I hear Recife's got a fun old party going on in the run-up.'

Small talk continued until they reached the highway, when the rumble of the tarmac dissolved any more conversation. Halfway to Recife, the Australian took his leave with a nod. He clambered on to the roof and unhooked his backpack, waving as he headed back down towards the beach.

In the interests of time, Ben had suggested they dry-cleaned their route with countersurveillance measures only once, leaving their combi and then hailing another for the remainder of their journey. It wasn't much, but the only way to keep nerves at bay was to treat each step into the unknown as a practical field operation on final selection weekend. This was why, Ben reasoned, every piece of field training in their probation year had been a living hell of chaos. Nothing in the real world ever truly went to plan. Instructors (mostly SAS officers on leave) took a particular and sadistic delight in throwing wrenches into proceedings – sometimes, quite literally.

They continued their dry-cleaning moves when they reached the bus station. It was a mud and concrete affair, jumbled over an undulating square of ground, a low-rise ticket hall glowing in the centre like a fluorescent furnace. Even at three in the morning, the place was mobbed. People waited, slept, argued, kissed and in some cases danced. Hundreds of men and women hefted bags of fruit and vegetables in every direction. Hundreds of others simply stood and stared, watching the crowds. Cutpurses and con artists of every stripe were here, and Ben felt the scrutiny on the back of his neck.

The bus schedule on the wall of the ticket office stated the first bus to Fortaleza would leave from Stand 11 at 0315. On their fourth tour of the site, Lucy checked her watch – ten minutes before departure. They had agreed not to show their hand until the last minute, boarding only when they were sure they were the final passengers on board. But now the man selling tickets in the hall had disappeared. They were sticking out, of course, as highly visible bleary backpackers with multi-coloured clothing. Lucy swatted away unwelcome stares and kept in between Nat and Ben. Diesel engines rumbled into life, spewing up black vapour and dust that choked the early morning air. As first light approached, overnight buses arriving from further afield began roaring up the station entryway. Nat narrowly avoided decapitation from a low-slung wing mirror as it swung in a violent arc around the corner.

Every minute brought more people, more crowds, the throng living and breathing of its own accord, a fluid entity with nowhere to flow. Drivers leaned on their horns at the slightest delay and the nerves around Ben's eyes began to throb with the noise, the stress, the jostling, unsettling energy of the place.

They might not get a space on this bus at all, he thought suddenly. They might have to fight their way on.

Stand 11 was certainly a popular spot. A crowd was gathering, spilling off the cracked paving and on to the tarmac below. Ben caught Lucy's arm and she jumped. *We should go*, he whispered, and she nodded in accord. Turning back to Nat, Ben paused to adjust his backpack when he heard a mighty yell he recognized immediately as Lucy. Wheeling around, he could see her sprinting away through the crowds after what seemed to be a small boy. She had left her backpack on the ground. Ben strained to see in the half-light and made out Lucy's head as it weaved through the throng. Ahead of her, ploughing a path, was the boy. He had her moneybelt in his hand.

'Thief!' she shouted, as all eyes turned to the chase.

'Stay with these,' shouted Ben. Nat glared at him but nodded. He dragged Ben's backpack towards him with his foot.

Ben powered off the pavement and into the swirling chaos of the concourse. He ran out in front of a Rio-bound luxury coach that blew its horn so loudly he was nearly blown into the path of a combi. Between two more incoming vehicles, Ben could see the boy now, moneybelt in hand, straps flapping in the breeze, doubling back now and hoping Lucy didn't follow into the traffic.

Big mistake, thought Ben.

He scrambled underneath an idling coach and waited for the little legs to flit past him – shooting his hand out and catching the kid's ankles. The little guy went flying, landing hard and painfully in the dirt. He cried out and scrambled to his feet again, kicking away like a mule, but Ben held fast. The kid must have been ten years old at the very most. A scar on his cheek and a fiery defiance burning in him. Ben took the belt back, whacked him around the ear and sprinted away. The kid, bemused but happy to get away with it, ran off towards the entryway.

'Ben?'

He could hear Lucy's shouts above the engines. He tried to shout back but got a lungful of exhaust fumes.

'Ben!'

He could see her now. He waved her moneybelt like a semaphore. She jabbed her finger in the direction of Stand 11. A bus was pulling away. Ben sprinted back across the concourse. He found Nat where he'd left him, surrounded by three backpacks.

'Those fuckers tried to get your stuff,' shouted Nat, pointing at a crowd of women pretending this was nothing to do with them. Ben glanced at them and looked back for Lucy. But she was nowhere to be seen.

Nat joined him, scanning the crowds. 'Where the hell did she go?' There was no sign of her. Anywhere.

'Stay here—' shouted Ben as he ran out again into the tumult.

'Bus is leaving! One minute!' spat Nat in his wake.

Ben took a quick 360 of the bus station. There was no way he'd find her in the crowds. He checked his watch and sprinted back to find Lucy standing accusingly over her backpack.

'Where did you get to?' yelled Lucy.

'Same to you—' said Ben, but Nat's voice was loudest.

'The BUS!'

Ben and Lucy wheeled around to see a coach chugging out of its stand. The doors were closed, the seats filled. Lucy ran out in front of it and strained to look at the destination card in the driver's window. It read 'DIREÇÃO PORTIMAO'.

She waved back to Ben and Nat, shaking her head.

Ben and Nat hefted their backpacks on to their shoulders and ran to the other stands. Ben felt Lucy's arm on his shoulder.

'That one!'

The Fortaleza bus was backing out of an entirely different stand now, number 17. From the sound of the labouring engine it seemed about ready to roar off down the exit ramp. Ben dropped his backpack and dived out in front of it. The driver blasted his horn, but Ben would not back down. Playing the 'entitled tourist' came easily to him, but it wasn't until Lucy arrived that the doors finally opened.

The driver hefted himself down the stairs and opened up the luggage area at the side of the bus. Nat helped him throw the rucksacks inside. A large tip finessed their progress into the last remaining seats and was also useful in distracting the driver long enough for Ben to get a good look at the milometer.

They sank into their seats and let the adrenaline dissipate into their blood. Ben kept an eye on their speed and calculated they would not need to get off this thing for half an hour. At current speed, at least.

'Seriously, Lucy,' asked Ben after a while, 'where did you go?' Although he was talking to Lucy, he was not looking at her. Nat was in the window seat next to her. Ben was in the seat behind, next to a tired-looking man eating sunflower seeds.

'What do you mean?' said Lucy eventually, half turning to look at him.

'How come I got to him before you did? You had a head start.'

'I got lost in the crowd.'

The man next to Ben spat a sunflower seed on to the floor.

Twenty-Four

Vauxhall Cross, London

The Chief's office was on the eighth floor, a corner suite of course, and decorated – rather disappointingly, Tremayne thought – in IKEA flat-pack furniture. The Chief's real name was Thomas Newton but he had been referred to by his American cop-show moniker ever since he had ordered someone audibly to 'get the hell out of my office' in his first week.

The Chief had arrived at the Service under the auspices of economy. Now that there was so much money sloshing around the building, Tremayne was surprised to see the Chief had never allocated any of it for refurbishment. He did, however, have a very suave line in pink Oxford cloth shirts. Pastel colours never suited Tremayne, but the big man managed to pull them off with aplomb.

And he was big. A competitive swimmer in his youth, the Chief's back was as wide as the leather Ektorp armchair that tanned itself quietly in the corner of the room.

The big man in the pink shirt stared at the balding man with the glasses and smiled.

'I'm pleased you felt the need to talk to me personally,' said the Chief. His voice had a healthy, wholewheat substance to it, as if it would do you good if you somehow managed to ingest it. 'I like to encourage communication. We all know what happens when it all breaks down.'

Tremayne wasn't, in fact, sure what happened when it all broke down. But he nodded all the same. After a moment's pause, Tremayne realized this was the Chief's nonverbal way of telling him it was his turn to speak. So he spoke.

He told him all about his concerns over Greco.

The Chief had spent his entire career being able to nod sagely at anyone talking to him, communicating in that silent gesture the sense that he knew exactly what was being discussed, that he was in the process of digesting it and that he agreed – but only up to a point. Now he was at the top of the tree, however, and he had nothing to prove. But force of habit made him do it again.

He'd never heard of an operation called Greco.

He did, however, know a man called KB.

He knew him very well indeed.

The Brazilian bus had rattled its way out of the urban sprawl of Recife, heading north along gleaming tarmac. The sun was beginning to peek over the trees, blinding Nat with a spotlight of orange as he slouched in the window seat.

Ben made his way back from the front of the coach.

'Forty-eight,' he announced. He slipped into the seat behind them. 'Two left, get ready.'

'Three, actually,' said Nat, and held up his hand-held Global Positioning System as if to prove his point. He'd been measuring their accumulated distance ever since they'd left Recife.

Ben glared at him. 'How long have you had that?'

Nat shrugged. 'About six months. Why? You want one? When's your birthday?'

Lucy shook her head. 'You and GPS, Nat. A marriage made in Dixons.'

'I like to know where I am.'

'You might have told me,' said Ben.

Nat pulled the blind down, wincing in the sun. 'You might have asked.'

At exactly fifty kilometres north of the bus station, Lucy, Ben and Nat were deposited by the side of the road by the driver. He'd maintained his commitment to only stopping at registered bus stops, but as luck would have it, there was one not a hundred yards down the road. Ben shoved a few notes into the driver's hand.

The driver did not help with their bags, but only descended to close up the baggage area once they'd retrieved their luggage from the boxes and produce inside. As the bus pulled away into the distance, Ben felt a sudden chill. They were sitting ducks out here, he thought. Cars flashed past them at suicidal speeds. The isolation and the bizarre directions had put all of them at distinct unease. And so far, the only reassurances they'd had were a strip of cloth and a telephone call. It might be according to Winthrop, but it was still unsettling.

After half an hour of waiting, Nat had had enough.

'A brush past will occur, that's what he said, right? Bollocks to that.'

'During this time,' said Lucy. 'He said, "A brush past will occur during this time".'

'So,' said Ben, 'it could already have happened.'

It was then they heard the phone. An electronic trill. For a moment, the three of them were paralysed. Instinctively, they all reached for their pockets, knowing full well they had jettisoned their own phones long ago. The roadside verge had no payphones in sight. Beyond the tarmac, only trees and scrub.

Lucy was the first to locate the source.

'Nat,' she smiled, 'your bag is ringing.'

Ben and Lucy tried to suppress their laughter as Nat dived for his backpack in a blind panic, his chubby fingers fumbling with the plastic ties and buckles. Eventually, a small zipper on a hidden side panel revealed the still-ringing cellphone. Nat brandished it like a trophy. Lucy put out her hand to receive it, but Nat had already pressed the thing to his ear.

Ben and Lucy watched dumbfounded as he walked calmly away from them, finger in his ear. Ben wondered how they'd slipped the phone in, but he remembered the kid. Either he'd done it himself before stealing the moneybelt or he'd been used as a distraction. Ben also knew full well that any luggage on a South American bus was fair game. He'd seen kids leaping on top of minivans, ripping off the rucksacks and jumping off again before the owners inside knew what was happening.

It didn't take Nat very long to turn around and walk back to them, pausing halfway to stamp on the phone with his boot heel.

'You going to tell us what they said?'

'Wrong number,' smiled Nat.

'Try again.'

'Retrace your route two clicks. Order coffee.'

Ben gave Lucy a despairing look.

'It's what the man said.'

Two kilometres down the road, a small roadside café was doing moderate business at a junction. It was called Barbao. The interior was small and the table at the back of the grimy structure was empty. Four chairs beckoned. Avoiding the stares of the breakfast crowd of regulars at the bar, they took up occupation.

Their *cafes com leites* were long cold when a man appeared from the bead curtain that separated the eating area from the kitchens at the back. He was tall, with a tan the colour of teak.

It was Roger, the Australian.

He'd changed, however. Gone were the flipflops and brightly coloured rucksack. Gone too was the chirpy Aussie accent. In his jeans and sneakers, he could have passed for any local. Which, Ben suspected, was exactly who he was. Ben noticed for the first time that his bare arms were badly scarred. He tapped his trouser pocket to make sure the Swiss army knife was somewhere he could use it.

Roger smiled thinly at them and placed a brown envelope on the table.

'You're here for the tour?' he said.

Lucy nodded, as she slid the envelope over to her. She began to break the seal when Roger's hand clasped hers in an innocent but painful grip. Both Ben and Nat bristled at the physical contact and shared a glance – they would both move if this got any further.

'Deliver this – intact and unmolested – to the address on the front.'

'Think you've confused us with someone else,' said Ben, not meeting his eye. 'I think it's the Post Office who does deliveries.'

'Your tickets are waiting for you there,' continued Roger, without a pause.

And he was gone, strolling out of the front door into the strengthening sunshine. Lucy turned the envelope over. The address, in spidery writing, was a well-known international hotel chain in Recife.

'So, open it,' said Nat.

'Judging from the broken bones in my hand,' said Lucy, 'I don't really think he wants us to.'

'It's a test of trust,' said Ben.

Nat stood up and stretched. 'Well, enough of this bloody

subterfuge, that's what I say. We can steam it. It's fine.' He grabbed the envelope but Ben caught his hand.

'No.'

'I can do it with my eyes shut.'

'I know. Still. You're not doing it.'

Nat had a solid line in defensive facial expressions. He deployed one now, that of the aggrieved genius held back by ignorant cretins.

'Or maybe it's a test of our ability to open the bloody thing, and by delivering it intact, we show ourselves to be worthless. How about that?'

The stand-off was beginning to attract attention from the owner. Lucy's heart skipped a beat when she realized one of the diners was still in his police uniform.

Nat's skills at nuancing letters from their envelopes had indeed become legendary during training. This, however, was not to be his day to shine.

'We're going to deliver this thing,' said Lucy. 'And that's the end of it.' Ben nodded in solidarity. And for once, Nat had nothing to say.

Contact Four

Twenty-Five

Recife
1450 local time

The city of Recife is arranged in a confusing array around bridges. The older town of Olinda, the original settlement of the Dutch, was in fact the primary tourist destination. The place was a composite, old and new, sand and concrete, a palimpsest of what was possible with planning and what surely follows in its absence. Early in the morning, the triangular sails of fishing boats, known as *jangadas*, dotted the ocean past the reefs that gave Recife its name.

Most visitors to the city avoided Recife itself altogether, choosing to stay in the safer and prettier Olinda. The address on the package took Ben, Lucy and Nat far away from the heritage sites and cafés, and into the heart of the chaos of downtown Recife.

The Hilton was located in a strip of international chain hotels on the western side of the city. Local politicians and businessmen outnumbered the prostitutes at the bar, but only just. Bored waiters shook lukewarm cocktails and slid them on to coasters.

The elevators operated only with room keys. Nat suggested they book into Room 540 'and drill a little old hole in the wall'. Good tradecraft but bad timing – Lucy was adamant that if they were to receive trust, they first had to show it. Bypassing the bank of elevators, they ascended to the tenth floor via an emergency exit stairwell. The corridor was deserted.

Ben led the way. Room 541 was located at the very end of the hallway, around the corner from a large picture window that offered a view of the city back towards the beach. The walls were a dirty salmon colour. Disinfectant and carpet cleaner mingled in the air conditioned air. It all made Ben feel ill. Ben was starting to think that Nat's suggestion might have been the right one – perhaps the room above, he was thinking, and they could find a vantage point through the ceiling. Before he had time to vocalize this, Lucy had knocked sharply on the door. He glared accusingly at her. She flashed a look back that seemed to say: *what was wrong with that?*

Calm footsteps inside, a quiet turning of the lock. Ben slid his hand into his pocket and gripped his Swiss army knife. Trust or not, there was no reason not to have insurance.

The door was opened by a broad-shouldered man in a brown pinstripe suit. His black hair was swept back on his head, glittering with wax, which had the unfortunate effect of making him resemble Count Dracula. He was preternaturally clean-shaven.

He regarded them sternly for a moment. His eyes dropped to the package in Lucy's hand. He smiled politely and beckoned them inside.

The room smelled of fresh coffee and cigars. A window was open, a light breeze rippling sheets of hotel stationery that lay in a pile on an old bureau.

The man shut the door behind them.

In his tight suit he could have been moonlighting as a nightclub bouncer. He waved the three of them to a flowery sofa and began pouring coffee into four cups. 'How can I help you?' he smiled. His accent was quite a shock – he had the rich dark plummy tones of a Latin teacher at Eton College. His tongue was the colour of claret.

Lucy kept her best Texas Hold 'Em poker face. 'We were told you might be expecting a package.'

'So you do have something for me.'

'In principle, yes.'

The man chuckled and brought the tray over to the small coffee table in front of the sofa. He perched himself on the arm of a chair by the window.

The aroma of freshly brewed coffee wafted up from the tray into Ben's nostrils. He desperately needed a hit of quality caffeine and knew the others felt the same. But they had no idea what was in these cups. They had not seen it being prepared. They could not accept. Training taught them that much, at least. The lowest ebb is the most dangerous time.

'Now then,' said the man, waving an encouraging hand towards the tray. 'Jamaican Blue Mountain. All very fresh. A little insulting to the Brazilians, I know, but good coffee is hard to come by on this bountiful continent, for some reason.'

'We're good, thanks,' said Nat. Ben caught his eye. They were on the same page for once.

'We'd like to know what the deal is,' said Lucy.

'The *deal*,' smiled the man, 'as you put it, is simple. I have no idea who you are. You could be three tourists taking an extreme risk.'

'Highly unlikely,' said Nat.

'But yet it's undeniably a professional awareness of just those small probabilities that keep us all, if you will, breathing.' He smiled a humourless smile. 'The way you can remedy this is to hand over something that would convince me otherwise. That way, we can begin to trust each other. Which is, after all, the point. Is it not?'

Lucy looked at Ben and Nat. They both nodded. Lucy brandished the envelope and placed it on the coffee table. The man sat up to reach for it, but Lucy pulled it back from his grasp, keeping her hand firmly on top of it.

'Just one question,' said Lucy. 'For the sake of argument, a theoretical one.'

'For the sake of argument,' said the man, sitting back calmly. 'A good cause. Very well.'

'Let's say that the delivery of this package into your hands is enough to convince you that we are serious.'

'Yes, let's.'

'All right. So, if that's true, what then?'

'You had expressed interest in a tour, I believe?'

Lucy pushed the envelope towards the man. He examined the seal carefully. Then in a flash removed a flick knife from his jacket pocket. Ben's hand twitched to his own blade but stopped short when he saw the man was merely using the weapon to slice open the envelope. He replaced the knife and quietly shook out the contents.

A series of photographs slid into his lap. He examined them one by one, placing them face down on the table in front of him.

He reached over to the telephone and hit three buttons. Into the receiver, Ben heard him say:

We've fin - ished our coffee

He lingered on the word 'finished' as a bow player would remain tenuto on a note – not long enough to change the value, but too long for it not to change emphasis. Ben felt this

142

subtle adjustment and didn't like it, feeling somehow it denoted something else, that this was not simply the information being delivered. Ben was moving his eyes to the door now. The man listened intently for a few moments, then hung up. 'Very well,' he smiled back at Lucy on the sofa. 'The next question may be difficult for you. Do you have any preference for country?'

'Country?' asked Nat.

'You will be placed within our . . . within the *apparatus*, but we try to avoid putting people where they know they will be unhappy. I'm sure you understand.'

Three faces on the sofa stared blankly back.

Lucy sat forward. 'Wait, that's it?'

'There are a number of formalities, of course: new identities, papers, money and so on. But yes, that *is* "it". Unless you can think of anything else . . .?'

Nat smiled. 'Well, personally, I've always liked the sound of the Cayman Islands.'

Ben was not smiling. The man had noticed this and now turned and flashed a reassuring grin in his direction. 'And what about you? Do you have any requests?'

'Just one,' said Ben. 'We've identified ourselves by bringing you that package. You have not.'

A look of startled astonishment washed across the man's smooth features. 'I didn't think I needed to.'

Ben moved quietly but pointedly to his feet. It wasn't panicked, it wasn't calm – just confident. 'I think I will have that coffee now.' He walked over to the still-simmering coffee pot. The man in the suit was also on his feet, striding perhaps a little less calmly to the phone. In the reflection of the metal coffee maker Ben saw the man's hand migrate to his jacket pocket. Ben's fingers twitched.

'Of course,' said the man, 'you're nervous. I understand. It's a big leap. From loyal subject, to fugitive, to . . .'

He stared off into space, up and to the right, as if searching visibly for the word in the ether. He did this a lot. It added a strange tension to everything he said.

'To what?' asked Ben.

'I hate to say the word, "traitor", but I suppose, theoretically, "according to Hoyle" as the Americans would say . . .'

Lucy was on her feet now. Nat still sat on the sofa, his head full of Paradise Beach, Grand Cayman, yellow bikinis, pina coladas . . .

'Wait, say that again.'

'Calm yourselves for a moment, please, sit—'

Lucy moved to Ben's side as the man punched another number into the hotel phone. 'I don't think I want to do this any more.'

'To be blunt about things, it doesn't really matter,' said the man. 'You already are.'

He turned over the photographs. They showed surveillance shots of high-security installations, individuals on their daily routines, oblivious to the intrusion of the camera lens. In some shots, entire families ate and drank and talked together. The bread and butter of espionage.

Then he produced some newer pictures.

They showed Lucy, Ben and Nat talking with their Australian friend on the bus. Meeting with 'Roger' again, at the café. The envelope in their possession. The series was assembled to make it look like a routine clandestine mission.

'The man you met is one of our hardest-working couriers in the region. By alleviating his workload this morning, you are now officially working for the First Directorate. My congratulations on a job well done.'

144

Lucy watched Ben as he seemed visibly to quell the urge to throw the pot of hot coffee. Her heart was pounding, her face drained of colour. She could hardly speak.

'First Directorate of . . .?'

'Sluzhba Vneshney Razvedki.'

The SVR. The twenty-first-century rebranding of the KGB.

Nat was playing catch-up on the sofa. 'You're Russian?'

'Of course,' smiled the man, his eyes crinkling. 'Why, what did you think I was?'

Twenty-Six

The Cabinet Meeting Room at 10 Downing Street might not witness agreement on many issues, but on one topic everyone there was probably unconsciously unanimous: the Prime Minister was late.

The briefing was only supposed to last forty minutes, but Sir Michael Wyndham, coordinator of security and intelligence at the Cabinet Office, decided the way things were going it might just last a little longer than a hard-boiled egg in a saucepan. He looked at his watch again, salt and pepper eyebrows raised in ill-disguised dismay. It was the PM's first week on the job, it was true, and like an excited puppy he was bounding from meeting room to meeting room without pausing for breath.

Fingers drummed quietly.

This was to be the first 'wisp' briefing of the new Cabinet. In the maelstrom of attention on terror threats and religious fanatics, longer-term security planning was falling by the wayside. The French historian Fernand Braudel once coined the phrase 'wisps of tomorrow', referring to the forces of long-term danger we generally ignore in our all-consuming obsession with the present.

Sir Michael was musing that 'tomorrow' was probably on the cards for everyone at the table too when the door burst open and the PM floated in, a half-hearted apology trailing after him like bad aftershave.

'So glad you could all make it,' he smiled, and Sir Michael wasted no more time. He tapped the dossier in front of him, which the Prime Minister began to flip through as if speed-reading. In reality, he was counting the pages and dividing by minutes. It was only ten thirty and it had already been a very long day.

'I should stress, Prime Minister, these are emergent threats,' said Sir Michael. 'Our window of action on these is long term, but it is no less important than the immediate concerns facing the country today. My colleagues from SIS will brief you on each of these in turn.'

For the next fifteen minutes, the PM listened carefully as the men in pastel shirts from Military Intelligence Six described ten areas of what they called 'important future focus', 'emerging markets' and 'future tipping points'. Ten countries and groups where states might fail, networks might grow and, one day, develop from their bad seeds to threaten the security of the entire country. The PM heard them all with great interest and was keen to hear more. The avian-looking man in the grey suit explained that more information was pending.

The PM then addressed the Chief. 'I take it there are ongoing operations in this area, then? As well as the usual agents in place?'

The Chief shook his head. 'Not at present.'

KB also shook his head.

He was lying. And the Chief knew it.

The meeting was scheduled abruptly, as soon as they both returned from Downing Street. There were to be no exceptions to KB's immediate attendance. To his horror he didn't even have time for coffee.

When KB sauntered in, the Chief closed the door behind him and wheeled him round by the shoulder of his jacket.

'Greco, KB?'

'Sorry?'

'What the fuck is Greco?'

KB cleared his throat to draw a line between this awkward moment and the professional tone he now adopted. 'My department is supervising fifteen live operations worldwide at the present time, all concerned with dual-use technology . . .'

One of the Chief's hangovers from his previous life as a management consultant was a facial expression he called the pregnant furrowed brow. 'And?' he asked, adopting the pose perfectly.

'And Greco is one of them,' said KB, wincing slightly as the sun rounded the corner window and hit him in the face.

The Chief went silent again. The pink of his shirt brought out the blue of his eyes. When he stared like that, thought KB, he was actually quite scary.

'Greco is a comprehensive survey of these emerging threats around the world, with . . . I will call it a dual-use focus.'

'You and dual use,' said the Chief. 'You're the only man I know who looks at medical imaging equipment as the most serious threat to humanity.'

'The vacuum pumps alone—'

'I know,' sighed the Chief. 'The pumps. I know.'

'Well, in this case, the dual-use component isn't clear cut yet. But it will emerge.'

The Chief furrowed his brow again. 'Why isn't it clear cut? And emerge from what?'

'The data,' said KB.

The Chief sighed and looked at his Patek Philippe. The problem these days was the counterfeit shops even faked the

148

mechanisms inside the bloody things. He coveted the strap more than the face, sometimes. Perhaps that's why Beverly had left him last year. For all the show, he'd just been faking the mechanism. 'Why didn't you mention Greco to me before?'

'I wasn't planning to at all. Not until we'd had a few successes. You've done the same when you've been in my position.'

The Chief uncapped his fountain pen and removed a sticky note from a large pile emblazoned with *Chelsea for the Cup*. He wrote the word 'GRECO' in elegant capitals. 'Have you ever considered naming your operations something a little less . . . esoteric?' he asked, as he replaced his pen carefully in the holder. 'Operation Desert Storm, for example, was quite apposite and to the point. It does, to coin an advertising slogan, what it says on the tin.'

'Yes, it does,' grimaced KB, clearly missing his point.

The Chief sighed. 'Hence my confusion. It's an odd choice of name.'

'Well,' said KB knowingly, 'considering its inner dynamics, I was going to call it Ponziani or Relfsson, but that would have been obvious. Lopez would probably be just as good, but more suited to a CNI-based operation. So naturally, I settled on Greco. It seemed most apt.'

The Chief had recognized the acronym for the CNI, the Spanish version of MI6, but nothing else that came out of KB's mouth made much sense. His old friend could have been talking Ancient Finnish for all he could work out.

KB held the uncertain silence between them as the Chief's phone began to purr. 'It's named after Gioachino Greco.'

The Chief nodded again, as if to say: *well, obviously*. He'd known KB too long, and owed him too much, to pursue this any further. The man had a plan and all would be revealed in good time. 'Just keep me in the loop,' he said as he picked up the receiver.

All in good time, thought KB as he walked back to his office and looked forward to a celebratory mug of peppermint tea. He paused by the doorway.

'By the way,' he said, 'how did you come to hear of it?'

'Strange coincidence, but, as it happens, it was Bill's son. You never said he was working for you.'

'Very true,' smiled KB as he left. *Although not for much longer*, he thought.

The Chief watched him go and, locating the word 'Greco' again on his memo pad, added a small, exquisite question mark beside it.

Twenty-Seven

L ucy was still rubbing her eyes. Nat sat stunned, staring out of the hotel room window. *This is not happening*, he seemed to be saying. *This is not the way things are.*

But it was, and they were. Visions of Siberian exile danced in his mind. Sugar plum fairies in Lithuanian *ushankas*.

'You accepted an invitation,' the man in the suit was saying. Ben shook his head and tried to speak. But the man simply continued his train of thought. 'You contacted us, followed our instructions, made a telephone call. You sought us out. When we asked you to perform a task, you willingly acceded. We are merely responding to that overture.'

A pall of silence fell over them.

'We were looking for – something else. Something very much *else*,' spouted Nat, tears welling in his eyes.

The man held the silence that followed his outburst and then sighed. He adopted a tone like a schoolteacher approaching a deeply untalented student.

'Let me try and make this as simple as I can,' he said. 'What you call "Contact Zero" is an elaborate fabrication. A fiction we created years ago to encourage . . . well, people like you, to be perfectly honest. It's not as if insurance underwriters are going to run off and seek out a fugitive spy network when they lose their jobs.'

Lucy could feel Nat's accusing eyes blazing at her. But she

kept her cool and tried to focus on the man's words. The room was spinning and she had to concentrate very carefully on drawing breath. Perhaps sensing her discomfort, the man calmly poured a glass of water from a bottle and handed it to her. She knew she could not accept and this made her all the more nervous. She gritted her teeth as the man continued: 'You must understand this from our position. We can't just walk into Vauxhall Cross and sign up able-bodied traitors. You know as well as I, entrapment is a nuanced business. Choosing which levers to use is an art form. We developed the idea of a fugitive network of spies to . . . I suppose . . . appeal to a field agent's emotional landscape. You play out grand roles, do you not? Heroic stories, thrilling escapes. The world is too mundane *not* to believe in such a thing as the Contact Zero network, wouldn't you say? Yet, sadly, that's exactly how the world is. It does not exist. It lives on, of course, in the hearts of hundreds of men and women just like you, but only in the realm of fantasy. You are now, I regret to inform you, as of this moment living very much in the real world.'

Ben felt his kidneys ache and, listening, had to agree. This was real all right. He had to admire their chutzpah. 'Very clever.'

The man shrugged off the compliment. 'It's only a tool. One of many. We have a similar myth circulating in the CIA. To them, I believe, we are known as the Sanctuary. Or is it the Cloister? I think that's it. Rick Ames was recruited that way, you know.'

A heavy silence filled the room and Ben realized his mouth was still gaping open.

'Do you mean Aldrich Ames?'

From 1985 to 1994, the nine years that he worked for the KGB as a mole, Aldrich 'Rick' Ames single-handedly sold on the names of twenty-five key sources within the Soviet Union to their masters in the KGB, where many of them received what was euphemistically referred to as *vyshaya mera*, the highest level of punishment. The very idea that Ames came to the Russians through the same route as they had made Ben's spine turn to ice.

The man in the suit saw their reactions and nodded sympathetically. 'He was treated badly, you know, before he worked for us. He nearly died in Mexico City. They said it was hard drinking, but it was us. But they took him for granted, until he was – cut adrift, as you say. He made an approach to what he thought was sanctuary. He no doubt found himself in a hotel room not unlike this one.'

'No, Ames had money problems. He had that mistress, the big spender. He approached you in Langley.'

The man shrugged. The gesture said: *you can believe what you like*.

'He was not as troubled by the truth as you seem to be.'

'That's because he was a traitor,' snapped Lucy.

'Beauty, loyalty, reality . . . all of these are in the eye of she who beholds. You know that as well as I.'

'Do you think we'll go along with you?' asked Ben.

The man smiled warmly. 'A very good question. It all depends. These photographs will of course make their way to your handlers at MI6. So, in a sense, they will already presume you are working for us. Even if you are not.'

'We're not interested in what they think any more,' said Lucy.

'Very wise. But even so, your unfortunate situation has no finite end. We've learned, over the years, that people like you are often left floundering alone by their governments. They cease to be useful and they are dropped. Their capture, their death, may be certain if they attempt to return home. This can also happen in any industry, you understand. Yet they also face persecution wherever they lay their hat. So, many years ago, under the guise of what is known to you as Contact Zero, we at the Russian Foreign Intelligence Service began to offer our services as an . . . employment agency. Now. If you have any scrap of wisdom left, I suggest you listen to what I have to say.'

Ben walked over to the window as the man talked. He stared at the horizon and tried to work out how, after everything, they had ended up in a worse position than before. Between a rock and a harder place. The man half turned on the sofa to include him in the sales pitch. *Because that's what this is*, thought Ben. *He's trying to sell us a job.*

'Naturally, we have many safe houses around the world,' continued the suit, 'many false-flag businesses, fronts, the entire infrastructure of espionage. And these things need, well, administration.'

'Housekeeping,' said Nat.

'The very same. And it takes a lot of manpower. Far more than we can usefully recruit through . . . official channels. Thus it is our policy to open our doors to whoever agrees to live by our rules. What is the phrase? "As one door shuts, another one opens." It's not glamorous, I will admit. But it is secure, and you can live out your lives in peace, under the protection of the SVR and First Directorate Security Detail. We can even arrange to transport your families and loved ones to visit. It takes time and money, of course, but it can be done.'

'Wait,' said Ben. 'You just said Ames worked for you after seeking sanctuary. But he wouldn't have signed up if it was just for housekeeping.'

'Well remembered and well put,' smiled the man. 'We rather took advantage of his position. In a rare move, he was forgiven by Langley soon after he'd given up hope and contacted the sanctuary – i.e. us. Naturally, such a situation was too delicious to ignore. His allegiance was already with us when he returned to Virginia. Rick was also, as you know, very motivated. After his arrest, it was agreed that from that point on we would employ recruits only in low-level jobs.'

'One problem,' said Lucy. 'For you, I mean. Our government already thinks we're not worth saving. So blackmailing us into becoming traitors won't help you persuade us. We want nothing to do with this.'

The man toyed with the pictures in his hand. 'A little too late for that now, I think.'

'Forget it,' said Ben.

'Please don't jump to a decision. I understand this is hard to take in, but the world is a cold and brutal place. Particularly for people like you. If you feel ideologically challenged, you might sleep more easily knowing that you are simply a clerk, a lowly cog in a very complex timepiece.'

Ben just stared a hole through the man's head. The man, quite wisely, calculated it was time to wind up his sales pitch.

'The suite across the corridor is ready for you. There are clean sheets, hot showers, room service, false papers, an entire infrastructure all waiting. A new life. All you have to do is go through that door. If, for some reason, you wish to spend the rest of your life as a hunted animal, a global vagrant, then you may leave. We will honour whatever decision you make. We are both from the same profession and we hold you and your work in great esteem. But if you leave us, do not try to contact us again. If you do, we will take steps to ensure your continued silence. I trust you will make the right choice.'

The man stood up, bowed politely to each of them and left the room. It was several minutes before anyone spoke.

'No way,' Lucy said. 'Absolutely no way.'

Ben and Lucy stared at Nat, who was now on his feet.

'Radical point. What have we got to lose?' He was walking slowly towards the door.

'Nat,' Lucy called out. 'Wait.'

Nat turned. By the time he realized what was happening, Ben was slowly manoeuvring himself between Nat and the door.

'Clean sheets,' said Nat, his voice rising with anger and frustration. 'Hot water.'

'Don't do it,' whispered Ben.

'A new identity. This is what your fairy story's been about, Lucy. The reality's not so pretty, I admit. Turning traitor isn't exactly guts and glamour. Playing janitor to the bloody KGB. It is, however, staying alive and living a *life*.'

'How do you know that, exactly?' said Ben. 'Because of what our friend just told us? Come on.'

'It doesn't make sense,' Lucy was saying, half to herself. 'It just doesn't.'

Nat was silent for a moment. Then spoke softly. 'I want my money.' He turned towards the door and faced Ben. 'I don't know what you're doing standing there, Benjy,' he said.

'Think about what you would be doing. Just think.'

'I am. Believe me.'

'I'm just trying to make sure you don't do anything rash.'

'Rash?' said Nat, pointing at Lucy with a sarcastic chuckle. 'Try emailing an SOS that's picked up by a foreign intelligence agency. Try talking us into calling them up on the *telephone*, Ben. How's that for chucking chance to the wind?'

Lucy imagined their argument could surely be heard beyond those doors. Perhaps that's exactly what the man in the suit was hoping would happen. *They're probably back there right now*, she thought, *holding their sides*. She lowered her voice. 'Nat, I don't trust that man and I don't think you should either.'

'It's the best offer I've had in a while.'

Lucy knew he was right. But she could not accept that this was the only way out. As much as she was trying to persuade Nat away from this, she was trying to persuade herself. 'Just remember you'll be putting your life in the hands of someone you've spoken to for ten minutes.'

'As opposed to following a length of cloth halfway up the Brazilian coast.'

'This is a bigger decision, Nat, and you know it.'

'Well,' said Nat, with a sharp look at Ben, 'ten minutes or not, maybe I'd be safer with him than in here. You know how things can get. Hardly need to remind you.'

Lucy shook her head. 'Come on. We're all friends here.'

The one thing about Nat that reassured Ben was his inability to disguise his feelings. True, he was brilliant at the conversational legerdemain you needed in the job (at least, Ben observed, for toadying up to the higher echelons). But Ben had noticed, in the year and a half he'd known him, that when Nat felt genuinely threatened, his true feelings bubbled up. You had to know where to look, but they were there.

And they were there now.

Without another word, the three of them walked across the room and opened the door. Across the corridor, the door to the suite beckoned. The smell of freshly brewed coffee and pastries wafted in. *Nice touch*, thought Ben.

It was Nat who led them down the hallway now and down ten flights to the street.

And, as they emerged blinking into the sunlight, it was Nat who began to speak. A car roared past as they turned a corner.

Two men selling Amazonian souvenirs saw Nat's backpack and called out. Nat ignored them, walking blithely on.

'I wasn't going to follow through,' he announced as he strode ahead of them. 'You know that. Right?'

No one said a thing. Nat was not comfortable with silent audiences and turned to confront them.

But he was alone.

Even the souvenir sellers were gone. Bright sunlight beamed through a break in the clouds, bleaching the pavement white and filling Nat's vision with a silver haze.

For Nat, such moments always seemed to proceed frame by frame, as if he was starring in the DVD extras version of his own life. He heard a diesel engine to his left and noticed from his peripheral vision that a van had pulled up beside him. The windows were blacked out. Suddenly the side doors slid open, but the light reflecting off the buildings was too bright for him to see much inside apart from the green spots he was trying to blink away. Behind him, he could feel someone's breath at his shoulder, as the hairs prickled up on the back of his neck and a tingle of fear snaked its way down his spine. Before he could turn and run, he felt the blunt end of a 9 mm automatic at his back and a forearm against his skull and two pairs of strong hands propelling him inside the vehicle.

As the doors slammed shut, Nat felt the ampoule of liquid plunge into his thigh, the soft velvet weight of unconsciousness easing him gently to the floor. The last thing he heard was the sound of Ben and Lucy groaning beside him and a man's voice close to his ear.

'Ssssh,' it said.

Twenty-Eight

As Ben woke he thought he was having a heart attack. There were stabbing pains in his chest and his left arm was knotted in agony. He self-diagnosed even as he endured the pain. Cardiac arrest? It was possible but unlikely unless from acute stress. Aneurysm? Too conscious for that. He felt for awareness in his limbs. Spatial dimensions came to him. Both his hands had been forced behind him and tied together. It was from his bound wrists that the climbing rope had been wrapped and then slung over the crossbeams of the room.

He could not feel the floor underneath him. He realized that this was because he was quite literally dangling from his hands. Because they were yanked straight behind him and tied together, his shoulder joints were taking the strain. Ben realized he'd woken once before, as they'd dragged him from the van. He remembered the crunch of gravel underneath him, the sudden scent of jasmine. He tried to work out why he'd fallen back asleep. The drugs? It was possible. His arms behind him, his chest heaving, the answer hit him – he'd passed out from the pain.

Underneath the blindfold, his eyes were a firestorm of red and white sparks. Breathing was an excruciating act of will-power and courage. Inside his mind, a remnant of memory assaulted him. *This was known as Palestinian hanging*, it said to him. *A Foreign Affairs briefing had outlined it; Turkey was found guilty of this a while back. That guy in Iraq. Funny what you remember*. Another minute of this and his nerves and ligaments might be beyond repair. He'd be a rag doll. A minute after that, he might asphyxiate.

His brother's eyes staring back at him now from the black pool of memory. Ben was surprised he had the strength to be frightened. He tried to cry out but he had no breath to speak.

Despite himself, he began to panic. He knew this was the worst thing he could do but there was no stopping him now. They say an animal that is being hunted down and tranquilized will awake from the sedative still trembling with all the same adrenalized muscle contractions and heart rate of the chase, since all the body's memory since it passed out was of escape, of flight. Ben, too, couldn't remember the last time he'd been fully awake. But he knew he must have been running. He couldn't help himself. He thrashed against the ropes.

A moment later the tension eased and he was on the floor. He felt the pain ebbing. The lactic acid swirling around his muscles, draining gently through his lymphatic system.

'What is your name?' said a voice. It had the same polite tone as the man who'd answered their call to the 'Samaritans'. Lucy had been closest to the receiver, but Ben had remembered its clear tenor. A voice of reason.

Ben said nothing.

'Who do you work for?' it said again.

Ben shook his head.

He felt himself being dragged to his feet.

For an eternity, he stayed here. Free from supports, he began to lean, to stumble. He tried to sit down. Arms immediately grabbed him and dragged him up to his feet once more. He was not permitted to sit, fall, lie. He began to force himself down, to collapse like a pile-driver to the floor, but over and over again the arms would catch him, beat him, force him up. Sometimes it was the handle of a broom or the butt of a rifle. There was no wall to lean against, no way of supporting his weight. His ankles swelled. The pain was excruciating. He slowly turned the dial and the signal faded inside. What was left was pain no longer, only the ghost of a signal. White noise.

Finally, a voice came again. Had it been an hour? A day? A week? No other certainty than the voice. The voice was now his metronome, his sun rising, setting. Ben's tongue was dry. He knew he was dangerously dehydrated. The standing torture was something they'd worked on, he remembered, in their final days of training. They'd even role-played it once. The trick, he seemed to remember, was in the tailbone. Point your tailbone straight down to the earth. The lower stomach then compensates for the adjustment in posture and stops your hips cutting off circulation. He tried it. It didn't seem to work. Again, the voice.

'What is your name?' it said.

And again, Ben said nothing.

Moments later, he felt his neck jerk back and a bag descend over his head, pulled tight with twine. Weak from hunger, thirst and exhaustion, his ankles crumbled away from him.

He was half carried, half dragged, over stone. A cool draught on his face. Outside air smelled sweet.

His knees jarred with every undulation of the ground. He willed himself to lift his legs and began focusing on those steps, those simple actions – raise the foot, plant the foot, raise the foot, plant –

He pitched forward and felt his cheek on the stone again, cool through the fabric of the bag, his own breath warm against his face. A knee found its way to the back of his neck. That voice again.

161

'What is your name?'

Ben said nothing.

The pressure on his neck increased. Ben wondered how many pounds per square inch it would take to snap his vertebra.

'Who do you work for?'

Even if he could have spoken, Ben could not find the breath to do it. He might have said, *that's original*, he thought. But even the effort of thinking was too much for him. After what seemed like a maliciously long pause, the owner of the knee removed it and dragged Ben once more to his feet. His knees crumpled and two hands supported him from the armpits.

Four more sets of footsteps followed him.

A smaller space now, a metal door that sounded like a cell. He was stripped naked. Ben even thought he heard a flashlight click as his buttocks were spread and gloved hands probed and searched. He was lifted up again, re-dressed and forced to walk once more.

A short frogmarch led to gravel underfoot. He heard a vehicle start up, doors open. *Another taxi ride*, thought Ben as he felt himself shoved forward. His shins slammed against a sharp metal ridge – a larger vehicle. He hissed in pain. The pressure behind him was there again and he scrambled up and on to the cool ridges of metal inside the vehicle. First one, then two more bodies joined him. The doors slammed and he felt a leg against his. Instinct told him who it was. His ears confirmed it.

'Ben—?' Lucy sounded far away. She had probably been subjected to exactly the same ordeal as he had. She had a habit of disconnecting, too.

'Yep.'

Nat groaned.

162

Confusion, pain, the hot stale darkness. Ben's head hit Lucy's as the van powered away. From the number of potholes they felt on the hard floor, it did not leave rural back roads. Thirty minutes later, Ben calculated, the engine died again. He knew this was not a reliable reference point or guide; they could have been driving in circles to disorientate them for all he knew. In fact, he almost expected it.

The engine cut out. All he could hear outside were birds. The sound of foliage in the wind.

The doors opened again. A swirling breeze welcomed them into the outside world once again, dragged by their feet and pulled up by their armpits. Lucy struggled briefly until a kick to her kneecap silenced her.

They were led across rough ground, down a steep slope, and eventually felt gravel underfoot again. Strong arms moved Ben's hands behind him. A rough wooden fence served as a hitching post as handcuffs clicked into place. He could hear Lucy whimpering to herself. He heard a blow, perhaps a foot to a knee. The whimpering stopped. The strike had sounded painful, even from inside his own private agonies.

Silence now, with only the wind and his own breathing to measure time. More footsteps on the gravel. Several sets, possibly as many as five people, Ben estimated. A paranoid thought arrived in his head.

As he heard the guns opened and loaded, the paranoia was merely confirmed. He was about to protest when the familiar voice carried over to him on the wind.

'The first obstacle thrown in your path stopped you all in your tracks. How do you hope to be part of a cause if you are ready to drop your guard at the earliest convenience?'

A feeling hit Ben in the stomach like molten lead.

'Russians?' the man said. The scorn was heavy in his voice

163

now. 'The SVR? You were so keen to believe that was the truth you ignored the very skills you need to survive. Then you were so keen to discount the revelations that you exposed yourselves to maximum risk, and why? Because you were desperate. So desperate to feel safe, you did not think. We do not help those who cannot help themselves. Weak links are not welcome here. They are only broken.'

The words tore Ben in two directions. His heart soared, his hopes dissolving fast. Does that mean –

'*Ready.*'

Another sound rippled on the wind. Ben knew it well. It was the safety mechanism of a rifle being flicked to the 'off' position. It happened again, again, again.

Wait. Four times?

'Tell us your names and we promise we will aim between your eyes. Stay silent now, you have our word the first shot will not be enough to kill you. And neither will the second or the third. You may have to wait days before you die. Thus I ask. What are your names?'

A voice piped up from Ben's left.

'The bags smell great, by the way. Pine-forest fresh.'

Ben whipped his head around in the direction of the words. It wasn't Lucy or Nat. He was right, they were not alone. And the accent . . .

It couldn't be.

The man was dead.

Worth the risk in any case. Ben filled his lungs. 'Jam Jar?'

'That you, you bloody English poof?'

'*Aim.*'

The voice was Jamie Gallagher's. Far from dead. He was, as ever, the Lazarus man. Four of them lived. Four of them had survived. This far.

'You've got the wrong guys here, pal,' boomed Jamie. 'We're nobodies. You're about to execute a bunch of spotty-arsed neds, d'you hear me? A bunch of lilywhites!'

If Jamie said anything else, Ben did not hear it. All other sound was subsumed by the crack of four rifles being fired. The explosion of white inside Ben dissolved into a negative, resolving gradually to the face of his brother John, smiling down on him at his passing-out parade, framed silver and gold by a halo of the sun.

'Lilywhites'

Twenty-Nine

London
Seventeen months earlier

The day had dawned bright and frosty, but the cloud cover soon returned, and by the time Ben was running for his bus, the London air was wet with drizzle. The permanent English monsoon.

He'd had a few first days in his life. All of them, bar two, had been unmitigated disasters. His first day at primary school had been a blur of tears and stares. When he changed schools at twelve and moved to Bristol, it had been a day of knuckle punches and Chinese burns. First day of university, again in Bristol, he had managed to sleep with the daughter of his senior lecturer. Nothing wrong with that, apart from the ensuing heartache and tear-ridden calls when he told her their love could never be. In his life, only his first pint and first taste of sex had scored any marks in the plus column.

At this point, he felt, it was time for a hat trick.

We are all grown-ups now, he thought. Different ages, backgrounds, life experiences. And one common goal, the fast-track training programme. Beyond that, a life of clandestine service to your country, not to mention some pretty fascinating days at the office. Compare and contrast with his college careers service. It had seemed to Ben that if he squinted for long enough, all entry-level graduate jobs started looking vaguely the same:

Executive Assistant Associate
Associate Executive Assistant
Associate Assistant Executive

And, of course, 'Sales'. He had held fast against the tide that pulled many into accountancy, battled his way around the hordes channelling their talents into marketing – be it dog food, scented soap, chocolate biscuits, luxury yachts . . . these people all seemed to Ben to have such astonishing *direction*. They were all arrows whose flight to target was assured.

Ben wasn't even sure if he was an arrow at all.

Or a boomerang.

Much to his surprise, he'd ended up where he was going. He hadn't even been aiming all that long. It was all bizarrely simple. Finding the blind and frenzied diaspora into blue-chip graduate traineeships unsavoury at the very least, Ben had briefly entertained a doctorate until remembering that the alabaster-faced creatures he spotted in the university library were all probably his peer group. He mentally struck that off the list as soon as it appeared.

Bored and in a belligerent mood, he took to the Careers Advisory Service computer and found the Foreign Office Fast Track web page. To his surprise, under 'Diplomatic Service Economists' and the obligatory 'Executive Assistant' headings was a far more entertaining menu button. It said simply, 'Secret Intelligence Service'.

Not that secret, Ben had thought. *It's right here.*

Even more to his surprise, this supposedly clandestine organization had a few breezy paragraphs on the next page. It mostly extolled the virtues of working for the Fast Track

170

Intelligence Branch. Ben noted the PO Box number and a final – he thought slightly obvious – warning.

Please note: potential candidates should not divulge to others their application to SIS. Failure to observe the confidentiality of an application may affect eligibility for employment.

Ben read it twice just to make sure and smiled. Keeping secrets? Not divulging? At least here was something he'd be good at.

The letter inviting him to interview arrived four weeks later. The first stages were simply Foreign Office selection procedures, generic Civil Service exams that Ben took with the same wry detachment as when he'd applied in the first place.

Four weeks after that, things got a little more serious.

Ben was invited to a 'chat' in an unmarked building in St James's. He wore his best suit and turned up on time. The woman interviewing him had, through no fault of her own, such a spectacular mole on her chin that Ben had to restrain himself from staring. He thought perhaps it was some sort of bizarre test, that the content of their conversation was relatively immaterial – what mattered to the selection board was how he held himself when faced with the Mole. A friend of his claimed that he had failed his Oxford interview when the director of studies stayed behind the *Financial Times* for the entire duration of the session. The failure stemmed from the candidate's complete inability to attract the professor's attention. Ben certainly didn't believe the story, but it was an entertaining idea all the same. He quite enjoyed mind games and even if the mole wasn't meant as such, he vowed to tell a good yarn when he was rejected. This kind of place didn't hire people like Ben. Knowing this relaxed him, gave him more than his usual dose of confidence.

Still, they had a very pleasant chat, all the same. Most of the hour was spent reminiscing about his pre-college trip around South America, funded through weekends spent working in a petrol station kiosk. Everyone else at university seemed to have been given round-the-world tickets as a prize for leaving school. It hadn't bothered him, he explained. It felt more satisfying to be self-sufficient. His interviewer agreed and shook his hand as he left. Ben tugged at an invisible forelock. *Much obliged, ma'am, so very kind of your ladyship to see me.*

When the telephone call came to congratulate him on his job offer, Ben vowed never to underestimate himself ever again. True to his word, he told no one.

The drizzle did not let up as the bus complained its way through London traffic. Bus lanes had been built to avoid traffic jams, but an unfortunate consequence was that the lanes were now clogged with buses. It was only as Ben dried himself quietly on the upper deck that he remembered he was wearing the same suit he'd worn to that final interview.

As he swiped his new card into the security gate, it also occurred to him that he had on the same shirt, tie and socks. He wondered how polished the others would be.

When he entered the lobby, he had to laugh.

The probationers stuck out a mile. There was no real reason why they should – there had been a gruelling selection process to get this far and Ben knew none of them. But somehow, lilywhites are lilywhites, whatever industry you're in. Living proof that sometimes, yes, you *can* try too hard.

There were pinstripes, bow ties, A-line skirts and square heels that would have looked frumpy on the Queen. The women either looked ready to teach Religious Studies at an all-girls prep school in Lincolnshire or primed for the catwalk at

London Fashion week. The men were the same, except for a ponytailed freak in a sports coat and bow tie, and a vast Welshman with a beard. Most sported off-the-peg suits, shaving cuts and schoolboy haircuts. Ben himself had only been in London for a week and like most of the other trainees had signed up for a recommended list of secure flat rentals in Pimlico. Ben's grotty little attic space was just on the habitable side of damp, cheap enough and near a few pubs and a barber. On a whim, he'd popped in the day before for a 'tidy-up' for his first day. To his horror, the resulting car wreck of a haircut made his head look like a pineapple. He had to smile when he realized that at least two other guys there had exactly the same haircut.

One of them was looking at him and grinning. He walked over to Ben. His suit was sleeker than most. The collar of his shirt was more Jermyn Street than Oxford Street. He pointed to his head.

'Small bloke with ginger hair?'

Ben nodded and smiled.

'I'll just tidy it up around the sides, sir,' said Ben, imitating the Scottish burr of the dwarfish man who'd cut their hair.

'James Gallagher,' said the man, shaking Ben's hand. 'Call me Jamie.'

'Ben Sinclair.'

'Well,' said Jamie, looking around them as regular employees trooped in through the security gates and eyed the fresh talent on display. 'This all seems rather excellent, I'd say.'

Jamie's accent was pure silver spoon English, yet the man himself answered only to 'Scotsman'. He was one of the particular breed of Highland dwellers whose accent jars oddly with their tartan tendencies. Jamie's family had a small pile near Loch Torridon that they freely admitted their own forebears had casually stolen during the Highland Clearances. Jamie thus belonged to a bizarrely confident clan who regarded everyone south of their postcode as a 'Sassenach' – despite a wholesale R. P. accent that set jaws and fists a-clenching in Glasgow. Ben had always quietly resented that English Home Counties genus of yahoo that presumed some form of exclusive ownership of class and taste, despite actively demonstrating its complete absence in their own lives. He had never met anyone like that until university, and even then they seemed to orbit around each other, terrified to socialize outside of the caste. Ben knew Jamie was from a different tribe entirely and he grew on Ben immediately. Something in his eyes had substance. He had known pain, Ben reasoned, true pain, and he respected that.

'I think I'll reserve judgement for now,' smiled Ben.

'Good plan. Good plan.' Jamie stared off into space for a second and then turned back. 'You don't play tennis at all, do you?'

Ben shook his head.

'I was rather hoping to set up some regular doubles.'

'If I hear of anyone, I'll be sure and let you know,' said Ben. Jamie grinned and stared at the man walking smartly towards them from the lifts.

'This way please,' he boomed from an unreasonable distance. 'If you'd all like to follow me.'

The ten lilywhites followed.

And for the first few weeks at least, they tried to do what they were told.

As it turned out, they all practically lived on the same square mile of London real estate. A few London natives still lived in their own flats on the fringes of the city, and Jamie, whose parents also seemed to live in Hertfordshire, had free run of their mews house in Marylebone. Early on in their training, this had earned Jamie the nickname of 'Jammy Bastard', which quickly and quietly shortened affectionately to 'Jam Jar'.

But the vast majority were effectively neighbours. The proximity meant that as far as parties were concerned, almost everyone was in staggering distance of each other. An informal support system developed, with wake-up chain-calling for early mornings, car pools to off-site locations and, every so often, a shoulder to cry on.

The first two months were exclusively theory. A gruelling set of lectures, seminars, technology classes and no small amount of continuous assessment meant the pressure on the ten new probationers was immediate and frantic. Braided into this was a sense of frustration. They had all signed up for different reasons, but avoiding an ordinary office job was probably a priority for all of them. And yet here they were, back at school, forced to sit in small plastic chairs and make notes with their Pentels in the margin of their spiral-bound notebooks.

Top of everyone's list of pet hates were the orienteering theory classes, discursive ramblings on the nature of GPS systems, global coordinates and the Winthrop System of locating dead drops, brush pasts and so on. If there was ever a revisitation of second-year geography class, it was here. Perhaps joint top were the equally impenetrable electronics lectures. For some reason film and television have always seemed enamoured with spy technology – the wondrous technological universe of Bond, the brushed-chrome gadgetry of TV spy shows. Yet the reality for most recruits was that the detailed operation and maintenance of electronic tools was about as appealing as being the systems administrator of a pet food company's local area network. The kicker was, in this particular industry, that tiny grey malfunctioning part could very well one day save your life.

For Nat, however, there was still residual glamour in 'stuff', as he described it. He became a top student in all electronic flavours of training, happily spreading his knowledge to the less fortunate amongst the intake. It might have been an attempt to broadcast his generosity to the girls, advertising his sexual prowess through his willingness to flaunt his brainpower to other needy members of the tribe. For the most part, it didn't work. Everyone was just too subsumed with ring files, flash cards, mind maps, memorizing security codes, and learning how to operate a burst-transmission USB flash drive from a mountain bike without attracting suspicion.

It was no wonder the parties were off the hook.

Jamie had agreed to host the first 'bash', seeing as his square footage and integrated sound system practically qualified his house as a nightclub under local council regulations. The invitations to this particular evening had been printed at considerable personal expense on heavy embossed cards (a needlessly profligate touch) and included details about parking that bemused Ben greatly – seeing as he could hardly afford tube tickets on his probationer's salary, let alone run a vehicle in central London.

In spite of this, Ben enjoyed Jamie's rambunctious enthusiasm for life immensely. He knew that his apparent ignorance of financial pressures rubbed some people up the wrong way, but to Ben, Jamie embodied the very essence of the old-school MI6 he'd read about as a child. A public school boys' club, a place of adventure, public service and derring-do along the way. It was part of the same spirit that had entreated cherry-cheeked nineteen-year-olds to sign up in the Great War, the sense of combat as sport, where score was kept with corpses. He was about as far away from Ben's life in Hartcliffe as the stars were from the moon.

The party was a marker in their training calendar. This was the end of the pure theory. They had a weekend to digest and recover. And on Monday, the practicals began. Jamie decided the theme was 'Whisky Galore' and had bought in cases of Macallan to grease the wheels of fun. But Jamie hated the stuff himself, he claimed, preferring tequila.

'From what I understand,' said Jamie as he upended a bottle of Jose Cuervo into a cocktail shaker, 'they pit us against the trainees across the river. You know, MI5. Obviously they send the more experienced lads after us as we get better, but there's some kind of annual wager that goes on around the upper floors. At least, that's what my brother tells me.'

Ben kept slicing the limes. 'Your brother's SIS too?'

'Not really. He's not a Friend, he's Foreign Office. He comes and goes.'

'What kind of wager?'

'Serious dosh, apparently. Big bloody business, so I'm told. It's bigger than the Grand National.'

The doorbell rang and Jamie flipped a remote control into his hand. The sound system began to kick in and, with his hands full, Jamie grinned at Ben.

'Get that, would you?'

When Ben opened the door to Lucy, it occurred to her that he wasn't that bad-looking close up.

Two hours later, Jamie had entreated everyone to join him in finishing off a line of tequila shots. Ben had quietly demurred, until probing from Jamie had resulted in an honest admission: 'I don't like who I become on that stuff.'

Claire, who had taken an instant shine to Ben, insisted that it was a rite of passage. Excused of future behaviour, Ben lined up a glass and imbibed.

After that, the party seemed to change gear a little.

There was Chris Dunlop, who would not have looked out of place with a Harris tweed sports coat and leather patches to match his donnish spectacles. Despite the phlegmy eyes and baby fat around his cheeks, it was rumoured he could run forever.

There was Alexandra Munro, 'Alex', a pointy-faced young woman who had recently divorced her husband and sought to radically change her life.

And then there was Nat Turner.

Ben had come across people like Nat while at university and his instinct had always been to avoid them. He found them in larger groups of talented, friendly people, catching tans off everyone else's sunshine.

Despite his instincts, however, he needed to learn to get on with him. After all, he lived in his building. And in this line of work, hiding your true feelings was surely just part of the job.

Sometimes, they helped each other get better at it. One evening someone had suggested they play a game of straight face – a person in the centre of the room was forced to maintain sangfroid while everyone else tried to provoke them with as much stimulus as possible. Claire challenged anyone to sit through the entirety of Suzanne Vega's 'The Queen and the Soldier' without 'tearing up'. Nat challenged anyone to do the same 'without laughing'.

Ben prowled from room to room, never seeming to settle. Jamie had strung fairy lights around trelliswork on his roof terrace and Ben sought out a quiet moment from the fray to smoke. Whilst up there he was cornered by Andy, the bearded Welshman. His breath smelled of real ale and Ben noticed he had a habit of rubbing the crown of his head with his palm during awkward silences – of which there were many.

Back downstairs, Ben caught Lucy's eye alighting on him on several occasions, though never for long enough that one could call it a 'look'. It was more of a passing glance, as if her gaze were busy on the way to focus on something much more important, and was simply enjoying the scenery along the way.

While Lucy was taking stock of the party, Nat was busy taking stock of Lucy. He had taken over stewardship of the bar when he first arrived, trying to insinuate in some way that he too was hosting the party. His cack-handed attempts to chat Lucy up had not fazed her in the slightest. In fact, Ben watched in awe as she politely deflected his attentions on to Claire, somehow managing to leave both of them with the feeling that they should have been talking together all evening, and Lucy was merely getting in the way.

She grabbed her coat soon after, chatting bright-eyed and smiling with Jamie by the balcony. As she left, she made sure her path took her past Ben.

'Excuse me,' she'd said.

Ben just nodded and smiled.

She'd paused just a little too long before walking on down the stairs and, despite himself, he heard his insides murmur something to him.

Secreted away in darkest Pimlico, the stucco-fronted settle-ment-cracked façade of Number 25 was one of fifty-two in the street, and it stood out like a shadow on the lung. If passing you might have imagined it a grand old place to live; in reality the building was effectively a squat with a posh address. Off a central staircase were five bed-sits and a shared kitchen and living area. On the top floor was a studio flat. Nat's second-floor bedsit had a view of a wall on one side and a streetlight on the other; the windows were grey and fingerprinted by countless previous incumbents. The guttering was broken and he often heard the splattering of overflow from his housemates' baths at close range.

Nat sat alone in the light of his laptop monitor, the single gas fire roaring on the far wall too weak to push the heat to his side of the room.

Lucy had knocked him back. But that was fine. He had stepped away with his pride intact. More importantly, he'd taken note that the good-looking guy who lived in his building hadn't left with her either. They'd spoken briefly, but that seemed to be it.

He quietly removed Lucy's mobile phone, which he had gently stolen from her bag after mixing her drinks, and placed inside it a small RF transmitter, the size of a miniature paperclip, securing it with a fast-acting adhesive in a hidden cavity just above the battery. Turning back to his computer, he booted up a tracking program that the computing staff had loaned him for educational purposes only. RF transmission could be detected within a two-mile radius and was superior to GPS as a short-range tracking device. The flashing beacon on the map showed his exact location in London SW1. Soon, it would show Lucy: where she walked, where she drank, where she worked, where she slept.

Thirty

The wars in Iraq and Afghanistan had persuaded the recruiting departments of all major government agencies in the UK that they needed to find a new kind of intelligence officer. At least, one that could run five miles without collapsing with heart failure, one who could swash and not buckle. In the past, in their desire for analytical diplomats and the appropriate group-think brain, the MI6 recruiters had failed to realize that working undercover overseas exacted a huge physical toll on their officers. Strong hearts, quite literally, were now a matter of necessity.

Theirs was the first intake, Ben surmised, that had at least half of their number drawn from Special Forces or other elite military cadres. Ben himself did not belong to this demographic, although he had regularly trained with two university friends who'd made it to the Special Boat Service selection, and when the time came for the physical exam, he'd passed at instructor level.

Even Andy the bearded Welshman had a quiet sideline in triathlons and a resting heart rate of forty-five beats per minute.

As the days turned into weeks it became quickly apparent to Ben that, although there were many things that united them as a group, there was one thing that divided them.

Money.

The vast majority of the lilywhites in Ben's class were children of a moneyed class – predominantly public school and ivory-tower-educated. Alexandra Munro, a self-styled blonde bombshell despite her sharp and pointed features and soulless eyes, had learnt to ski at Klosters, where her father had once served on security detail for Princess Margaret. Jamie, a.k.a. Jam Jar, had the most cash, it was true, but he was also the friendliest and most generous of the bunch. That didn't stop the gap becoming a chasm on social occasions. Bottles of wine were bought, cabs hailed, all without even a nod to the idea that perhaps not everyone had their credit cards paid off at the end of every month by a personal banker at Coutts. There were several boisterous dinners that ended with a drunken 'let's split the bill' – completely negating Ben's assiduous budgeting. He had never known a time when he looked at the left side of the menu. Generally, on the rare occasions he ate out, his eyes stuck to the numbers on the right.

Despite the monetary castes – Lucy and Ben considered themselves 'untouchably skint' – the ten of them bonded together and began to enjoy the simple give and take of academia.

After two months of classroom work, all but Lucy admitted to the frustration of being cooped up. The potential energy of the seminar room turned the place into a pressure cooker of blistering intensity.

Finally, in the third month, the chance came to break free. Field training had begun – or 'monkey see, monkey do' as several instructors called it. This seemed to suit everyone much better, and frayed tempers began to piece themselves smooth once more. The Class A personalities that predominated in the year's intake suddenly had to make choices – to cooperate, and thus show their 'team player' colours; or compete, and stand out as individuals.

The countersurveillance training module was at first a simple case of following trainers around the streets of London. Backstreet circuits took probationers from Southwark up to King's Cross, Marylebone back down to Waterloo. It was a life-size game of espionage Monopoly. London's taxi drivers spend years learning 'The Knowledge', committing the routes and byroads of London to memory. The trainees of Vauxhall Cross found themselves au courant with most of Zone One by the time Christmas was approaching.

Everyone, it seemed, had a strategy.

The problem was, it was the same one. They had memorized the unofficial textbooks. In particular, the ones written by disgruntled ex-spies. One particular tome had specified a neat trick to rid yourself of a tail pursuing you on foot. Since their goal was to follow you without drawing attention to themselves, the suggestion was simply to slip on a pair of rollerblades. If you did it quickly enough, you could then look back and see who was now running after you trying to keep up.

Lucy had tried this during the first round of MI5 vs MI6 cat-and-mouse in full knowledge that she would not break sweat. Unfortunately for Lucy, her pursuers had read the same book. She had cut in to Hyde Park and was gliding around the Serpentine with a grin on her face until she turned round to find a horde of other in-line skaters keeping up with her. She had no idea who was who, and by the time she reached her checkpoint, she'd been failed by the assessor.

After foot surveillance, though, came the cars.

Barry, their Scotland Yard trainer, had doggedly pursued his tactic of dry humour in the face of wholesale disinterest. Special Branch had been with them from the beginning and Barry in particular had a truly pathetic line in 'women driver' jokes. Nat, however, began to look very nervous during the evasive driving briefing, and eventually admitted that he couldn't drive. At all.

So, while the others were put through their paces, Nat was despatched to a windblown intensive driving course in Norfolk. It drove a stake through the heart of their grandiose ambitions to beat MI5. Andy the Welshman had calculated it already – it would probably come down to Nat. And since Nat was still parallel-parking around traffic cones, it was not going to be their year.

Nat, however, had other ideas.

He returned to training with a freshly minted provisional licence and a weekend to absorb enough evasive manoeuvres not to kill himself or others during the final round.

The pressure was immense – not just from his colleagues, but from everyone in both buildings. The lilywhites – and Nat in particular – began to realize this annual drive-off was the upper echelons' equivalent of toad racing.

The team over at MI5 was overconfident. News of Nat's new licence had reached them in a matter of nanoseconds, and allowed them – perhaps unadvisedly – to rest on their laurels.

Because Nat had a secret weapon.

His driving was not only new, but appalling. He drove like a blind ninety-year-old peering over the steering wheel of a Morris Minor. He sat too far forward, white knuckles on the wheel, sweating, hardly ever emerging from second gear except when he was trying to wind the window down and found himself shifting to reverse by mistake.

The MI6 pursuit vehicles were dumbfounded. They had no idea what to do. They were used to the Ben Sinclairs of this world, who slipped in and out and sometimes it seemed directly *through* traffic and evaded them with such sublime speed and grace that at the end of one run they emerged from their cars and grimly applauded.

In Nat's case, there simply was no pursuit. They practically rear-ended him at every turn. He would change lanes without indicating, stall, make illegal U-turns and drive so slowly that council cleaning vehicles would overtake him, blaring their horns in a fury.

Rather than evading them, Nat entrapped them – a rare and highly risky gambit. Because, of course, the MI5 pursuit vehicles were also being assessed on their ability to follow without being seen. Nat's speed was so slow that there was no chance of them ever doing that – they had to travel at Nat's speed or slower. The assessor, who had no idea that Nat was so wet behind the ears, declared it the 'most audacious driving I have ever seen', and awarded the MI6 probationers full marks.

The celebration had lasted through the night, with Ben and Jamie parading Nat on their shoulders through the lounge bar of the Green Man. Derek, the landlord, who normally loathed the young pretty things who patronized his establishment, was happy to conduct a lock-in when Jamie put his black Amex card behind the bar as collateral.

At two in the morning, Ben excused himself and headed home, shortly after Lucy had departed, which left Nat alone despite his constant stream of chat-up lines. Somehow, as the conquering hero, he felt he deserved to get the girl. He trailed back to Number 25 and logged back on to his computer.

He'd been tracking Lucy ever since he'd placed the RF device in her phone. He didn't really know why he'd done it other than the sheer daring of it. His recruiter from Oxford had told him training gave the enterprising officer carte blanche to experiment. While group think was admired, individual enterprise was sometimes lauded above all else.

And anyway. He just wanted to keep tabs on her.

The marker displayed on his screen showed that she was close – and moving closer. He knew she lived just around the corner and so there was nothing that exciting about the prospect of her going to bed. That said, late at night, he had often logged on just to check up on her – he'd frequently said to those that would listen, 'I like to know where I am.' It seemed these days to apply to Lucy just as much.

But something about her route troubled him. She wasn't going her usual way. To his growing excitement, the beacon was flashing towards Number 25.

Downstairs he heard the front door open. Did she have keys? He couldn't work it out. His heart was accelerating with excitement. Surely she wouldn't . . . well, it was possible. After all, he was the hero of the hour.

A single set of footsteps on the stairs. The ceiling above him creaking as Ben got into bed. Nat was confused. Then he realized – maybe Ben had her phone. Maybe she'd left it at the party and he'd retrieved it for her.

He resisted a temptation to call it and find out.

An hour later, he tired of the chase and fell asleep.

Around 3.30 a.m., he heard a ringing. At first, Nat thought it was the doorbell. But the tone was wrong.

It was coming from upstairs.

Ben heard the sound too, waking with a start from a semi-slumber. He'd fallen asleep fully clothed on the bed.

It was Lucy's phone. She'd left it behind in the pub and, unsure what was done in such situations, he had hung on to it with the full intention of giving it to her tomorrow. But Lucy had clearly realized her mistake and was calling from a payphone to settle her nerves.

186

'Hello?'

'Please come down. Quick.'

Nat heard the footsteps skitter down the stairs. Then he heard the door buzzer sound. Andy and Claire emerged from the first-floor bedroom. Chris emerged from the second-floor landing. Soon all the residents plus Claire were standing in the hallway, staring out at Lucy.

She was soaking wet and in tears.

'My flat's flooded,' she explained. 'I don't know what to do.'

Lucy camped out on the sofa for a week. The flat was large enough that they could both dress and undress in privacy or darkness, depending on preference. Ben put up an old rattan screen to help separate their living space, but on rainy nights in, they just slobbed on the sofa with a takeaway anyway. It was a polite ballet that made them both smile at the bare bulb in the bathroom. It was after she came back from a weekend visiting her parents that she moved things on.

'What if I moved in?' she said. 'And split the rent?'

'To the house, you mean? I don't think we have another bedroom—'

'To your bit. Your room. It's big enough, isn't it?'

The reality hit and he nodded numbly. The more she told him, the more he felt sorry for her. Ben had no idea Lucy was as badly off as him. His first weeks in London had nearly given his bank manager a stroke. The lowest level of Civil Service stipend put anything but monkish good behaviour at break-even. Having fun cost. And there was nothing like working next to people whose effortless ability to live like princes put the Saudi royals to shame.

The answer was yes.

They both knew what would happen if she stayed any longer,

but, somehow, it didn't seem to matter. No one was getting married any time soon. They were both attracted to each other. Very much so, in fact.

Thus, the night after they agreed, Lucy walked over to where Ben was sleeping and slid quietly next to him under the covers. Their union was entirely tacit. No words were needed at all. Not even the next morning, over coffee. They simply fell into step.

Two weeks in, she told him about the tattoo on her ankle. For Lucy, that was as intimate an act as anything.

For Nat, sitting in the glow of his computer monitor, the flashing dot of his quarry now blinked every night above his head. He made plans to pay back the pain, somehow. As Christmas approached, he finally thought of a way.

Thirty-One

The first ransom note appeared before anyone even realized she was missing.

'WE HAVE HER,' it began. 'DEMANDS MUST BE MET BY FRIDAY.'

The entire message was constructed from newsprint cuttings, stuck on to a sheet of copier paper in a jagged line. 'Very old school,' Nat said later. The note had been posted to the trainees' current supervisor on this rotation, Paul Bradley, and it was he who broke the news to the team.

'It is unclear,' he said in his sonorous baritone, 'what those demands are, but it would be churlish not to guess.'

A day later, another note.

This time, with a difference. The note also included a body part.

'DO NOT MESS US ABOUT,' came the accompanying message, 'WE IS SERIOUS.'

Bradley had looked a little shaken as he addressed the class that morning. 'What I am about to show you may shock you. However, we cannot turn away from this situation as it is a learning experience for you, a real-world crisis here on our doorstep.' His huge fingers held up the body part, a lock of hair, the platinum-blonde fibres visible against his dark suit.

The hair was Clarissa's, almost certainly.

'I need not tell you, Kevin is particularly upset at this time.'

No one, to be fair, was surprised by this.

Sergeant Kevin Meades, ex-Fusiliers, three-time SAS reject, now led the in-house security detail in Vauxhall Cross. His haircut was as cheap and short as his temper, lignite eyes set deep under the shadow of an icebreaker forehead. In the thirty-eight years he'd been conscious in the universe he had accumulated all the warm charm of a frayed noose, all the bonhomie of an acid bath, and was a man from whom a smile was extruded only by industrial cold-drawn process, like a length of copper pipe.

It was bizarre then, but somehow not surprising, that Sergeant Kevin Meades was also chief architect of the MI6 Christmas decorations. And like the manager of a department store, every year Kevin took pains to implement his vision long before the leaves turned brown.

The KLH, or Kevin's Little Helpers, were by tradition plucked from the unfortunate probationers in that year's intake. And unlike Jury Service, there was no crying off. Kevin Meades had a fastidious obsession with the Christmas holiday. The full complement of lobby-level security guards were issued with small Santa hats the night before December 1 and were obliged to wear them until 11.59 p.m. on Twelfth Night.

The highlight of Kevin's Yuletide blueprint was the tree that graced the centre of the atrium, and specifically the top of it. Clarissa, as she became known, was a reproduction Victorian angel, a remnant of chintz from a long line of chintzes, and was universally loathed by everyone in the building. Not as much as they loathed Kevin, of course.

Kevin relished his position of authority over inferior crea-tures and he did not relent in exercising it. Inside the gates, the staff had power over him. But ever since papers had migrated from the upper floors on to the streets of South London, it had been decreed that security details had the power to prevent the exit or entrance of anyone they suspected of wrongdoing. Kevin's attitude was guilty before proven innocent.

There was nowhere to come back at him, either. He invited a sharp word or a fierce stare. He drank it in, his lifeblood. It was a universal truth that hurting Kevin somehow would be good for everyone.

When Clarissa first appeared, when the gleam of pride in Kevin's eyes was first identified, the angel became a prime candidate for kidnapping.

The originator of the ingenious plot had been Nat. Late one night, as he decked the mezzanine with boughs of imitation holly, he found himself level with the top of the tree, eye to eye with Clarissa. He had not acted, of course, but in his plain view horror at the ridiculousness of his situation a plan of action had hatched in his sleep-deprived mind.

Over drinks at the Green Man, he had announced to the assembled masses that it was time Kevin Meades was taught a lesson. He'd had his fun with probationers before. But not this year. Not these lilywhites.

The trainees had decided that this was something they could not let the man do alone.

The inclusion of body parts had been Lucy's idea. Simply nicking Clarissa off the tree would not serve as punishment. To truly succeed in their task of removing probationers permanently from Kevin's Christmas chain gang, he had to be humiliated. This was Psyops rotation after all, and a chance to learn some field-tested negotiation techniques.

Paul Bradley clearly felt the same. Even as Kevin's protests fell on deaf ears on the upper floors, Bradley carried on with the pretence that Clarissa's kidnapping was indeed a matter of the gravest severity.

'Clearly,' said Bradley, 'this is someone who fully intends to follow through on their threats. This was only the second communication, and already there has been an appalling act of violence visited upon the victim. This hair has been sent with one purpose, to demonstrate a willingness to kill.'

The next day, as if to underscore his thesis, a wing appeared.

By the time Friday had rolled around, there wasn't much of Clarissa left to negotiate for. Nevertheless, a settlement was reached, and from that point on the decorations would be the responsibility of general staff only. After a weekend of glue and intensive care, Clarissa was back in one piece atop the giant fir, a gift from the Etterretningstjenesten, Norway's foreign intelligence service. Despite the generous gesture, it was regularly swept for bugs – both organic and electronic.

To celebrate their victory, the entire probation year posed for a photograph in front of the tree. Ben recalled the moment when the camera flashed, red dots before his eyes, the dark and isolated figure of Sergeant Meades watching coldly from the balcony above.

Ben wasn't entirely sure, but he seemed to be staring directly at him.

Thirty-Two

There were good days and bad days, but the rhythm of life in training and with Lucy began to glow inside Ben. It started to provide him with a bass line, giving his world solidity, form, substance. The structure let him let go. Some days he even felt like one of those Labradors on dog food commercials, bounding around with exuberant energy: wet nose, happy tail.

In the mornings, he would run with Jamie down the Thames to Tower Bridge and back again. It was a punishing slog, but as the weeks wound on, he found it was the only way he could expel the anticipatory tension that fizzed and crackled around his bones when he woke.

The regular exercise only served to buoy him further.

Once the probationer programme got a head of steam, however, there soon wasn't much time to kick back and relax. Sometimes, he didn't see Lucy for days apart from her unconscious form on the mattress beside him. When their schedules permitted, they'd share a can of cheap noodles on the sofa, watching fuzzy black and white TV. Every week they pooled the money they saved not eating lunch in an envelope and bought a bottle of champagne and a Chinese takeaway. A few times, they enjoyed it together in the bath.

And they would make love, and cling to each other, neither one saying a word.

Gradually, gently, Ben allowed himself to feel something

he'd never really felt before. That he belonged. This was a new kind of family, one he'd probably not see for years at a time, but one he was still proud to be a part of. Despite the character clashes, despite the genuine loathing he felt for some of the more spoiled sections of his team . . . well, they were family.

You had to love them.

There wasn't really any choice.

He celebrated his birthday at Pollo's, a cheap and occasionally cheerful Italian restaurant in Soho. Lucy was there, as were Jamie, Andy, Claire, Dan, Chris. The drunker they got, the more fabulously indiscreet they allowed themselves to be. Outside, they practised drunken tradecraft and talked themselves out of a night in the cells.

It was a wonderful evening, a hungover and sexy morning, and the first weekend off Ben could remember where no thoughts of home intruded, no future concerns, no guarded moments. He was young, on his path, and thinking only of the present.

Two days later a letter arrived for Ben from Personnel. He was to attend a disciplinary hearing with staff psychologists and the deputy head of recruitment. He arrived early and was kept waiting forty minutes before being ushered into a room with a panel of four cold-eyed suits. A fifth chair was placed to the side of the table, in which sat Sergeant Kevin Meades.

The implication of the panel was that although no evidence had come forward to identify the 'vandals' who had 'terrorized' the hard work of Sergeant Meades, the name Ben Sinclair had come up more than once. This was, he was reminded in words that echoed off the high ceiling, his final warning.

He'd called Lucy from the road but she wasn't picking up.

He used the time to hit the supermarket for the first time in weeks.

At the same time as Ben was leaving her another message from the sauces and pickles aisle of Tesco Metro, Lucy was sitting in a triple-glazed office on the fifth floor of Vauxhall Cross. Smiling sympathetically at her across his desk was the very helpful manager with the glittering eyes who had taken her intake of probationers somewhat under his wing.

Lucy had been crying, and was here with a plea.

'I want to stop,' she said.

'But you've behaved impeccably,' KB had said, 'and done only what is being asked of everyone else.'

'Everyone else wasn't encouraged to form a relationship with someone and then drop it,' she told him.

'Everything you've done is part of your evolution. Every stage of this training is more awareness of your limits. I told you the function of this. Being an officer isn't something you can punch on a time clock. It dominates your life because it simply *is your life*.'

Lucy nodded, half in understanding, half in loathing – but of who, she wasn't sure. 'What if I want to stay?' she asked eventually.

'Where?'

'With him.'

'As in, remain in the liaison?'

Lucy nodded.

'Well,' continued KB, 'the point of it was to achieve a goal. This you have done. You can of course do whatever you like. Just don't think it will look very good on your CV that you are still fraternizing with someone from across the river.'

'He's still part of my intake, though. He's on my team.'

'He is, certainly. He is no doubt many other things too. But these were the rules of the road laid down to you. This is a year of the utmost importance. You are here to learn. To be the selfless intelligence officer I know you can be, and soon.' Lucy got up and paced over to the window. 'Perhaps you should ask yourself,' said KB, 'what would he do?'

By the time Ben arrived back at the front door, he was in no mood to share his space with anyone. He was laden down, half crippled with shopping bags, mostly tins of the baked beans that Lucy seemed to demolish in hours. He half debated turning around and booking into a hotel for the night to spare her his bitterness but resolved instead to cook comfort food until she came home.

Opening the door, it only took him a few seconds to realize she'd moved her stuff out.

Thirty-Three

B en's ears rang painfully in the darkness.

They were still ringing when the hood came off. Even as his eyes struggled with the light outside, his mind was frantically trying to work out why he was still alive. Gently the realization came that the only reason his heart was still beating was probably that the bullets had been blanks.

He was also pleased to discover that he had not soiled himself. A glance to his right told him that Nat was not so lucky. A dark patch was spread liberally across the front of his crotch.

Two men with rifles stood thirty feet away on a small rise of ground. Ben recognized one as the clean-shaven man from the hotel room. He was now dressed in casual clothes. The other man was taller; with deep-set eyes. Closer still was a third man. His face was scarred badly, and salt-and-pepper grey flecked his unkempt hair. He could have been any age between thirty and fifty. All that was clear was that his was a life that had seen much pain.

The four of them had been tied at regular intervals to a fence. Behind the fence, a steep bank hid them from sight. In the distance, Ben could make out the ruins of a structure or a series of structures. A farm, perhaps. He felt his stomach lurch as the man began to speak.

'In 1944 an underground movement developed in rural

Czechoslovakia. A network of freedom fighters working against the Nazis. Several Allied paratroopers were in hiding in a network of safe houses throughout farmland and villages in the southwest of the occupied country.

'The lives of these men depended on the network keeping absolute control of information. The people who needed to know told no one else. One day, one person in that chain made a mistake, and hinted to another person outside that circle of the paratroopers' existence. Twelve hours later, the paratroopers and the network of freedom fighters were dead. The safe houses were exposed and razed to the ground, some were locked and set fire to with the host families still inside. The codes used by the network were compromised and used against Allied forces still arriving in the country.

'There is no limit to the amount of care with which a network must proceed. No cap on the demands it will place on its members. This is only a small taste of what is to come. I cannot stress more strongly that your trials are only just beginning.'

Nat managed to clear his throat and fill his lungs in the silence that followed. 'So is this . . . I mean . . .'

Ben turned his head and for the first time caught sight of the man ten feet to his left. Jamie Gallagher grinned manically back at him, eyes blazing with life. The Lazarus man was alive and well indeed.

And Jamie was way ahead of everyone, as usual.

'Look,' he shouted. 'Is this Contact Zero or what?'

The man looked surprised for a moment, and said nothing. Then, slowly, a curious look crept across his face, as if Jamie had just asked him if there really was a Santa Claus.

Contact Three

The journey was a trial, but the crossing was a torture.

Sweet was not a tall man but stowed away thus, as a chicken in a coop, his will eroded to the nub. The coach was worse. It had taken twelve hours from Calais, the roads sodden and so waterlogged in places it was a miracle the driver didn't ask every passenger to heave and push them south. Still, at the end of every traveller's thoughts is his destination, and Sweet felt sure his would arrive eventually.

And of course it did, and his heart soared just to see his old home once more. His work here was not yet done. His mind raced at the thoughts of old friendships renewed.

Not that they would be aware of the renewal, Sweet thought. At least, not at first.

Some twelve miles outside the main ville was a cluster of modest dwelling houses and a maison de maître, known by almost everyone in the region as la maison de maîtresse.

Claudette had been waiting for him, she admitted. Sweet had to laugh, in spite of himself. All this time? he asked. I am truly blessed. She had laughed with him and pressed his face to her bosom. An attic space had an entrance hidden behind her bed, which concealed a small stone stairwell. As she entertained her consorts in her boudoir, upstairs Sweet was working on what would come next.

Such an inspirational sound, smiled Sweet, was human pleasure resonating beneath one's feet. Each day, Claudette would bring him food, and each day, Sweet would leave a king's ransom in coins for her in return.

Then, one day, the food did not arrive.

Sweet, a man of regularity, a man of principle and craft, was anxious. Over and above his concern for his protector, however, was his work. His gut sometimes led where his head did not, and at this moment his thoughts were so twisted he had no other option but to follow. He removed his papers and burned his plans, committing them to memory as the flames flickered in the grate.

Creeping to the stairs, he waited until darkness entombed the house before emerging.

She was indeed in bed, the lady of the house, sliced open with an épée, ravaged and mutilated beyond any limit of human decency. The boudoir was now a charnel house, her body a warning.

Sweet grabbed what few possessions he had left and fled into the night. He had surrogates here, of course, a family to help him achieve what needed to be done. But, one by one, his visits became nothing more than marches of death. Whoever he had touched in his previous life was gone.

It would be ten days before he discovered the truth about their deaths. It would be ten months before he found another friend.

Thirty-Four

They had been delivered back to the stone floors of what appeared to be a rural barn. Cold night air seeped through the cracks in the old timbers of the door. The rafters showed damage from where, one by one, they had been strung up. The man with the scar had not uttered a word since the van had pulled up outside. Once their hoods had been removed, he had not exactly been talkative. But the mood was changing. There was a sense that this was transactional, that both parties had found themselves here, both sides as blameless as each other, doing what they had to do.

Two other men in casual clothes had brought water and blankets. The four of them had folded up inside themselves, cautiously absorbing this new reality. It was taking them a while to sink into the new situation, like a hot bath.

Most present in Ben's mind, however, was the simple thought: Jamie Gallagher was here. Jam Jar, the Lazarus man, had made it. He glanced over and caught Jamie staring back at him. Ben just looked away and shook his head. This was all too much.

Gradually, the surprise and delight of seeing him brought back other memories. Ben tried to remember his own rule. This is not the time, or the place, for that.

Eventually, one by one, they found their voices.

Lucy shivered, but it wasn't from the cold. The man with the scar was standing patiently by the door. She turned to him. 'I don't understand. The Russian business . . .'

'A test, naturally.'

'Which we passed,' added Ben.

'Yes.'

'And, erm, the firing squad?' asked Jamie. 'To measure our grace under pressure perhaps? Or something a little more sinister?'

'To establish how far you were prepared to go to preserve the truth.'

'Which we passed, presumably? Flying colours?'

'That is why you are still alive.'

Jamie exhaled sharply. 'Good-oh,' he muttered. 'Good to be alive. Alive is good.'

Okay, thought Ben.

'If you're not Contact Zero,' ventured Lucy, attempting a different tack, 'and I'm very much presuming you're not . . . then perhaps could you please tell us who you, in fact, are?'

'And the shooting at us. Tell us about that,' snapped Nat. 'The shooting at us with fucking blanks.' He sat slightly apart from Ben, Lucy and Jamie, still evidently embarrassed about his lapse of control under fire.

'We are merely links in the chain,' said the man. 'Cogs in the mechanism.'

'Pretty serious bloody cogs if you ask me,' said Jamie.

Lucy let out a laugh, despite herself. Ben turned to see her staring admiringly over at Jamie. His arrival had cheered them all. Despite himself, Ben felt a twinge of jealousy.

An arid stare pierced them. 'Sanctuary is not simply something you are awarded. It is something you earn. To find it you must first prove your worth. We needed to find out if you could withstand whatever comes next. Whether you'd be secure enough to carry knowledge of this network away with you.'

'So what *is* our next step?' asked Jamie.

The man's eyes were impenetrable.

'Our network survives only through the strength of the individuals who comprise it. So, first, you must rest and recuperate.'

Nat crossed his arms and peered at him sceptically. He could have been a PhD supervisor analysing a student's latest essay. 'Why don't you just try and find sanctuary yourself?'

'We do not need sanctuary because we have done nothing wrong. We merely help along the way.'

'Samaritans,' stuttered Nat, 'don't tend to knee people in the neck.'

The man was turned away from them now. His mind clearly on other things.

'No more questions now. We can offer food, water, protection while you sleep.'

'A proper little bed and breakfast. Sounds all right to me.'

The man seemed to smile at this. He was almost tickled by it. He turned once more to face them – his eyes glowing with both pity and compassion.

'Your struggles, I'm afraid, are only just beginning.'

Thirty-Five

T he Chief hardly had time to think about the present, let alone the future. He had no energy, inclination or will-power to worry about the past. There was so much more to be getting on with.

Yet in spite of the deluge of paperwork, he made one or two exceptions. In certain specific cases, the past troubled him a great deal – the dim and distant, the medium term, even the very recent. It pestered him like a hungry cat. The Chief was still trying to make sense of his reprimand meeting with KB. He knew that the man was a talent, he had worked with him for so long over the years and, despite his dreadful toadying and freelance directions, he was one of the few in the building who actually produced results. And these days, ever since perfor-mance-related pay had kicked in, that was what mattered.

The Chief was busy on several other pieces of business when a secretary arrived in front of him with a sheet of paper – *the research you ordered*, the secretary explained. The Chief was just about to retort that he had no memory of ordering anything when he glanced at the sheet and recognized his error.

The document was titled 'Greco'.

He thanked the secretary and shut the door.

Sitting down behind his walnut desk, he reviewed the document carefully. He knew he shouldn't, he knew he could easily have let the matter slide and let KB inform him at his own pace. But there was a concern tickling its way out of his subconscious and he simply had to know a little more.

The document was a history lesson, a potted one at that. Gioachino Greco, it explained, was born around 1600 in Calabria, Italy. A man of lowly birth, he seemed, however, to have a propensity to spend increasing amounts of time in grander circles, with men of high position and, clearly, extra time on their hands. A closer look explained why.

Greco was a chess player.

An extremely good one, in fact.

The Renaissance, it seemed, was also a nascent time for the game of rooks, pawns, kings, queens and, particularly, bishops. The Chief found it ironic that chess blossomed under deeply religious cultures, and it seemed equally apt that the game itself offered a snapshot of how power had migrated within Christian culture – from the clergy to the nobility.

Greco, the Chief discovered, was also a competitor, travelling widely and winning many challenge matches at home and abroad.

All very interesting. But why name an operation after a chess master, unless simply to marvel at the ingenuity of its creator? The Chief couldn't understand it. And he was damned and blasted if he was going to show weakness and ask KB for an explanation.

It was then that he saw the final paragraph and everything started to become clear. At least, as far as Greco was concerned. But, thought the Chief, if this was the reason KB named this operation after him . . . if this was the *essence* of Greco . . .

The thought troubled him very much.

Thirty-Six

In his dream, Ben was laughing. He was with his brother John in the kitchen of their parents' first house in Bristol. John was thirteen, Ben was six. The dream never allowed him to hear the comment that started it all. Knowing John, it would have been a fart joke. It seemed to cut in to this moment after the event. But the room filled with purple streamers of laughter, gales of it, towers of it, transporting and engulfing them as they fell to the floor, clutching their sides.

They stayed there, in the dream, unable to rise from the carpet, launching into ever louder shrieks of hysterics until, as Ben rolled and tears stung his eyes, he heard the sobs and his brother's voice groaning, and, as his brother's hands grabbed at his ribcage, his stomach, Ben leapt to his feet and saw John, trying to keep it all in, a gaping hole, his insides, pink and red in the void of his belly and then the howls of pain and the foul smell of innards and the spreading pool of black under him.

All the while, standing there, over him, Ben. Just watching now. Even as John's pleading eyes burned up at him, his bloodied hand extended up, Ben felt himself impassive, cold.

Spectating.

Ben emerged from sleep as if he'd been holding his breath underwater and gasped. Shaking the fug from his brain, he felt the eyes staring at him from the other side of the room. He was in a spartan dormitory, once perhaps the neophytes' sleeping quarters until they earned themselves the prayerful solitude of a monastic cell. There were plain white walls and six metal bed frames lined up in a row. Four of the beds had thin mattresses laid out upon them. Ben felt the rough edge of a thick blanket against his skin. Recollections drifted back to him. They had talked, eaten and retired to bed. The nervous energy of the past few days had drained them all and, despite feeling he would be too nervous to sleep, it had come with ease. Jamie, he knew, had quietly promised to keep watch over them all, but from the looks of things all four beds had been used. It was like something out of the Crimean War. He half expected Florence Nightingale to waltz in through the door. Instead, he saw one of the men from the firing squad. He was loitering just outside the door. Perhaps he was on guard duty. Perhaps, Ben thought sleepily, he was selling something.

'There's still some breakfast left, if you want it.'

Ben showered in cold water and dressed in his newly washed clothes. He hadn't asked for them to be washed, but they had appeared on the bottom of his bed, folded and aired. It was more than faintly ridiculous. He imagined his mother popping out of a side door – *just did a few loads for you, dear*. Ben was trying to work out why he felt anxious when he saw something was missing. He turned quickly back to the guard who stood once again in the doorway.

'Shoes,' said Ben. 'I had shoes.'

The guard shrugged, then remembered. 'They were washed. They had blood on them, so – I think they were put somewhere else, to warm.'

Ben was still waking up. It seemed to him a little odd that the guard was taking such an interest in his footwear. He was young, a few years older than Ben, perhaps. But his eyes seemed decades more advanced. He was still standing there, loitering in the doorway.

'I'll show you,' he said.

Ben was too tired to protest, and followed him.

The man led him down and through older corridors of the main building; some rooms once housed wine; others now lodged rats. The man began to talk quietly to him as they walked. It quickly occurred to Ben that the man wasn't that interested in his shoes after all.

The Crimean War theme was continued in what appeared to be the mess hall. Within the ruins of a converted monastery complex, a new refectory had been constructed, making use of the old tables and benches.

Ben found Lucy and Jamie eating. They were talking in low voices and stopped as he approached. Ben felt his stomach twitch. Conspiracy sounded something like this. And was that stubble rash on Lucy's chin? Probably not.

All the same, Ben was suddenly feeling . . . *raw* was the wrong word. As he sat down, he realized what it was. He felt *permeable*. And he was trying desperately to seal himself up again as soon as possible.

'You took your time,' said Lucy.

'Slept the sleep of the dead.'

'Join the club.'

Ben felt Lucy glancing down at his hand as his fork quivered slightly in midair. He wondered whether he should say some-thing, perhaps a comment about his aching muscles, but decided against it. Nat joined them after a few minutes. He kept his voice low as he ate. 'There's six of them that I can see. Top man, Mr Personality, I mean, and three guarding this set of buildings. I've seen two more on a patrol around the outside.'

Lucy's eyes flashed. 'They let you outside?'

'I saw them through a window. Two people held me up. Four people nearly shot us. Six.'

The Samaritan with the scar watched impassively from the doorway. When breakfast was over, he invited the four of them into a spartan living room and reiterated his message: he could provide 'safe harbour', room and board, for three days. After that, should they need any more help, they were on their own.

And, at the end of three days, they would be given the name of a 'friendly face' – another link in a chain that could lead to Contact Zero.

Not that the Samaritan had any guarantees about that. 'It's need to know, I'm sure you understand. Anyone who gets this far tends to want to go further. But later on, I'm not so sure that's true.'

Ben saw a memory flash in the Samaritan's eyes. 'You've tried yourself?'

The man shook his head. 'As I told you, there was no need.' *Denial*, thought Ben. *He's tried all right.* Ben saw that Lucy had spotted the same thing. Their eyes met in complicity.

It was King Ethelbert, in 600 AD, who first brought the idea of sanctuary to English shores. For a seventh-century fugitive, reaching a holy and sanctified place was not enough. To gain legal sanctuary from harm and due process, a door knocker was sounded or, instead, the poor sod might gain access to the interior and sit on a stone seat known as a 'frith-stool', named after *frithu*, the Anglo-Saxon word for peace.

There was a final element to this first form of sanctuary, however. There was a time limit. Some thirty days or so from achieving it, the fugitive was bound thereafter to 'abjure the realm', and leave the country forever.

As far as this Brazilian sanctuary went, abjuration was not

yet on the agenda. A combination of sleep, three meals a day and some gentle exercise was all the three of them could manage. The grounds of the monastery were crumbling in parts, but mostly habitable. It was unclear how long the compound had been abandoned by the holy men, but the cells and prayer chambers were clearly well used in the past. Now, the monastery's refectory served as the social hub of their stay, with the great oak table maintained with care, benches, wooden bowls and talk.

There was much to discuss. Jamie, for one, had some explaining to do. 'I'd been working a group of Muscovite transplants,' he said. 'Odessa's full of them, the so-called snow birds. Coming down to the sea to make money, get drunk, gamble, screw and do deals . . . I was only really getting started.

'I came home after work and had an invitation to a reception in this hotel on the other side of the lake, about forty minutes by car. I knew a few people I was interested in would probably be there so I signed up.

'Two idiots were waiting for me in my hotel room. They chloroformed me and I suppose they were trying to smuggle me out and into a van. But this old thing—' he patted his shoulder, the scar where the snow fence had once skewered him – 'this thing saved my life. It aches a lot these days, very painful, and I think they must have thrown me into the van on to something sharp. Anyway, the pain was excruciating but it was enough to wake me up.'

'What happened?'

'I faked them. I pointed a torch to the driver's head and told him to slow down. Instead he tried to crash the car. I got thrown about in the back and Mr Bright Spark in front went through the windscreen with his mate. So I changed clothes with one of them, gave him all my papers and set fire

212

to the thing, called the police and waited to see what happened.'

'But wait. Your death was reported. Why didn't you go to the embassy and report back alive?'

'Because there was only one person who knew where I lived, and I suspected that's the person who'd sent the invitation. They presumed I gave my real address. I hadn't, I'd given him a backstop flat I'd rented under another name. The postcard arrived there, the invitation, and I knew the embassy was in on it. I was being targeted. God knows why.'

'How did you know how to get here?' Lucy asked.

'Same as you did. Archivist rotation, right?'

Lucy nodded. Ben could see Nat was starting to bristle with scepticism.

'And you just happened to remember the right code to broadcast?' Nat sneered.

'No. I just happen to be better at remembering things than you are. Come on. We all heard about the rumours. Some of us pursued them a little more than others. Lucy and I are both scientists. We're curious people.'

'You certainly are,' said Nat.

'Odessa's a long way away,' said Ben.

'So is Vauxhall Cross.'

'Your point?'

'We've all come a long way, baby.' Jamie smiled. The tension dissolved slightly.

'It's just a bit odd if they sent you all the way to South America.'

'Maybe this is just where the rat run begins. If I was building a sanctuary, I think I'd look around here. South America's the fugitive Club Med. Hate to say it, but all those Nazi war criminals didn't hole up in Tokyo. Those bastards all headed down here.'

After another night's sleep, Jamie felt a craving for exercise again and asked if his hosts might find him a pleasant running trail. But they would not allow him outside the monastery grounds, and so Ben, Jamie and Lucy were forced to jog through cloisters, over wells, and around in circles until they felt the burn.

The next day, Ben sprinted ahead – knowing that Jamie would follow. Lucy, who preferred to set her own pace, pretended she was planning on stretching anyway.

The two men ran in step for a minute or so before Ben spoke. 'Did you call your brother?' he asked.

Jamie glanced at him. 'My brother?'

'The one at the Foreign Office.'

'Oh. Well, yes. I did. As it happens.'

'What did he say?'

'You'd really like to know?'

Ben said that he would.

'Well,' said Jamie, 'he said my career in SIS was effectively over. That if I came back to the UK I would most likely be arrested. That it could seriously damage our family name.' He paused, thinking, far away. 'Not a very helpful conversation, I must say.'

'I'm sorry.'

'So am I.'

'The newspaper report said you jumped.'

Jamie changed gear and slowed things up a little.

'Not everything one reads tells the truth.'

'I suppose that's right.'

'Another example could be the Black Sea. Don't believe

214

everything you read about the Black Sea or Bulgaria. Things like that.'

A dark look from Ben. As he drew breath to protest, Jamie continued, eyes glinting with foreknowledge: 'But I gather from the others that we're not talking about the past,' he said, looking at the ground as he spoke.

'We've got the rest of our lives to sort it out. If we ever get there.'

'I hate to be philosophical about it, but we *are* in the rest of our lives,' said Jamie. 'We're in the middle of them right now. So I don't know about you, ya English poof, but I've got things to do with mine.' And he burst ahead of Ben and hurdled a wall. Ben accelerated and caught up with him, but even after what they'd been through, Jamie was the alpha male. He was hardly panting as they walked back to find Lucy. Ben was hyperventilating.

In addition to the physical rehabilitation, the time was a much needed mental space. The long-term effects of torture are well documented. Unless the brain has time on its own terms to heal, it too can hobble a person for life.

As the third day drew to a close, a new feeling of possibility seemed to infuse all four fugitives. Ben, particularly, had a new-found energy about him. He talked at length with Jamie, hearing more about his experiences in Odessa. There was still respect there, between the two of them. It had an edge, but it was there. Nat spent his time with Lucy, who had taken pity on him. He confided in her that it wasn't the gunfire that had caused his 'accident', but the hoods. He had always been claustrophobic, he explained. Lucy's words of support helped repair lost pride.

She also knew that Nat was the jealous sort.

He'd felt threatened by the history that Lucy and Ben had

shared. She understood this, and took steps to include him. She needed all three of these people as close to her as possible. That was another advantage of sticking together.

It's harder to betray someone when you're sleeping in the same room.

By the morning of the fourth day, he was back to something near to his old self.

'Yo,' he announced to the others as he arrived late for breakfast. But no one looked up or smiled.

'They've given us till sunset to leave,' said Jamie without emotion.

'They're kicking us out?' said Nat.

'It's all we get,' said Lucy. 'Guess the next lot are coming through. Or something.'

'Well, they washed my clothes, so they get my vote.'

'Mine too.'

'Didn't that strike you as weird?' asked Jamie through a mouthful of bread. 'Struck me as a bit fucking odd.'

Ben nodded and looked at the spread of food before them. For the first time in as long as he could remember he was genuinely ravenous. He longed for a cigarette.

'I got the feeling this wasn't a permanent gig,' said Ben, looking at the holes in the ceiling, the grass growing from between the floorboards.

'Oh, we're camping all right,' said Jamie. 'That's what all this running around has got us so far. A sodding camp site in a monastery.'

The man with the scar appeared through a door at the far end of the dining hall. 'A mission, in fact.' The four turned to look at him. 'We found this place several years ago. The original owners were tempted by our offer to manage it and, so, it's remained in our care.'

'Who is "we", exactly?'

'The Samaritans.'

'But not Contact Zero?'

The man merely smiled politely.

'Okay. We're here. We're back on our feet. Now what?' said Ben. Lucy eyed this new energy with interest.

The man with the scar narrowed his eyes and surveyed him, betraying a little surprise at Ben's brusque tone.

'We help to guide you to the next step.'

Ben turned to the others. They all nodded with the same look – *we're not staying here, that's for sure.*

'Very well,' said the man with the scar. Despite their constant attempts, he had not divulged his real name. The only way to get anyone's attention was to call them 'Samaritan'. Nat couldn't stomach this and had resorted to a simple 'Hey, you'. The man joined them at their table. The scar may have been grotesque, but the eyes were warm and convivial. 'In that case, I'm afraid we will have to ask you to indulge our obsession for privacy once more. I'm truly sorry. But I'm sure you understand.'

As he spoke, the man held up one of the hoods that had nearly suffocated them all four days previously. Nat shuddered at the sight of them. 'We'll use blindfolds this time,' he added. 'I am told they are far more comfortable.'

He walked them to a courtyard fringed with overgrown jacaranda trees and palms. A Jeep's engine was turning over noisily on a circular track that disappeared under rusted iron gates. Their four pieces of luggage were tied securely to the roof of the vehicle, and then the man turned to them again.

'We have one other request. You all take one of these.' He opened his palm to show four white tablets.

'Got to be joking,' blurted Jamie.

'Maybe he's taking us clubbing,' murmured Nat, looking subtly to Lucy for a reaction. She was too focused to respond, and Ben saw his disappointment.

'The only alternative is another phenobarb ampoule to the thigh, but these are far more gentle on the stomach. We can't truly release you into the world once more without some insurance and security for ourselves. I'm sure you understand.'

Lucy took a pill between her fingers and peered closely at it. 'Valium?'

The Samaritan gave a noncommittal shrug. 'A variation on that theme.'

Ben took the pill from Lucy and swallowed it, dry. Nat stared open-mouthed at his recklessness, but after Lucy and Jamie followed suit, he grudgingly popped the pill. 'Chin chin,' he said.

Once the blindfolds were on, each of them clambered into the back of the Jeep and lay flat, like a corpse. A blanket was laid over their prone bodies, and, without a word of farewell, the journey began. In the darkness, through the growing numbness in his limbs, Ben felt Lucy's hand reach for his and squeeze it. He knew this was simple instinct, familiarity, the need for comfort. He knew this because he yearned for it too. He tried to squeeze back, but in the time it took for the thought to register, the effort seemed too great. He drank in the darkness when it poured over him, welcomed it.

Thirty-Seven

It was raining when the four of them came round. The drops were like slugs of ice hewn from a block. They were lying in a circle on the edge of a plain of rough ground, harsh grass and rocks. Ben shook the moisture from his eyes. Puddles were forming around them in the mud. There was no sound bar the drumming of the rain.

As the others came to, Ben was climbing down from a tree. Lucy, on her hands and knees, vomited. Jamie rocked on his haunches and stood unsteadily up, helping Nat to his feet moments later.

'There's a road half a mile west,' said Ben.

'You're up early,' croaked Jamie. 'Right then. How about some scrambled eggs and bacon on bruschetta?'

Ben raised his eyebrows. *If only.*

Lucy opened her mouth to the raindrops, swirled them and spat. 'What about the bags?'

Ben pointed over to a small patch of earth nearby where a tarpaulin had been laid, their luggage concealed under a light camouflage of branches and palm fronds.

Jamie raced over and heaved the tarpaulin off. Nat joined him and promptly tugged it back over. 'And now you're just getting it wet.'

'That's because I want to check my stuff.'

Ben walked over to Lucy as the disagreement blossomed

over by the tarpaulin. She folded her arms and stared back. He smiled grimly. 'How do you feel?'

'Like a bowl of rat's-nest soup.'

'What do you think it was they slipped us?'

Lucy sucked her teeth for a moment, screwing up her face. 'Probably phenobarb again, from the looks of things, the bloody liars.' She held up her hand, a slight tremor in the fingers.

A shout from Jamie made them turn. 'Take a look at this.' There was a fifth bag under the tarpaulin, a small grey day sack, with two empty pockets on either side. They hestitated a moment before opening it. Lucy dived in and unzipped the main compartment. Inside, basic rations: four bottles of water, some crackers, some chocolate. Below that, wrapped in plastic, a paperback edition of *Tamburlaine*, a play by Shakespeare's contemporary, Christopher Marlowe.

They huddled under the tarpaulin to examine it.

'How thoughtful,' Jamie said, 'reading matter.'

Ben thumbed quickly through the pages. It was a yellowing Penguin edition, the kind of well-thumbed volume you might find in a beachside guesthouse next to a James Michener novel or a Go Mexico travel guide from 1988. Nat took the book from Ben and re-examined each page in reverse. No signs of microdots, inserts or otherwise. Lucy leaned over him and flipped the pages back to the frontispiece.

'There,' she said.

She pointed to a scrawl of numbers on the page, just underneath the top corner where a price appeared in pencil. There were two lines of them:

49.25903
122.77428

And nothing more. The rain was easing up now, and Jamie took charge of the luggage. He heaved off the tarpaulin, rolled it up and secured it on his own backpack. As Ben watched, he realized that all of these people were bringing something to the table. Lucy had her strategies. Nat had his languages, his technical know-how. Jamie was an action man who'd lie down on barbed wire for them without hesitation.

Ben wondered if they'd start to realize they could do all this without him. He vowed to make sure that never happened. Nat poked his head in between Lucy and Ben as they stared at the numbers.

'Another phone number?' said Ben, realizing he was talking out loud.

Nat sniffed loudly. 'No.' And walked away.

Ben followed him. 'It's a catalogue number, a library classification?'

Nat paused and shrugged like it was the most mundane question he'd ever been asked. 'Doubt it.'

'So what is it then?' asked Lucy. With the attention back on him, Nat was finally prepared to share.

'Could be any of those things. But those numbers in that sequence could also be a measure of latitude and longitude. If you ask me, that's a GPS location.'

Lucy peered back at the numbers. 'Are you sure?'

Nat opened up his rucksack and was relieved to find everything as he'd left it – his palm-held Global Positioning System was close to hand, the battery still at half-capacity. He began inputting the numbers. A moment later, he was peering at the screen, savouring his moment of superiority.

'And if *that's* true . . . I guess we're going to Panama.'

Thirty-Eight

T he Chief almost admired KB for his arrogance. His presumption. He ran over new epithets in his head as he opened the door to KB and showed him in.

For a man summoned under extreme duress to see the head of the entire Intelligence Service, KB seemed remarkably poised. He also held a small manila envelope tucked under his arm.

'I take it,' smiled KB as he sat down, 'you have worked out my little *stratagem*.'

The Chief smiled back as he held KB squarely and firmly by the neck, yanking him over the back of the chair. He held him in balance for a second as he leaned in close.

'I have been led to believe that two of our latest recruits to go into the field have died or gone missing on their maiden postings. I also gather they have somehow come under your remit. You had better tell me everything,' he said, and let go. The chair rocked forward again and KB breathed deeply, brushing himself down. He seemed to have been expecting far worse.

'May I show you something?' he said, rubbing his neck.

The Chief just stared from his desk.

KB retrieved the manila folder from the floor and stepped gingerly behind the Chief at his desk. He placed a series of photographs in front of him.

The Chief held them up. They were an odd collection of shots – all of them long-exposure. They all showed car lights, beams of red and white, weaving around a large metropolis.

'Taken without such an exposure, you don't see the movement,' said KB. 'But leave the aperture open, and one can see the trails. It's quite, quite beautiful.'

'Your point, if you have one.'

'We need information on young networks. Unknown quantities. Wisp material.'

'Indeed.'

'It is easier to understand something when it's in motion, is it not? I believe astronomers call it the "red shift" if it's departing.'

The Chief swivelled in his chair. 'Greco,' he growled.

KB sighed and faced him. 'Gioachino Greco was a chess innovator. He is the man who effectively invented the gambit. The sacrifice of a minor piece to achieve a stronger position in the long game.'

He had expected the Chief to start making notes at this point. He was slightly worried when he discovered he was not. He cleared his throat and continued. 'When a piece is sacrificed, the opponent is often bemused. They become so fixated on the loss they don't realize that their next few moves are irrational too. They do things they don't expect. They act without their usual care and attention.'

'You sacrificed these people.'

'The only way to get a snapshot of an organization is when it is in motion.'

'You *sacrificed them* . . .'

A strangled, exasperated yelp emitted from KB's throat. 'By gambiting a small number of very junior operatives, we are getting a phenomenal fast-forward insight into groups who could put *thousands* of lives at risk in the future. What do

223

you do when you think your friend's not telling you the truth? You call everyone you know and ask them what they think. This is exactly the same idea. And we are suddenly in a position of comprehensive knowledge whereas yesterday we were blundering around in the dark. To my mind that is a harsh but defensible truth. The sacrifices we make today are protecting us and our children ten, twenty, thirty years from now.'

'We are not making those sacrifices. They are.'

'We are both aware of what the stakes are.'

'You gambited two young lives.'

KB fidgeted slightly in his seat. 'Seven, actually.'

'My God!'

'Although I'm told another one is unaccounted for. So perhaps six is the final count.'

'There can be no justification for this,' said the Chief, picking up the phone.

'There can, Thomas, I assure you,' said KB. His voice was supremely confident. The Chief's finger wavered over the button marked 'OPS'.

'Do you still dream about Berlin? I know I do.'

The Chief broiled in the silence.

'If you work together you learn to understand certain nuances. Your love of the f-word, for example.'

The Chief did not move.

'And your love of brandy. Your ups and downs careerwise—'

'What is your point?'

'Most breakthroughs happen by accident,' said KB, deliberately delaying. 'Penicillin was discovered when Fleming left a Petri dish out when he shouldn't have. When I concocted Greco I did it with simplicity in mind – to pursue these seedbed groups, to gain a foothold in their power structures, panicking them into showing us what made them tick. But along the way, something amazing occurred.'

The Chief waited for KB's ego to savour the anticipatory silence.

'I realized the operation had a *dual use*,' he said.

The flourish appeared to be lost on the Chief. KB continued. 'In fact, it had a secondary use that was far more important. The gambit, as such, was relegated to number two.' He paused to crack a knuckle.

'So what became number one?'

'It occurred to me even as I had the notion that, by sacrificing these agents, I might motivate some to find ways to evade the inevitable – and escape.'

'Where?'

KB fixed him with lizard eyes.

'Where do you think, Thomas?'

Silence bar the chiming of a carriage clock on the mantelpiece. *So that was why he mentioned Berlin.* The Chief leaned in close to KB. 'I'm not talking about this.'

'You and I both know what it would mean—'

'No—'

'That it's a question we are both dying to answer. Is it real? Does Contact Zero exist? Where? How is it funded?'

'That's not the point of this.'

'Oh, but you and I both know it is. The two of us, more than most, I would say, would be delighted to know *exactly* what's going on where Contact Zero is concerned. Wouldn't you say? Like I said, I still dream about Berlin.'

'We both agreed we would not talk about that again.'

'He was dead. We know he was dead. And yet we both still worry. Why? Neither of us saw the body. We'd worked with the man for years and neither of us saw him die. He disappeared.

225

He knows what we did to him and he disappeared and had the temerity not to wash up on a beach somewhere. Which leaves one horrific possibility.'

'He's not still alive.'

'I doubt it. But he could be. He could have found Contact Zero for himself. He could be there, old bean. By dismantling Contact Zero . . . we dismantle him. Erase him from our memory. And we can sleep again.'

The Chief was silent for a long time. At least two minutes went by. He stared at his desk, moved to the window, glanced back at KB. Consumed, it was clear, by memories.

'In any case . . .' the Chief trailed off.

KB smiled – he had hooked his fish.

'In any case, there's no way of knowing that anyone would survive that kind of sacrifice. Deliberately blowing their cover means a death sentence.'

'Unless they are good enough to survive.'

'No way to be sure about that.'

KB moved to the window and gazed out over London. He'd choose this office one day too, if or when he took over. 'There is, actually. Though it takes a bit of planning.'

'You helped these people?'

KB stared down at a tugboat pulling a barge full of refuse downstream, towards the Thames Barrier. 'Just a little. To get them on the road. Playing percentages, you understand.'

The Chief closed his eyes and sighed.

'But don't worry. From now on, I'll only help the one who's working for us.'

Thirty-Nine

That the Samaritans would send them on another cross-country journey was not surprising. One part of training that Lucy had never tired of was the case studies, stories of the espionage operations of the past decades. One story had always stayed with her. A covert MI6 cell in Sudan, fighting Bin Laden in the nineties, were under such immediate threat from sabotage that they were forced to move from safe house to safe house every night for a year. The constant motion, the lack of sleep, the dependence on others who could, at any time, cost you your life – these were the daily pressures of a field officer on active duty. She felt it was a prime example of the need for trust between team members. To live like that for a year, you had better know each other very well.

Passage to Panama was possible over ground, but too dangerous. Even the intrepid Jamie agreed that a passage into the country through the Darien Gap was not advisable without a trusted guide. Since trust was the thinnest material on the ground at that moment, and since the Darien was overflowing with guerilla warfare, brutal killings and a seemingly endless parade of kidnap, torture and robbery, the plan was a nonstarter.

They flew instead to Guayaquil, Ecuador, and then on to Costa Rica. Paying cash at all times, travelling on separate tickets in the same cabins, they looked after each other, and it paid dividends.

Flying to Costa Rica meant one more buffer between their actions and their intentions. Taking a local bus as far as the highlands on the road to Rio Sereno, they chanced their arm on the border crossing just as they were closing up for the night. The guards had run out of tourist cards on the Panama side, and, with a modest bribe, at 5.59 p.m. four more 'budget travellers' had their passports stamped.

Once on the other side, they approached the first tourist agency they could find and bought their way on to a night coach to Panama City. Arriving the next morning, Ben's anxiety began to grow. They were finding it all so easy, using bribes whenever an obstacle hit their path.

From now on, he knew, it wouldn't be so easy.

The Colón Free Trade Zone functioned as one giant piece of financial flypaper. The lack of restrictions on most imports and exports made it a nexus for money laundering, drug smuggling and human traffic. There were plenty of people in this country who operated outside the law. In fleeing here, they had replaced one danger with another.

With its towering office blocks of concrete and steel, being in the city was a little like standing next to a giant's well-appointed brushed-metal kitchen units.

A Global Positioning System can orient a person to within an astonishingly close distance of a target point. As they approached their goal it was becoming clear to everyone that their cover of four student travellers was wearing thin – the majority of people they were passing on the street appeared to be businessmen and women.

But sheer curiosity pushed them on, until finally, turning a corner, Nat pointed a well-gnawed finger at a blue-grey office tower on a street corner.

'That's the mark.'

Jamie and Ben staked out corners while Lucy and Nat investigated the lobby. A serene corporate scent put them both at their ease – a ploy, perhaps, to encourage commerce in the sweet-smelling air conditioning.

There were nearly a hundred names on the information board, but all MI6-issue GPSs have one extra feature normally unavailable to consumers at Circuit City – vertical elevation. Nat estimated the target at sixty feet above them. Factoring into this the height of the building, Lucy calculated a low floor. Only one name on the board was a low-floor corner office space. The notice board read: 'ALVAREZ, DR J'.

Retiring to an internet café outside the commercial district, they quickly uncovered his speciality – plastic surgery.

'We'll follow him home,' said Jamie. 'It's too exposed to make contact in an office building.'

'Why go to that trouble?' said Lucy. 'He might do home visits.'

Ben saw that Jamie was blushing slightly as he backed down to Lucy's suggestion. He was not, Ben was sure, a man who was used to being countermanded. Lucy called the doctor's number from a quiet payphone in the lobby of a tired old hotel. An astonishingly blunt receptionist explained the only way of meeting the doctor was by appointment.

Lucy, growing impatient after the hours of travelling, took a risk. 'He was recommended to me by a friend from Brazil.'

The receptionist went quiet for a moment and came back in a friendlier tone: 'The doctor says it is better if you make an appointment and come in. I see he has a cancellation for this afternoon. How is that for you?'

Three hours later, Ben and Lucy, clean and smart in newly purchased preppy clothing, reached the bank of elevators and pressed 'UP'. A woman was striding towards the open doors but Lucy punched 'DOORS CLOSE' in time for her to be denied. The elevator jerked slightly and then moved smoothly upwards.

The corridors had thin carpet and blank walls. No attempt had been made to provide signs or other forms of orientation. The only reference points were the numbers on the doors: 512, 514A, 516 . . .

They reached Suite 532 and rang the bell.

Inside, a fishtank bubbled next to a row of plastic chairs. a grand old couple waited in a corner. Behind a small cubbyhole in the wall sat a young woman in a grey speckled tracksuit top. Her hair was midnight black and greasy, tied back with a bright yellow rubber band. Her glasses were purple. Long green nails completed the ensemble. She looked as if someone had been flicking different colours of paint at her all afternoon.

'You are here to see the doctor?' she smiled.

Lucy nodded and gave her false name.

'We will need to see proof of payment, a credit card, something like that . . .'

Ben stepped in and peeled a handful of $50 bills from a billfold in his pocket. The receptionist glanced at him as she took the cash and began typing into her computer. She pushed a clipboard towards Lucy and asked her to fill in a form.

As Lucy scribbled lies in capital letters next to him, Ben tried not to look at the receptionist. Instead, he removed the copy of *Tamburlaine* and began to read. Was this what he was supposed to do? He tried to look like he knew. In a few seconds, he felt faintly ridiculous, and simply held the book in his lap.

'The doctor will see you now.'

Dr Jesus Alvarez brought new life to many in Panama. In his mind he was performing the miracle of Lazarus every day on

230

the poor and unfortunate of the world (although, he would be the first to admit, it was generally the rich and insecure who were his clients).

He was a hangdog gerbil of a man with impish eyes flashing under the lids. Portly if not paunchy, he had the puffiness of a beer drinker and a roll of pink flesh unfurling like a window blind over his shirt collar. The first words in Ben's mind were 'doctor, heal thyself'. Dr Alvarez smiled at them both, ruing the male partner's loyalty in attending the appointment with his patient. He would have liked to talk to her alone. His breath smelled of alcohol and peppermints.

'I'm very pleased to meet you, Mrs . . .?'

'Kinnear. My husband John.'

Ben nodded politely but did not blink. Alvarez shifted in his seat. 'How can I help?'

Lucy smiled as Ben removed the book from his pocket and placed it on the desk in front of them. The doctor regarded it blankly and returned his lizard gaze to Lucy. His eyes *flicked* like a tongue down her nose, neck, chest, waist, thigh, a trained and lascivious eye.

'You were referred to me – us,' said Lucy after she'd recovered, 'by a friend.'

'From Brazil, you said. Carmen told me. To whom precisely do I owe the honour?'

'We'd rather not say,' said Ben, picking up the book and returning it to his pocket. He had clearly made up his own mind about the doctor and Lucy was more than happy to agree with him.

'To augment or reduce, for you, I think it's not advisable,' said the doctor. 'Your nose could use a streamline, of course, and the chin implodes a little into the neck, with those lines. But otherwise, unless you had specifics in mind, or a problem underneath your clothes, I—'

Ben smiled at the doctor. 'How much did you say a nose job would cost?'

'For medical tourists like yourselves, a special rate applies. Four thousand US, cash if possible.'

'We'll think about it,' said Lucy, and grabbed Ben's hand with the full intention of crushing it. Dr Alvarez held the door open for them with a smile and announced to Carmen that he was ready for his next patient.

'Thank you for your time,' said Ben.

Carmen the receptionist rose quickly from her seat as they left, reaching Lucy at the door and smiling as she pressed a small slip of paper into her hand. Instinctively, Lucy took hold of it as Carmen said. 'Your follow-up appointment will be tomorrow.'

Lucy began to shake her head – 'I don't have a follow-up' – even as she and Ben glanced down to read the note together, which simply stated an address in downtown Panama City and a time in the early hours of the morning.

Forty

E ven from the taxi it was clear that the neighbourhood was getting seedier by the yard. With each block that eased by, Ben could see the number of cafés diminish in proportion to the increased incidence of pawn shops.

Soon after that, the pawn became porn. There were vacant lots, tyre fires and a lack of streetlights. Eventually the driver rapped a hairy knuckle on the partition and stabbed his finger at the sidewalk.

'This is her! This the place!' he grinned. His teeth were mostly gold. There was no room for doubt. It was definitely a strip club. The biggest clue was the enormous sign outside, declaring 'GIRLS GIRLS GIRLS' in tasteful metallic-pink neon. From behind the dark doorway and the presumably Uzi-packing security guard, a pounding beat of dance music spilled out into the early morning air.

'Keep going,' said Ben. The driver half turned in confusion but soon got the message. He dropped Ben and Lucy off around the corner of the next block. The cab following them, containing Nat and Jamie, did the same.

They were an hour early. It was no mistake – they all had some work to do. The first steps of dry-cleaning were baby-sized – a thorough walk-through of the surrounding area. Escape routes, rooftop sightlines, any number of mundane factors that might be life savers under more pressing circumstances. Staying alive was all about taking these paranoid musings into account. To be foreworried is to be forearmed.

A refuse container, overflowing, beneath a solid window frame. A doorway that offered enough shadow to hide three Orson Welleses. Ben saw both out of the corner of his eye as he slowly circled the streets surrounding the club.

Eventually they descended on the front door. A stony-faced bouncer heard the European accents and unhitched the velvet rope. Tourist dollars were always welcome.

Inside, the club was a black hole. Hardly any light managed to escape from the one focal point, a pole-dancing stage in the centre of the room. Surrounding the stage were booths and tables, thronged with melancholy business suits and whooping packs of young men. Dotted around the club, other performers were entreating men to pay for private dances. One or two disappeared through a number of doors in the mirrored walls. Finishing an enthusiastic routine was a girl in her teens. The smile beamed a form of exotic promise, but the eyes were on autopilot. Unsure what to do next, Lucy smiled at a waitress who guided the quartet to a table in the centre of the room.

They sat for ten minutes, one eye on the club, one eye on the show.

Lucy was about to suggest they take a tour of the place when she felt a hand on her shoulder. Wheeling around, she came face to face with the girl from the stage. 'Dance?' she smiled. Lucy took a step back and tried not to look horrified, then she realized that there was someone standing behind the girl. It was Carmen, in a dark but seductive business suit. She made no attempt to show she recognized Lucy or any of the others. Her face was pure commerce.

'It's one hundred dollars for a private dance, plus a bottle of champagne for fifty dollars. One hundred fifty.'

234

Lucy nodded. Carmen smiled thinly and let the girl lead the way, winding through the tables of businessmen to a small black door to the side of a mirrored bar area. As she pulled the door open, she turned and stared at Ben, Nat and Jamie. They had been following Lucy and the girl. Carmen looked them up and down and turned back to Lucy, the client.

'You can bring your friends too, if you like.'

Lucy and the girl disappeared through the door. Nat caught Jamie's eyes gleaming in the eighties disco lights.

The girl led Lucy and the boys down a red-carpeted corridor and into a small room at the end. By the time they'd arrived, a bottle of champagne was sitting in the middle of the room, on ice. Carmen was seated next to it. She threw the girl her jacket, and she crept into a corner, shivering, to have a cigarette.

'Nice place you have here,' smiled Nat.

'I need the money,' snapped Carmen. 'Now, please, show me the book.' Lucy made a move for her jacket but Carmen held up her finger. 'I warn you, I can call security at any time, and, believe me, they will kill you if I yell loud enough. So don't waste my time.'

'We weren't planning to,' said Lucy, and fished the Marlowe play from her pocket. Carmen's eyes lit up as she saw the cover and flipped through the pages hungrily. Reaching halfway, she examined the page numbers. Unnoticed by all of them, one of the pages had been torn out of the centre of the book. She surveyed the book for another minute and then returned her stare to Lucy. It took them aback to see her eyes were wet with tears.

Jamie had kept his eye on the girl in the corner. She didn't appear to understand anything. 'Well?'

'My father can help you,' said Carmen, and dismissed the girl, who handed her jacket back as she left.

'Where is he?' asked Lucy when the girl had gone. 'Can we meet him?'

'You have to meet him. He's the only one who can tell you what to do.'

'Where can we meet? Where is he?'

Carmen moved forward to whisper in Lucy's ear. Her eyes nearly popped out of her head.

'And how the hell are we supposed to do that?'

As the sun came up, the four fugitives shared a drink in the hotel bar. They needed it. Lucy explained more details. Carmen's father was a man called Michael Church. All four of them had read about his exploits in their probation year. But they had only known him by his MI6 codename – Summer. And everyone knew where Summer had ended up.

The problem wasn't finding him. The problem was finding a way to talk to him.

Forty-One

S ummer had been recruited from Cambridge University in the spring of 1975 when his tutor had slipped his name to the Director.

His early career was unremarkable but workmanlike, neither excelling nor falling behind. It was only later his supervisors realized this seeming mediocrity was deliberate; he was simply working to ensure he did not become anyone's pawn in a game of below-the-waterline politics in his first few years.

When he became convinced that his tenure was solid, he began gently to prove himself. A tour in Germany and another in Moscow showed the management echelons what they had long suspected – Summer had the makings of a top-flight intelligence officer. His recruitment levels were second to none. His networks were solid and their product was reliable. So good was he in this regard that several internal investigations were launched during this time to check up on him – his managers felt, perhaps, he was *too* good. Their concerns were misplaced. He really was that brilliant.

He was moved to Nairobi, Kenya, at the turn of the decade and while working for the British High Commission his marriage collapsed. Two months later, he began a relationship with a local woman who worked at the US Embassy. When he declared the liaison to his superiors, he was told to cease the relationship as it contravened security protocols. Reluctantly, he did so, but two months later the woman approached him to inform him she was pregnant. She gave birth to a baby girl, who was then named Carmen. In spite of his managers' wishes, Summer maintained contact with both mother and daughter.

In an effort to stymie further contact, or the restart of their relationship, Summer was transferred to a covert paramilitary posting in the Sudan.

Alone and isolated in his new position, Summer began to look with hard clarity at every aspect of his life.

And then came Operation Kidglove.

It was, at first glance, a simple protection detail. His involvement was need to know and, as far as Summer could see, his special skills were purely as a heavyweight. He was right.

The asset, ████████████████, codename Trinity, was a reputable businessman whose factory premises had been purchased by a Khartoum-based leather goods manufacturer. It had come to Trinity's attention that the men behind the purchase were connected to an individual called Osama Bin Laden. This was 1994 and, apart from high-level intelligence summaries and the first World Trade Center bombing, most of the world had not heard of the man. Of course he was very well known to the intelligence world.

Summer had to accompany Trinity from safe house to safe house in Khartoum, securing his safety until such time as agents from MI6 and the CIA could sit down and debrief him in full. For eighteen months, Summer lived and worked with this man, who had, he said, agreed to name many individuals associated with the factory purchase. Word had got out that the man was collaborating with foreign governments, and keeping him alive and away from the clutches of both the

Sudanese intelligence goons and Bin Laden's guerilla heavies became a draining and terrifying experience.

Summer was waiting for his government to act.

But they would not.

Summer knew that Trinity would not wait forever, that this was their chance, definitively, to *know*.

No decision was made.

Abruptly, in 1995, the asset lost patience and disappeared. Summer was furious. He complained to his supervisor in Vauxhall Cross who posted him to a counternarcotics and gun-running operation in Colombia. In 1996, Sudan was pressured by the UK and US into kicking Osama Bin Laden out of the country. He fled to Afghanistan, and the world would be changed forever.

Summer did not know that the cataclysm was coming to the world in 2001. For him and many others, it came earlier, in 1998. The embassy bombings in Nairobi and Dar es Salaam, in Tanzania, sent shockwaves around the world and confirmed that Osama Bin Laden had not been idle in exile. The explosion in Nairobi was also a personal cataclysm for Summer – the mother of his child was killed in the blast.

His handlers at MI6 wrongly decided that the best thing would be to allot Summer a chunk of vacation time. Unfortunately, a month on a beach in Goa only served to isolate the man and compound his growing concerns that his intentions had been manipulated. That the Service had tainted him and his family. If his work had been recognized, if he had been allowed to complete his job in Sudan, *maybe* Osama Bin Laden could have been contained. *Maybe* the embassy bombings might not have happened.

The maybes nearly killed him.

In that month, Summer began to realize he really did have

principles after all. He began to feel betrayed by his employer. A well-written but badly typed memo had found its way to the deputy director's desk but the office had discounted it as some form of prank. Gradually, when the memos kept arriving, it was clear that Summer now had a beef with the Service and what it had done to him and to the world.

For Summer, the worst was yet to come.

A year later he had been posted on a covert mission to aid the Colombian rebels in their guerilla war against the drug lords, providing training and arms-smuggling skills. He had long since re-established contact with his daughter, now in college. One night, while visiting her as she travelled in Ecuador one summer, he came clean and told her the truth about himself, his job. She took it all on her young shoulders and simply asserted to him what he already knew to be true – he had to do what he could live with, and no more. A week later a source in the Bogotá office reported that a man by the name of Michael Church – a known Summer alias – had been talking to a journalist about his misgivings over Sudan. Sources had been mentioned.

A midnight summit was called on the sixth floor of MI6 headquarters. The decision was made that such behaviour was getting too dangerous even for such a valuable asset. He had, it was explained, been warned about this sort of thing already.

One morning, on his daughter's twentieth birthday, he was tipped off by a friend in the police that a warrant was out for his arrest. He had been falsely accused of training and gun-running for the wrong people. The winds of accountability had shifted and everyone was looking for a fall guy. Namely, him.

Alone and unwilling to drag his daughter into the mire, he fled to Panama. And disappeared.

Nothing was heard of him for two years. The man had become a ghost. Then one day he chose to step back into corporeal form. There were specific reasons why he chose to re-emerge. Namely, his daughter Carmen. A boyfriend had decided to get physical with her (in fact, a tactic of the Panamanian intelligence services to flush him out). The ruse worked. He called round uninvited to the boyfriend's house after a hospital admitted her with concussion. He had pushed her down the stairs. What Summer found instead were forty police – armed, ready and waiting.

He was arrested and thrown into La Joya prison, an institution with all the characteristics of Alcatraz, without the petting zoo or the warmth of human kindness. Because of his contacts in the paramilitary world, he found himself loathed and lauded in equal measure. He was quickly transferred to 'maximum security' – for his benefit, as well as those outside. He discovered he had trained some of the guards in close-quarter combat, which they then turned gleefully back on him. Eventually, he earned respect as a survivor.

Not one of the guards or his fellow inmates knew of a secondary role he played. One that he had vowed to hold fast to despite his incarceration, a vow he had made in his invisible years, to his invisible friends in something known only as Zero.

Forty-Two

La Joya prison had been built in response to continued outcries over the appalling conditions at Panama's own version of Alcatraz, Coiba Island. La Joya stood on a vast circular depression of reclaimed swampland in the district of Chepo and San Miguelito some sixty kilometres outside Panama City, part of a larger prison complex with two other facilities – La Joyita and Tinajitas.

As it turned out, conditions at La Joya weren't so great either. In the summer the heat attracted thousands of mosquitos, which found ample breeding grounds in the stagnant pools of water that lay hidden in the heaps of old tyres and burnt-out cars that littered the surrounding countryside. The La Joya site itself looked more like a concentration camp than a prison.

There were two perimeter fences, each with ten feet of steel mesh topped with razor wire. Four observation towers punctuated the vast oblong, manned with snipers on six-hour shifts. There were almost no visiting times permitted, and all applications by relatives were vetted by the prison administrator himself.

Although the entire complex was deemed a maximum-security installation, a separate whitewashed wing had two additional gates and was regularly patrolled by a guard on horseback. The added security around this wing was not, as a casual observer might presume, to keep the inmates in. Those unfortunate enough to find themselves in the maximum-security wing of a maximum-security jail like La Joya were either politicians or ex-drug lords. Both of these groups of people had plenty of prices on their heads, and most of the people qualified to collect this money were also doing time in the main prison area, some two hundred yards away. Word travelled fast amongst inmates and guards, records were kept of who was sequestered where, and, with a thriving black market in knives, razor blades and cellphones, it wasn't too difficult to pinpoint a target or two. Despite the constant circulation of prisoners in the wing, it was not possible to keep identities secret for too long. Indeed two months before Carmen pressed the piece of paper into Lucy's hand, a local mayoral candidate imprisoned for the violent rape and murder of his opponent's daughter was found beheaded in his cell. The verdict was suicide. The fact that the only weapon found in his cell was a plastic spoon did not feature on the report.

Michael Church a.k.a. Summer, had been in the maximum-security wing for five years. He had no plans to escape, and he knew in his heart it was far safer for him to be here. Besides, he had a job to do.

The overcrowding problem in the rest of the prison did not apply here. There was no such thing as solitary confinement of course, but here at least hammocks could be strung across rafters under the thin metal roofs.

Had they still been working for Her Majesty's Secret Intelligence Service, the four fugitives would have had access to NEXUS, the MI6 intranet that allowed entry to the SIS network of embassy files around the world. From here they could have called up the latest satellite data on the compound, identified weak areas of security, even read reports from previous researchers and chargés d'affaires about the governor, his drinking habits, his favourite bars and sexual proclivities.

Alone and on the run, they had none of these tools.

All they had, in fact, was each other.

But they still had to get inside. And, somehow, speak to the man known as Contact Three. Failure was not an option.

After a full afternoon of research and brainstorming, the fact was, no one really knew how to do it. Panama was a transit point for aliens, primarily from other countries in South America seeking to reach the US. Some of them were trafficked into indentured servitude, their travel facilitated by a network of alien-smugglers, travel agents, hotels and safe houses. Some of these people would have relatives. Some of them might be guards. But bribing the guards was simply too vast a project, too great a risk.

In any case, if word got around that they were spending freely, by the time they got inside the prison walls they would have no money left. Or worse, they would be unable to buy their way out again.

As dawn approached they agreed they would not be making any moves in the next few days. What they needed was background. They decided to set up camp in a faceless hotel on the northwestern outskirts of the city. From the upper floors, the road to La Joya was partly visible, hidden from the prying eyes of the city by a fringe of palm trees on the edge of the swamp.

Checking in required a little more planning if they were here for a day or two. Drawing straws, Jamie and Lucy agreed to pose as a couple, Ben and Nat would check in separately as buddies travelling their way back up through Central America. They ensured their rooms were on the same floor, the fourteenth.

Ben and Nat did not exchange words as they cleaned up in the room's bright-pink bathroom suite. As Nat was taking a shower, Ben opened Nat's bag and did a speedy inventory. He had three identities with passports from the usual suspect countries – New Zealand, Canada, Australia – that were overt, plus the old-school PDA with its obligatory GPS system, a tube of hair dye (blond) and a long, serrated hunting knife.

At no stage during his brief search of the bag did Ben take his eye off the bathroom door. Working on a hunch, he himself had once tricked a girlfriend into thinking he was in the shower. He had watched from a crack in the door as she calmly helped herself to some cash from his wallet while the water ran. So impressed was Ben with this barefaced betrayal and subterfuge he had continued seeing her for a few weeks after that just for the entertainment value of what she would do next.

That night, as Nat curled up on the floor (he had lost the coin toss), Ben let his mind slip back to memories of her, of light freckles on her shoulder, her mezzo-soprano moan . . .

Ben woke up like a whip crack and studied the semi-darkness for a second. Blinking the sleep away, he immediately realized that Nat was not in the room. At least, he wasn't asleep – he already knew the sound of the man's pig-after-a-truffle snoring. Silence. Then: voices. Muffled, low-key. They were coming from the corridor. He heard footsteps and more hushed talking and, slipping out of bed, recognized one of the owners of the voices as Lucy.

What was there to talk about at three in the morning?

Ben tiptoed to the edge of the door and listened. Outside in the corridor, the personalities talking were Lucy and Nat, but not the voices' content. The instrument, not the melody. He peered out of the fisheye lens. A distorted carpet stared back at him. They were further down the corridor, presumably outside Lucy and Jamie's room. He could not hear Jamie's voice in the mix. He had to presume he was still asleep, and this was between the little man and the ice queen.

Shivering, he padded back to the bed where he located his socks and draped a blanket around his shoulders. Pushing the door open a crack, he peered outside and saw the emergency exit door to the stairs gently clicking shut.

Nat had woken Lucy ten minutes earlier and dragged her quietly away from the sleeping figure of Jamie. She had taken a few seconds to wake up and quickly surmised that this conversation should not take place in the reverberating space of a hotel corridor. The emergency stairs were not alarmed and the door was thick enough to hide their voices.

The air was thick and close in the stairwell, the stone steps cold. Lucy's impatience began to grow as Nat returned to his circular argument.

'I don't like it, Lucy.'

'You two have made up your minds and you're set in those views. Fine. Live with it.'

'I just don't trust him.'

'I don't much trust any of you right now. Sorry to say. Nothing personal, it just seems . . . practical.'

Nat was picking absent-mindedly at a scab on his finger. It made Lucy feel sick. 'I don't care if you trust me or not. What I don't like is the idea that I might have to trust my life to *him.*'

'Truth be known, Nat, my back is probably safer with him than with you.'

'That's only because he cares about you.'

'Stop it.'

'I'm sure that's why.'

246

'Can I go back to bed now?'

Nat studied Lucy's face. She had pillow creases down one side of her face. *We both sleep on the same side*, he thought, and briefly mourned what might have been, even though he knew in his heart his chances had always been the same as a snowflake's in Hades.

'He's a good man,' said Lucy. 'Deep down, he really is, I promise. And you can whistle ironic love ballads all you want, but that's the truth.' And she left him there, in the muggy stairwell, and padded back along the carpet to her room, hoping she was right.

The garage level began on Sub-basement 1. Stall 1515 was in the far corner beside an emergency exit door that glowed green in the shadows.

Stall 1515 was occupied at this early hour by a Lincoln town car with blacked-out windows. The man sitting on the driver's side knew there were dangers at this time of night in being so brazen in arranging a rendezvous. But important matters do not go away unless they are resolved and as far as he was concerned, not to mention his master, he wanted this resolved *right*. That said, time was up and this was now edging into the realms of the foolhardy. He checked his watch and reached for the ignition.

A cigarette flared in the far corner. The driver stayed his hand. Janus had shown up. His heart jazzed. It meant there was progress. The man walked over to the passenger side and got in. As was agreed, the handler kept his eyes on the steering wheel at all times.

'You're late.'

'It was hard to get away.'

'Fill me in.'

'I'm still working all this out.'

'There is nothing to work out. You are the linchpin of a very important operation.'

'Yeah, well, thanks for springing that on me.'

'We had to let you believe that you were in the same position as the others.'

'Why?'

'To maintain plausibility. Look, what has happened is a tragedy. It's a major leak. But needs must, and we are taking advantage of the situation. That is all. Operations are greenlit for stranger reasons, believe me. In any case, if we'd told you what we were planning from the start, you would not have been so convincing.'

'So you just let me think I was in trouble.'

'You were in trouble. You are in trouble.'

'I could have died.'

'Indeed. But you didn't. With some judicious help – our help – you stayed alive. Which meant you were still qualified to continue with this operation. Which is why our contact approached you in the monastery.'

Ben inhaled deeply for a long and shuddering breath. 'Can I make an observation? One. *You're welcome*. And two. For future reference, your man on the inside of the monastery is a liability.'

'How so?'

'His approach was not exactly subtle.'

In fact, the appeal for Ben to follow, to collect his shoes, was so surreal that Ben had been deeply unsettled by it. Ben supposed that it sounded so bizarre that it must have been entirely innocent. It wasn't, of course. He led Ben down a set of stairs to another isolated corridor in the maze of rooms and hallways that comprised the rest of the monastery. He'd locked a door behind them and just before Ben wondered if this was some esoteric seduction technique, the man had come clean. He was an SIS agent, placed in the Samaritans.

And he had been waiting for him.

Ben had not been that impressed and told the man in the car exactly what he thought.

'We needed someone in there. And he's all we have.'

'And I'm all you have.'

The man cleared his throat. What he really meant was *what the fuck do you mean by that?*

'Are you in any way conflicted about this mission?'

'No. But I told you. This is all a bit raw. What you're asking me to do . . .'

But no compassion here. The man looked straight ahead as he interrupted: 'What is the latest?'

Silence. Then: 'We've made first contact.'

'The ultimate contact?'

'Hardly. He's a link in the chain. A treasure hunt.'

'Name?'

'Still working on it.'

A considered breath. 'You're protecting him.'

'What if I am? He's just one step closer to what you want. That's all. And if I find out someone's wiping up after me, if more people wind up dead . . .'

'You have my word.'

'I am so very reassured.'

The man placed a small device on the dashboard. It weighed about three ounces and looked like the memory card for a mobile phone. 'You will no doubt be searched again. This is a transmitter. Make sure it avoids detection.'

'You've done this before, haven't you?'

The man continued: 'Once you have found the location of

this sanctuary, this is the signal carrier. Send a burst transmission to the nearest embassy, then follow up with a call as instructed. But only at Zero, do you understand?'

'Then what?'

'You will be taken care of.'

'How?'

'You will be secure and alive.'

'That's a little less than I was hoping for.'

'Listen to me—'

'No. No. *You* listen to *me*. I am only just getting used to this idea.'

'An honest answer.'

'What if this thing's not a place? What if it's a person?'

'Then improvise as best you can. Our time is up.'

Benjamin Sinclair nodded and slipped out of the vehicle. For all of his concerns about his mission . . . he was doing it for other reasons. Any recruitment requires leverage of some sort. All spies have motives. Mostly, they are financial. Others find solace for their betrayal in ideology.

For Ben, it was a strange combination of loyalty and revenge. He wanted to do right by the person who had supported him. And he wanted to do wrong by everyone else, to get those bastards back for what they'd done.

Forty-Three

The next morning, Nat called a meeting around his bed like a romantic novelist conducting a signing *au lit*. He announced he had a plan that could get them a face-to-face with Michael Church. The methodology was simple, to the point and had a precedent.

Bribery.

'Not to get us in, you understand, but to get him out.' He eyed them all individually, convinced of an enthusiastic response. But only Jamie seemed to nod in accord.

'Could work,' said Jamie, 'could work . . . You're not talking about buying freedom or anything. Right?'

'No. A day pass. Twenty-four hours. He could even see his daughter. She's not seen him for years, she said.'

Lucy shared a look with Ben and bit into an apple, talking in between chews. 'You mentioned precedent.'

'Happens all the time back in Cuba. I met a bloke who brokered conjugal visits for prisoners. He had a standing agreement with the guards. They just turn the other way as the customer leaves – along with a couple of heavies while he's out there, obviously – and then they get him back before the numbers are counted in the evening. No one knows he's gone, no one knows he's back. We could do the same with Michael Church. He gets a little holiday, we get our information. Everybody wins.'

Jamie sat forward on the edge of the bed. 'Right. And how exactly do we contact these guards to bribe them?'

'Well, they're all PNP, I think. National police force.'

'So?'

'We just – ask around.'

Ben cleared his throat. He knew his silence had been noted by the others and he had to make them think it was simply because he'd been pondering their next move. He was, of course. But he was also still trying to work out if anyone had seen him come back up from the car park the night before.

'Suppose,' he said, 'we actually manage to locate a few guards prepared to do this. How exactly do we guarantee they bring us the right man? Are we going to rope Carmen into this? Force her to cooperate? Expose ourselves to more risk?'

Nat stared at the table, trying to control his flushing temper. 'We use a photo, Ben, to check.'

'I'm talking about when they turn up,' said Ben, voice rising, 'and parade someone completely different in front of us, demand double the sum we agreed on and leave us with absolutely zero option because they've already seen our faces.'

'He's got a point, my friend,' said Jamie.

The four of them returned to their breakfast and tried to dissolve the awkward silence that had fallen over them. Ben felt Lucy's gaze on him but tried hard to ignore it.

'How about this,' she ventured, 'for an alternative?'

Lucy explained her thoughts over the room service breakfast and despite Nat's disappointment at having his plans shot down by Ben, he too was soon in accord. It was all the more exciting because Lucy not only had a plan, but it was one that might, in all probability, actually work.

The fact was that, despite the dangers of the prison system, there had been survivors, those who had paid their dues to society (and, more importantly, to the politicians who had put them there in the first place) and emerged blinking into the rest of their lives. Lucy therefore had concluded that there were no doubt many people alive in Panama City who knew the inside of the prison, its architecture, its staffing procedures and, with any luck, its vulnerabilities.

For her plan to work, they would need a consultant.

Ben listened carefully to her ideas and realized they already had a useful way of finding one.

Carmen broke for lunch at two thirty, still exhausted from her earlier subterfuge and worried sick, as always, about her father. Ben slid into step with her as she walked to her favourite café. She was pleased to see him – but not surprised.

'Do you have a minute?' Ben asked.

'It depends,' she smiled, 'on how it's spent. Time, as you can imagine, has become the most precious thing to me in the world.'

'We need to find a couple of people. First, an ex-inmate. There must be people in this city who've done time in La Joya, even those who have met your father . . .'

'It's possible. A lot of crime in this city. A lot of inmates.'

She was playing, and Ben let her. They walked on for a minute in silence. Finally, Ben tried again.

'No one springs to mind?'

Someone clearly did but she wasn't saying anything. They passed Nat and Lucy walking in the opposite direction; Jamie, he knew, was keeping watch from the other side of the street. Ben hoped she didn't feel threatened. He also hoped, however, that she knew they meant business.

'What about the second person?'

'We also need someone who knows how the prison gets its food.'

A thought seemed to *click* into place.

'Meet me at the club, eleven o'clock,' she said. 'I'll see what I can do.'

The rest of the day was spent in libraries, internet cafés and phone booths, compiling intelligence on whatever scraps of open-source information they could gather. Posing as a graduate research fellow from the RAND Corporation, Lucy established the number of security guards; Jamie, using his previous cover as a well-meaning schoolteacher, asked about the political situation at the prison; Ben, compiling an entirely fake directory of local businesses, divined a more or less comprehensive list of the names and functions of all the private firms which did business at the prison site – cooks, cleaners, medical staff, drivers. Nat helped himself to two small fire extinguishers from the corridors of Carmen's office building.

At ten that evening, adrenalized with their progress, they returned to the club. They were more careful this time – any petty criminal will tell you it is never advisable to return to a covert meeting place at the same time of day. Their training had underscored this several times; it was the espionage equivalent of returning to the scene of the crime. They all travelled separately and ensured their taxis dropped them off at an entirely different venue.

As before, they dry-cleaned the area. They began to close the circle. The kitty had financed four non-contract cellphones with a two-way walkie-talkie function. Set on vibrate, and operated with cheap earpieces, they weren't exactly the British Secret Service's finest communications equipment but, for cheap improvisation in hostile territory, they weren't half bad.

'Clear northside,' said Ben into his microphone.

'Ditto, westside,' said Nat, overemphasizing the latter word as if he was an MC on a rap record.

Ben closed his eyes and tried not to let the irritation bleed through into his work.

The circle moved closer still.

Forty minutes later, they all converged on the site. It was under a minute to the rendezvous time.

The club was shut.

Before anyone could speak, the sound of an engine reverberated around the walls of the alley from the southern end, where it broadened into a T-junction. A pair of blinding headlights fired down from a vehicle as it turned into the alley proper. The car was an SUV, it seemed, or a truck – it was broad enough to hit the edges of the brick and metal structures on either side.

It began to accelerate towards them.

Ben tried the door to the club but it was locked. There was no real crawl space between the step and the doorframe. Anyway, there were four of them, and for now he needed all of them to be involved and alive.

Jamie was already running away from the vehicle. Lucy joined him. Nat, momentarily paralysed, tried to half-heartedly climb up the drains on the building opposite the club. He fell down and joined Ben at a sprint. The vehicle was roaring down after them now. But it held back from Nat's heels as he ran.

As they rounded the end of the alley, the horn blared.

Ben squinted back and saw Carmen at the wheel. She beckoned. Ben hesitated for a moment, then whistled at the fast-departing Jamie before he disappeared around the next corner.

Ben looked Carmen in the eye and he could tell she was scared. He opened the door for Nat and Lucy as they got in. He joined Carmen in the front as Jamie rounded the corner.

Momentarily confused, he was about to turn and run again when he saw Ben in the passenger seat and understood.

The car was moving as Jamie leapt in the back and closed the door. Carmen threaded the SUV through the narrow alleyways and emerged on to a highway. She did not use the brake.

'Care to explain what's going on?'

'Insurance. For my protection, as well as yours. The man we are going to see is not a man to be approached lightly.'

The car speeded up and headed into an area to the south of Panama City known colloquially as 'Carne'. It was labelled as such by the local police, who were, it was rumoured, dead meat as soon as they entered.

The structure was vast, situated on a square of dusty scrub amongst iron fencing and scorched earth. Carmen had driven the final mile without talking. Ben admired this young woman, who had lost her father so many years ago but clearly not his street smarts.

Carmen parked next to a sign that had been shot out by automatic gunfire. On one side a dusty track snaked into a makeshift parking lot. On the other, visible from the approach road, a grid of railings that seemed to feed through two large double doors. In the distance, mazes of ramshackle homes, a township of sorts, where burnt-out cars fought for space with shacks and feral dogs in packs.

Carmen turned to them as they walked in convoy towards another heavy metal door on their side of the building. The man they were visiting, she explained, had owned this place for years. Even during his sentence, it continued supplying the prison.

'At first, please, let me do the talking.'

She caught Ben smiling in admiration at her.

'Two for the price of one?' he said. She nodded grimly.

The smell was overpowering. The floor sloped away gently to a large grid of hooks, hoses, bloodstained concrete and slabs of raw meat. It might have been a trick of the light, but Ben noticed several carcasses by the far wall that were still moving. The abattoir was clearly still doing good business. From somewhere, Ben heard a door creak open. The sound of a shotgun being primed echoed around the walls.

'Show yourself,' went a voice. It sounded brittle, the whisper of a broken man. It seemed a miracle it carried on the air at all and didn't dissolve into vapour.

Carmen tugged Lucy's sleeve to make her turn as a man walked out of a glass door in the far wall and stood there, staring at them from the shadows. The man might have been thirty-two, possibly thirty-three, but certainly no less than thirty-one stone. His vast girth was contained in bright green trousers that were held together by what appeared to be a length of shipping twine. His shirt cleaved hard to his torso, dotted with large patches of sweat. The overwhelming impression was one of a walking human egg. He peered out in their direction and blew a cowlick of white hair from his eyes.

'Hugo,' said Carmen.

'*Reina*,' smiled the man. His teeth were rotten. He stared at Ben and the others, and gestured at them with both barrels.

'*Los amigos de mi papá*,' she told him. He absorbed this slowly and then beckoned them through the glass door. Beyond was a large office area, a mess of papers and receipts, where Hugo helped himself to another glass of rum from a half-empty bottle in the corner. Ben watched the man's lungs judder with effort as they strained to fill his body with oxygen. He mused that without the gun he was no threat whatsoever, because of his complete inability to run after you if he turned nasty.

257

But drunkards with shotguns are slightly less relaxing.

Carmen explained that his four visitors were keen to know everything they could about the maximum-security wing of La Joya. Hugo asked why and, after seeking permission to speak from Carmen, Lucy told him part of the reason.

The man shook his head, clearly unconvinced.

Lucy mentioned they'd be happy to pay for his time.

Hugo began to smile.

A short discussion later, he pulled a roll of butcher's paper across his desk. He plucked a small pencil from a drawer, drew the blunt tip across his tongue and began to draw. The paper was waxy and the pencil too light to be visible from a distance. But the detail was clear up close, which was all that mattered. Ben watched his huge fingers move rapidly, his red tongue flicking as he spoke.

'I know this place as well as anywhere in the world,' he explained between giant breaths.

In his ten years inside for manslaughter, Hugo had forged a strong friendship with the catering staff – his work in the kitchens (as well as his financial support of the catering workers' families outside) ensured that he received a steady supply of Belgian chocolates smuggled in from European ports, as well as double portions that were, in contrast to the rest of the prison's food, vaguely edible. Naturally, he also received the choicest cuts from his own warehouse whenever the delivery was organized.

As it turned out, this was perfect preparation for what Lucy had in mind.

Forty-Four

At 5.30 a.m. every Monday the catering staff at La Joya Penitenciaría received their weekly order of meat from a number of respected processing centres and abattoirs around the city.

Following a telephone call from a friend in the despatch office at Juarez Meat Products, a young kitchen worker called Esteban made sure he was on shift to collect the sides of beef that were to be processed that day into the weekly stew.

As his friend had explained, there were three more sides of beef being delivered than usual, and these were to be stored in a particular place within the kitchen area. Esteban didn't really understand why anyone would want to do this, as there was little ventilation under the floor, and the meat was usually refrigerated on arrival. Still, he was under obligation to the friend for many favours before, including this job, not to mention the tacit continuation of the health and vitality of his family, and he asked no questions.

Of course, these slabs of meat were not intended for human consumption. Quite the opposite. They had been prepared specially for a small species of diner known as *Calliphora vomitoria* – the common bluebottle.

To appetize the beef for these new tastebuds, shreds of already putrefying meat had been inserted into the centre of the slabs, like pimiento into an olive. Lucy, a biologist via her bachelor's degree, took pains to ensure that the small additions were already adequately populated by maggots. When the slabs arrived at the prison, from the outside they both appeared and smelled completely normal. Inside, they were a silent, writhing mass of glistening white larvae.

It would only be a couple of days before they transformed.

The next forty-eight hours were spent amassing what Lucy referred to as 'a small dressing-up box'; Ben preferred to think of it as role-play research. Working independently, the four purchased matching plastic coverings, gloves, spray cans and goggles. At the end of the first twenty-four-hour period they had the majority of their tools. By the morning of the second period, Jamie and Lucy had obtained a vehicle by posing as a well-meaning expat couple and paying over the odds.

By Lucy's calculations, the next morning would be their window of opportunity.

Esteban knew nothing of the plans of Lucy, Ben *et al.*, but knew quite a lot about following instructions. At the end of his shift, he was responsible for touring the maximum-security cells, connected to the kitchen by a dark and airless corridor. As he served the inmates through their hatches, he recalled his instructions and made sure to drag the handful of raw meat in his hand across the rough concrete breeze blocks that formed the walls of the structure. A thin and invisible line of grease and beef fragments embedded themselves into the grooves of the wall.

His final act that night was to return to the flooring to check on the sides of beef he had buried two days before. To his surprise, he could feel a low vibration under his feet as he stood there, a noise perhaps.

Almost like a buzzing sound.

*   *   *

It took a few more days for the pupation of the maggots to evolve to a winged stage. Burrowing their way around the inner cavities of the meat, the larvae born as females ventured no further than the space around the humming carcasses, returning almost immediately to begin to lay their own eggs in the moist flesh that had delivered them into the world. As the kitchen workers trudged above them, the new colony of flies began to thrive, born into the very epicentre of bluebottle paradise. When their number became too great, the more intrepid members of the clan found their way into the cracked and rusting vent system, through mouseholes in the floorboards, the void walls of the structure itself. The trails of grease and rotting flesh on the walls drew the rest up and out and into the low corridors and humid cells of the entire block. Soon the prison was a prehistoric soup of flies, vibrating as one. The first Michael Church knew about the infestation were the whistles of the inmates in his corridor. The men in his bunk room were snorers, they had no problems with sleep. For Church, every night was a challenge, every noise a jolt from peace.

This night, it was the whistles. He listened again as his hammock creaked like a metronome in the hot fetid space. Another whistle, but this time, in the background, a new noise. The low drone of insects.

It was then he began to be aware of the air in the cell. There were small vents at the top of the walls, badly designed and mostly blocked with soot and dust and old cigarette ash. But through the cracks small black dots were appearing. They too were buzzing.

By first light the entire maximum-security wing was a cacophony of noise. Prisoners shouted and screamed, banging their fists against the brown rusted doors all along the building. They scrabbled for the barred windows, the panels in the doorframes. Outside, the guards were even more vocal, cursing and shouting at the tops of their voices as the swarms spiralled around them. Underneath it all, the low pulsating drone of teeming bluebottles.

The chief administrator of the prison was in bed with his wife when the call came through from his deputy. The guards were demanding transfers or at least the chance of evacuating the building for decontamination. The deputy knew full well that the place was already overcrowded; there was literally nowhere to go apart from outside, and no semi-sane administrator had the *cojones* to allow the personalities in that block out in the fresh air during a time of chaos. In any case, a riot only spreads from block to block. The maximum-security unit was too far away for any other inmates to hear their catcalls or comprehend their complaints.

The decision was made. Both guards and prisoners would remain in place until the exterminators arrived. The deputy assured him a team would be contacted as soon as possible. As he replaced the receiver, he tasked his immediate junior to find a suitable company that was vetted for prison security.

It didn't occur to anyone that the white van pulling up thirty minutes later outside the prison gates might not be the company they had contacted to alleviate their suffering. After all, the two men getting out of it looked the part completely.

Ben and Nat both wore plastic headgear and goggles that further disguised them as just another duo of sanitation workers. Underneath the plastic, their cheap cellphones were permanently conference-calling Lucy and Jamie, who sat at the wheel and in the back seat of the van respectively, the waxy pencil-drawn map of the maximum-security wing spread between them.

When Lucy had mooted her plan, Nat had not been enthusiastic. The plan itself was fine. His role in it was not. Reluctantly, he referred the others back to the incident with the firing squad. As he'd told Lucy before, it wasn't the guns that had worried him, it was the hoods.

Nat was borderline claustrophobic. 'I'm just worried what I'd do if I was under pressure in there. I think someone else should step in.'

Ben was impressed by his candid admission. But he knew, with the rest of them, that Nat's Spanish was not only flawless but an important tool. As well as being an electronics expert, Nat had an extraordinary facility with languages. Ben could hear the music in words, it was true, but Nat could sing them. He commanded a bewildering array of dialects. Despite his concerns about the enclosed spaces of La Joya, there was no way Nat wasn't going in with Ben, and Ben told him so.

All Nat could think was that Ben was trying to flatter him. There was an ulterior motive, Nat thought to himself. It set him all the more on edge.

Nat and Ben had negotiated the first two gates with some ease. Nat's tonalities were beautifully officious and the threat of the governor's wrath should they not be permitted immediately to enter the maximum-security compound was so palpable that the guards practically thanked them for their time. Word had already spread about the infestation, it seemed, and Ben felt a blast of confidence inside. This might just work.

There was a hundred-yard concrete pathway through the dried grass and weeds to a third set of fencing and razor wire. Ben and Nat approached carefully and the guards were only too happy to let them in – as they stepped through the gates, they could see why. One of the two-storey whitewashed structures was surrounded by guards, smoking, chatting, glancing back in evident discomfort at the darkened windows of the prison block. As they walked closer, Ben could see that the windows were only dark because of the fury of airborne activity inside. The place was a ferocious standing swarm of flies, and the guards, with typical brutality, had decided to lock the prisoners inside.

Nat asked a guard some pertinent but distracting questions as Ben whispered into the hands-free microphone that was taped to the inside of the hood. 'We're at the east door.' A pause and then Jamie's voice returned: 'Straight in, corridor, ten yards then a right. Follow that to another door and he should be on your left.' Ben signed off with a *check that* and walked over to Nat as he received a small bunch of keys from a guard.

'He'd rather we went in alone,' said Nat in his officious Spanish.

'I don't blame him,' said Ben, trying to sound like the man who never has to make decisions and leaves it to his more intelligent partner. 'It doesn't make any difference to me.'

The guard seemed not to care either. Nat unlocked the door and the two men walked carefully inside and were immediately engulfed in a buzzing mass of black flies, a solid wall of revolting stench that vibrated like a heat haze.

It was at about this moment that a flaw in the plan occurred to both men. They might have brought about the means to get into this prison block, perhaps even to speak to the man known as Contact Three. But they were entirely unqualified to deal with the actual job of extermination. The packs they wore slung over their shoulders were nothing but souped-up fire extinguishers. They only had a limited amount of time before someone began to twig that the flies were not going away.

First things first, however.

Ben led the way, ensuring the door behind them was locked securely.

The floors were wet. Underneath the pulsating drone of the flies was another noise – human screams, shouts for mercy, for salvation, blue murder. Nat let off a few bursts from his firehose to let everyone in the building know they were being seen to. 'Stay in your cells!' he shouted. 'Extermination team!'

'The air!' shouted some inmates. 'You'll poison us!'

'Special chemicals,' improvised Ben, 'harmless to humans.'

They reached the end of the corridor where, as promised by Hugo's drawings, a T-junction allowed them a sharp turn to the right. Nat and Ben moved quickly now, swatting away the insects, practically swimming their way through. They reached the far end of the corridor to find there a blank wall.

Nat fumbled around in the semi-darkness for a handle, a panel, anything. But there was nothing. Ben turned away from the wall to talk into the mike. 'Problem. T-junction, right turn. No door.'

Ben couldn't hear the rustling of the butcher's paper as Jamie frantically scoured the plans for signs of a mistake. But he knew the pause on the line wasn't hold music. 'Give me a minute,' said Jamie eventually.

'Not really spoilt for time, mate.'

'That's what the plans say. There should be a door—'

'Well, there isn't one. Is there any other way back to the main cell block?'

'Through the kitchens. Double back, take the left hand of the T-junction. The corridor then bends back around to the right and round again. There must be two entrances, and one's been blocked off.'

'Take your word for it,' said Nat.

Ben rapped Nat on the shoulder who gave the thumbs-up.

The interior hallways of the structure, as well as wet, were uneven. Running back to the T-junction, Ben lost control for a moment and clattered to the ground.

Nat regarded him coolly. For a moment, Ben thought he might walk on, but instead he sprinted back and heaved Ben to his feet.

They followed Jamie's directions and accelerated past administrative offices, a guard's ready room – no pleasure palace – and finally passed what appeared to be a library. Ahead were the kitchens, where the noise, smell and chaos were at their height. The floors were swimming with filth, a charnel house of putrefaction and decay. The floorboards that Esteban had calmly lifted several days before were now a writhing mass of black wings. Nat now followed Ben to the far door. Ben's ribs ached and he reasoned they'd been bruised in the fall.

On the other side of the kitchen area was another, heavier door.

Nat heaved it open and the two men ran inside, slamming the door shut behind them.

Abruptly, the buzzing receded and they found themselves in a sea of calm. The infestation was not as bad in here.

Four sets of doors were set on either side. At the far end on the right, the final door, Ben peered through the peephole in the metal doorframe. Two men were seated next to a large candle that was burning in the hollow of a broken toilet bowl. One of them was a wiry man with a thin moustache. The other had blond hair, blue eyes and a long beard. He was a packet of muscle and sinew, more of an extreme athlete than a prisoner.

The man saw the eyes staring in and calmly turned away. Nat fumbled with the keys. Ben looked at his watch, and a shudder of anxiety travelled up his spine as he realized that the bona fide extermination team might well be arriving soon. 'Any signs of trouble?' he asked into the mike.

All he got was static. The fall had probably damaged the cellphone in his pocket. *Damn it to hell . . .*

Nat brandished another key and the lock clicked open. As they opened the door, the man with the thin moustache rushed at them, knocking Ben to the ground. If the man got out of the building, Ben knew, the guards would soon follow and their distinct lack of progress would be questioned.

Nat whipped around and sprinted after the man. Nat might not have been quick off the mark but he had a low centre of gravity which kept him steady on his feet. The man with the moustache was too busy with the flies to pay enough attention to the terrain and went over on his ankle as he hit the kitchen. Nat tackled him by the knees and dragged him over to the pots and pans, delivering a knockout blow with a large casserole dish. The cut in the man's head began to attract more bluebottles and, in a misplaced act of sympathy, Nat dragged his unconscious body back towards a large industrial cooker.

Back in the cell with the blond man, Ben stood and kept an eye on the small barred window which looked out on to a courtyard in the middle of the structure. There were still flies in here, roaming lazily, unaware perhaps of the orgy going on just down the corridor.

'Carmen sends her love,' said Ben.

The man nodded and smiled. 'Please return the sentiment.' His eyes filled with tears and for a moment Ben thought he might crumble.

Ben cleared his throat. 'We don't really have much time . . .'

Michael Church shrugged and told Ben what he needed to know.

When he had finished, Church regarded him in the half-light. A distant metallic *clunk* was heard from the corridor.

Ben was distracted but intent on his question. 'Has anyone else found you? Before us?'

The man nodded. 'Two years ago, a man came. He was posing as a chiropractor. Giving adjustments to the prisoners. It was quite an ingenious attempt.'

'What happened to him?'

Church shook his head as he stood up. He felt Ben's eyes on him, this sad lonely man.

'I can't remember.'

'I learned all about you. What you did. In training.'

'And what do you think now that you've met the great man in person?'

Ben summoned his best, most generous smile. But Church saw through it.

'A piece of advice. You might beat the system for a while. A decade, even. But then, one day, they'll find a way through. And break you into little pieces.'

'I thought you were doing okay here.'

'I am. But, believe me, this isn't the way I'd planned for things to turn out. When I started, I had a lot of reasons for what I did. Now? All I want – ' his eyes were glistening with tears – 'is for Carmen to live her life. It's why I'm here.'

'Can't you get out?'

'I'd be killed as soon as I stepped into freedom,' he said. 'Here, at least, I'm safe . . . and so is she. My own life is immaterial of course. I stay here only for her.' Ben nodded, and Church suddenly took him by the shoulders and drilled a stare into Ben that made him catch his breath. 'Only trust those who have as much to lose as you.'

Ben managed to extend a hand. Michael Church took it and

gave a cold and clammy shake. Despite the man's physically imposing exterior, inside, the man was already gone.

'I suppose you'd better start your work,' he said.

Ben realized Nat had not come back and ran to the door that led to the kitchen. It was locked. From the other side, he could hear the ceaseless buzzing of the flies. Ben hammered on the metal frame.

He spoke into the microphone and called for Jamie.

Nothing but static.

He kicked, hammered, shouted through the joins. His ribs jarred with each impact, each lungful of anger. He hissed through the hinges.

'Let me out!'

And from the other side, he heard him.

'Don't know if I can do that, mate.'

Ben rocked back on his heels. He'd wondered if Nat's paranoia would get the better of him in here. He'd let him get the upper hand. Ben chastised himself for losing his focus there. Still, they needed the information from Church. At least he had one bargaining chip.

'What's the problem?'

To Ben's complete shock, the door opened. Nat stood there with a uniformed guard, holding a handkerchief to his face. Ben had misjudged the moment completely. It wasn't a plot against Ben. It was a ploy against this new threat in front of them.

'Clear?' asked Nat. The corridor behind Ben had few insects inside. Ben understood immediately and jumped into character.

'Get out! You'll contaminate the place again! This area is clear!'

He pushed the guard back into the kitchen. The escaped

prisoner was nowhere to be seen. Out of the corner of his eye, he spotted a foot protruding from behind a large industrial cooker. He hoped Nat had only stunned him. Ben slammed the door behind him.

'There are too many for our chemicals. We need to go for reinforcements,' explained Ben.

'I was just telling the captain exactly that,' shouted Nat and gestured to the guard.

Lead on, it said. *And hurry up about it.*

The same guard escorted the men to the gate. Lucy, who had heard the rest of their conversation via Nat's cellphone, had already driven there in the van to pick them up. Jamie still crouched in the back, the butcher's paper spread out on the flat back seat. Nat turned to the guard and shook his hand as he stepped into the van.

'Please ensure no one enters until we return. We would hate to waste all of our work so soon.'

The guard nodded, green in the face from his ordeal inside the putrid corridors.

Lucy gunned the accelerator and they were waved through the exterior security gates. Five minutes down the approach road, they turned on to the asphalt and saw an exterminator van turning left and heading down to the prison.

'Well?' asked Lucy as Ben and Nat disrobed and changed into their tourist garb once more.

Nat stared at the road ahead, eyes bulging from their sockets. His breaths were rapid and shallow, his skin a mix of alabaster and green. Ben was shaking.

'Give him a minute,' he said, and vomited.

They moved hotels that night, rotating their covers and checking in under different names. Lucy asked Ben to pose as her

270

husband. He agreed, much to Nat's disappointment. But somewhere inside Nat's bitterness, a gleam of forgiveness was breaking through. The operation in the prison had certainly been successful. Ben had spent the following hour explaining every last detail of Church's instructions.

They all agreed to move the next day. A stiff drink in the bar followed a ritual burning of the evidence in the hotel furnace.

Lucy offered to sleep on the couch. Ben declined, but his smile had been full of gratitude. She hadn't meant it in a seductive way and he hadn't taken it as such. He knew, like she did, that she was telling him it was all right. And, complicit together, she would be looking out for him like he was looking out for her.

Ben could not sleep on account of his heart, which hammered into the mattress with such ferocity that he could hear the springs echo in retort. He could remember the smell of her hair, her cool flesh sliding into bed beside him that first night in Pimlico. The visions were sharp and clear, hitting him in waves. The mist of memory was tainted once more by anger, the red face of betrayal. Lying here in the dark only brought it home more strongly than before. The day he'd been reprimanded by the personnel board. The day he'd been framed for a harmless Christmas prank. The day he'd come home to find Lucy had moved out, without a note, without a call, without a scrap of common decency about her.

These were small slights, of course.

Paper cuts to the heart, nothing more.

But then there was the Gauntlet, the final assessment.

The two days that changed it all.

Forty-Five

Coco Solo Container Port
Panama

The Schwartz family were repatriating to Israel. An intergenerational *aliyah* brought about by the death of the family patriarch, Sol, meant they were shipping their copious belongings from Hancock Park to Haifa in a 'panmax' container vessel owned by General Cargo Consolidated LLC, one of five subsidiaries of the Nim Israel container corporation.

The *Europa* had a capacity for 750 standard-size containers both above and below deck. Since new arrangements with Panamanian authorities now calculated fees based on 'above and below' loads, the company had recently agreed to take additional cargo space for paying passengers. Some were even permitted their own domestic arrangements. The Schwartz family, for example, had absolutely no idea that one of their bedroom sets was used, like many others over the years, as a temporary studio apartment for the exclusive use of ocean-going fugitives.

There was no specific paper trail for the verbal agreement that existed between the management of General Cargo Consolidated LLC and those seeking Contact Zero. If a wary eye was cast over the directors, however, and a great deal of database research and forensic accounting was conducted, it would have been revealed that the chief operating officer of the corporation had a cousin called ███████████████████, a man who had been arrested without charge for two months before it was realized that a mistake had been made. During that time in prison, ██ ████████████████████████ and had extended an open invitation to all members of the global intelligence community to use his cargo routes as covert entry points into the country. Except ██████████████████, of course.

Thus it was that the good ship *Europa* coasted to a two-mile stop alongside Gatun Locks on the eastern side of the Panama isthmus. It was three in the morning and there were several dock workers making their final rounds before charging the section with water . . . The four ex-lilywhites skirted past the far side of the lock and made for the cargo bays to the bow side of the *Europa*. Ben had piloted narrow boats on the Warwickshire waterways but this was something on a slightly bigger scale. The fall from the dockside into the dark sliver of water below could easily be fatal.

As they moved slowly through the shadows, their forms were picked out by an infrared scope. If her files had been correct, Collins was looking at Ben Sinclair, Lucy Matthews, Nat Turner and James Gallagher. Considering who had tasked her in the first place, it was them, undoubtedly. Satisfied, she prepared to move again. She had been following the four ex-trainees ever since they had left the monastery gates in Brazil. Her orders were clear and no grey areas remained. She enjoyed such work, the lack of no-man's-land. The IRA had given her regular employment on that basis.

But with the death knell of the Struggle, there seemed to be a lack of places that could use her specific form of expertise. In fact she was a double-team talent. As well as being one of the best trackers in the mercenary world, she was also adept at extracting confessions through her ability to dislodge a person's kneecap with a few whacks of bicycle chain.

She knew they were planning to board a vessel – no one who crept down here in the middle of the night was ship spotting – and all that she needed was the name and the time. A simple telephone enquiry would suffice the next day. She was in a good mood. The journey out of here would be two days at the very least – generally ships hit Jamaica before continuing on to Europe or West Africa. Sometimes they even made the journey nonstop. Collins realized she could take a holiday on this job. Aruba, perhaps, or Curaçao. She returned to her scope, suddenly enjoying her mission more than any she could remember.

True to Michael Church's word, their phone call to the harbour master (another ex-inmate for whom Church had helped negotiate a scar-free jail term) had resulted in a time and a place. The exact location was a loading bay with a single container, open and dark at the far side. No dock workers, no security cameras. It was clear what was being asked of them.

'I've changed my mind,' said Nat.

Lucy held him by the shoulders.

'It'll be okay, I promise.'

'Forget my psychological issues for a moment. In my book that's called a sitting target.'

'It's also called our way out.'

'You told me we'd be hitching a ride on a cargo ship. You didn't tell me it would be in one of those things.'

'This isn't the place to really discuss the matter in detail,' hissed Jamie. 'Perhaps you two would like to engage in a full and complete discussion from the privacy of that steel container over there?'

Ten minutes later, the four of them were huddled in the far dark corner of the structure, amongst the cellophane-wrapped furniture of the Schwartz family. Hidden by a three-piece suite and a four-poster bed was a small fridge, a mountain of bottled water and a small chemical toilet. A studio apartment at sea, Ben mused. No turn-down service, but it would do. The two bright headlights of a vehicle blazed inside briefly as they approached, and as the front portion of the container slowly leaned to and shut, Ben realized it was a forklift. As the final sliver of light disappeared from their world, a thought occurred to Jamie that he chose to vocalize to the rest of the group.

'How exactly are we going to breathe in here?'

Of course, there were airholes punctured throughout the structure, an elementary ventilation system. Spindles of faint, artificial light, presumably, Ben thought, from safety lighting in the cargo bay, provided some visibility inside. Ben examined the place in detail after discovering the flashlights taped to the back of the fridge. Clearly, this was not the first time this container had been used as a human traffic carriage. It was a custom model, adapted from the standard-issue aluminium-sided structure to better accommodate both the cargo and the more valuable stowaways in some modicum of comfort.

Eighty feet above them, the captain was informed by the lock master that the gates were now open and the path was clear for him to proceed. The shipping company was electronically invoiced by the Canal Authority for the privilege of using the facilities, and a course was set for the Straits of Gibraltar and the waters of the Mediterranean.

Ben had prepared for this journey with the precision of a Swiss watchmaker. He knew each of his cohort's emotional temperatures, their dispositions towards him and their likelihood of suspicions. He calculated that even in Lucy's newly friendly intentions towards him, she could be as paranoid as him. It made no sense that she would begin a sexual relationship with him, however, and he relegated her to his second place of risk. Jamie, for all of his physical stamina and icy professionalism, still retained an emotional connection to Ben, he felt, and was team-oriented enough to see the common goal of 'reaching Zero' as a far more important and likely need for all – Game Theory playing out, in fact, where cooperation surpassed individual need every time.

It was Nat, then, who gave Ben the most concern.

He had rifled through Nat's luggage, it was true, in the hotel room. Had he made a mistake? He'd been as careful as he could with zips, folds and so on, but it was possible that Nat had been more diligent than Ben gave him credit for. He'd presumed Nat's late-night conversation with Lucy had been about him. Lucy had made no mention of it, even though Ben had referred to overhearing voices on that night in Panama City. This only served to make him even more convinced.

It made sense, therefore, to embrace the man as fully as possible. Sun Tzu had said it; even his father had mentioned it a few times – if in doubt, embrace your enemies as close as you can. Better to be stabbed in the back than stabbed in the front.

But something was bugging Ben. One day into the voyage, he realized what was making him worry: Nat was taking it all very well. Far too well. Ben reasoned that Nat had recognized Ben's attempts at friendliness and identified them – correctly, as it happens – as part of a larger strategy.

Ben decided to ease off for a while and see where it took him. It didn't take long to find out.

One week into the journey, Nat began to break. It had been hard for him in the prison. It was ten times worse on the boat. There simply was nowhere else to go. In the heat, the darkness, the stagnant oppressive air, Ben heard Nat begin to talk to himself. A murmur, sometimes more, but it was starting to be a constant feature.

Ben knew the form. Nat was talking himself sane. Since no one else could know the pain he was feeling, only he could administer to it.

But it made him a dangerous travel partner.

Particularly where Ben was now concerned.

Ben tried to ensure his periods of sleep coincided with Nat's REM slumber – the moments where he was deep enough into unconsciousness that it would take at least twenty minutes for him to emerge once again. Knowing that his safety, and possibly that of his mission, depended on minimizing Nat's inquisitiveness, Ben felt a few bags under the eyes were a small price to pay.

The only incriminating object in Ben's possession was the narrow-band burst transmitter given to him by the handler in Panama. To begin with, he had worn the object underneath a Band-Aid to the right of his belly. But in the heat and humidity of the hold it had begun to peel off, and so Ben had transferred it under another plaster, this time to his chest.

Night and day were not perceptible to the four fugitives in the hold. But they knew a routine would allow them the highest chance of surviving the ordeal without too many psychological scars. The air was more rancid than usual and the heat unbearable. They agreed that an 'early night' was the most sensible precaution.

A small metallic *clang* jolted Ben awake – despite the constant hum of the engines, any change in their environment was immediately noticeable.

'What was that?' Nat's voice whispered from the corner.

Ben pretended not to hear, opening his eyes wide and starting to feel around his sleeping area. The seas were rough and the small metal transmitter had disappeared from Ben's chest.

The fucking thing had slid off.

As the boat climbed another wave, the *clattering* sound returned – and it was headed for Ben. He saw a speck flash past him but restrained himself from diving for it. He couldn't show any concern.

'Dunno,' said Ben. 'I might have dropped a coin.'

'Doesn't sound like a coin.'

Nat was coming over now. Their conversation had woken Jamie and Lucy, who rubbed their eyes and sat up from the areas of floor that served as their sleeping quarters. Ben tried, as casually as possible, to lean back and place his body, or at least his arm, in the path of the transmitter in case another movement of the ship sent it skittering back down towards him.

But the seas were uneven and, instead of rising into the next swell, the ship was skewered starboard. The piece of metal flew across the width of the container and *clanged* into the aluminium sides. Now Jamie and Lucy were on their feet.

'The hell is going on?' mumbled Jamie.

'Ben's lost a coin,' said Nat.

'Go back to bed, ignore it,' said Ben.

'That keeps making a racket, someone's going to come down here and see what the problem is. They'll think one of the tie-lines has come loose.'

Ben knew he had to act now. He kept his knapsack close to

hand, aware that there was a small scattering of change in a zip pocket.

'Can you see any tie-lines loose?' asked Ben as he deftly unzipped the pocket and removed a coin.

Nat, Lucy and Jamie had briefly glanced away from him to the tightly bound furniture in the container before them.

'Of course not,' said Lucy.

Nat glanced at Ben warily. 'Why do you say that, Ben?'

'I say that, Nat, because even if they do come down here, even a cursory check will show there's been no movement of cargo. Okay? Just an observation, if that's all right with you.'

Ben walked over to where the last impact had occurred, unsteady on his feet. It had been a few days since he'd walked. He'd kept fit through sit-ups, but had ignored basic coordination.

Nat was stirring himself to join him, but a pitch to port sent him back to the ground. Ben willed himself to keep steady and reached the far side of the container.

'What are you doing?' asked Nat.

Ben crouched down. 'I thought I heard it over here,' he said, locating the small metal object and replacing it with a coin.

Nat was on his feet now. 'Wait.'

Ben clasped the transmitter in a clenched fist.

'You missed it. There it is.' Nat bent down, his belly spilling over the edge of his boxer shorts. He came up triumphantly with the coin.

'Yours, I believe?' He offered it out to Ben, glancing briefly down at his clenched fist.

'Keep it as payment for a job well done,' smiled Ben and walked carefully back to his sleeping area. 'Try not to spend it all at once.'

Nat watched him complete the entire distance before sitting

down. He noticed that despite the uneven flooring and the unsteady movements of the boat, Ben did not put out his hands instinctively to keep his balance. One of his fists remained clenched.

'Thank you,' he said.

The last time they'd spent this long in each other's company a man had died. Nat wondered how long it would take for the same thing to happen again.

'Probationers'

Forty-Six

T he poet, artist and borderline lunatic William Blake was most famous for two interwoven pieces of work – the *Songs of Innocence* and the *Songs of Experience*. Both featured a series of poems that had divided critics and fans alike for centuries. The first three months of training were, for most of the intake, a variation on this poetic theme – and, like the *Songs of Innocence*, were mostly a repetitive cycle of infantile exercises whose true meaning and significance would only emerge much later.

Once the role-playing exercises had begun, Innocence was a long bitter way down the river. The world of Experience was upon them.

It was during their first live countersurveillance assessment that Ben became convinced that Nat had taken an instinctive dislike to him. It didn't help having him as a close-quarter buddy on his team. When the man next to you is as untrustworthy as a bear in a butcher's shop, you know the future will not be pretty.

He meant to cause him – if not pain, then trouble. Ben could feel it, like an interference pattern on a television.

There had already been shots across the bow, of course.

Ever since Lucy had moved out there had been a perceptible shift for the better in Nat's behaviour. But that had only been the mask. Even Jamie, not the most perceptive of people, had noticed. He'd been standing with Ben when Nat and Andy had passed in the cafeteria. Andy had enquired a little overloudly to Jamie just how his hangover was.

The implication was that Ben had not been invited to yet another social gathering. A progressive, quantum creep of isolation was surrounding Ben. And he had no real idea why.

Jamie had reassured him, as usual. But as the probation year wore on, Jamie took on more of a Neville Chamberlain optimism that, although refreshingly blithe, was disappointingly wrong most of the time.

The live countersurveillance exercise required a spotter and a lead. Following one person is hard enough. Following two requires enormous planning and safety in numbers. But being the prey isn't easy either. A bizarre large-scale form of choreography has to be deployed. It involves intense cooperation and understanding.

At every step of the way, Nat helped Ben get caught.

It wasn't through any overt mistakes, although there had been a few of those. And aside from tripping him up, which occurred only once 'by accident', – there could be no foul called.

Whatever the method Nat employed, it began to work. Ben felt his hold on training start to slip. His initial burst of enthusiasm and ability was waning fast. Instructors were unhappy with his progress. Socially, he was isolated, his relationship with Lucy over. She was still, he realized, avoiding him. The subtotal was a shroud of discomfort that covered Ben as the nights grew colder in January.

He'd even discovered, much to his bewilderment, that Lucy wasn't as poor as she'd made out. It was, after all, one of the main 'excuses' she'd mustered as the reason they should live together in the first place.

One day, quite by chance, Ben had visited a bookshop in Notting Hill Gate. Stepping out into the weak winter sunshine, he'd noticed a soft-top Mercedes with hazard lights flashing by the bank. A bus was honking loudly behind it and a traffic warden already had the car in her sights. Ben marvelled at the brazen confidence of whoever owned the car.

Then he saw her.

It was Lucy.

Grinning in apology, Lucy Matthews ran back from the ATM and slid back into the driver's seat. Ben took note of the numberplate and traced it through a friend in Scotland Yard. The plate was tagged 'S', meaning it was owned by an intelligence officer. A few guarded questions told him exactly which one.

The conclusion was as simple as it was brutal. Lucy had lied. About money, about herself. It did not make any sense. He toasted goodbye to the hard month of January alone, with a whisky on his sofa. Far from belonging, Ben was starting to feel like the loneliest man in the world. As far as KB could see, it was all going very much to plan.

Forty-Seven

Les Portes du Soleil
Franco-Swiss border

Two weeks into February and the team was skiing.

The resort of Avoriaz, no less, a lesson in languages and evasive winter driving – with just a small break for on- and off-piste activities around the Portes du Soleil region of France, perched on the border with Switzerland. Not, of course, that either government had any idea. It was high season still and thronged with poseurs, enthusiasts and intelligence officers.

Everyone, it seemed, enjoyed their winter training.

Clive, their terminally cheerful SAS ski instructor, was built like a cable car and was about as subtle as an avalanche. He was wide-eyed and loud, enjoyed pointing out French special forces, German BND agents practising ice climbing and even, he told them with a gleeful grin, a chalet on the Swiss side owned and operated by the CIA.

'Bullshit,' said Nat.

'Try skiing near it tomorrow. See how far you get.'

On the bus up to their own billet, Ben kept himself to himself. He'd begun to realize that what had happened to him with Lucy and Andy were not isolated moments. One by one, the other probationers were starting to take against him.

Little by little, he was being edged out of the group.

Ben was quietly determined to find out why.

The first day of ice driving had been a spectacular washout – literally. Within minutes of their arrival, an unnatural mild spell had kicked in and had destroyed half of their winding course through the mountains.

But there was still plentiful snow and ice on the upper slopes. So, to improve morale, the instructors agreed a few high-altitude black runs would sharpen up reflexes. A helicopter ride took them up to a pyramidal peak.

Ben was not a good skier. He had resented the inherited ski skills of the upper-middle-class kids at Bristol, who presumed that everyone went to Méribel at least once a year. To compensate, or possibly to spite himself, Ben had taken to an artificial slope at the Avon Indoor Ski Centre, to lay down some insurance if he ever needed to hold his own. He was glad of the experience now. He had not anticipated that any amount of their trip would be spent on the slopes – it was, after all, sold to him as a winter-weather driving course. Jamie, true to form, was more than happy to lead the way, carving perfect turns through the woods, around rocks and even, at one stage, catching air over a ravine. He had already skied the 'brown run' at The Wall, of course, and needed bigger challenges.

When Clive suggested a final run home, Jamie had other ideas. He was only just getting started.

'What about this Yankee chalet then?' he'd asked.

Clive shook his head. 'You can slap eyes on it, but that's it.'

He dragged them over the border, down a tortuous black mogul field and then suddenly broke right, off piste. Ben was terrified. As the others laughed and slalomed through the trees, Ben snowploughed erratically around the trunks as best he could. It reminded him of the nursery slopes, with five-and six-year-olds whizzing past him at every turn.

He finally caught up with the team's tracks as the forest thinned to nothing. Below, a hidden valley untouched so far by ski resort developers. And in the centre, an opulent-looking private residence.

'See the ring of trees?' asked Clive. 'That's wired for sound and vision. Like I said. Not a good idea.'

The MI6 trainees gazed down in wonder at the good life.

'I wouldn't recommend defecting, either.'

'Looks all right to me,' smiled Lucy.

'Yeah,' said Clive. 'But it's full of bloody Americans, innit. Try getting a decent brew down there.'

Clive led the way back through the trees and over into France. True to form, Ben was left to make up time on his own. It took him two hours to navigate his way back down to the chalet for lunch. It was a two-storey affair, surprisingly luxurious by SIS training standards, and featured a long entrance hall for boot removal, moving into an L-shaped dining area that abutted a kitchen.

Ben clattered in through the door, kicked the remainder of snow off his boots and sat down heavily on the bench. From the look of the jackets hung up on the hooks, everyone was back from their high-altitude adventure. As he unclipped his left boot, Ben was aware of something else – not only were they back, but they were in the next room.

What's more, they were talking about him.

'I don't understand Ben, I have to be honest,' Chris was saying. 'The guy just has this way of annoying me. It's sort of a talent, if you think about it.'

'I was watching him this morning,' interrupted Nat, 'in the van. We were trying to include him – right? – I think we were definitely trying, and all we got was this static – this – white noise . . .'

'Maybe he just tries too hard,' Jamie added.

Thank you, thought Ben. *Jamie, the eternal optimist.*

'Hardly,' came Lucy's voice, a cruel chuckle in her tone.

'What was that thing with his brother again?'

The voice belonged to Nat – and Ben froze.

'Oh, God,' droned Alex, in a tone that suggested she'd just remembered the name of that new personal shopper at Harvey Nicks, 'he died, didn't he?'

'That's right,' chipped in Andy, 'he was stabbed in the street.'

'I read the clippings . . .' It was Lucy now who Ben could hear, his heart hammering in his throat as he heard the most sensitive part of his life laid open on a slab. 'Can you believe that? Stabbed in the middle of Bristol.'

'Well,' said Nat, pomposity dripping from every syllable now, 'growing up on a council estate, you've got that sort of thing coming to you.'

Ben quietly inhaled through trembling lungs, and stood up as Alex spoke again. 'I suppose you almost expect it in a way. They're all such bloody savages.'

The room seemed to implode on Ben even as he heard the murmurs of agreement filter in from round the corner.

Ben strolled into the fray at that moment, bright and sunny, in the first stage of an experiment. The room glanced up at him in a microscopic breath of panic before acting normal. It was Nat who filled the silence, presuming and hoping that Ben had heard none of the last two minutes.

'Well, good people, though,' he continued randomly, as if his conclusion made some kind of sense to what had come before. 'I've never been myself. Oh!' he blustered, 'seeing' Ben. 'Hello, hello. Thought we'd lost you to the Yeti or something.'

'Sorry I'm late,' smiled Ben. 'Nursery slopes were a bitch.'

Many people laughed at this, people who Ben knew for a fact had a negligible sense of humour. Those who laughed loudest, Ben noted, were those who'd been cruellest.

'So,' said Ben after Nat and Andy got up to pretend to do something in the kitchen and allay their frayed nerves, 'what are we talking about?'

Ben savoured the half-second's pause of guilt.

'Fondue,' smiled Lucy, effortlessly, 'fact or fiction?'

'Seriously.'

'I am serious. We were wondering whether we should invite Cap'n Clive to team drinks after the class this afternoon.'

Clive was someone no one in their right mind would want in the same restaurant. Lucy *was* nervous, thought Ben. She just wasn't showing it. Ben looked closely at Jamie. He could see the flushed cheeks that suggested regret. He wondered if he'd ever admit it to his face. Ben turned back to Lucy.

'You want my opinion?'

'Of course.'

'Do it. No sense in freezing the man out, is there?'

'Well put,' said Nat from the kitchen. 'He might be an arsehole, but he's *our* arsehole.'

'But Nat,' smiled Ben, 'I thought that was you.'

And the laughter started once more.

The temptation to inform each of them, in turn, that he'd been listening all along was impossibly delicious. But Ben quickly realized that this premium knowledge offered a fascinating insight into how his fellow probationers dealt with lies. He began to look for patterned behaviour that might come in useful at a later date. Nat laughed when he lied; Lucy toyed with her hair. All of them sounded melodically conflicted . . . innocent phraseology all of a sudden had an exclamatory quality about it, as if it were being read for the first time in a bad play by an even worse actor. Words not so much dressed up as wearing a clown suit.

With each interaction, Ben kept a tally. He used this chance moment to create a taxonomy of these people, as if they were butterflies in his own private case. Rather than be hurt by it, he was grateful for it. To be empowered over others, without their knowledge, provided security. And security was something to be thankful for.

When the team returned from the Continent, Lucy had tried to engage Ben in conversation. His complete lack of interest had concerned her, and later that same night Lucy drove back to Vauxhall Cross and parked in a VIP space normally reserved for visiting dignitaries.

KB had been sipping peppermint tea, in the middle of a game of internet chess. He had even turned his flat screen monitor around for her to look at his choice of move.

'You said you were having some problems?' he smiled.

'I'm just not comfortable with this any more.'

KB nodded, allowing the silence to denude her confidence. He rose to his feet and padded to the window.

Lucy felt the need to fill the void. 'I don't care if he's what you say he is or not. I think I've proved the point.'

'You've proved yourself a fine recruiter. You've also proved to me you have the ability to dissociate yourself from your emotions when making large career decisions.' KB smiled down on her. 'This part of your training is over. You've passed with flying colours.'

The anxiety flooded off Lucy's shoulders.

As she left, KB complimented himself not only on his way with words, but on his long-term planning. There was a chance, of course, that none of these young people would survive what would hit them on their first assignments. KB understood the odds involved and he felt ready to accept them. Because as far as he could see, if at least some of them couldn't overcome a little local difficulty, then they didn't deserve to be here in the first place. And they certainly would not survive a search for Contact Zero. This training was only a cold shoulder in a long line of hardship. It was about time they grew accustomed to it. After all, he himself had survived those long cold winters in East Berlin on a diet of potatoes and betrayals. He sided with Ayn Rand on this one. Survival of the fittest was, in this case, the only option.

He felt the overwhelming need to find some clay, perhaps, and fashion a pot with his hands. The way he felt now, he could mould anything.

He placed a call to a chap called Neville in the Archives. He wanted to be sure his gossip muscles had been working properly. Information, as he knew, was power.

Contact Two

Forty-Eight

Israel

The ship docked at a deep-water berth off the Eastern Container Terminal at Haifa after three weeks, four days, seven hours, twenty-six minutes.

The four of them were considerably thinner, greyer and more mentally unstable than twenty-five days previously. Had they disembarked a few minutes later, it is accurate to say that Nat would have strangled everyone, including himself.

Thrown to the sides by the pendulum motion of a crane, Ben held on to Lucy. From the outside, all was peace and calm efficiency. Not that they could tell, but outside their temporary coffin Haifa was living up to its Hebrew name – pretty shore – washed red with a perfect sunset. Somewhere beyond the military installations, three German-built submarines patrolled the underwater Med, their nuclear warheads at a constant state of readiness. For all its beauty and commercial activity, Haifa was also the main naval base for Eretz Israel. Ever since the Crusaders had passed through here in the twelfth century, the town had seen warriors and commerce in equal measure.

The container was unloaded by a dock worker who was earning at least double pay compared to his colleagues, not that they were aware of it. He did this once every six months, perhaps. He asked no questions.

The cargo container was transferred to a remote corner of the Nim Israel storage yard and left for the night. The driver knew that by the time he picked it up the next morning, the box would be a little lighter and the outer door would have been resealed. He always knew to place the cargo exactly where it should have been in the first place, file a misappropriation paper with the customs official and worry no more about it. The anomaly was easily missed in the crippling volume of trade that came through the port on a weekly basis.

Thus it was that at two the next morning, Ben, Nat, Lucy and Jamie emerged blinking into the shadowy waterside hinterland of an industrial cargo yard.

They had had three weeks at sea to prepare for the next stage of their plan. Church had told Ben what they had to do. They were here to find a woman called Hannah Rosen. A family in Jerusalem could help. There was just one problem. Hannah Rosen was a 'sleeper' and they had no idea how to wake her up.

Forty-Nine

T he Chief had asked KB for a report, but KB had not replied. Concerned his friend was avoiding him, the Chief paid a doorstep call to his office. He found him sitting by his phone, staring at it.

'Problems?' asked the Chief.

'Solutions,' smiled KB. 'I neglected to tell you one last detail about the Greco procedure.'

'I'm all ears.'

'I took the liberty of employing an insurance policy. Should our plant get any innovative ideas.'

'That's why you've been avoiding me?'

'I know how you hate surprises.'

'Who is it?'

KB told him.

The Chief's eyes widened. He'd heard about what she'd done to her enemies on the Falls Road in Belfast. 'So long as she's on our side,' he said grimly. 'God help us if she's not.'

As it happened, Collins was fully on the side of her paymasters. She'd never drunk more Mount Gay rum in her life.

She'd spent two weeks in the British Virgin Islands, bonking the odd bartender to oblivion, shopping and so on. When she was through she stopped off in Puerto Rico for a final week-end's blowout. There had been a spot of trouble getting to the airport, when the cab driver had taken a shine to her emerald eyes and tried to take a detour to his brothers' house. She knew something was up when he began talking quietly on his cellphone and the meter stopped running.

She had decided not to get physical unless he touched her. He first attempted to explain they were stopping for gas, but her silence merely frustrated him and only bolstered his ardour. His two brothers emerged with a knife and a crowbar. The driver laid a hand on her breast and stuck out his tongue lasciviously. 'Don't worry,' he told her, 'if you don't move, you'll escape with your pretty face intact.'

By the time she had finished with them, it was the men who could not move, their kneecaps shattered and pummelled so far around their joints that their legs were rendered almost avian. Their screams were mute, however, as their faces were so badly mutilated that their jaws were left permanently agape. It also didn't help that their tongues were ripped out and shoved into their eyesockets. It seemed a shame as that meant they could not see the true scale of her pre-emptive revenge. But at least they were conscious enough to experience the short, agonizing minutes that remained of their lives. Collins always left them alive.

She charged the taxi and made for the airport. Settling into her business class seat, she thought how great it felt to be ahead of the game again. She'd made sure the flight arrived at least four days before the scheduled arrival of the cargo ship. Many was the time on a surveillance operation that she found herself catching up to stand still. Here, the groundwork was done, provided to her in a stout manila folder at the start of her mission. Once she'd found their trail, it was easy. The rest was a simple case of follow the leader. And there was a guarantee of action, too. That's what her client had told her:

whether his mission succeeds or fails, we need to take him down.

She mentally took apart her high-powered rifle in her mind's eye and reassembled it. Life, it seemed to her, could not get much better than this.

Fifty

A local bus would be too much, they agreed, after the stresses of the container. Almost as soon as they were on the ground in Israel, paranoia had taken hold, seeping into their psyches like a fever. Not to mention the fact that Nat was close to losing a grip on his sanity following their voluntary detention at sea. Lucy confided in Ben with a look that she was worried about him.

They had put as much distance as they could between themselves and the boat as soon as possible, crossing Haifa to the northwest and reaching the promenade at Bat Galim beach. They found some public toilets and scrubbed, shaved and drenched the ocean ordeal from their bodies.

After drying off in the sun, they devoured breakfast in a coffee house on the promenade near the cable car station. Haifa was similar to San Francisco – you needed the coffee shops to negotiate the hills.

'This is what I don't understand,' jabbered Nat in a whisper. 'There is no rhyme or reason to this. Here we are in Israel. Before we were in Central America. Where next? The Vatican? Antarctica? The moon? I think this is all one great big cosmic joke at our expense.'

Nat's eyes were bloodshot and watery. His foot was tapping with unconscious manic energy on the metal chair, the clanging sound attracting the attention of passers-by. Jamie, Ben and Lucy exchanged a look that said: *yes, I think so too*. As they left and followed a re-energized Nat back up towards the main street once more, their hearts missed a few beats when he suddenly took a detour and strode towards a soldier on the other side of the street.

Unable to shout out or drag him back, they simply had to stand and wait, coiled like springs, ready to move. When the soldier started pointing helpfully down towards a collection of minibuses, they breathed a sigh of relief. But the impulsive act only made Ben even more concerned. Nat had the appearance of someone slowly mulling something over in his mind, and overcompensating with rash decisions that could have done with some of that brainpower instead. Ben knew that if it came to it, he would have to find a way of leaving this man behind. He did not want to resort to violence. He simply wanted to get the job done. Having him around was fine. Having him around and actively snooping was a whole different story. For now, he would have to embrace him.

They caught a minibus towards Jerusalem. At several points along the way, Ben found himself checking behind them for familiar cars. It made no sense to feel they were under surveillance, but he was helpless to stop himself. It made him feel a little better that several other of their fellow passengers were doing the same thing.

The *Sheirut* ducked and dived its way through West Jerusalem and deposited them at the northwest corner of Zion Square. Emerging into a seedy tourist trap was not what Ben had imagined the cradle of the Judaeo-Christian world to be like. Several moth-eaten youth hostels crowded around pedestrian throughways.

The address they were looking for was in Nahlaot, a short walk – they discovered after a few failed attempts at directions – through Mahane Yehuda market. This was the first neighbourhood to have been built outside the Old City walls, replete with old buildings, cobblestone streets and small courtyards.

'I don't feel comfortable just door-stepping this guy,' said Ben.

'Same here,' said Jamie.

'So, let's take a look and—'

Nat was already powering ahead with Lucy. Ben glanced at Jamie who shrugged in solidarity. The two men let the matter drop.

Number 38 Shiloh was as run-down as they come, hidden between a ramshackle set of grey, rickety old houses. The structure at Number 38, however, was a single family home. Nat and Lucy conferred with Ben and Jamie – one for the front, one for the back. By the time they reconvened, Jamie had a plan.

'Anyone else see that cat flap?'

Lucy and Ben concurred that they had.

'Well, then,' said Jamie. 'We're all right.'

They checked into a youth hostel. As the others signed the register, Jamie sidled over to the ancient, idle payphone in the corner and memorized the number. Sitting on the edge of his bottom bunk (Ben took the top), Jamie sourced some paper and a pen. Ben and Nat looked over his shoulder as he wrote: 'YOUR CAT HAS INJURED MY CAT. PLEASE CALL ME TO TALK ABOUT MONEY.' Then he added the number of the hostel phone. No one was fluent in Hebrew, and so the note was left in English.

Pushing the note through the mailbox of Number 38, Jamie noticed the same police numberplate cruise past again. Not one to take coincidences lightly, he smiled at the others as he returned to them.

'Turn around, keep walking.'

Nat, Lucy and Ben smiled back at him, did exactly as he said. Jamie strolled with them, noticing the police car turn off the square and disappear.

'Any particular reason?' asked Nat after a few strides.

'No half-measures round here,' said Jamie.

They hurried back to the hostel, where Nat and Ben took turns in scaring off any poor soul trying to use the payphone. In the age of the text message, they were lucky. And, after only a few hours, the phone rang. Jamie grabbed it, but passed the receiver to Lucy. It was an old man, and he sounded irate.

'My cat would never do such a thing,' said the voice.

'Pardon me, sir, but—'

'And I tell you this, conspiracy to defraud money via cat injury is still conspiracy whichever way you look at it. Proceed with extreme caution, young lady.'

'Mr Rosen?'

The phone went quiet for a few seconds. Lucy thought she could hear opera playing in the background.

'No Mr Rosen here,' explained the voice. 'You have the wrong person—'

Lucy bit her lip and pressed him. 'We're looking for Hannah Rosen—' she was raising her voice now – 'and we were told you could tell us where to find her.'

Another pause on the line. 'Hannah Rosen. I see. Well, I cannot help you there. I cannot tell you where she is.'

Lucy's heart skipped a beat. 'But—'

'But I can tell you how to find her.'

His tone sounded indignant. Lucy smiled to herself. Semantic point. But never mind.

'Should we come to your house?'

'Of course not.'

'Then how—'

'You should go to the Wall. Where men and women pray together.'

The line fell silent.

'But – what does Hannah look like? Will she know us?'
But he'd already hung up.

The old man replaced the phone. His name was Eric Meltzer. For nearly sixty years, he had fulfilled his side of a long-standing agreement – to pass on information when asked the correct question. In this case, when asked about a Miss Hannah Rosen. And, for nearly sixty years, after passing on the appropriate directions to find her, he had picked up the telephone and contacted a man known only to him as 'My Learned Friend'.

He dialled the same number now. The call was picked up on the final ring – just before Eric was about to give up and try again. The other side did not announce himself or even give greeting, but Eric knew he was listening.

'Someone called this morning asking for Hannah,' he explained. 'I told them how they could find her.'

'Thank you,' said the voice. 'And God bless.'

Eric never knew who or where this Learned Friend was within the city. All he knew was that, on the first of every month, ten thousand shekels would appear in an offshore numbered account whether he passed on this information or not. He also knew that if he ever failed to pass on such information, or betrayed anything of his dealings to any other person, the payments would end abruptly. He did not care to explore what else might also transpire.

Deciphering old men's riddles was not part of Lucy's espionage training. Tradecraft was. But despite the bizarre instructions from the man on the phone, the goal appeared on the surface to be relatively simple.

'So we meet her at the Western Wall,' Nat muttered bitterly. 'That's nice and anonymous.'

Of course, the holiest site in Judaism was a strange location for a clandestine meeting. The predominance of the faithful, tourists with cameras and paranoid security services, not to mention the checkpoints to enter and leave the Jewish Quarter of the Old City, meant that an attempt to meet someone without attracting attention, let alone speak to them, was next to impossible.

Lucy agreed it was odd. The security was massive; then again the crowds would shield them. In any case, there was no other option but to turn up. Half an hour later, a taxi dropped the quartet off at the Jaffa Gate to the Old City of Jerusalem.

They approached a security checkpoint for people entering the Prayer Plaza. The *Kotel ha-Ma'aravi*, or the 'Wailing Wall' as it is also known, had been a focus for violence, as well as faith, for centuries. There was no way of avoiding a search. Ben had foreseen this and ensured he removed the transmitter from his body, hiding it between the frame of his bunk and the clammy wall before they left.

Once through the checkpoint, they emerged into the grand vista of the main plaza. The wall itself rose some sixty-five feet above them, discoloured below six feet, where the hands of countless millions had touched the surface in prayer.

A duo of police strolled past and eyeballed the young tourists as they loitered around the fenced observation area.

'So what now?' said Ben as he eyed the crowds.

Lucy surveyed them too. 'He didn't say.' But her eyes had already picked out the solution to their problem. 'Wait, we've got this wrong.'

'How can we have got it wrong? Unless there's another wall he was talking about?' asked Jamie.

'Right wall, wrong place. I'll be back in a sec.'

And Lucy began to walk around the fence and head straight

for the wall. 'Oh, shit, Lucy,' hissed Nat, 'wrong way . . .'
Immediately, two elderly men rushed at Lucy and shooed her
towards a smaller section of wall to the west.

'I see what she's doing,' said Ben, and grabbed a paper
yarmulke from a custodian at the entrance to the prayer area.
He glanced over at Lucy, who was being harangued by two elderly
ladies and helped into a sombre array of unflattering clothing.

Where men and women pray together.

He wasn't just describing the Western Wall.

He was describing a *specific point on its length.*

The *mechitza* is the fence that sections off the wall's span
between the sexes. The men receive the lion's share of wall
space for their devotions; the women, the smaller remainder.

Ben and Lucy arrived at the wall at the same time. Without
looking at each other, they tried to mirror the devotions of the
men and women on either side of them. All the while, they
kept their eyes on the wall. Specifically, on the cracks between
the stones.

Close up, one is able to see a staggering number of small
white scraps of paper shoved into the gaps between the stones.
These are *kvitlach*, prayers written by the faithful, personal
messages to God.

Ben had realized, with Lucy, that their contact had mentioned that the wall would only show *how* they could find
Hannah Rosen. The where would come from something else.

Namely, Ben had realized, a scrap of paper.

Someone was using this holy site as a dead drop.

A little insensitive, thought Ben. *Ingenious, but insensitive.*

As Ben and Lucy tried to dissolve into the crowds at the wall,
a telescopic lens had picked them out pointed from the
ramparts of the Old City.

It had cross hairs in the centre.

Collins was crouched in a comfortable position, fixing her lens now on Ben Sinclair. She noticed the other two beside the far barrier, engaged in an animated discussion.

At this rate, Collins thought, they would attract a security patrol before too long. As she crawled away to find a new vantage point, she saw that she was right.

Back down by the wall, Nat appeared at Ben's side as he scanned the papers in the cracks. 'You're nuts,' he whispered. 'You can't take people's prayers out of the wall. My dad was a nonobservant Jew and even he knew that.'

Word began to spread among others at the wall. *Look at her, the tourist at the end. And those two. What are they doing?*

A severe woman in glasses began admonishing Lucy in Hebrew. *You're not here to talk!*

Jamie, back at the barrier, could see the growing commotion and noticed it had not gone unmissed by the security forces nearby. If they didn't do something to quell the problem soon, she'd create another, bigger problem out here.

For Lucy, luck was at hand. Wedged just to her right, a join just to the left of the partition, was a *kvitlach* that seemed thicker than the rest. There was writing just visible from the crack. It read: FOR HANNAH. Checking no more attention was being paid to her, she wrote a prayer of her own and, as she pushed it in, she removed the other scrap of paper to her hand.

Then the woman in glasses was in her face now.

'I'm sorry, I just – I changed my mind!' Lucy said.

She turned and walked away, full of apology and embarrassment. Ben and Nat had already peeled off and joined Jamie by the barrier.

'Got it.'

'Well, that was offensive,' said Nat.

'Wasn't my bloody idea to hide it there, was it?'

'I suggest we disappear, before anything else,' said Jamie quietly, as one of the cops spoke into his radio.

There were no objections.

They headed towards the Dung Gate and took Batei Makhase as it curved alongside the southern wall. They tried to keep a balance between the fascinated tourists they were trying to be and the increasingly nervous fugitives they actually were.

The road curved enough to allow their peripheral vision to check their progress. Surely, by now, they were clear?

A guard was following them.

Two, in fact.

They headed north, back to Hashalshelet, the Street of the Chain, which took them west again, along pristine streets, into the centre of the Jewish Quarter.

'We're going to have to split this up a little,' said Ben to Lucy as they strolled.

'What's the message say, Luce?'

'Series of directions.'

'Can you memorize what's on that paper?' asked Jamie.

'There's too much of it. Not at a run.'

'So we need to cut loose,' said Nat.

Ben had already worked it out. 'Lucy, Jamie, you break left as a lovey-dovey couple. We'll square the circle, parallel up and meet you next turn.'

It was classic 'box' counterespionage evasion. Without a knowledge of the narrow streets and alleyways of the city, it would be harder than usual. But there were crowds, open spaces, steps. The conditions favoured the prey over the pursuer. Even if Israeli security forces were considered by most intelligence operatives as among the world's elite.

What's more, Ben wanted very much to stay close to Nat. The move was instinctive and strong.

'If not, see you at the hostel.'

'Not if we see you first.'

The four of them were approaching the Cardo, the site of a covered market. Just before the junction proper, Lucy pulled Jamie excitedly to her and pointed, waving to Ben and Nat. They looked like an impulsive couple thrilling at the sight of the hustle and bustle of the ancient town. At the same time, Ben and Nat marched off north, into the souks on the edge of the Muslim Quarter.

The two officers behind them barked into their radios and split up. One followed Lucy and Jamie, the other strode after Ben and Nat as stall traders called out their wares.

Jamie dragged Lucy through the throng and immediately stepped into a puddle of luck. A birthday party was spilling into the already crowded Cardo. Unable or unwilling to run, the security officer pushed his way through the celebrations. Jamie cut left and Lucy cut right, leaving him with no option but to take one or give up the ghost.

He chose Jamie and cut left in pursuit. But before he could catch up with him, Jamie had already doubled back to join Lucy on the Cardo once again and accelerated their pace into the streets of the Armenian Quarter.

Ben and Nat were not so fortunate. Their pursuer was like a shadow, glued close to their wake. Here was a balance. At this stage there was no showing of hands, no acceptance that this was a pursuit at all. The officer was investigating suspicious activity; they were trying to communicate a relaxed and nonchalant air at the same time as eradicating the tail as quickly as possible.

Nat was instinctively following Ben's lead – perhaps he'd taken the disastrous training episode during probation seriously after all – and Ben could feel that he had control. He tested the connection, cutting back on their route without warning, down

Aqabat al Saraya, up El Wad . . . Nat stuck to him, responding like a horse on a bridle, without complaint. He was scared, thought Ben. He's relying on me.

As they rounded another corner, they passed another security guard who was checking a stall owner's papers. The guard looked up and stared at them. Ben's eyes widened in pretend panic and a sudden explosion of speed powered him away. Nat, panicking, broke into a run and followed.

'Hey!'

The guard, unsure what was going on but concluding it was surely not a promising situation, sprinted off in pursuit.

Ben jinked left on to the Via Dolorosa. The steps were large and the going was tough upstream, past an endless countercurrent of kids weaving, running, leaping down . . .

The steps were frustrating and dangerous to run on. They were too large for single paces and too small for a solid rhythm – sometimes two strides took you up, sometimes three . . . there was enough to be concentrating on without worrying about the next step.

Ben let Nat catch up with him and ease ahead.

As he did so, Ben also made a move.

Nat didn't see it coming.

As he overtook, Ben suddenly checked sharply back and sprang left, across Nat's wake. As Ben passed his kicking heels, he delicately flipped Nat's right ankle upwards, jamming it into a knot with his left. The overall effect was like an umbrella in a bicycle wheel. Nat screamed in surprise and torpedoed painfully to the ground. As he impacted with terra firma, Nat's jaw connected with the hard stone step ahead of him and blood and several teeth scattered. Ben heard the commotion but did not look back. He only picked up speed as he dived through a carpet shop and powered his way through to the back, where a small entrance opened out into a narrow thoroughfare.

Back on the blood-smeared steps, Nat sucked in great gulps of air, his head a kaleidoscope of pain. He crawled agonizingly to his feet only to be tackled by the guard. The pursuing police officer had been caught out by the change of pace and arrived panting moments later. The guard on the ground pointed to the carpet shop and the officer ran through it in pursuit of his quarry.

Reaching the other side, he realized his task was futile. Without a good look at the suspect, he had no description to give. He radioed in to his station as he walked back to Nat. One suspect apprehended, one still at large.

'Suspected of what?' yelled Nat through the blood and tears. He craned his neck, looking frantically for Ben, but all he could see were the blank indifferent stares of strangers as the handcuffs *clicked* . . .

Back in the hostel, Ben worked fast. First he unpicked his Canadian passport from the seams of his overcoat and removed the small plastic sachet taped to the underside. Checking the bathrooms were empty, Ben left clutching a towel and the sachet, returning ten minutes later with considerably blonder hair, and the transmitter safely back under a Band-Aid on his right-hand side.

He retrieved Nat's bag from under his bed and removed his GPS from a side pocket. He then kicked it back under the bed, hefted Jamie's bag from his bunk and looped it on to his shoulder. Running over to the female dorm, Ben located Lucy's and did the same. No one blinked an eye.

By the time he hit the reception area, he was sweating. He pulled his hood over his new hair and settled the bill in full.

He moved outside and found an area of garbage cans against

an alleyway. From here he had a good vantage point of the hostel. He checked his watch. Knowing Jamie and Lucy, they would have taken about as long as he had to lose their tails and were headed back here.

Almost three minutes later, a taxi pulled up outside the hostel and Lucy and Jamie sprang out. Ben sprinted over to Lucy and back over to the alleyway. Confused and panicked, they joined him moments later. Ben handed them their backpacks and kept talking.

'Major disaster,' he said.

'What's happened?'

'Nat got nabbed. He pushed over a security guy—'

'Oh – shit—'

Lucy sucked her teeth for a moment and came to a decision. 'We have to go back—'

'Where? The police station?'

'To tell them—'

'He's done nothing wrong, he's unlikely to be on any database, but those extra passports in his pocket aren't going to win him any friends. He could be locked away for days.'

'So we wait for him.'

'Listen to me. He is not going to take us down with him, all right? They might get lucky. They might have friends in the British Embassy. There might be a mugshot of us on the wall of their cafeteria for all we know.'

Jamie sighed, bit his lip. 'Ben's right. It's too risky.'

For the first time, Lucy's eyes betrayed fear – she was no longer the owner of the casting vote. 'You're just going to abandon him?'

'If I screw up, Lucy, feel free to do the same to me. I mean it. We have to move on. Change clothes. Change skin. And make our rendezvous with this sleeper before she wakes up and leaves.'

They found a public toilet where Jamie shaved his sapling beard into a finely tuned goatee. Lucy, meanwhile, heart thundering, changed into a preppy outfit, with flat shoes and three-quarter-length trousers, as befitting a French tourist abroad.

The three of them then hailed a taxi. With Lucy in the middle, they stared down at the set of directions they'd retrieved from the wall.

On the paper was the word ROSEN with a series of street names, some marked with turns, others simply outlined in basic steps that made the document resemble a twenty-first-century treasure map. Perhaps, thought Ben, that's exactly what it was.

Left on Ha-Zanhanim. Continue as it becomes Sultan Suleiman . . .

The taxi took them as far as it could. To ensure privacy they asked him to pull into a hotel, the Metropole, that Jamie spotted a few blocks outside the main thrust of their route. Once they were outside, they moved quickly. Jamie had taken charge of the orienteering and all of them were sensitized to every police siren, every shout, every stare and jostling passer-by. The directions took them east along the north wall of the Old City, past Herod's Gate and then south towards the Garden of Gethsemane.

Ben had not given the consequences of his mission a second thought until this moment, perhaps because he never allowed himself that luxury under normal circumstances. All distractions were unwelcome. But then these were not.

He was aware of the tension inside him and understood its meaning. But there were higher powers at work, deeper betrayals already in the fossil record. And nothing could be done to turn that back. He was doing everything he could. A tragedy had occurred, officers cut adrift. What was happening was a natural outgrowth of that. The Service needed to locate

Contact Zero because without commitment there can be no loyalty. That was what KB had explained to him. The very existence of Contact Zero threatened to unravel all the Service had worked hard to build. If all an agent had to do was pull the ripcord when things got rough, where was the responsibility to make good? It was like giving back the car when the ashtrays were full. Ben understood the point. Loyalty was vital for survival. And KB knew how he felt. More than anyone.

He would complete his mission and stay alive. If asked, who would do less, or more?

The last recognizable direction was just south of Gethsemane. After that, the directions were all in paces – north, south, east, west.

It was pretty clear why.

Before them spread the western face of Mount Olivet, also known as the Mount of Olives. Almost every square foot of the surface was covered in graves. This was the Jewish Cemetery.

'I'm starting to get a bad feeling about this,' said Jamie.

'Starting?' muttered Lucy.

Most Jews, when they die, are buried with their feet facing Jerusalem. Those buried in Jerusalem face the Golden Gate. Those with enough leverage find themselves on the western slope of Mount Olivet.

Hannah Rosen was one of those with leverage.

They found the grave minutes later. Below her name, the inscription: 'Beloved daughter and sister, none knew thee but to love thee. Hannah Rosen, daughter of Yosef Rosen. Died on 23 Nisan (5706). T.N.Tz.B.H.'

Ben, Lucy and Jamie stared down in bewilderment at her grave. As they did so, the perfect circle of a telescopic lens picked them out from an eyrie inside the walls of the Old City. As his contact had informed him, someone had indeed come looking for the ever-beautiful, ever-perfect Hannah Rosen. What the contact had failed to inform him . . . well, it was no matter now.

The man gazing down the telescope drew back and walked down through the tower to his study. The chamber was tiny and set into stone so old and wise the learning sometimes made him heavy with sadness – there would never be enough years to fill his head with the knowledge that surrounded him.

Like all priests in the Coptic tradition, his black robes flowed behind him as he descended the stairs and emerged into the bustle of Aqabat al Saraya, the street across from the Church of the Holy Sepulchre that had been his home for more than thirty years.

Unlike most Coptic priests, Father Daniel had been born in Basildon, Essex. A tortuous and painful route of life had found him here, in his study rooms set into the very walls of Old Jerusalem itself.

He wondered to himself whether these young fugitives would have what it took to make the next step. He had seen those seeking sanctuary stop here, shrivel and die with defeated hope, so timid were they of doing what was necessary. He wished them well. It had been so long since anyone had got this far. He hoped they had the staying power to wait. He was confused, however. The contact had said there would be four. His eighty-year-old legs ached and his hip, though much younger than he, was bothering him again. He ignored the pain and forced himself into a brisk walk. The least he could do was to be punctual.

They'd stayed staring at the grave for half an hour. From the sounds coming over the Golden Gate from the Old City, police activity was intensifying. Ben was scanning the horizon, deep in thought.

'Think about it,' said Lucy. 'She's a sleeper. Our contact in Panama tells us to wake her up. Well, here she is. She died in 1946. What now? Start digging? Is it a code? A clue? Another bloody riddle?'

Ben shook his head. 'We're not digging. We've already drawn attention to ourselves down at the wall. We can't risk any more security patrols picking on us.'

'And yet,' said Jamie, 'it seems logical that we should.'

'How is that logical?'

'This is Jerusalem, correct?'

'Unless it's changed names since I was last here, yes.'

'Possibly the most paranoid and security-conscious place on the planet?'

Ben weighed this carefully and nodded. 'Just about.'

'Do you think, perhaps, this all has something to do with testing us? Didn't our meeting in Recife end up as a test? Wasn't meeting our man in La Joya the same? Why not this?'

Lucy sighed. 'What if it is, Jamie?'

'Well, I'm beginning to think this thing is a circle.'

'What do you mean?'

'I mean we may just end up exactly where we started. Cast out, alone and dispensable.'

Ben stared at the horizon as a wailing siren filtered over on the wind. 'That's where we are now, I think.'

'But now, you see, *now* we have hope. And hope is dangerous because hope can make you do things you wouldn't normally do. Such as following hidden messages to Jewish graveyards.'

'Contact Zero, Jamie. Focus on that.'

'I have. And it's an idea, Lucy. It's still an idea. And I don't know whether it'll ever be anything else. I'm just scared I want it to be true so much I'll do anything to make it so. Including ignoring the brutal facts in front of my face.'

316

'The Samaritans were real. Michael Church in Panama . . . You have to believe we're headed in the right direction.'

But Jamie was biting his lip again. 'What I believe . . .' He stared out at the city. 'I don't know what I believe. We're standing in the centre of world religion, a place of such certainty, so much belief, and I don't really know where mine has gone. Or if I ever had any to begin with.'

Lucy shook her head but wasn't going to argue any more. The silence held them.

An elderly man in a flowing black robe and with a halo of white hair picked his way through the grave sites. Instinctively, they stepped back. The man did not look at them. He was intent on the grave. He knelt down, producing a candle, which he lit with a cheap lighter. He knelt and prayed for a moment, and then finally held their gaze. His eyes blazed with spirit, intelligence and no small measure of tragedy.

'I thought there were four of you,' he said.

Lucy opened her mouth to speak but Jamie stepped in.

'Just the three of us.'

He nodded and stood up slowly. He winced as he took a step back to view the Golden Gate. 'It was sealed up, you know. By the Sultan. He knew that the Jews and the Christians believed if the Messiah came, he'd arrive here on this mountain and enter Jerusalem by that gate. So, the Sultan bricked it up in the hope it would stop him. If you ask me, that is wishful thinking. If you can negotiate a Second Coming but not a brick wall, you're not doing a very good job, are you?'

'Do you know Hannah Rosen?'

· The man smiled – far away, fleetingly.

'I did.'

Fifty-One

H is name was Daniel Sherman. In the summer of 1945, when Daniel returned from a Special Operations Executive combat posting to take up a full commission with MI6, a general election was held in Britain. The Labour Party promised that if they were returned to power, they would allow Holocaust survivors to emigrate to Israel and pledged to act for the establishment of a Jewish national home. Labour won the election but then, in a move seldom seen in politics, turned away from their election promises.

In October 1945 Jewish dissident groups united in a combined rebellion against the British administration in Palestine. In response, Britain ordered a crackdown. It was under these circumstances that Daniel Sherman was posted to Jerusalem. On June 17, 1946 an attack took place in which nearly all of the bridges connecting Palestine with its neighbours were destroyed. Almost two weeks later, the British began a two-week sweep-up of those suspected of anti-British activities. A countrywide curfew was proclaimed and nearly three thousand people were arrested throughout the country.

During this time, Daniel had been stationed at the King David Hotel, the south wing of which housed the British military command. Over the first three months of his tour, he had begun to feel conflicted about his country's involvement in the Holy Land.

He had begun to drink – not excessively, but consistently – at the bar in the hotel. It was a popular nexus for business and pleasure, Jewish and Gentile. He had worked all weekend, just as he had the previous weekend, and drowned his sorrows as usual on Sunday night, served as ever by a beautiful young girl called Hannah Rosen, who worked behind the bar at the hotel at weekends.

Monday, he explained to her, would have been his first day off in three weeks. But it was not to be, he continued. 'Bastards have me in here again, eight o'clock tomorrow morning.'

'Well, I'll be here after noon.'

'Well, Miss Hannah. You just saved my life.'

As it turned out, Daniel nearly saved hers.

The day of the 22nd was a day of business as usual in the British military command unit at the King David. Daniel spent the morning managing the egos of his commanding officers and keeping his mind on the job.

At precisely 11.59 a.m., he sauntered into the bar and sat down. He would take an early lunch, he had decided. And with a following wind perhaps the lovely Hannah might even join him to boot.

She was ten minutes late, but that didn't bother Daniel. She couldn't join him for lunch, however. To compensate, he decided to have a drink at the bar before he ate.

At almost the same time as Hannah was pouring his soda water, a man was planting an explosive device deep within the structure of the hotel.

Two minutes later, two telephones rang simultaneously: one with the telephone operator at the King David, the other in the editorial office of the *Palestine Post*. On both, a female voice explained:

'I am speaking on behalf of the Hebrew underground. We

have placed an explosive device in the hotel. Evacuate it at once – you have been warned.'

Oblivious to the imminent threat, Daniel and Hannah were talking. He had instantly jettisoned all lunch plans as she began to tell him of her childhood, her parents, her love of music and dance.

He excused himself to the bathroom and stood at the urinals, contemplating how on earth he would ask this girl out on a date. Two senior officials were relieving themselves next to him. To Daniel's surprise, they were talking about the telephone threats to the hotel.

'Do you know they even tried to persuade me we should evacuate?' said the first.

The second man was an indignant as he was aloof. 'We don't take orders from the Jews.'

'Quite.'

Ben hurried back to the bar a changed man. But she was nowhere to be found. He circuited the bar and spied her chatting with the manager of the restaurant. A pang of jealousy hit, replaced immediately by fear. *He knew what they meant. A warning was a warning. The Night of the Trains had shown they meant business. This was deadly serious.*

They must leave, now.

He pulled her gently but firmly to one side. 'Come with me for a moment,' he smiled.

She grinned back and pulled away. *I have to get back to work.*

'You don't understand, we have to leave. We must leave.'

Hannah stared at the nice British man she was starting to like. She felt the gaze of her manager on her back.

'I'd love to come, I would—'

Exasperated, Daniel walked away. He would never forget the smile of regret that was on her face as he left. A little over ten minutes later, at 12.37 p.m., an explosion ripped through the southern wing of the hotel. All seven storeys were completely destroyed. Had Daniel returned to his office instead of the bar, he would have been prevented from leaving the building. In a show of confidence in their own intelligence, and scorn of all others, the majority of the government secretariat and command structure were in their rooms when the bomb went off. Hannah, in the bar below, was crushed to death by debris.

The next day, Daniel Sherman tried to resign from his post at MI6. His handlers would not permit it, so instead he made his position untenable. He found God and fled to Egypt, where he found the Coptic faith esoteric and sincere enough to atone for what he knew to be a great many sins.

Twenty years later, he was approached by a trusted source in London to act as a 'stepping stone' – a point of contact for British spies caught out by their governments, those seeking sanctuary from the poisonous world they had chosen.

Fifty-Two

F ather Daniel talked as they walked slowly through the graveyard. He was flanked by Jamie and Lucy. Ben brought up the rear, keeping one eye on the horizon around them and one ear on the gravel beneath their feet.

'We must be vigilant, of course. The security services are on alert after a spate of vandalism on these graves. It's usually blamed on the Jordanians for some reason but I understand they are trying to be more diligent these days.'

'How long have you been part of Contact Zero?'

'I have never been part of it. I believe it is part of me.'

'I still don't understand.'

'I second that,' muttered Jamie.

Daniel smiled. 'The problem with this city, you see. This is not a place to find answers, it's a place to find more questions.'

'But the message in the wall, the subterfuge . . .'

'Protection.'

'For whom?'

'For us, of course. For "them". It's no good having a network of intelligence officers – ex-intelligence officers, I should say – without having some means of testing people. This is a paranoid city. The fact that you managed to contact me without too much trouble is very encouraging.'

Daniel could see the three of them were hiding something. He decided not to pursue it. On the few occasions where he'd been summoned to brief new candidates, he found them not exactly willing to share their dirty secrets with him. Priest or no priest, confession was not easy.

'Did you hear about Contact Zero in training?'

'No. In the war.'

They were all listening now.

'So what is it?'

'We weren't sure, the same as I am now. I have never reached that far into the network. I simply know that this is where I belong, this is where I will stay. In the war, we had a safe-house network in France. It was run by the Resistance, but it had been assembled much earlier.'

'In the Great War?'

'Actually, rumour has it, in the sixteenth century.'

Lucy stopped walking to take this in.

'That long ago?'

'Have you by any chance,' asked Daniel, 'heard of a man called Christopher Marlowe?'

Ben cleared his throat. '*Dr Faustus. The Jew of Malta. Tamburlaine the Great.*'

'The very same.'

'We were given a sample by the Samaritans.'

'A little tease, I'm afraid. We are proud of our history. The rumour is, he was the one who began it. Contact Zero, I mean.'

'How on earth could he do something like that?'

'The man was a spy for Queen Elizabeth. He was sent to France to root out Catholic plots against Her Majesty. He pointed the finger at most of the plotters in Rheims while he was there on natural cover. When he was retired early, he protested. So they faked his death in Deptford – a drunken bar brawl, allegedly, and he swam the Thames to embark on another life. So the story goes.'

'Marlowe faked his death?'

'He didn't. Walsingham did, Sir Francis Walsingham, the Queen's spymaster. He sent him back to France to complete his mission. But the joke was on him – they had used him only to parley with the enemy. He had – and you'll appreciate this – ceased to be useful. He was part of a deal and he was compromised. So he fled into the night. By this stage, he'd amassed a small fortune from the stage and his various clandestine investments through the years. He used the money to set up a trust. A small but ever expanding network of safe houses. But not for official spies. For the likes of us. The ones who cease to be useful. The ones who fall through the cracks.'

'And that's Contact Zero?'

'That's how it *started*. What it is now, I believe I don't have much of an idea.'

Jamie sighed. 'That word again.'

'Started?' asked the priest.

'Believe,' said Jamie.

'You must be exhausted. Come. I'll waste no more of your time.'

Daniel removed a small sheet of paper from his robes but held it tight to his stomach for a moment.

'Our problem, as I see it, is that we are not dealing with monks. Holy men who recant their sinful lives and give themselves to God . . . they do not, on the whole, take orders lightly. In the case of intelligence work, there are often multiple masters, layers of the onion, if you like. Then there is the whole lying business. People – I'm sure you're surprised and shocked about this – lie all the time.'

'How awful,' murmured Ben under his breath.

'Contact Zero offers sanctuary. The ultimate refuge. But refuge from harm needs discipline to endure it, just as a life on the run requires it. We need individuals psychologically suited to a life in exile – not just from the country they love, but from themselves.'

'I thought that's what the Samaritans did,' said Jamie.

'They're just the sea wall. They stop us from being flooded. We are the filtering mechanism. We now know you're physically able to join our network – you've proved it by being here. But are you ready on the inside?'

'Of course,' said Jamie.

'Do you know the story of Rahab?'

Ben glanced at his watch. He was concerned the old man was savouring his stories too much. Time, he knew, was not on their side. Nat might even be released from custody soon. They could literally bump into each other on the street.

'Rahab. The harlot who helped the spies,' said Ben.

'The innkeeper, please. Everyone's so quick to judge a good-looking woman in this world. It always amazes me.'

'What about her?' asked Lucy.

'The story of Joshua and the spies is always referenced as a means to introduce the concept of the White Lie, the beneficial untruth. On the one hand, says religion, don't tell lies, lies are bad. On the other, Rahab is okay because her lies were good lies, they let good triumph. Therefore, where do you draw the line?'

He looked directly at Ben. There was no change in heart rate, no discernible nerves. Ben had been expecting it, in fact. In his experience of holy men, they always sniffed something untoward out of him – particularly if morals were on the menu.

'The less hurt there is in the world, the better, in my opinion,' said Ben.

'Well said, young man, well said,' smiled the priest, and handed him the paper. 'May we all protect ourselves from the slippery slope.' Lucy and Jamie peered in to read the document. When they had finished, Ben took out a lighter and watched the message burn into cinder and dust in the earth.

'I must leave you now. Be strong for one another and remember: sanctuary is sometimes only to be found within.'

'That's not very comforting,' said Jamie.

'It's not meant to be, I'm afraid.'

Fifty-Three

The Chief had called KB in for a nightcap. KB noticed his friend was drinking again, but was pleased to see the portions had diminished since their heyday. The Chief couldn't sleep all night, he'd been saying. He'd been running things over, and things were not good. The same question, turning over and over.

'Do you honestly believe that Bill's still alive?' asked KB.

'The man was not to be underestimated.'

'Don't you think, if Bill was alive, he'd have done something by now? He'd have made a move?'

The Chief drained his glass and refilled it. KB reviewed his position – *maybe the portions had reduced, but the frequency was still right up there.*

'Put yourself in his position. You place your trust in two men who betray you and leave you for dead. You know you possess information that could ruin them both. What do you do? Spring back immediately?'

KB shrugged. 'Possibly—'

'Or do you bide your time? Wait until you see them relax, gain security, build families . . .' The Chief looked around his office with some degree of melancholy and regret. 'And scale great heights. That would be the time to strike, no? Not when justice is swift, but when the fall is longest, hardest, cruellest.'

KB had gone a mild shade of green.

In all of his theorizing about Bill Tremayne, he'd never considered that he would play *such* a long game. Vengeance over time . . . does it multiply or divide? He'd always thought the latter. But now . . . the Chief's paranoia was infectious. He shook it off.

'I refuse to believe it. Why now?'

'Why not? What made your original choice call off work? Why did Marcus Tremayne get put in place? I saw his face and nearly had a heart attack.'

'Personally, Thomas, the resemblance doesn't bother me. He's received his marching orders.'

The Chief sighed deeply, a punctuation point to the discussion. He seemed mightily relieved.

'Then it's settled. Greco is not only useful, it's essential. Just one thing puzzles me. You selected one of the intake to be our agent in place.'

'Correct. He is leading the charge to Contact Zero. And when he discovers the truth, he will lead us to it. It is, after all, the plan.'

'How did you know he'd accept? The mission, I mean? After all you did sacrifice him – and his career – to Greco. Then you ask him to remain loyal to the organization who dropped him and betray the very people who are helping him stay alive?'

'In my book, everything is possible, Thomas. It's just a matter of planning.'

Fifty-Four

T hey calculated the level of risk they were taking against the need for speed and secrecy. A night bus through Israel was never a relaxing experience, but Ben and Jamie in particular insisted if they were to get to the next stage, relaxation should be the last thing on their minds. But Lucy was having none of it. They were taking a taxi.

What's more, she wasn't leaving the city without one last search for Nat. But he was nowhere to be found. His rucksack had been confiscated back at the hostel. And there was no way the three of them were sending out a search party.

Ben was spectating again. He wondered what it would feel like, watching himself tear apart on the inside. He wondered if he could ever make that happen.

He was aware of Lucy, inhaling slow, calming breaths as she walked beside him, and right at this moment Ben desired no more than this: to tell her everything. To open up inside, to account for all he was and all he was trying to do. There was no avoiding this outcome, he had wanted to say. How could it have been any different?

But he couldn't, of course. Not only was he loyal to those who donated loyalty first, he was a realist. They walked on towards the hotel, the taxi rank and the unknown.

The unknowables would announce themselves. But the certainties he knew: the people he'd given himself to had toyed with him, played with him, dropped him and betrayed him. His friends and his enemies, all had done the same.

All were responsible.

They had weaponized him, like a dose of anthrax.

The Gauntlet

Fifty-Five

I t was called the Gauntlet because of its severity. Like the live exercises during the previous 11 months of probation, the final assessment had no safety net. Unlike the others, there were no staffers on hand to take notes or assess progress. This mission was isolated, true, definitive. It was scheduled to last up to forty-eight hours and their final assessments were based in part on the dossiers the probationers would acquire during its duration.

It also required no small amount of stamina. Special Forces selections were often forty-eight or even seventy-two-hour marathons of sleeplessness and brutal physical effort. The MI6 gauntlet had a secondary challenge – finesse. This was not just a yomp across Dartmoor.

It was the defining moment of their lilywhite lives.

The first section involved a conventional business cover to Alexandroúpolis in northeastern Greece. From there, the team was tasked to cross covertly into Turkey, a tough assignment made more dangerous by the preponderance of unmarked landmine zones dotted around the border. Reaching the coast, they received a relay signal and located a dead drop that identified their supply landing zone. Camping out in the wilds, they laid infrared flares along a flat stretch of grassland and, despite Nat's insistence that their watches were slow, that night a drone appeared over their heads and a cargo plane flying in low over the Black Sea deposited two large supply containers on the infrared landing strip.

The cargo itself was simple. Inside were two inflatables with powerful dual-mode engines, and a new set of orders. The two teams divided up and synchronized their watches – the next time they'd meet would be Istanbul.

Silent and nervous as hell, the two teams set off into the choppy windswept chaos of the Black Sea. Jamie was charged with navigating the inflatable with Lucy, Ben, Chris, Nat and Dan hunching low on both sides through the moonless night, buoyed by tides and a sense of optimism.

Two hours later, they saw the crags of a rocky shoreline. They had passed the border into Bulgarian waters. If they took themselves too far north, they would hit a naval base near Sozopol. Their mission lay some fifty miles south along the coast. They kept as close as they could to the centre of a channel that split the shoreline in two and continued some ten miles inland. The channel narrowed as it turned west towards the interior; to the south, the shale and sand that made up the sea bed formed a rippling gradient that fanned gently up to the banks of sand and brush on the shore. This was their target and they were on time. Their inflatable was an eight-seater with a minimal draught that made it more a hybrid hovercraft than a boat, but the two silent outboard engines behind would not operate in depths under three feet, and so the engines were cut some sixty yards from the wash and the six of them slipped quietly into the freezing water to push the craft to shore.

Nat consulted his GPS handset and signalled the others to a spot four feet north of the highest band of silt, seaweed, driftwood and other detritus. Ben looked at him quizzically and gestured further up the shore to their right – there, the sand and brush melded together in twisted roots and weeds. Nat glared at him and pointed back at the spot in the sand. Without another glance in his direction, Nat ran quickly to the tree line and crouched down. He looked busy, but Ben knew full well the man was having a quick rest and trying to avoid what was coming next.

The remaining five crew members removed small shovels from their knapsacks and began to dig. An hour later, they had a hole some three feet deep and twenty feet in diameter, more than enough to contain the inflatable. Twenty minutes after that, the shoreline was clear of footprints. There was no sign that any human foot had touched this beach since the last high tide.

The other four members of their assault team were, according to Ben's watch, arriving right now on the other side of this promontory. They would conduct their exercise through the night and be gone by the time the sun came up.

This gave them four hours to complete the project.

More than enough time.

Then again, Nat was commanding officer.

They reached a hillside bluff that offered some respite from the unsettling wind that whipped at them from somewhere over Crimea.

The objective, in fact, lay some two miles to the north. A piece of new construction was under way, picked out by satellite photos shown to them in the warmth of Vauxhall Cross two days before. It was their job to survey the site, ascertain any potential military application, photograph it comprehensively and get out.

Nat tasked Lucy and Dan as the vanguard, with himself and Jamie as the conquering heroes, and Chris and Ben bringing up the rear as the also-rans.

The ground was uneven and Nat's pace was unsure. The site had no obvious security, and it was unclear whether the workers were staying on site. No canvas was visible, nor any vehicles. The team got to work and two hours later returned to the bluff. Nat was red-faced and peacock-like.

As they rounded the bluff and approached their landing site, his expression deflated. The beach had disappeared.

The six of them stood for a second and tried to make sense of it all. The area where Ben had indicated they should dig was still beyond the dark and ominous waters. But everything else was liquid.

The tide had come in.

And somewhere, down there, under several thousand tons of water, was the boat. Their only way out.

It took all of Lucy and Jamie's persuasion to talk Nat back from issuing an SOS. This was the most important challenge of their short careers, they argued. Eventually, Nat capitulated.

But once dawn approached, Ben knew their task would not be easy.

'We're exposed as hell out here,' he said to Jamie.

'Tell it to the captain, pal.'

Ben knew he was right and approached Nat, who was staring back down at the dark sloshing waters below the tide line.

'Don't say it,' he snapped as Ben approached.

Ben swallowed the slight and kept going.

'First light is two hours away. There's no cover out towards the site, and we don't want to risk being spotted by workers. Perhaps I should investigate the southern side?'

Nat stared at him. His eyes were watery and full of anger. Ben presumed the anger, while directed at him, was really a misfire. Nat was lambasting himself and he knew it.

'I was about to suggest the very same. Take Jamie with you. He knows what he's doing.'

The inference, Ben realized, was that he did not.

Ben and Jamie traversed the headland and found the perfect spot. Half a mile from their landing site, hidden from the construction to the north by patches of trees and a steep drop to the ocean, there was enough cover to camp and maintain sightlines in all directions, including the water. They reported back to Nat, who agreed.

Forty minutes later, they were dug in amongst the gorse and . . . Jamie peered out at the dark water and nudged Ben as he pointed. A faint rippling could be heard. Jamie fumbled for his infrared binoculars and picked out the second team heading for home. Ben shook his head, but said nothing.

'The Greeks called it the "inhospitable sea", you know.'

Ben shivered and saw that first light was approaching across the sea to Chechnya. 'Sounds about right,' he said.

As the night turned into morning, tempers began to fray. With no rations and no water, their situation was becoming problematic. Nat, despite his leadership position, seemed the crabbiest of all.

'My mouth is sealing itself shut,' he moaned. 'A cool glass of water, that's all I need.'

'Cup of tea might be nice too,' muttered Jamie.

'Or a croissant,' smiled Ben, 'with praline spread.'

Nat flashed them a fierce and petulant look.

As the light improved, car noise filtered over from the site, followed by the sound of light construction. The hammering and sawing continued through the day. Ben followed the arc of the sun in the shadows he saw in the long grass. Then, as night fell, the construction noise dissolved to nothing and the vehicles grumbled away once again. By Jamie's calculations they had another few hours and then the tide would have receded far enough for them to escape. Ben reasoned they might even score points for organization and lateral thinking. Despite Nat's basic mistake, they had completed the mission and were home free bar the waiting.

Nat seemed to have other ideas.

'I'm going to have to find some water,' he said. 'Or I'll die. Who's coming?'

The blank stares did not seem to dissuade him from his mission. As the stars came out overhead, he began to raise himself from their position and head for the edge of the trees. Jamie caught up with him.

'What the hell are you doing?'

'I can't function without some water. I'm serious, I'm fucking parched.'

'We're all fucking parched, mate. And we'll be in a Turkish bar in six hours. Leave it till then. Nice gin and tonic'll sort you out. Or whatever it is they serve down there.'

Nat seemed to hover, torn. Ben got to his feet and came over beside Jamie. The mere act of his standing seemed to turn Nat's head around. 'You can come with if you like, but I'm going. There's got to be a freshwater stream or something. Come on.'

Ben looked back at Lucy. She signed at him: *where are you going?* He signed back: *water divining. Back soon.*

It was like managing an impatient child. At several points Jamie had to physically squash Nat to the ground to avoid broadcasting his silhouette to anyone within a two-mile sight-line of their position.

A mile past the camp, they found a small track, possibly used by the construction workers. On the other side, another bluff, possibly a lake, although the light was playing tricks on them. A stream could be heard, trickling over stones. Nat shot the two men a victorious look and, before they could react, took off over the rocks and stones towards the sound.

As he stumbled near the source of the noise, a dog began to bark.

Nat froze and dropped to the ground. Ben and Jamie were already in cover. The dog continued to bark and Ben's stomach began to twitch as he saw a light come on behind the trees. Hidden from their line of sight, a small cottage lay some twenty yards behind the trees.

Moments later the beam of a flashlight probed the darkness. Ben knew if they kept in position, it was unlikely that the owner would venture out this far to check. But Nat had other ideas. He scrambled noisily to his feet and ran back to the two men.

The flashlight swung around and caught his ankle just as he dived to join the other two. A male voice shouted. No response. Another shout, followed by the sound of a pump-action shotgun being primed. Somewhere on the wind, Ben thought he also heard a baby crying.

This, Ben knew, was the time to run.

He threw a rock to the man's left and the three of them broke right and tried to rethread their steps through the rocky terrain and the darkness. The man heard them and set off in pursuit, shouting gruffly, presumably their third and final warning in Bulgarian.

They were fortunate, thought Ben, that the man had not released his dog. From the bark, it didn't sound like a tracker, simply a canine alarm bell. But the man was gaining on them. Perhaps he didn't need a dog.

Nat was running back towards the camp. Jamie yanked him up an incline that led back around to the bluff. Ben agreed with the idea. In the darkness, there were more places to hide, fewer sightlines even with a flashlight.

Ben could hear the man as he ran. The Bulgarian was softer

now, breathless. Ben heard an electronic beep and realized with horror that the man had just made a call on a cellphone. The police, Ben presumed. Or the army. With the naval base fifty miles up the coast, a chopper could be here in minutes.

The next few seconds, for Ben, occurred in slow motion. When he remembered them later, he could smell the salt air and hear the scrabbling sound of feet and hands against rock. But the panoramic tragedy was fluid, almost frozen.

The sound of the Yellow Pages ripping in two filled the air. Ben knew it well – it was the sound of ripping tendons. A yelp in the night air and the skittering smash of a flashlight on stone. The beam cut out and all was dark and silent.

Jamie froze too, holding Nat by the shoulder like a shepherd training a dog. Ben turned his gaze back to the bluff. The darkness showed only rocks, scrub. What looked like a mound of earth near the edge of a sharp drop was exactly that.

Below them, however, he could see another shape.

Face down in a series of rock pools, some thirty feet below down a steep drop, was the man. His hair wafted moonlight-grey in the pool. Blood soaked the rocks around him.

Nat appeared at Jamie's side.

'Fuck. Let's get out of here.'

'We have to go down,' said Ben.

'And screw up the mission? I don't think so.'

Screw it up any more than now, thought Ben, *and it hits the record books*. 'That man is drowning to death.' He turned to Jamie. 'Stay here for me, all right? I might need a hand up.'

Jamie nodded and slapped him on the back. Jamie was the mountain goat, but Ben knew the descent wasn't too difficult. He found copious handholds as he descended, and leapt to the ground beside the man. He turned him over and checked his pulse. He was still alive.

Perhaps a better way to put it was: he was dying, but not yet dead.

Unwilling to shout back up at the cliff, Ben thought for a moment about using the man's cellphone to call for medical attention. But a quick search revealed no more phone. In the dark, Ben wasn't sure where it could have ended up.

The man was bleeding, a head wound gaping and sighing thick warm pulses into the rock pool. There was nothing he could do. He scrambled back up to the top of the bluff, where Jamie yanked him up.

'He's dying,' said Ben.

'No phone?' asked Jamie.

Ben shook his head. They'd been thinking the same thing.

'We can call in from the radio,' said Ben.

'The tide,' hissed Nat. 'Come on!'

'No.'

Ben stood for a moment, torn again. A dying human being versus the dying human inside. He thought of the baby's cries from the cottage. Had someone just lost a father?

He was back in Bristol, back with John.

The blood in the gutter, the stream from the wound.

Torn in two. To stay or to go.

Just like this.

'We go back.'

'We call it in, Nat, come on. Who cares—'

'I care. And you will too if you don't obey my orders. I am the commander on this mission and I am instructing you for the final time to cease insubordination and adhere to my command. Is that understood?'

Ben pushed all thoughts of saving the man from his mind and followed Nat and Jamie back to camp.

Nat said nothing as they reached the others, throwing

himself into command mode again. Soon all six of them were back on the beach. The tide had receded just enough to allow them access. But it was still wet, sloppy, heavy sand, and unearthing the craft took longer than they thought.

Exhausted, wet and – he now saw – blood-soaked, Ben balanced on the inflatable as Jamie took them out of the headland and back into the Black Sea. The wind and the fog nearly froze him solid where he sat. Jason and the Argonauts had once sailed these waters in search of the Golden Fleece. Ben hoped he'd never see them again as long as he lived.

Back in London, the news was not good. The body had been found and, although there had been signs of a struggle and foreign prints at the scene, the murder case was demoted to the Bulgarian version of accidental death.

It didn't take long for an inquest to emerge. In order to assuage the furies of the upper tier, a summary series of interviews and debriefs was held.

Ben faced his inquisitor with courage and answered his questions honestly. The man was small and almost like a starling, Ben thought. He also sparkled reassuringly with a deep intelligence, a man who seemed to acknowledge his frustration at the tragic turn of circumstances, their political ramifications and their inherent and intractable sadness.

Ben had seen him through the months of training, even spoken to him. He hadn't given him a second thought, truth be told.

His name was KB.

Two weeks later, the same man called for him to come to his office. Ben knew the others had by now given their depositions. He wondered whether they might all have to do probation again.

'I'm afraid I have some bad news,' said KB as Ben entered. He didn't even have time to sit down.

'Okay.'

'The events of your selection weekend have resulted in a variety of very colourful accounts of the night. But one thing has been very clear. Everyone involved seems to blame you for what happened.'

Ben didn't hear what the man said next.

His eyes clouded, his stomach knotted in pain and he found himself fumbling for a seat. It was a standing wave of vertigo.

'Say again,' he gasped. 'Say that again.'

'The most damning testimonies were from the two men closest to the incident. Nat Turner and James Gallagher.'

'Jamie? But he was there—'

'Mr Gallagher in particular took pains to point out your lack of direction at a time of stress and your inability to follow orders.'

'The man was dying – we could have saved his life—'

'Both he and Nathan Turner felt that you allowed your past trauma with your brother to interfere on an SIS operation. Now I do not know what really happened on the exercise, but I should inform you that I disagree most strongly with the panel's recommendations,' said KB.

But Ben was no longer capable of listening.

'They were right there with me – it was his fault!'

KB shook his head, more at the situation, Ben could tell, than his sudden loss of decorum. He allowed Ben the space to compose himself. There were no tears, no visible signs of emotion. But the turmoil inside had clouded his mind. He walked to the window and stared out.

There was a filament of rage inside Ben now, glowing white; it drew itself up into his throat. He felt it might burn him from the inside out. His instincts controlled it, quelled it, but it scared him too to know, for certain, it was there.

'I understand how upset you must feel. From what you told me, there was more of a collective responsibility in this case. However, you were, I'm afraid, identified. There was until today a recommendation that you be released from the programme entirely.'

Ben stared at the man who held his future in his delicate little fingers.

'But I am vouching for you. No one likes rocking the boat. And there have been a few occasions when the Gauntlet, as I believe it's still called, gets a little . . . knotty. So this is what I propose . . .'

Ben listened quietly as the man with the large grey eyes saved his professional life. He could stay on, the man explained, and graduate from the probationers' programme. The man added that although it might be difficult to find a maiden posting for him, he would personally underwrite it.

He would do this because he respected Ben's strength.

In the midst of disloyalty and betrayal, he held his own and did his job.

It was madness to allow such a candidate to slip through SIS fingers. KB was decided. He had spoken to the Chief and vouched for Ben's continued service. The Chief had, in turn, assessed the situation and awarded him a clean bill of health, plus a first posting. What happened after that was up to Ben.

KB patted him on the shoulder as Ben absorbed the news. 'This is a place you belong,' he explained.

Ben asked him if there was anything else he could do. The man said there was. One day, he said, at some point, he would ask Ben to do him a favour in return.

Fifty-Six

Tremayne was disappointed but not surprised. He had been sure his appeal to the Chief would have been received at least with a modicum of appreciation.

But no, no, and no. There was no room for whistleblowers in office politics. A bureaucracy welcomes criticism as much as a mafia family loves gossip. Their threats, Tremayne knew, were only lip service. They wanted him out of the picture and they'd found a corporate way to do it.

The Chief and KB watched him go from the atrium, clutching a black bag and escorted by Kevin Meades towards the security gates for the last time. The emails KB himself had sent from Tremayne's terminal had forced poor Sara Turnbull, after some encouragement, to complain of harassment.

Which, they had explained to a confused and bitter Tremayne, left them no choice.

They watched Tremayne pass through the gates and leave, his shadow disappearing around the corner.

'Satisfied?' said KB.

'I think you were foolish to even consider the man for the job.'

'As you may recall,' said KB, 'as far as everyone was concerned at the time, there was no job. By causing any ripple at all, I was putting myself in danger. I doubt he even knew his father that well.'

'Any news?'

'What kind of news are you talking about?'

The Chief flicked his eyes to a passing suit and smiled.

'You know what kind I mean.'

'I told you, he's been tasked to find it. When he does, he'll let us know. You don't leave burst transmission beacons turned on 24–7, you know. They tend to attract attention.'

The big house was echoing more than usual when the key turned in the lock. His breath was a mist in front of his face. Grand and old and frozen like an ice floe, the halls were full of memory, even now. Here, where his father once strode noisily through the night, always working, never ceasing, it now stayed silent and echoed only to the dustpan and brush of Joan, the help.

A letter was waiting for him in his tray, placed there no doubt by Joan in a fit of organization. Oddly, it had no stamp. But perhaps a messenger had delivered it and Joan had kindly taken it in.

Tremayne opened it and stared. Inside, a plain bonded sheet. Addressed to him and dated that day, an invitation to a fishing trip. What made the thing so shocking was that it addressed him by his childhood nickname. What's more, it was all rendered in the forceful steady lines of his dead father's handwriting.

Contact One

Fifty-Seven

Stamp's dream was interrupted by the phone. His arms pockmarked to pincushions, he resembled a shamed priest in a brown cotton cardigan that hung awkwardly from his bony shoulders. Asleep, his mouth gaped open, a small sliver of drool spreading lazily over his mound of 500 thread-count pillows. His phone was set to vibrate. It was buried under a rosewood suede jacket that was folded in his Puma bag. The bag was on the sofa in the living room. Despite these insulations, Stamp still heard it as clearly as a B-movie scream. He had no problems with the call, a text message from a person he had never met nor had any wish to.

That said, he did enjoy social contact. It was always an education to see people up close with the naked eye. Just so long as no one tried to shake his hand. Proximity had its downsides. Stamp lived well in a large house with dark walls and echoes. His footsteps were light so as not to wake his neighbour and alert her to his existence so early in the morning. She knew what normally happened when he left so early and he didn't want her to worry.

He looked at the message that had just arrived and concluded there was still time for breakfast. Stamp had once lived a life of regret and poverty and had been making up for it ever since. This included his heroin. Take needles, for example. There were addicts who blindly pumped their cheap drugs into their bloodstreams like porn stars. Stamp sought out only the best. As a young man he'd worked as a nurse in a drop-in centre in Soho. His understanding of his own musculature and blood flow was such that he could administer an intraspinal injection to himself practically whilst doing jumping jacks in the dark.

It was a great myth that all drug paraphernalia was much like any other. You wouldn't do the Dakkar Rally on a Vespa, he would argue; you wouldn't suck Margaux or Pomerol up with a straw. Class A drug use was much the same. Stamp's morning routine consisted of simple, high-end equipment. First, a 'bluetip' – a 25 g insulin needle offering a minimal puncture wound but solid product flow. In addition he had located a manufacturer who had happily lengthened the bevel slightly with a laser, allowing for a more comfortable angle of entry. Second, a small customization on his part, a 2 cc Pyrex syringe barrel, nearly double the standard size, offering both the convenience of dishwasher-safe cleaning with what was for Stamp the equivalent of a venti caramel latte with extra foam. Most importantly, of course, the drug of choice had to be pure. Stamp had once exacted a cruel revenge on two men who had tried to pass off brown tar heroin to him as something much more luxurious. They hadn't anticipated his customized needle set – which clogged up with anything less than premium grade.

After washing his hands with antibacterial soap, Stamp would then use a stainless-steel heirloom teaspoon, filter the drug through a carefully shaped circle of Indian cotton and dissolve the substance in pre-boiled Evian, adding a small dab of powdered vitamin C to speed things along. His morning tourniquet was normally an old blue Hermes tie of great sentimental value, pulled tight in a slip knot with his gleaming white teeth.

Stamp normally prepared his morning hit listening to the

BBC World Service. Today, there was a programme about farming in Zambia. After a vigorous cleanse of his cratered forearm with an alcohol swab, he laid it out on the cool granite slab of his kitchen counter, tapped away the air bubbles and, as he learnt how mechanization was helping tobacco and maize make a comeback for smallholders, injected $500 worth of heroin into his bloodstream. He would repeat this three more times during the day. The only things that changed were the radio programme and the colour of the tie.

He considered himself not so much a heroin addict as an enthusiastic yet consistent aficionado. For some it destroyed their careers, their lives, their libidos and their health. For Stamp, it only seemed to augment his existence in every single way.

His introduction to it could not have been easier.

Working for British Intelligence in the Balkans had been about as stressful as it was possible to get. Stamp had first been assigned duties stopping arms shipments from Hezbollah reaching distribution hubs like Mostar. They came in through the Croatian islands, via shrines like Medjugorje, and out to those who paid for them. He began to learn the way guns and drugs were almost a barter economy. Each could be sold on, retaining its value.

Then came Kosovo, and Stamp found himself liaising with the KLA, the Kosovo Liberation Army, whose armed struggle was also funded mostly by drugs.

It didn't take long for the pressure-cooker work to push Stamp to jettison vodka in search of a new way to release the pain. ███████████, a friendly contact in the KLA, informed him he knew just the way to do it. Stamp joined him in his farmhouse for a night that wiped his tortured consciousness clean for a few hours. He awoke the next morning to a new purpose – to repeat that experience again, again, again, again.

Six months of cheap smack rendered Stamp incapable of active duty. Despite his strong network of contacts, there was nothing he could do to rehabilitate himself. Rather than manage his addiction and come to his aid, his MI6 handlers tried to frame him for smuggling the stuff himself, informing the UN contingent who in turn passed his details on to Interpol.

Stamp was conscious enough of his handlers' bad feeling to jump town before they got to him. Friends in the old smuggling routes took him away and a period of cold turkey – in Turkey, as it happened – gave him enough clarity to seek sanctuary from people who knew the meaning of betrayal. Contact Zero. Ten years later, he found himself here. Happily reunited with his drug and grudgingly affiliated to a network that had admittedly been good to him, despite its sniffy attitude to his daily grind. They probably resented the fact that Stamp didn't need their money – he had discovered something that many other ex-spies had not. If you knew how to play the game just right, crime didn't only pay, it did so frequently, in large amounts.

Stamp released the pressure on the plunger and felt the euphoria tingle down his spine and dissipate out to his fingertips. There was a sense of excitement about the day already. He flushed a blood-spotted cotton swab down the toilet and assumed one of the many yoga asanas he found prolonged the flow of the drug around his system. If the contact had been correct, he would expect a delivery by midnight.

Fifty-Eight

C ollins watched the old man in robes limp away. Adjusting the scope, she refocused on the group, who she noticed had an intent about them she had not seen since leaving Brazil. She also noticed Ben Sinclair absent-mindedly smoothing out an area to the right of his stomach. She knew Ben was supposed to have a transmitter – she was babysitting the man after all. But that was sloppy tradecraft. It was like touching your wallet when you're scared of pickpockets.

She tailed the three of them to the youth hostel. *Perhaps searching for number four?* She felt scorn for the sentiment. If I was them, she thought, I'd keep moving as fast as I can.

She found another vantage spot – this place was full of them – and followed their progress towards the north side of the city. She was about to pull back and pack up when Jamie stared right into her lens.

She hit the deck and froze. Waiting a few seconds, she peered through the viewfinder again. The three of them were walking away now, back towards the hotels on the other side of the city wall. Collins looked for any other signs of curiosity. Just as they turned the corner – there it was. Another casual glance in her direction. He looked confused, however, and Collins surmised she had not been seen.

It still took her heart a few minutes to calm down. Taking a taxi from a rank outside the Metropole, the trio were suddenly in a great hurry. Collins had also noticed a small but telling moment as the three got into the cab. Jamie had invited Ben to get into the back seat after Lucy. But Ben had refused. Jamie had then got into the car, followed by Ben. The front seat of the car was not on offer, she could tell from the plastic screen divider in the front. But why the musical chairs? Collins suddenly remembered the small gesture – the touching of his side.

There was no reason to feel awkward about sitting flush against someone else unless you were worried about what they might discover when they pressed against you.

Collins hailed a cab from the same rank. She instructed the driver to obey her directions and look forward to a hefty tip if he kept silent for the entire journey. The man look one look into Collins's hard green eyes and nodded.

The tip was going to be huge. There were nearly sixty miles on the clock by the time Ben, Lucy and Nat were dropped off at the port of Ashdod. But it was time, not money, that was more valuable to them. Obeying the priest's instructions to the letter, they registered for a tourist cruise that would take them up and around the coast towards Tel Aviv.

They were in no mood to talk. Leaving Nat behind had been hard on all three of them – in different ways – and the cab journey had been a sustained and icy stretch of silence.

Ben felt the plaster peeling off again.

He had only a few Band-Aids left to secure the transmitter to his side. He thought about wrapping a bandage around him, even taping the thing down. But the plaster offered a quick removal in emergencies, and he decided to stick with it for the time being.

They were looking for the Sunset Cruise line. After a

worrying few minutes walking up and down the advertising hoardings, Jamie spotted a bored-looking ticket hawker by a small sign with a tiny English translation.

It didn't seem like it, but Father Daniel had implied that this was the safest way to their next contact. They boarded at four o'clock. The sunset cruise to Tel Aviv was more of a party boat than a chance to contemplate the rotation of the earth. Ben and Jamie fended off the attentions of a couple of girls from NYU; Lucy had the same pleasure with a virologist from the Ben Gurion University.

As the sun began to die, the captain announced that it was 'time to get wet'. Almost as one, half the boat disrobed and leapt into the sea. Ben, Lucy and Nat looked at each other in panic. This was not something they had anticipated at all.

Ben, in particular, was beginning to look pale.

'Okay, shirts off, into the water.'

'We're fine, thanks,' smiled Lucy. 'All the same.'

'Come on,' grinned the first mate, 'live a little.'

'Honestly, this is perfect,' said Jamie, rubbing his face, trying to summon a scintilla of bonhomie.

The first mate leant in close, eyes sparkling.

'If you don't get in the water, it won't work for you.'

From somewhere he could not see, he heard the *chug-chug* of a diesel engine. The first mate could hear it too and flashed him a knowing look.

Suddenly Ben understood – they were to transfer to another vessel around the next headland. Panic seized Ben when he foresaw the practicalities – he realized that descending to an inflatable and boarding another boat would be too much of a strain on the plaster.

If the thing came off, the transmitter was going to Davy Jones's locker.

Jamie interrupted Ben's train of thought. 'They're going to waterproof our bags,' he explained. 'Lucy can go with them in the boat. The two of us should hop in the drink like the others and play snorkellers. That way we can go over with Lucy and keep the boat steady.'

He was already stripping off.

Ben hesitated because the motion of the boat and the nerves in his stomach were pitching and yawing and unsettling the hell out of him.

'Come on, mate, chop chop—'

'In a minute, all right?'

Jamie eyed Ben sceptically as he rolled up his shirt and shoved it in the top pocket of his rucksack. The first mate took hold of it and wrapped it tightly in Cellophane before adding it to the others, both already encased in their own clear plastic chrysalis.

Ben saw Jamie and Lucy talking to the captain and then to each other. A look between them sealed it. They were going. Jamie beckoned him. Ben made the international sign for 'dodgy stomach' and pointed to the stairs below. He flashed three fingers – *three minutes!* – at Jamie, who rolled his eyes but lingered.

When Jamie and Lucy turned away again, Ben scurried below, down the stairs and into the less than delightful head. The ship's toilet was a low-slung chemical nightmare, and the space so small that Ben's elbows were thudding against the sides as he felt for the transmitter.

He wondered whether it would be worth the risk of transferring it into his moneybelt or even a small zip pocket in his rucksack.

But if it was loose, it could be searched, dropped or – worse – found.

He decided that he would make contact and demand delivery of another. It was a ridiculous way of doing things, he thought, and if he gave it any more concern it would distract him. He ripped off the plaster and clenched it in his fist.

He flushed the head to keep up appearances and returned to the deck where Jamie was waiting to haul him up.

'Shirt off and in we go! Come on!'

Jamie's hand missed a small metallic portion of the transmitter by a centimetre. Ben grinned, nodding, as he could see Lucy crouching unsteadily on a small inflatable that had been lowered from the back of the boat.

In the water all around, men and women were swimming, laughing, snorkelling.

Jamie stood at the edge of a ladder that led down into the water. The other vessel, another pleasure cruiser, was idling innocently some hundred yards away. The two craft looked interested in one another, but not connected.

Ben realized that he had no way of disposing of the transmitter until he was safely immersed. And to do that, he needed to be close to Jamie and follow him in. Ben waved at Jamie – 'in you go, you're making me nervous for fuck's sake' – and wished he'd just flushed the stupid thing down the head.

It also didn't help that Lucy was staring at him now.

'You okay?' she called from the boat.

Behind them, it was party time in the water. The perfect blend of innocent and highly suspect activity in the Med. A powerful outboard started up – Jamie turned to look, as did Lucy – and Ben seized his moment, walking to the side to pretend to get a closer look, and releasing his grip on the transmitter in the process.

He heard the *plop*. He wasn't sure anyone else had.

But Jamie and Lucy were still distracted. Jamie glanced

back, irritated now. And Ben stripped to his shirt and his boxer shorts. He walked confidently over to Jamie who was now clambering down the ladder.

'You're wearing that in the water?'

'Don't want any sun on my back,' Ben explained, hoping it sounded convincing. Jamie shrugged, happy he had his escort. The two men sank into the lukewarm water and swam alongside Lucy, who navigated the small inflatable over to the second cruiser.

The transfer took less than fifteen minutes.

They were hauled into the second craft by older men in a hurry. As soon as Jamie's foot left the ladder at the back of the craft, they were chugging away again round the headland. Lucy checked the horizon for signs of navy or coastguard. A deck hand smiled at her. 'Home free,' he said.

'That's the idea,' she replied.

She shivered in the breeze, splashed by the foam from the powerful engine. She glanced down at Ben, who was bending down to inspect his rucksack. The water clung to his boxer shorts, showing every nuance of his lower body.

She noticed the shock of the water hadn't been too shocking, at least on him.

Ben looked up to see her looking.

Jamie, towelling off to the starboard side, saw the entire exchange.

It took them over sixteen hours to reach the island of Korčula, an island just off the Croatian coast northwest of Dubrovnik. As they approached, Jamie explained that several of the usual suspects from his placement in Odessa had passed through this place many times. Business was as brisk as it was brutal. Odessan gangsters liked to kill with the silenced Glock and the Uzi. Croatian gangsters preferred to kill with their bare hands. Like the lamb you slaughter for the pot, they would say, 'the meat is always sweeter when it breaks under your own fingers.'

The priest had given them an address on the island. He admitted he didn't know who the contact was. This was the inherent frustration for the spy on the run – each contact was a stepping stone along the way. But the stones themselves could only see one step ahead. At this address, Father Daniel had explained, they were to announce a password and accompany the occupants to the mainland town of Dubrovnik.

The boat bypassed the forty other pleasure cruisers vying for space in the island's exquisite marina and moored instead around the coast in one of the hundred quiet coves. Without a word, the crew lowered their inflatable and, diving in, towed it to shore and deposited the bags. Rowing back to the craft, they loaded Lucy, Jamie and finally Ben and took them into the shallows. Half an hour later, the boat had disappeared again around the headland, its engine still thrumming in its wake.

The farmhouse was set back from the main road, a few miles outside the main town of Korčula, a stunning old city that reminded Ben of Mdina in Malta, with perhaps the old roofs of Cuzco. It was possible of course that the courier had set them up and led them directly into a trap. But the mental and physical exhaustion that descended on the trio moved them into a more direct approach. They took a cursory stroll around the property. It seemed to be innocent enough.

Lucy strode towards the door and knocked heavily. Ben and Jamie held back. It was far less threatening to have Lucy do the preliminaries.

The door was answered by a woman holding a caterwauling

baby. From Ben and Jamie's viewpoint, she appeared to be pointing down the road. Lucy smiled, thanked her and left.

'Wrong house,' she explained. 'It's that way—'

Jamie looked behind her and saw two men stride out from the side of the house with high-powered rifles. Ben saw the men too. The rifles were pointed at them.

Fifty-Nine

The standoff at the farmhouse abated as soon as Lucy shouted the code word. The woman who'd answered the door, it seemed, had not understood Lucy's faltering accent and instructed her husband to defend her.

The two men walked to a van and unlocked the back. They disappeared into the house and emerged once more with two large rucksacks. Placing the bags under an old rug in the back of the vehicle, they threw the keys to Ben and clambered into the front. Then it was suddenly clear what was being asked of them. They were a taxi service. Ben quietly handed the keys to Jamie, but Lucy grabbed them.

The men directed her in grunts and shouts – left, right, yes, no, straight – until they reached the car ferry which took them to Orebic, on the Pelješac peninsula.

From there, Lucy followed the signs to Dubrovnik. The old city was a walled sanctuary from the sea, a patchwork of red roofs and gleaming stone.

On arrival the men from Korčula unloaded the van, then struggled under the weight of the two rucksacks as they walked.

'Any thoughts at this time?' whispered Jamie.

'None,' said Ben. 'Let's just do what they ask.'

'I'm glad you're so comfortable with that,' said Lucy.

The men flanked the trio once they were in the main square.

The marble tiles on the ground practically glowed in the sunlight – all around were bell towers, high apartments, glorious architecture.

They kept walking until they reached a café at the entrance to a long, narrow street flanked on either side by high apartments and offices. Sitting in a miserable semicircle, Ben, Jamie and Lucy watched their new business partners drink endless coffees. The square was audible from here and still clearly full of tourists. Hours passed. As the sunlight waned, the sound of the crowds thinned out.

One of the men scribbled a name on a scrap of paper.

He followed it with an address. He pointed at the words and then at them.

'We're going there?' asked Lucy when she saw it.

The men nodded – but when Lucy began to pick up the rucksacks, they slapped her hands away, grumbling in Serbo-Croat. Without Nat, there was no communication here. Both Jamie and Ben bristled, but Lucy had it under control, grabbing the man's wrist and staring right back at him.

With enough respect earned, she released her grip.

'A sixth sense tells me we need to fetch someone,' said Ben.

The men gestured again. *Go and bring back*, he was saying, it seemed.

'Okay,' said Ben, 'how do you want to do this?' As he spoke, Ben realized that the longer he left it without calling back for another transmitter, the more he risked hitting Contact Zero without any means of communication with KB.

'Well,' said Jamie, 'let's go see what they say. My feeling is, they'll be the second part of this piece of commerce.'

'I think so too,' said Lucy.

Ben didn't mean to, but he touched Lucy's hand as he

362

gestured towards their companions. 'Let me stay then. Make sure these lads don't get up to anything.'

Jamie considered it for a moment, and perhaps welcomed the chance to get away from Ben and have Lucy to himself. Lucy seemed to feel the same way.

'Done,' said Jamie.

They both hurried off into the maze of stone and tiles of Dubrovnik. Ben waited for two full minutes before moving. There was a payphone on the inside of the café, near the gents' toilets. The men probably had cellphones, but he didn't want to chance asking them – a conversation on how to split the bill might last all week. He bought a coffee for the change and filled the phone up with pieces of silver.

He felt like an animal at a watering hole. Huge focus in one direction could mean no focus in another – and mean the end of it all. So the eyes flicked and circled to ensure no predators intruded – it was lucky they did—

Lucy was walking back into the square.

He was about to replace the receiver when he remembered these payphones disgorged their spare change in a noisy torrent after disconnection. So he placed the receiver on top of the phone and picked up his coffee in one smoothly timed movement. Her gaze settled on him just as he strolled idly outside, as if quietly ready to enjoy his caffeine hit after a bathroom break.

'So soon?' said Ben.

She glanced at the phone but was too adrenalized for the thought to land. 'We're ready to go.'

The men kept on with the refrain – *bring them here*. So, as the crowds thinned out even more, they moved back out to the shadows of the narrow street. Ben's mind still buzzed with the near miss, not to mention the missing transmitter. He would simply have to plan a little better next time. But there would be a next time.

There would have to be. And soon.

Ten minutes later, two more backpackers arrived, with Jamie. At first they smiled, nodding at the fellow travellers in front of them. But they looked a little out of place in their hiking gear.

The men from Korčula stepped forward and took the rucksacks from the new arrivals, opening a zip pocket briefly to gaze inside. The 'travellers' did the same with the other rucksacks.

Ben was still trying to work out who was doing what to whom when the shots rang out.

An automatic. Long range.

The man beside them exploded in a fountain of red. Before the other three men could react, three more kill shots had floored them in a matter of seconds. Ben wheeled around and scanned the rooftops – this was a sniper. And a very good one.

Lucy had also realized this and pushed both Ben and Jamie flush against the wall. They stood bloodied, frozen in shock amongst the fallen men and blood-soaked bags. Almost immediately a Range Rover roared out of a cross street, lights blazing. Jamie was ready to run but Ben saw the weapon pointed from the window. At this range, with this shooter, it was suicide.

'The bags,' came a reedy voice from a doorway.

They could do nothing but stare—

'The bags!'

Still they couldn't locate the sound.

'Put them in the back and get in. Do it or you're dead.'

The bags flew in and they clambered in with them. The car roared out of the square, and through the old streets as if it owned the city. Which, given the income of the man at the wheel, was quite possible.

Sixty

T hey could not make out much from his profile, but he had a languid confidence to him, a brown sweatshirt on bony shoulders. His driving was fast, entitled, suicidal. They flew past the old city and north, through the modern heart of the town that extended in both directions on the coast.

'Very nice,' the man said suddenly, pulling into a small cove off the highway. A drain led from here to the ocean, masked by trees. 'Come along.'

Ben glanced at Jamie and Lucy and saw they were as terrified as he was. The man opened up the back and began hefting a rucksack from between their bodies.

'I thought you were here to help. *Come on.*'

Ben slid out and grabbed hold of another rucksack. The man stopped him with an iron grip.

'Not those ones. Just the dirty ones.'

He tapped the second rucksack that one of the men from the island had carried. Ben followed the man to the drain. The man opened the rucksack to reveal bag after bag of white powder.

'Yes, it's what you think it is,' he said as Ben stared. The cash value of these bags was staggering. 'Now shut up and help.'

And the man began to do a very strange thing – he was dumping the drugs. Ben's face must have prompted him again.

'Please.'

As Jamie and Lucy watched, Ben and the man unloaded the white powder into the drain. As a final act, the man placed both rucksacks in an oil drum nearby, doused them with petrol and set them alight. Clambering back into the car, he turned and faced the three of them sitting stunned in the back.

'It's not pretty, I know. But people like us need to take what we can get, don't you think?'

He drove for an hour along the coast to a small village framed by trees and the light stone walls they had seen in Dubrovnik. A narrow lane skirting a row of modest garages served as a temporary parking space. The man opened one of the garages and hefted the remaining backpacks into the darkness.

'Well then,' he squinted, 'who's hungry?'

Lucy had heard of the addict officer Stamp. As part of their ongoing mental health management, the staff at MI6 regularly employed Service-sanctioned psychiatrists to share their thoughts on the pressures of the job. One such psychiatrist had used the Balkans as an example of 'what not to do'.

They were eating dinner in Stamp's palatial apartments overlooking the Adriatic. He'd offered them showers, a change of clothing, and dinner. They had taken him up on everything, although, he noticed, they kept watch for each other too. Very sweet. He could feel the accusing stares from the other side of the table and smiled, rolling up his arms to show off his scars. He knew what they were thinking and he didn't care.

'I don't know what the others have told you,' he explained between mouthfuls of organic beetroot salad, 'but I can guess. Stay true to yourself, sanctuary is both within and without . . . all that crap.' His accent was a bizarre cross of East End barrow boy and a prelate from the Whispering Gallery. Talking to him

366

was like talking to someone from beyond the grave. Every conversation was a séance.

He sipped a Pinot Noir he'd been saving from the cellar and pined for a hit. He knew he should wait, however. These kids were suffering slightly from sensory overload. 'I, you may have realized, am not an idealist. I am a realist.'

'Just tell us what we need to know,' said Ben.

'Not so simple, tiger, not so simple. I've not had able-bodied helpers around for a while. You want the next contact. I know you do. I have it. But first you do something for me.'

'We already have.'

'You've been to trade shows? This neighbourhood is sort of the same. Round "these parts", it's an equal proportion of Westerners, Russians and pornographers. Intelligence, drugs and the sex industry all intersecting under your feet. Since you're here, and staying with me, I'd appreciate a favour in return. After that, of course, I'd be happy to sort you out.'

'May I ask a question?' said Lucy.

'That's very . . . American of you,' said Stamp, smirking. 'But yes, you "may".'

'Is this what you do now? Set up drug deals, kill all participants and take the proceeds?'

'In a word, yes. I know it sounds like a teenager caught smoking by their mother, but . . . everybody's doing it. And as you saw, I bin the filthy stuff afterwards.'

'And keep the money.'

Stamp shrugged, gesturing at the antiques that lined the walls.

Ben stood up from the table and examined a mask on the wall. 'Ethiopian?' he asked.

'Rwandan, I think,' smiled Stamp, returning to his salad. Before Jamie or Lucy could react, Ben was behind the man with his bread knife pressed hard against his oesophagus. The serrated edge nudged into Stamp's leathery flesh without cutting it. Ben realized he would have to apply a great deal more pressure if he wanted to do some damage – the man's throat was like a turkey's . . . all sinew and gristle.

'I am tired of making small talk,' growled Ben.

Stamp chuckled.

'Now that's more like it. A fellow realist. Bravo. Keep going.'

'You might have paid off the local law enforcers around here, but we are sitting ducks. We have been through too much to sit here and take this from you. We are not your fall guys.'

'Bravo again,' said Stamp.

'Who do we speak to? Where do we go?'

'You go to where the money is, my friend.'

'Where's that?' asked Lucy, glancing up at Ben, who was still holding tight.

'In the cupboard there. Right-hand drawer.' Stamp was gesturing to the hand-carved French oak drop-down eighteenth-century bureau. Jamie walked over and opened it. Inside, a cigarette case.

'Bring me the fags.'

Jamie brought them back over but kept them on his side of the table.

'You can let go of me now, you've done your negotiating.'

Ben stepped back but did not return to his seat. The knife stayed out and his eyes did not leave Stamp.

'Just keep your hands where I can see them,' said Ben.

'Will do, Detective,' smiled Stamp, knowing what was coming next. He turned his smile on Lucy, who was holding the metal case between her fingers. 'Go on, my friend, open it.'

She popped the case open. Inside were two business cards from a Swiss bank in Zurich she'd not heard of before.

'It's a family affair, very discreet,' continued Stamp. 'They do all my banking too.'

On the back of each card was a handwritten number.

'You should open a bottle of bubbly you know. You're so very nearly there. Mazaltovulations.'

Ben felt a surge of panic. If this was their end point, he needed to get his hands on another transmitter. But so far the chances of contacting the SOS number he'd been furnished with had been negligible. Too much risk.

A road trip to Switzerland, however . . .

That might prove possible.

'This network needs worker bees. Every month, ten thousand dollars is deposited in each account. The pact is sealed once you take money out for the first time. The agreement's pretty straightforward. For half the year, you make yourselves available to the network for deniable operations around the world. They've got an arrangement with most risk-management firms. They prefer to use us fuckups as there is no history of corporate espionage on our part – at least not much – which there can be with recent stand-up retirees of the Service who might jump ship to another operator. We're low maintenance, apparently. We offer a strings-free team of extremely able operatives who can be deployed anywhere in the world within minutes if necessary. Explains quite a lot that goes on in the world, if you ask me.'

Lucy struggled to keep up. 'And you're part of this?'

Stamp might have heard her, but he wasn't paying attention. 'You know . . . you jump through hoops. Get your badge and your certificate. Then, once you're free, they say – you have to earn your keep. Think of it like fishing, they say. Give a man a fish, he can eat for a day. Teach a man to fish and he can eat for a lifetime – well, no, actually. They have to fucking well get up

369

in the morning and bloody well fish, don't they? Otherwise, they starve. Or until overfishing ensures fish stocks plummet. Still, better than nothing, right? Fuck, no. I signed up, joined, whatever you want to call it. But work for a living? For them? No thank you very much.' He turned to Lucy, apparently aware of her question for the first time. 'I am part of the network, but I don't take their coin. I make my own money, freelance. As you can see.'

Ben noticed in the ornate mirror behind Jamie's head that dawn was approaching. He saw his own reflection framed there and a wave of intense loneliness broke hard and square in his chest. He felt now as he'd felt that day on the pavement, his brother's life seeping into the gutter, his own voice caught in his throat. Was that what their lives were to become?

He heard Lucy speaking and inhaled deeply.

'But there are only two cards here. And three of us.'

Stamp looked up at Ben, then back to Lucy and Jamie on the other side of the table. Somewhere, a grandfather clock chimed four.

'Yes.' His eyes were glittering. Discomfort, it seemed, was a sorbet to him. 'I was getting to that.'

From the rocky shore, Collins kept watch. She'd already popped enough crystal meth to make her heart power the city's electricity for a week. She'd noticed the move with the knife in the bay window. Impressive. Nothing like the kill shots in the square, of course. That was Olympic stuff. For the first time in her life, Collins felt that she truly desired an autograph.

Her attention flicked to a police launch skimming calmly along the waters off the coast. By the time she'd looked back at the orange light of the window, the figures had gone.

Damn it.

She scrambled back up the rock and caught a glimpse of the foursome as they stood on the balcony. For a second, Collins thought she felt another gaze levelled back at her.

Sixty-One

S tamp excused himself from the discussion to savour a hit in the bathroom. As he tied his green hospital-grade tourniquet in a celebratory double bow, he wondered if it really was that easy to fool an intelligence officer these days.

He exhaled slowly as the plunger plunged, and sank quietly into downward-facing dog.

Outside on the balcony, futures were being decided. Jamie was looking out to sea as first light approached, gripping the railings and shaking his head. The reality was as brutal as it was clear. There were two places left at the next stage. One of them would have to stay behind.

Lucy had already formulated a farewell speech. But Jamie had beaten her to it.

'I won't listen to you,' said Jamie. 'I've made my decision.'

'But here, Jamie? Him? The man is a scumbag,' said Lucy.

'The closer we get to this Contact Zero thing . . . the more I'm wondering whether it's even something I *want* any more.'

Ben shook his head, but Jamie wasn't finished. He was focused on Lucy now.

'I don't have to stay with him. I don't have to do anything but find my way. It's beautiful here. I'll work it out.'

'Please . . .'

'Ben. Tell her I don't change my mind.'

Ben was relieved Jamie had volunteered so quickly. He was

not looking forward to justifying his place in front of Lucy. He shrugged and nodded, as he knew that those gestures were what was expected of a normal human being, betraying normal emotions.

'It's true, Lucy.'

'I don't care.'

'Just promise me you'll get there. Whatever it is. Animal, vegetable, mineral. Put it on the newsgroup. Our message board. That's still allowed, surely?'

'We'll try our best.'

When Stamp emerged back outside, he was as loose as a marionette. His pupils near perfect black ovals. A small trickle of blood ran down his forearm. In his state, he hadn't even bothered to clean himself up. Life was proceeding very well, and if he played his cards right, he might have an assistant for a few weeks.

'So,' he slurred, holding on to the French doors, 'do we have a winner?'

Ben bought a used car from a local garage. He realized with some concern that their coffers were now seriously depleted. Without Jamie's share of the float, they were starting to run out of money – and time. He quelled the temptation to snipe at her when he arrived. *She's no soft-top Mercedes, I know* . . .

The E71 took them up through Split and, eventually, into Slovenia and the foothills of the Italian Alps. In the hours of driving, Ben let the silence sit between them. There was nothing that could be said. Jamie had waved them off without ceremony. They were both, in their own ways, shocked by his sacrifice. And deep inside him, Ben could see how upset she was by it. Yet, now the decision was made, they had the business cards.

He needed that transmitter.

Stamp had shown them how much damage their job could cause. How the filth and lies could stick to your ribs and pull you down with it.

They were climbing, skirting north of Venice, weaving up towards the foothills of the Dolomites. Ben saw the signs for Milan and cut west, towards Verona and Trento.

Lucy was curled up in the passenger seat, half there, focused on the road. She hadn't offered to drive, and it wasn't bothering her that she hadn't.

A few cars passed and blared their horns. Ben started to realize that, despite the fresh air, he was exhausted. He slapped himself awake and the noise startled Lucy. She'd been asleep too.

'Bed,' she said.

Ben tried to agree but was too tired to form the words. The sign said 'Villa di Angeli', but really it was a motel. To Ben and Lucy, it felt like Castel Gandolfo. The 'concierge', Signora Sanga, showed them proudly to a small low-rise rabbit hutch of a room with chewing gum peeking out from under the welcome mat. Ben paid in advance and, by the time he'd shut the door, Lucy was passed out on the bed, asleep.

The sofa was just about big enough for him, but instead he took the cushions and laid them on the floor.

About ten minutes later another guest was shown to her room, with a window adjacent to *la stanza numero cinque*. The Signora felt sorry for her, as she did for all women who were forced to travel alone. *And such beautiful eyes*, she said to herself. *Like an angel*.

Ben lay there, on the cushions, staring at the ceiling. For some reason, he couldn't close his eyes just yet. He was in that strange zone of exhaustion where even falling asleep seems one labour too many. Instead Ben was savouring the stillness, the muted conversation from the room below, the sound of the cars whizzing by on the road outside.

Perhaps this was what sanctuary was all about, he thought. Perhaps this was what Lucy and Jamie and Nat had all been fighting for. And Ben, he reminded himself. He'd been heading there too, to begin with.

His fight was about something else now, and it was eating him up inside.

'Can I ask you a question.'

Lucy was calling to him from the bed. Her voice was sleepy and he wondered whether it was part of a dream.

'You just did.'

'Can I. Ask you. A question.'

'Depends what it is.'

'Never mind.'

Ben waited for her breathing to regularize and then stood up, walked over to the bed and got in between the covers. Lucy, half asleep now, did not flinch.

'What's this?'

'I'm fed up of the floor. And I'm cold.'

'So why are you bringing it in here?'

'Bringing what?'

'That cold you were talking about. I know how cold your feet can get.'

'For once, please. I need somewhere I can sleep.'

Ben allowed a buffer of mattress to stay between them.

'How do you sleep at night?' she asked.

'Not as well as I used to,' he said.

Silence for a moment, the sound of a TV commercial in the next room. Ben let the issue settle like a light snowfall. But instead of melting, it started drifting. He sat up on his elbows and looked at her. She stayed prone on the bed. He could see her lashes blinking.

Lucy seemed about to tell him something. But her breath caught and dissipated into the air.

'What?'

'It doesn't matter.'

Ben lay listening to their words, their little conversation, and realized, in the past few weeks, they were starting to mean more. What concerned him was that it wasn't something he could control any more. He was entering into new country and he felt it.

'Do you think we'll ever get home?' said Lucy.

He smelled her tears and felt her breath on his back.

'I hope so.'

Rolling over, she reached for him.

A sudden panic in Ben as he realized his plaster was also gone. Did she know? Had he told her? He couldn't remember any more. In the urgency of the moment, he thought, the dark passion of the motel room, it might not matter anyway.

In this moment, to Ben, nothing else mattered but *now*.

They rose and fell together, forcing the life back into each other, tasting hot fears and blood, the pain of running and the unknown. A falling into step.

There were no words.

They both knew.

It was the only home they had left and they both clung to it for dear, sweet life.

Four hours, ten hours, half an hour later – Ben woke up. He didn't remember falling asleep, he was sure of that. He only knew he couldn't quite focus yet. He glanced at Lucy, now foetal on the bed and half wrapped in the bedcovers. He smelled her on his arms and felt twelve months younger.

He finally zeroed in on his watch. Four o'clock. A solid five hours. He wondered how long Lucy might pass out for. He remembered fondly the day she missed her birthday, on account of her celebrations the night before. A strange thing it was to be greeted at your bedside by a birthday cake in the middle of the night . . .

The memory sharpened him.

Control, he remembered. There was a whole world out there that needed him.

Ben checked his pockets. He had enough euro coins for a call. He'd not seen a payphone on the way in, but perhaps in reception – had he been that tired?

He slipped on his shoes and started towards the door.

'There's a spring sticking into my navel,' slurred Lucy into the mattress. Ben changed direction slightly to make it look like he'd been going to open the curtains.

'Time to move,' he said.

'I understand the words you speak,' sighed Lucy. 'It's just hard to make it all happen.' After a few minutes she dragged herself to her feet and began trailing a sheet after her as she headed for the bathroom. She took a towel from the shower rail but it was comically small. Instead, she began to undress under the sheet.

Ben watched her in the reflection of the window.

'It's all right, I've seen it all before.'

'That's not the point.'

She smiled thinly and closed the bathroom door. Ben waited for the water to run before he set the front door on the latch and slipped quietly out on to the landing.

Once, Ben had indeed caught a girlfriend with this trick,

watching from the bathroom as she rummaged around his things. He'd told Lucy the story, in a moment of post-coital sincerity. He had probably forgotten this. But Lucy had not.

She opened the bathroom door a little wider to confirm her suspicions. He'd gone. She dropped the bedsheet. She was fully clothed.

What are you up to, little weasel?

A two-storey 'inn', the structure would have looked more at home by a desert road in Arizona, perhaps, or by a Nevada wedding chapel. An area underneath a covered walkway on the ground floor contained a line of vending machines and two payphones.

Ben charged the coins through the slot and dialled in a blur. He looked to his left past the machines as the dial tone morphed into a ring – the coast was clear. He looked to his right just as a male voice picked up – and saw Lucy standing there with her arms folded.

He hung up.

'Guilty,' he smiled ruefully.

'Who were you calling?'

'I'm sorry, I'm an idiot.'

Ben was licking his lips and Lucy noticed. *Funny the little things you remember*, she thought.

'Who was it?'

'I was calling my mother. Come on, you've wanted to do exactly the same. But I hung up, I don't want to jeopardize what we've achieved—'

'You're lying, Ben.'

'Not true.'

He was walking away now, to a set of stairs at the far end of the vending machines. 'We should get on the road.'

'Tell me what's really going on.'

Ben turned and walked back slowly towards her. He had a primal physicality when threatened, she knew. But she was on her guard.

His voice was calm and reassuring.

'What's going on is, we need to get on the road.'

Ben brushed past her on the way back to the room. She shuddered, pushing the feeling away, needing so much to look at him as the enemy now, she reminded herself. No more trust, no more memory.

Lucy felt for the nail scissors she'd swiped as she left the room. Enough to blind someone if you knew how. Enough to make you feel a little more secure.

Ten minutes later they were in the car and roaring out of the parking lot. Twenty seconds later, Collins was in position behind them. Fifteen seconds after that, a third car flipped on its headlights and powered out in the same direction towards Italy's border with Switzerland.

Sixty-Two

Lombardy, Northern Italy

The Citroën was struggling with the road ahead. It was the same on the inside of the car too. A light rain was strafing the roads, the windscreen, the distant mountain tops.

Ben was gripping the wheel and driving too fast and trying very hard to keep the demon inside from leaping out of him. 'Whatever happened to you, I don't know. But it was a tragedy.'

'What happened was what you already know.' Lucy's voice was defiant, tearful.

He'd hurt her before, his stomach told him. Gears meshing inside. At last, perhaps, some traction . . .

'What do I already know?'

'Oh, come on—'

'Claiming poverty. Moving in with me. Sharing my fucking baked beans and driving a Mercedes SLK. What's that all about?'

'You were playing the game just as much as me, matey.'

The surprise hit Ben hard.

'What game?'

'The – recruitment. The training.'

'What about it?'

Ben spotted an emergency parking place and roared the car to a stop. Lucy sensed danger and was out of the car before he could prevent her.

Outside, the wind was whipping down through the valley and up like the crack of a bullwhip into their faces. A squall of rain was lashing down now, swirling around them, the gravel and dirt under their feet turning swiftly to mud.

Lucy had her hand in her pocket, eyes blazing at Ben as his mind raced. She was accusing him. *She* was accusing *him*.

'What fucking game!?'

'The training. The recruitment!'

And she told him. She told the whole story of her first week as a lilywhite. The attraction she'd felt for him. The feelings she'd had. And the meetings, late and long-reaching, she'd had with a man called KB.

'He told me you were part of the training course,' she said. 'That you were seconded from Five, over the river. To keep you as close as possible. Make friends.'

'I was your first project.'

She took a deep breath. 'You were everyone's first project, Ben.'

Ben felt a dizziness descend. He wasn't spectating now. He tried to step outside the pain but he was inhabiting it all. The rain was lashing his eyes. He held up his arm to protect himself and saw the scissors in Lucy's hand.

'What are you trying to do, Lucy?'

'I'm trying to work out who the hell you just called.'

'My mother—'

'The truth!'

'Lucy. I wasn't seconded from anywhere. I was recruited just like you.'

'Don't give me that—'

'*Why would I lie?*'

Speculations raged inside Ben. His eyes watered. Watching himself, he saw a man ripped in two. Torn like a young life on a Bristol pavement.

'I'm still working for the Service.'

'You're what?'

'I'm supposed to find Contact Zero. And when I do, they will destroy it.'

Collins had seen the car power off the road and found enough room to U-turn around the bend of the road. She roared back down the hill and found a hard shoulder that offered a vantage point of the parking area. She could see the argument unfolding, if not hear it. The rain made lip-reading at this distance impossible.

She didn't need to lip-read what happened next.

Sixty-Three

As the rain came down

Lucy's grip on the scissors was loose and fluid. She couldn't run at Ben, that would be ridiculous. Even with her expertise in holds and throws, no one ran towards their target. You drew them in.

So Lucy ran.

Down past the car, towards the road. Ben sprinted after her, shouting, pleading in the chaos of the wind.

When he was close enough, she spun on her heels and kicked him in the groin. He doubled over in pain long enough for her to get his head in a lock and move the scissors to the soft throaty flesh under his chin.

'I will end you right now unless you tell me more.'

'That's all there is.' Ben felt the prick of blood above his Adam's apple and knew in this rage Lucy was capable of anything he was. Probably more.

Lucy tightened her grip.

'I'm serious,' said Ben.

'How could you do this? How?'

'Oh, shit.' It had only just occurred to Ben. The deaths. The list of friends around the world. He'd been told the plan evolved from that tragedy. But if he'd been manipulated, if he'd simply been the target for recruitment . . . that meant . . .

'After the Gauntlet, KB told me he'd save me from the sack. He told me he'd call back the favour one day – and that was fine by me at the time, let me tell you. After our covers were blown, when I came out to meet you – I was as convinced as you were that our year had just self-destructed. KB had a contact in the monastery. If there was a leak, he told me, they were working on it. But the situation had opened a window of opportunity – find Contact Zero.'

Lucy had dropped the scissors. The rage had gone. Only memory, and pain, remained.

'But I know now. It was murder. All of it.'

He grabbed for Lucy now, but it was only to embrace her as tight as his muscles would allow.

Collins watched them holding one another and concluded the worst. She had no proof yet, of course. But she hoped to, very soon.

The rain was easing but still Ben drove too fast, thought too much, spoke too loud. Lucy could only hang on and listen, numbed by what she was hearing. The car was lurching around the corners. She pinched off a wave of nausea and opened a window. But she knew this feeling was more from what Ben was telling her.

It was a careful and sadistic plan. KB had needed a mole to locate Contact Zero. To do this he had to find someone willing to turn their back on their comrades, to collaborate and then betray. To achieve this, he needed to ensure his target had good reason to feel aggrieved. What better than to introduce a child of struggle, a believer in meritocracy, into the effortless aristocracy of the SIS?

The slow-burn isolation of Ben through twelve months had achieved what was required. Lucy listened to his story and understood. It was a form of emotional Botox. Ben had been convinced of the worth of the plan but numbed to the consequences until it was too late.

A grimy roadside rest stop beckoned. Ben pulled in as the rain downgraded to a drizzle. They needed hot drinks and warmth. In a small booth at the back, Ben took her through it all, once again, from the beginning.

At a nearby table, Collins heard the confession in full, on a small but perfectly placed miniature parabolic microphone. When she'd heard enough, she left a paltry tip and returned to her car in the parking lot. She had her orders. Strictly speaking, she knew she should make a call right now. But instead, she shrugged and popped some chocolate in her mouth, savouring it as it melted. She knew what she was doing. She would call after it was done. She knew the roads around here well – Cles, Dimaro, Tirano – though she preferred them a little icier than now. Still, it gave her enough confidence to remove a high-powered automatic pistol and place it on the leather seat next to her. The BMW M3 had heated seats, she remembered, and flicked a switch on the dash.

The gun would appreciate that, she thought to herself.

Ten minutes later, she was back behind the Citroën on the road.

The gradient was getting steeper, undulating in ever increasing amplitude. The car didn't seem to mind accelerating, but Lucy didn't trust the brakes at all. Scratch that. She didn't trust anything any more. The headlights probed the road ahead but without high beams (possibly a luxury extra when the car had been built; perhaps an oversight) there seemed to be death looming at every turn.

'And now?' said Lucy.

'Zurich.'

Ben saw the *autostrada* signs ahead to Bolzano and realized they were overshooting their route to Zurich.

He headed west at the next interchange, Mezzolombardo, making for the pass near St Moritz. Ben decided in advance to avoid the Swiss toll roads once they passed through the border crossing. With this car in the state it was, there was a chance they'd get pulled over on a road safety issue. Best to stick to the back roads.

In his rear mirror, Ben saw the halogen beams were still there. *Italian drivers*, he thought.

Then thought again.

Sixty-Four

C ollins was biding her time. Unless they had picked up her
tail and were planning on losing her, she preferred to
make her move on more precipitous asphalt. The crappy little
Citroën had no such luxuries. And now the accelerator was not
responding. Try as he might, as the gradients increased, the
engine lost faith and Ben could do nothing about it. It was only
when the road levelled out between climbs that things began to
pick up again.

'You see it? Don't turn round,' said Ben.

Lucy strained to see anything in the side mirror, bent out of
shape by years of psychotic parallel parking on the side streets
of Dubrovnik.

'Wait. Slow down. More . . .'

Ben deliberately braked hard around the next bend. The car
behind revealed itself. Lucy recognized the grille and the
headlights as they turned with the car.

'Yep. Well spotted.'

'Any idea? Can you see?'

In the dark? With full beams in my face?

'Whoever it is,' said Lucy, 'they're driving a Beemer.'

Ben saw a stretch of empty straight road ahead and slowed
down even more. Even the most timid driver would pass. In a
BMW a gentle tap of the accelerator would take you past. But
the car stayed exactly where it was.

'Not good,' said Ben.

'No,' said Lucy.

Ben speeded up, grinding the gears on purpose, hoping the manoeuvre might be misinterpreted as bad driving. They were climbing hard now, sharp turns and undulations, tunnels and barriers.

And a long way down.

Ben nearly jumped when he felt Lucy's hand on his.

'I just want you to know something,' she said.

But Ben had no time to answer as a flash in the rear-view was followed by an almighty explosion from the axles.

The tyre, thought Ben – shot out.

Lucy whipped her head round and heard the report of another shot, this one richocheting off the harsh mountain rock that was now inches away from the window—

'Ben!'

'The thing's lost, the steering's gone—'

Ahead of them, another turn, a flimsy barrier all that remained between the mountain road and a thousand-foot fall on to bare rock.

Ben crunched the handbrake and spun the wheel. Enough juice to grind the remaining tyres around to the right and propel the Citroën towards a slip road on the right-hand side.

'The road—'

'I see it!'

The Citroën roared up the steep incline, the accelerator stuck now – the car giving its all – but the incline simply arced back over on to the mountain road again, and Ben hit the brakes as another explosion resounded and the rear window atomized, the bullet puncturing the door by Lucy's shoulder. The next one, she knew, would be the kill shot.

But the car had other ideas and, striking a boulder on the slip road, flipped over sideways and skidded to a halt.

Behind them, the BMW roared to a halt and the shadow of a woman leapt out on to the slip road.

Ben was dazed. Lucy moaned.

In the broken mirrors they could see her feet. The smell of petrol and brake fluid mixed with the alpine air. Ben heard a car engine roar—

Collins had already committed to stepping out into the road when a third car roared up behind her. There was no time to aim, fire or turn. It was the last mental snapshot of her life, bright lights blinding her as her back broke and the impact shunted her high into the air, bouncing off the ridge of the slip road and falling back down towards the road below.

A coach turned the corner. The driver had been speeding and tried to brake, to no avail. What was left of Collins skittered over the edge of the mountain road and was gone.

The third vehicle slammed on its brakes and the driver ran out to see the damage he'd caused.

Lucy was awake again too and was struggling with her seat belt. She heard the crunch of dirt underfoot as someone ran to the side of the car, crouched down and peered in.

He had to crouch quite far. He was very tall.

'Everyone okay?' said Jamie. 'Thought I dinged you for a second.'

Sixty-Five

Minutes later, they were winding through the mountain roads towards the Swiss border. Lucy sat next to Jamie in the front seat of a Mercedes with Croatian plates. He had the heater on, but there was something rotting in the system. It smelt stale. Lucy's nose quivered and she turned it off.

'When did you realize we were being tailed?'

'Jerusalem. I saw a flash on my eyeline when we were talking to Father Daniel. I'd been wondering whether the Samaritans might have sent someone to check up on us but that was where I made sure. I waited till the last moment then copped a look again, and there it was. A flash of a scope in the sunlight – someone was diving to the ground or turning away. They wouldn't sit somewhere where the scope was directly *in* sunlight, so they sat at an angle. But under pressure, you shift, you move quickly. Hence – I knew.'

'And you volunteered to stay behind.'

'For show, of course. To prove myself wrong. But I wasn't. I took one of Stamp's cars and she was back tailing you within minutes. I don't think she imagined she would have a tail herself.'

'You saved our lives,' said Ben.

Jamie shrugged. 'It's not me, laddie, it's the training.'

He smiled in the rear-view but caught Ben's dark eyes instead.

'What's the matter with you?' he said.

Ben didn't really know where to start.

The border officer accepted their passports (there was no reason to doubt their authenticity – they were all bona fide Irish passports made by an MI6 forgery artist on Saturday mornings). At this time of night, the officer warmed to Jamie's fluent French and seemed to take pity on the three tired souls in the Mercedes. Nevertheless, he paraded through the questions, did a cursory search of the vehicle, even managing to query the Croatian plates. But he was dealing with professionals, who eased their way past each question with exactly what he needed to hear. He waved them off with a mini salute, touching two fingers to his cap.

It took them all a few seconds to start breathing again.

Ben's explanation had silenced Jamie. Two hours later, they were on Autobahn E35 and he was still without words. Without warning he swerved off the highway and into a rest stop that was closed. But it didn't seem to matter to him. He needed air. Ben remembered how he'd reacted when he'd heard about Claire, Andy, all the others. News that large digests slowly, like swallowing a hunk of cheese. It had the same effect on Jamie as it had had on Ben – he had no idea why up was up or down was down. The world simply swirling around him.

'I don't understand,' said Jamie eventually.

'It's not that hard.'

'I'm talking about the Gauntlet. You said that you were told we all pointed the finger at you.'

Ben was starting to feel a tingling at the back of his neck.

'We were told to isolate you,' continued Jamie. 'To befriend you then isolate you. You were a sort of project, I suppose. But we were never told to pin the blame for the Gauntlet on you, too. Nat took the fall for that.'

'How?'

'A reprimand. A final warning. That sort of thing. It wasn't enough to kick him out.' His eyes were damp with tears. 'We would never have done anything like that to you.'

Ben nodded, taking it all on board. KB had lied about that, too. The final flick of the puppeteer's fingers. The clincher that led him to loyalty.

Unquestioning loyalty. Until now.

'I'm sorry,' said Jamie.

Ben shook his head, patting Jamie on the arm.

'There's only one person who needs to be sorry,' said Ben, a faraway look in his eyes. Lucy embraced Jamie warmly. The past was heaving slowly away, like a boat on the tide.

'Do you ever play chess?' said Ben suddenly. 'If you sacrifice a pawn, it can help you win the game. You might lose a piece, but you gain a stronger position on the board.'

Lucy flashed him a dark look. 'Who exactly were you thinking of sacrificing?'

'There are two numbered accounts waiting for us in Zurich. You have the details of one.' Ben looked at Jamie and handed him the business card. 'I want you to have the other.'

Jamie was still so entwined with his news, so busy revisiting every moment he could recall to cast it in this new light, that he had no idea how to react. He looked at the card but did not take it.

'No charity, please.' His smile was bitter, full of regret.

'None given. This is purely practical.'

'I don't see how.'

'I have something else to do.'

'I can't take this . . . in spite of everything, it's yours. Stamp said there were only two.'

'Firstly, I doubt I'd believe anything that man said. Secondly, they're numbered accounts,' said Ben. 'They're eminently transferable. No problem.'

Gingerly, Jamie took the card in his fingers. 'But what about you?'

'I'll be fine. As far as you're concerned, you should keep going. To Zero. That was the plan, correct? We've come this far.'

'I sort of thought this was it,' said Jamie.

'Do you truly believe that?' Ben gestured around the bleak tarmac and spotlights of the parking lot. A bitter wind blew in from the mountains. Occasionally a car would roar down the fast lane of the Autobahn. 'Would you say this is what we've been working for? A well-stamped passport and a Swiss bank account? A pension and a car park?'

'But they've all said it. It's a network. Get the bank account and you belong. We draw money and work when they get in touch. I mean it all makes perfect sense.'

'I think we need to make a distinction,' said Ben, 'between the Contact Zero network and Contact Zero itself.'

Lucy narrowed her eyes. 'You think there's a difference?'

'Contact Zero *is* a network, all right? Of course it is. It's not a place, or a person, or a thing . . . it's an entity in and of itself, a system. But is that *all* it is? I'm not so sure.'

'What makes you think that?'

'So far, we've done nothing but meet people. Parts of a chain. The Samaritans. Michael Church. Hannah Rosen RIP. Father Daniel. Stamp. All along, we've been imagining the chain leads somewhere. It doesn't. It leads back on itself. It's a circle. But once we've gone around it, we know what it is. We've done a recce around its perimeter. And now, we know how we can use it.'

'Makes sense. But use it how?'

'It just occurred to me at the border. You saw how he treated us. Irish passports. Nice car. Fluent French. Yet he still looked in the boot, shone a torch in our eyes. The world has changed.' He was pacing now, a man convinced of a truth no one else had seen yet. 'Picture this. A diffuse network, operating in small cells around the world. Part guerilla, part covert operations. A strict and secret admissions procedure that depends almost entirely on an antagonistic disposition towards the UK intelligence services. Structural and operational sections that form the connective tissue. A solid ideological base and a flourishing network of forged identities fuelled from many different parts of the globe. A customized system of finances that might well have its basis in old Templar monetary structures but has a more apt modern equivalent in the hawala remittance system. Sound familiar?'

Lucy looked at him, stunned.

'Al-Qaeda,' she said.

Sixty-Six

No word from Collins now for eight hours. No word from Sinclair. Tremayne Minor sacked but now untraceable at home too. No wonder KB was not sleeping tonight.

He tossed and turned in his silk sheets and sat on the edge of the bed. His apartment had a view of the Houses of Parliament, his own personal alarm clock as Big Ben struck away the hours.

He showered, dressed and took a late-night stroll from his house in Westminster across the Thames and into the main doors of 85 Albert Embankment. It didn't surprise him that Thomas was there too.

'You're sure he's made no contact?'

'A call was made to my SOS number from a payphone near Verona. Whether that was him or not, I don't know. It took me an age to trace the line in any case.'

'Then we should consider the operation dead.'

'Why?'

'Because the longer we hope for it, the bigger risks we will take. We have other operations ongoing, for Christ's sake.'

'For us there *is* no bigger fish than this. We will find out for *sure*. We will *sleep* with that knowledge full square in our skulls.'

The Chief watched the passion and fury flash in his old friend's eyes. 'Just be careful. We need evidence, not hearsay.

We need conviction, not rumour. Until he sends a signal, until we corroborate it ourselves . . .'

Oh, we'll corroborate all right, thought KB.

Instead, he nodded. Patience, the virtue of the bored. Patience, the excuse of millions for whom failure was an option. The key to success? *Visualize the outcome. And make it happen.*

Sixty-Seven

The noise from the Autobahn filtered in as Lucy and Jamie absorbed Ben's theory.

'I suppose it's nearly the same structural model,' said Jamie.

'It *is the same model.*'

'But if that's true . . .'

'I think Al-Qaeda borrowed from Contact Zero,' said Ben, 'even if they didn't know it . . . Which means the Contact Zero network *will* have a command structure, just as Al-Qaeda has Bin Laden and his deputies in the caves. It has to.'

'Why?'

'Because without it, it couldn't function. Even huge economies need direction. Without it, we wouldn't be here. I'm sure of it.'

'Are you saying, then, that they're connected?'

'It's possible. But unlikely. They're ideologically polarized for one.'

'Fugitives with a cause?'

'It's no doubt that people like Stamp represent a network that's flying pretty close to the sun. But that's not to say there's an overlap.'

Lucy smiled at Ben as he spoke. It hit Ben hard. His eyes began to sting. It almost felt like tears. What's more, he was in the centre of it, in the moment. He hardly knew where to put himself. He had to acknowledge it. He was crying. Instead, he reined back in – not from fear, this time, but for practicality's sake.

'Someone out there is in charge of all this. So please, go and find them.'

'How?'

'Zurich. The name on that business card. And please. If you find out . . . please let me know.' His smile faded slightly. He was already thinking about his next move. 'If I'm still around.'

Jamie opened the car door. 'Time to hit the road.'

Lucy and Jamie dropped Ben off at the town of Chur. A brief farewell and they were gone, heading north to Zurich. Ben wished them well and knew he had stepped into virgin territory. A sacrifice was important. It brought sense to the chaos. With dwindling funds and a limited time before KB knew the truth, Ben had no opportunity to dwell on past transgressions.

The future was much more pressing.

Right now it was full of vengeance.

Ben refuelled at a late-night café near the cathedral and located the jarringly modern railway station. He bought a ticket to Bern and jumped off at the last minute. Returning to a different ticket window, he purchased a passage to his true destination. He was heading southwest, towards Geneva.

Although this was a night train, Ben had no time to stop and sleep. He was running a course of action through his head and he wanted everything to click as efficiently as the *Schweizerische Bundesbahn* rolling stock he sat on. Two seconds after its scheduled arrival time, the train deposited Ben in Lausanne, on the north shores of Lac Léman. Even here, his eyes were on the time and the money.

It made him happy to spend the small amount of Swiss

francs he'd carefully hidden all those weeks ago in Peru. They had seemed so ridiculous then, lying in a bundle in a secret metal box. Now, he brandished them gladly to a clerk on the sixth floor of Globus-Grand Passage, a vast department store on the Rue du Pont.

In return, the clerk handed him the very latest hand-held GPS navigation tool. Despite its shortcomings compared to the SIS model, it would more than suit his needs now.

Ben checked his watch and calculated he had about seven hours of daylight left. He'd come to Lausanne rather than Geneva because he wanted to stay within the Swiss borders for his next move, avoiding if possible a second ordeal with the border-crossing officials. Trends of luck can change on the run, and Ben felt it better not to test it.

He located a local bus and rode it to Valais, sharing it with enterprising skiers hoping to find powder on the tip top of the Portes du Soleil. The mountainsides had been reclaimed by grass since the winter. He wondered if his memory would hold up without the snow to remind him.

One cable car ride and two hours of hiking later brought Ben through a forest of evergreens to the lip of a peak that spilled down into another valley beyond. There, halfway down, sat a palatial rosewood chalet, surrounded by two rings of tall pines.

He'd previously seen the place from the other side of the valley, on the edge of the ridge high above. It had taken him two hours to ski back home.

He stayed close to the tree line and crept up to the outer ring of trees. Removing his jacket, he took a reading from his GPS, obscuring the object in his hand from any prying eyes. And pry, he was sure, they would.

There was good reason. A 'hiker' soon appeared in a gap between the trees.

'No visitors up here, I'm afraid,' drawled the man. The German was good but the remnants of a Bostonian accent still lingered. *A few more language classes, buddy, and you'll be fine.*

Ben made his apologies in German and walked away. That would be close enough, he thought.

Two hours later, he was back in Lausanne and on the night train north.

He waited as long as he could in Calais before making the call. The payphone took a while to summon a dial tone, but Ben had at least an hour before the ferry sailed for Dover. He called directory enquiries and located the number for the American Embassy in Bern. He asked to be put through to the operations desk, where he calmly informed them that an attack was imminent against US interests around Avoriaz. Asked to elaborate, Ben hung up.

He switched payphones and dialled again. This time with enough one-euro pieces to buy the phone booth in its entirety. He recognized the voice on the other end, but not its tone. The words seemed perfectly reasonable:

But there was tremolo underneath it all. He'd never heard KB sound relieved before. Perhaps Ben had been in two minds about this next move. Perhaps he'd even been considering completing what he started. But this convinced him otherwise. There was an expedient nerviness playing out here.

'SOS,' said Ben.

'Tell me.'

'Well.' Ben thought for a moment. 'There's good news and there's bad news.'

'This is no place for games.'

'The bad news is, the transmitter's been damaged.'

'What?'

'The good news is, I've found it.'

'Say again?'

'I know where it is.'

'When you say "it" . . .'

'You know what I mean.'

Silence on the line.

'Then you should stay in place until we can—'

'You don't understand. There's no time. The thing you're looking for is not a person, it's a physical place. A compound. But it's mobile. The location shifts every six days. Everyone in the command structure is here, but they're leaving. What do you want me to do?'

Everyone? KB's voice began to rise, frustration creeping in, tightening the throat – they were *so close now*—

'Stay with it—'

'I could be burned at any time. They're more paranoid than anyone I've ever met.'

'Then – you're sure the transmitter's dead?'

'As a dead doorknob.'

More silence. A series of ominous clicks on the line. Ben saw the cars were already boarding the ferry. 'And so will I be if they catch me here waiting for you to say something. Look, I told you, it's a travelling circus.'

KB's voice was panicking now. 'Well . . . can you send a GPS location? Can you pinpoint it that way?'

'Affirmative. But if you're planning on doing something, I'd be quick about it. These people move all the time and, as I told you, I'm losing trust.'

'How long exactly?'

'I'd say about eight hours.'

'*Eight hours?*—'

'This is the best chance you'll ever have.'

And he hung up.

Ben strolled on to the ferry, wondering if his instincts were right. Contact Zero brought out the worst in people. They'd all fallen for the myth, been intoxicated by the very idea of it. And with only scraps to feed on, they'd nearly believed it into existence. As it turned out, for Ben, Lucy and Jamie, their instincts had been right. But there were other people who, he now realized, shared that obsession. There was a zeal about KB.

Perhaps KB wanted it too much.

Ben hoped that was still true.

Belief can do strange things to people.

So it was a place. He'd always dreamt it was.

The coiled snake of paranoia unfurled itself within KB. It existed, that's what he knew now. Perhaps that's all he'd wanted. Just to know. Memories of Berlin flooded back. *A control centre.*

But he needed more than knowledge.

He needed certainty.

With trembling fingers, he lifted up the phone to call Thomas. What would he tell him? How could he explain . . . ?

He replaced the receiver. These were defining moments, he felt. He punched in another number. The Irish black bag artist he'd tasked days before. Still no answer. She'd be forfeiting her second payment. He could hardly ask Sinclair where she was. He had no idea she even existed.

But what to do?

He'd often experimented with scenarios like this. If you

heard Bin Laden was probably in a terraced house in Birmingham, would you send in a strike? Troops? How much pain would you inflict if you didn't know for sure?

The world was full of decisions based on rumour and hearsay. Wars were fought on less. Could he afford *not* to strike?

So desperate was KB to believe in this mythic beast, he did only a cursory check on the GPS location Ben had furnished him with. It was indeed a remote site in Switzerland. It seemed entirely plausible. And by taking this alone, he might even garner most of the glory – even in the Chief's substantial shadow.

He knew the codes required to task the Increment. The Secret Intelligence Service's Special Forces detachment was on constant standby for precisely this moment.

There was no room for doubt.

But no time for certainty.

KB went on trust.

As it turned out, a very bad move.

Sixty-Eight

B en emerged from the ferry looking remarkably different
from when he went in. For a start, his hair was gone,
shorn and shaved with a six-pack of safety razors and a bar of
soap. He smoothed his bald dome back and adjusted the
frames of his thick-rimmed glasses.

With his new look came new clothes – a cheap suit and an
empty briefcase. He could have been selling mobile phones on
the Old Kent Road or trading nickel futures on the Bourse.

He stopped off at a Ryman's before fighting his way through
the crowds at Victoria Station, dropped down to the Victoria
Line and took the single-station ride to Pimlico. Being back in
England centred him. He passed payphone after payphone and
wanted so much to call his mother, his sister. *Happy birthday.*
Sorry I'm late. Something came up.

Number 25 had not been painted. It didn't look like anyone
had touched it at all. But still oddly welcoming, still a little like
home. Despite the new batch of lilywhites that Ben presumed
were staying there.

There was no way in at the door, of course, but then there
never was. Clambering over the steps, Ben dropped down to the
lower-ground-floor window that Claire had jemmied so many
times trying to get in to see Andy, they'd named it after her.

The Williams Window was closed but unlocked. Crouching
in the shadows, he heard the front door slam. Ben was terrified

and confused – he was sure the probationers would be at Vauxhall Cross by now. Until he remembered – the time difference. One hour. He cursed his idiotic brain.

A lucky break. Ben turned his watch back in thanks.

Fifty minutes later, he heard nothing more from inside. Seconds after that, he was in the hallway. The familiar smell of carpet cleaner and central heating hit him square in the face. So many dead. There was a reason he was here.

He had to get moving.

He knew there was a good chance he'd find someone's MI6 ID card. When Ben had lived in the house – in the small studio flat at the very top of the building – there was a small ceramic gnome for keys and loose change on a table by the front door. It was anyone's dibs to take what they needed. The cards were awkward, too big to fit in the credit card section of a wallet or purse. When on missions abroad, or even weekends away, there had been a sense of sharing. You left your card for others, in case they'd forgotten theirs.

Ben was surprised and delighted to see that some things never changed. He lifted a heavy plastic card out of the mountain of two-pence pieces and left by the back door. Crossing the small courtyard at the back, he hurdled a fence that backed on to a small alleyway and ran off in the direction of his old bus stop.

He walked along the south side of the Thames and said goodbye. The grey churning waters he remembered were calm today. It seemed to suit his mood perfectly.

At 85 Albert Embankment, a bald, suited man with a briefcase strode confidently past the security cameras and into a blind spot near a side entrance where he had once enjoyed a kiss with Lucy Matthews.

As he passed a plant pot, he quietly deposited his briefcase behind the foliage and continued nonchalantly on to the security doors. He swiped his ID card through the machines and hoped the optical recognition software had not been installed yet.

He was in luck.

He headed for the lobby bathrooms, removed his lighter and quietly held it under the smoke detector. It took only a few seconds for a piercing alarm to fill the atrium from the sub basements to the roof.

Being the SIS building, fire sections were zoned. But by using the lobby bathrooms, Ben knew a mass exodus was almost guaranteed from the offices along the central corridors and atrium.

He waited for a moment until the automated Tannoy began to relay evacuation procedures to the workforce. He heard the clatter and murmur outside and joined the throng as they left the security doors, now locked open.

He relocated his briefcase from the pot plant and left his jacket there instead. Now in shirtsleeves, he walked straight back in through the flow to the concerned stares of the security guards.

Walking to the centre of the atrium, briefcase still in hand, he stopped. Sergeant Kevin Meades was on duty and came striding down the adjoining corridor. He recognized Ben immediately, but that didn't bother Ben in the slightest. It would make things much easier. He looked at his watch and thought this was probably as good a time as any.

Ben smiled at Sergeant Meades and explained that he hoped he was looking forward to Christmas, that he needed to speak to KB, that the briefcase in his hand contained a bomb.

Sixty-Nine

Zurich, Switzerland

I t looked more like a town house than a bank. But the address on the card did not lie. The giveaway for Lucy was the security cameras. The Bahnhofstrasse might be out of sight from here, but Swiss banking was alive and well and very, very discreet.

Apart from those cameras of course.

They were bloody everywhere.

The name on the door said: KMCO EXPORT BANK.

They rang the bell.

Two minutes later, a buzzer sounded.

Lucy and Jamie glanced at each other as they were escorted to a small marble-clad reception area. A small LCD screen showed the financial channels, news tickers flashing manically underneath the presenter's hands as he spoke.

A rotund young banker with dandruff on his jacket walked in ten minutes later. He smiled unconvincingly and took them to a small computer room, where he consulted his records from the numbers they had furnished him with.

He shook his head imperceptibly, confused.

He picked up a phone and spoke in a whisper.

Lucy caught Jamie's eye. Would they run if challenged? Lucy believed they would. The banker excused himself and left the room.

They knew they were being filmed, and it made no sense to break the façade yet. It wasn't uncommon for clients to find themselves inheriting a bank account with no idea of its contents. Mad uncles and rich aunts were known to leave family heirlooms for forgotten nieces. So long as they had the account number, they were fine.

Eventually, another banker emerged. This one matched more of the stereotype: impeccable suit, a calm but inscrutable smile and glasses so thin it looked like someone had drawn over his face with a ballpoint pen.

He escorted them to another room and shut the door.

'I wonder if you might have a pass code?'

Jamie cleared his throat.

'My . . . grandfather left us these accounts. I don't know what that code would be.'

'A number, a word, it could be anything. You may type it in yourself if you like. But I warn you, if you make a mistake, you'll have to come back tomorrow.'

Jamie bit his lip.

Lucy leaned in. 'No one said anything about a pass code. Correct?'

Jamie nodded.

'So anyone getting here would have felt the same as us.'

Jamie nodded again.

'I want to try something. If that's okay with you.'

'Be my guest.'

Lucy sat down at the computer and pressed a single digit on the numerical keypad: '0'.

The banker had heard the single keystroke and smiled. 'Very good.' He turned and led Lucy and Jamie to an observation room before disappearing down the corridor. There was a large granite table and a small potted plant.

Jamie shot Lucy a look that she interpreted as: *well, here we are*.

The two numbers resulted in two safe-deposit boxes.

Both contained exactly the same thing: a small keyring with an ever-changing number digitized on the back. Their very own 128-bit original encryption key, fresh and new every thirty seconds. A small note in the boxes said they were to allow online access to their funds, as well as to receive secure messages.

Lucy was trembling. The truth was hitting home.

This was possible. Sanctuary could exist after all. She remembered something her mother once said to her. *Money doesn't buy happiness, dear, but it does pay off quite a lot of sadness.*

Jamie held up the final item in his box. Lucy saw she had an identical one and picked it up.

It was a postcard of La Rochelle, a port community on the Atlantic coast of France. The image in the postcard showed a lesser-spotted grebe. In small faded letters in the corner: 'ENJOY THE FAUNA OF CHARENTE-MARITIME'.

Jamie turned the card over. It was blank.

'What do you think?' Lucy asked.

'Insert the missing words, I'd say.'

Lucy looked at him. 'What words are missing?'

'Wish you were here?' smiled Jamie.

Seventy

KB descended via the central escalator and walked across the marble floor.

Some six hundred staff were gathered outside the security doors, peering in at the chaotic semicircle around a bald-headed man in a suit. At his feet, a briefcase. There was muted consternation, an English panic – a frenzy of whispers, why didn'ts and should haves.

KB finally stood opposite Ben and shook his head. Ben could see the Chief, eight floors up, gazing down from his eyrie. Ben could see he was on the phone. *Well, you're missing some good old gossip down here too, mate.*

'We don't want to buy your drugs here, sorry.'

Ben ignored KB, raising his voice to ensure the crowd could hear. He caught sight of body-armoured security guards with their weapons trained on him. His heart began to accelerate. He remembered to keep his cool.

'I just wanted to deliver some news,' said Ben. 'Is it on the wires yet?'

KB's face changed colour. 'Is what on the wires?'

Some thirty minutes before Ben walked through the security doors a blip had appeared on the Early Warning System of Station 12, a CIA-run alpine training school on the Swiss border near Avoriaz, France.

The reason was simple. At the same time, four very able SAS

personnel were completing a high-altitude high-opening (HAHO) jump from a Galaxy some 20,000 feet above French airspace.

Using their parachute cells as avions, they monitored their glide paths and ensured that they were landing on the Swiss side of a remote valley in the Portes du Soleil region. They worked hard on their cover stories, and this one had some substance to it.

By the time they landed, a reception committee was already driving out to meet them.

The embassy team, discovering the invaders were UK Special Forces, called their UK counterparts in disgust. A rippling wave of indignation spread all the way to the Foreign Secretary.

It was rippling into Vauxhall Cross right about now.

As KB stared down his nose at Ben, another whisper started up like a dust devil in the room. Word, it appeared, had come out about the aborted attack.

The US Embassy was calling.

So was the White House Defence Detachment.

A right little SNAFU for you, smiled Ben.

'What have you done?' said KB, forgetting where he was for a moment.

Ben stared straight back. 'I should ask you the very same question.' He saw KB's face fall when an aide whispered something in his ear. Up above, the Chief was turning red. And he was coming downstairs.

Ben could see the lilywhites here too, outside. He spotted them a mile away.

'Get the probationers in here,' said Ben. 'Do it *now*.'

Kevin Meades hissed at another guard, who ran into the crowds outside and started calling out names. Another guard ran to the phones.

'Not everyone. As many as you can find.'

They stuck out a mile, of course. Unlike the majority, these kids were scared. But he had one more thing to tell them all before he left. The guard assembled them before Ben, a surreal inspection of the troops.

'I'm just here to tell you that Contact Zero is a fantasy. One man believed that fantasy and tried to will it into being. The cost was too high, but he was still prepared to pay it. Six of this Service's finest agents. On their first postings. Future lilywhites, be warned. It's no fun being a pawn.'

From the looks on those lilywhites' faces, they agreed.

'This man is wanted by Interpol for drug smuggling and murder . . . !'

Official word came in from the Chief, who strode down the steps and scoured the crowd for KB. There are stories of men and women who are so shocked and distressed by news or events that their hair spontaneously goes white overnight.

For a moment, Ben thought it had happened to the Chief. Unfortunately, it was only a trick of the light as it haloed his head on his descent.

'Downing Street,' he said. And one by one the crowd dispersed. Kevin Meades leapt like a cat on the catnip and wrestled Ben to the floor. As he lay there, Ben pointed to his briefcase.

'I'm sorry about Clarissa. I didn't do it.'

'I know. I don't care.'

Under Kevin's full weight, Ben still tried to shrug. It didn't really work, but then it didn't really matter.

For once in his life, he'd done what was right.

And it felt very, very good.

Seventy-One

Israel

N at was still bubbling. Ben had put him here. He may or may not have tripped him, but he never came back for him. Outraged and upset, he'd festered for days. But the anger was subsiding – one of the reasons was Rachel.

Rachel was his assigned officer. Her green eyes had bored into Nat's for three days following his arrest. The one staggering thing about the Israeli security service, he had found, was how hot the women were. Her cascade of dark brown curls was pinned back and restrained.

It nearly drove him mad.

Perhaps this was a tactic, he reasoned.

Her questions had circled him. He had picked them off one by one. But the evidence of wrongdoing was nowhere. He denied knowledge of the others, apologized for wasting police time, and wished only to continue his vacation in the Holy Land.

Inside him, the truth. They had left him here.

When the betrayal had subsided, the context remained. Would he have done the same? If Ben had tripped? He would have run. They both knew that.

There was more to worry about than the past.

To find Father Daniel again was too dangerous. He was marooned here, he knew. To go on alone, too much.

And the thought began to strike him: even if he had the courage, the strength, the knowledge to take him further, finding Contact Zero might just mean finding Ben again. And although Lucy had her place in his heart, perhaps here, and now, was the time to let that go.

The authorities were doing the same to him, after all.

Rachel saw him to the gates of the station, her lips set in a timid smile. Even in his short time here, Nat's Hebrew had been coming along quite nicely, thank you. Shalom, he smiled at her as he left, realizing too late he was still missing a few front teeth.

Taking an inventory of his belongings in the hostel, he realized she'd written her number on his release paperwork. When he called her, he asked how long she would be at work. She told him she would be done with her commission within the year.

Nat told her he'd be happy to wait for her, and spent the rest of the afternoon pricing guesthouses by the beach in Haifa.

Seventy-Two

The peninsula did not appear on any maps, did not feature in any guidebooks or sailing manuals. Navigation charts referred to it simply as a hazard, although it was rare that anyone ventured quite so far out beyond the Charente-Maritime prominence on a boating holiday. In maritime terms, it was the equivalent of an old map stating, 'Here Be Dragons'.

Only the postmark and the faded message on a postcard had brought them here. That, and the lesser-spotted grebe.

Lucy and Jamie had bought binoculars, windcheaters and packed lunches. The taxi had dropped them as far as the paved road would take them. They would have to cover the rest on foot.

Two miles in on a muddy trail, Jamie stopped to train his eyes on the horizon. In the distance, cabins were visible. Chimneys with lazy strands of wood smoke reaching up towards the sky, blue and clear, wisps of cirrus streaking out over their heads. The sky felt vast here, like the lid had been taken off the world.

There were two men rambling towards them on the trail. As they approached, Jamie's gut began to tingle. He knew these faces – but from where?

As they passed, he remembered – they were the guards they'd encountered in Brazil.

The more they walked, the more they felt a strong sense of déjà vu.

They finally reached a small Breton cottage beyond a gate. Inside, a fire crackled. A man came to the door as he heard their footsteps. At last, thought Lucy, someone I don't recognize.

They had, however, met his son, on one occasion. Their first day on the job – back then, the lilywhites of the intelligence branch shared an awkward lunch with the lilywhites of the analysis branch. There, over smoked-salmon sandwiches, every new probationer had shaken his hand.

William Tremayne smiled at the young fugitives. They reminded him so much of himself. He longed for another adventure, but recalled to mind the pain and suffering it had taken him to reach sanctuary. As a young man he had conversed with his neighbours in a small market town. They were a quiet Jewish couple who had survived Dachau to reach the suburbs. He had asked them, in his teenage zeal, why they didn't want to live somewhere like London.

'Because too much happens there,' the wife had said.

Reaching this sanctuary, he had finally understood what they meant. He welcomed the two travellers with hot tea and toast.

'I presume you need to search us?' said Jamie.

William shrugged. 'If you get here, that's enough. I know who you are.'

He took them on a walk. The reserve was huge. It could maintain hundreds of people in perfect safety. Lucy felt herself relieved, but perhaps also a little sad. No one had ever said sanctuary would be a party, but even so . . . She pushed the thought from her mind.

'We are remote enough, and experienced enough, to ensure the safety of all comers. It takes some getting used to, but I enjoy it. My son has just joined us, you know. He's part of the reason you got here.'

Jamie could stand it no longer.

'So it's true then . . . this is Contact Zero?'

The old man smiled. 'This? No.' He beckoned them up the cliffs, to a promontory above the leeward side of the bay. A vast jetty thrust into the ocean. Moored there, in a perfect natural harbour, a Class I private cruiser.

'That is what I think you're talking about.'

Seventy-Three

Heathrow Airport

KB was wearing his charcoal-grey Armani suit. He often travelled business, but when circumstances led him to slum it in steerage, he always made sure he looked the part.

'Are you looking for upgrades at all?' he smiled at the check-in clerk. She nodded sagely and began tapping at her keyboard. In fact, she was hitting the shift key over and over again. She knew full well there would be no upgrades today.

'You might want to ask at the gate, sir,' she suggested.

KB turned and joined the queue that was shuffling through Departures and towards the security check. It was a less humiliating send-off than he had imagined. He could pick out the MI6 minders who'd been sent to babysit, to make sure he really was getting on the plane. He presumed they'd have a couple on the flight with him too.

Kazakhstan wasn't a direct commuter hop from Heathrow, after all. There were a few steps in between that might have proved attractive places to disappear.

It wasn't all doom and gloom, the Chief had reminded him as he heard about his punishment posting. The Chief's political muscle fibres were nippier than KB's and he'd managed to negotiate a quiet retirement. For KB, with a few years to run before a pension, an all-out sacking might have been the end of

418

everything. What he got instead was simply an ignominious dressing-down – nothing like the savagery he had anticipated when the PM had stepped into the fray. Sir Michael, who had chaired the enquiry, had remained a gentleman throughout. It paid, KB reasoned, to have friends in high places after all.

'Take it or leave it,' he'd been told over the table. 'A chance to eke out the final years to your pension. In the armpit posting of the century, of course, but I'd say in the circumstances, it's mighty generous.'

KB had to admit it was.

As his Samsonite rolling Tote slid quietly into the X-ray machine, he thought about the bottles of Scotch he would buy in duty-free. He decided to drink one on the flight to Ekaterinburg and another on the subsequent white-knuckle ride to Almaty, Kazakhstan, and the fleapit monitoring station that would be his home for the next four years.

He was still thinking about the booze when he realized his bag had not yet left the machine. The security guard was staring at his monitor, shuttling the belt forward, back, forward, back.

Another guard stepped in and the two men spoke in hushed whispers. They beckoned him through a heavy door and into an airless interview room. When the security guard opened the ergonomic central zipper of his Tote bag, it revealed what KB knew from experience was around half a million dollars' worth of cocaine.

As strong arms gripped his shoulders, he had to smile.

The symmetry of it all tickled him very much.

Seventy-Four

T he legal wrangles were taking longer than the sentence they were supposed to delay. But politics changes everything in human endeavour, and Ben knew his situation was getting worse by the day.

KB had been furloughed and the Chief had manoeuvred himself out of trouble. But his breach of MI6 security, the theft of the ID card – they alone were enough to stick him in jail until the rest of his hair turned grey. The new PM was keen to be seen to be tough on issues of national security. He was being made an example of.

The irony did not escape him.

All prisons were sanctuaries, and, he was sure, all sanctuaries felt like prisons eventually.

He was classified as a vulnerable prisoner, possibly out of spite. Thus he was banged up in his own block, complete with kitchen and gym, with all the other supergrasses and turncoats that the country had produced. He supposed another spy wouldn't hurt their image very much.

A fly in his cell had been bothering him all day. He finished another chapter of *Tinker Tailor* and went to sleep.

The next morning, the fly had a friend.

Coming back from breakfast, there were four.

Then eight.

It was turning into a party.

It wasn't just here, either. Ben had noticed a few kitchen staff quietly swatting away through the swing doors. And a few conversations about the weather had mentioned them too. 'Muggy week ahead,' he'd heard. 'Got two in my bunk last night.'

But the flies kept coming.

Twelve. Twenty. Forty.

By the end of the week the building was a living swarm. The governor had called an emergency meeting. Prisoners were banging on their cells with shoes, cups, fists. Campaigning lawyers demanded action.

The next morning, an extermination team arrived.

A local contractor, the governor had reasoned, was quicker than sourcing something from London. By the time he did that, the flies would have taken over.

Ben sat in his cell and willed himself not to hope.

It was too dangerous.

He heard the sound of footsteps and saw the white industrial smocks of a large-scale extermination crew. They were drilling into walls, floors. Pump-action insecticide.

Then the shouting started.

Guards were screaming. Prisoners too.

'Shut that thing off!'

A problem with the concentration. The chemicals were too strong. Reacting with the air, clouds of vapour were choking the block. An alarm sounded. Evacuate.

Guards ran to cells. Doors opened wide.

The governor made temporary plans. The gymnasium would hold the overflow until the problem was dealt with. A head count was under way even before the rest of the inmates had been taken through.

But some inmates had been taken to the infirmary. Others were still trapped in the building. The head count would take hours and the governor rued the day he'd listened to his career advisor.

The chaos spilled out to the gates. The extermination team vowed to return to their depot to change chemicals. No one noticed that the twenty-person crew contained one additional member, or that only four of the five vehicles signed in and out by prison staff took the same route out as in.

Inside the van, Ben stared speechless as his rescuers took off their protective whites and handed him a change of clothes. Two of them looked to him remarkably like Jamie and Lucy.

'Put these on,' said the one resembling Jamie.

Ben held the clothes for a second, momentarily paralysed.

'It's all right, I've seen it all before,' said the one resembling Lucy.

By the time Ben had his change of clothes fully on, he knew that these weren't doppelgängers at all.

Halfway to Newport, the passengers – now in ramblers' clothes – transferred to a rental car for the short drive to the docks. Jamie and Lucy walked with Ben down to the jetty. The weak sun hit his face and Lucy gently took his hand.

He looked at her face and she smiled and pointed to the end of the jetty. What he saw there took his breath clean away.

Contact Zero

Word came back to England of the death of Doux, or 'Sweet', the double agent sent back to France to continue the work of the late Kit Marlowe. Only a few knew the truth – that Sweet and Marlowe were one and the same.

After his death, his possessions, including the table, were bequeathed to Marcus Burnham, once an agent under Sir Francis Walsingham, then dropped like a stone and pardoned later.

He eventually found work in the library of Corpus Christi College, Cambridge, Marlowe's old college.

It was noted that the older Mr Burnham had never allowed any object to be placed on the old oak table he kept in his rooms. During a fire in the college buttery, Burnham was seen running back to his college set and heaving the top of the table down the stairs, so desperate was he to keep it intact.

The wax surface of the table was not all it seemed. For written into it, through pressure, was every contact, safe house, name and password that Marlowe had established in his two years on the run in France. The majority of his wealth was sent to private bankers under instruction to release funds only to those who could deliver certain words and phrases that Burnham found contained on the table surface.

Burnham made no copy other than his own memory.

And vowed the secret legacy of Marlowe would stay alive.

Seventy-Five

William Tremayne had joined the Secret Intelligence Service on a flight of fanciful innocence – to fight for his country. Too young to battle the Nazis, there had been an ideological brazier burning within him since birth and when he achieved his double starred first at New College, Oxford, his facility with languages and energetic zeal were not lost on the MI6 recruiters.

His expertise quickly became apparent – both a warrior and a diplomat, his skills lay in covert operations in hostile environments. In the Cold War he had been a central asset in the fight against East Germany. On a cold Sunday afternoon, he had been scheduled to meet his handlers, Thomas Newton and Karl Bernard – otherwise known as 'KB'. He knew them by other names, of course. But when the dust had settled on their betrayal, he made it his life's work to find out their true identities – and deliver justice to their door.

For their part, both Newton and KB were at the tail end of a very lucrative period of their lives. The black economy, they had discovered, was as potent a force in East Berlin as it had been in the Second World War. For those in a position to profit, and with the skills and contacts to do so, it was too tempting to turn down.

William Tremayne had suspected both men of private

enterprise, and, with the tacit approval of his station chief, he began compiling a dossier of their skimming operations.

This was why, when Tremayne made the rendezvous that cold October day in 1977, there was no one there to meet him. No one, that is, apart from a cadre of secret police.

When the Stasi took him away, Newton and KB had presumed the man was dead. But fifteen years later, a surveillance photograph of a project in Marrakesh caught KB's attention. Not for the Soviet mole in a clandestine meeting with his Turkish counterpart. It was the man pictured at the back of the room, the man unaware of the secret photograph. To KB, it was William Tremayne. Newton, suddenly finding himself in the line-up for Chief, stayed away from paranoid thoughts. He was dead, he explained. There was no way the man could have escaped, made it back over the Wall and survived all this time.

There was, KB had reminded him, one way.

Contact Zero.

Unfortunately for them, he was right on the money.

For William Tremayne, the years clicked by with steady monotony. He knew even if he showed himself again under a new guise, the bureaucrats would stop him in his tracks. There were no betrayals that went forgiven for those who worked behind the Wall.

He included himself in this analysis, of course.

He managed to sneak into the country from time to time, witnessing his son's school play, the funerals of both his parents, vowing at every stage to avenge himself on the man who had brought him to absolute zero. Only the strength of his will and his love for his son had raised him back above the water line. Love had saved the drowning man.

He knew enough to wait. For hubris, for the fall, there needed to be height. When word of Greco leaked to the network, he knew the time was now. He'd heard of the incident at the airport. And he knew to which Cotswolds hamlet Thomas Newton had removed himself. There was more revenge in the old bird yet, he reasoned.

For now, though, he was saving lives.

Seventy-Six

The boat cost twenty million US dollars, but was probably worth double that. It had been bought in cash and, although registered in Panama, it was effectively untraceable. On board was enough fake paperwork to convince someone it was a Swedish submarine, if need be.

William Tremayne piloted the boat into the Solent, powering out into the Channel. Below, Ben sat in the galley staring into his tea.

The interior was comfortable without being opulent. The money had clearly been spent on other things – mostly black boxes, Ben noted, with flashing lights. On the roof, as he'd boarded, he'd spotted at least three state-of-the-art satellite communications systems.

Jamie and Lucy were busy with maps and charts. They'd only had a few months to get to grips with life at sea. But they were enjoying it. He toasted them again in silent thanks. They nodded in return – *sorry it took us so long*. Ben held Lucy's gaze but could not, for the life of him, decrypt it.

'Command and control,' smiled Ben eventually.

'The hub. A mobile one at that,' barked Tremayne as he came down to join them. He was as vigorous as his son Marcus was self-contained. Marcus nodded from the bank of electronics that lay just off the main deck. There was enough countersurveillance equipment on board to monitor an entire country.

'Who funds all this?'

'You were told about Marlowe, I take it?'

Ben nodded.

'Well, compound interest is a wonderful thing. But we're not trustafarians. We sell our services to the highest corporate bidder – we are contractors, effectively. The most deniable you can get. Our clients are global-risk corporations who generally prefer it that we never existed, and that's the way we like it too. Not that they know they're hiring Contact Zero, of course. To them, we're merely mercenaries. But, as you can see, we're really much more than that.'

'So you sing for your supper?'

'Many of our members prefer to stay in our little nature reserve, others simply live where they desire, taking work when they're asked to. We don't try to impose too much.'

'Fair enough.'

'It's a good arrangement.'

'So where do we fit in?'

'I'm a little tired of travelling the world. I'm looking to settle into the cottage and read some books. I was wondering if the three of you would care to take over for a while? The admin's not too bad. And the views are amazing. Marcus would come too, of course.'

'I'll think about it.'

'A noble plan. Very well. Supper to come. And a night at sea. But I expect you'll stay on the deck. I'll let you finish your tea.'

Ben nodded, remaining seated at the large galley table that seemed far too big and grand to be part of the furniture.

Looking closer, he saw that the entire surface of the table was covered in tiny shapes . . .

Wait.

Not shapes at all, in fact – but writing. The table was

covered in a vast, swirling, minuscule array of the written word. From a distance, you could mistake it for knots in the wood, undulations in the waxed surface. But these were indentations, very much intentional.

As he read, the keystones of Contact Zero, the fossil record of all that had gone before, unfolded for him, rooted him there. He laughed, helpless, his eyes wet, never leaving the living document under his fingertips. The more he read, the more a cog inside him began to turn. This, in time, turned a gear that meshed with another. The bitter filament of anger that once glowed inside began to dissolve, replaced with another sensation. Belonging. For the first time since he'd held John in his arms as he left this world, he felt he mattered. He stepped into the feeling, embraced it, tuned himself in.

He looked up to find Lucy staring at him from the doorway. 'Hello,' she said.

Ben nodded, unsure if he was capable of anything else.

'Would you do me a favour please?' he asked eventually. Lucy nodded. 'Would you slap me, very hard, in the face?'

Lucy considered the request for a moment.

'I can do one better.'

Before he knew what was happening, Lucy grabbed his shoulders and kissed him tenderly on the lips.

'Thanks,' said Ben.

Bill Tremayne was helping Jamie plot a new course on the bridge when Ben and Lucy came to join them. The look on his face told the others: he was staying.

'I have one concern,' said Ben eventually. 'A distributed network of cells . . . around the world . . .'

'You're making a scary comparison.'

'Yes, I am.'

Lucy and Jamie looked at him.

'I think we all are.'

'What troubles you about that?'

'Nothing. It just – isn't there a way to use that? To target them, I mean?'

'A global network to counter a global network? It could work, I suppose. Better than using a sledgehammer to crack a nut. To be honest,' said Bill, 'we're still in our infancy where that sort of thing's concerned.'

'Infancy? The table in the galley tells me this network's been alive for over four hundred years.'

'Early days, as I say.'

Ben, Lucy and Jamie looked at each other blankly.

Bill Tremayne smiled. 'The Chinese Premier, Zhou En Lai, was once asked what he thought about the impact of the French Revolution. He said, "It's too soon to tell." That's how I feel about a lot of things. Everything is possible, with time. That's why I love the sea. We all get where we're going, eventually.'

'Where *are* we going?'

'Too soon to tell.'

'Let me put it another way. Where's next?'

The older man smiled.

'I hear ███████████████ is lovely this time of year.'

Acknowledgements

This book was possible only with the charity, assistance, scholarship, friendship and all round grooviness of many people I hope I remember to include here. Huge thank you to Nick Sayers, Anne Clarke, Emma Longhurst and everyone at Hodder for your enthusiasm and patience for this novel. To Jonny Geller, Ben Hall, Jane Gelfman, Bob Bookman, Chris Simonian – agents extraordinaires – for your counsel and wisdom. To my wonderful girlfriend Gabriela, words fail me at this point and I'm left with only the tip of the iceberg, which is this: I could not have done this without your incredible love, good humour, help, editing and cheerleading in the face of appalling self-inflicted deadlines. Thank you. To my parents Sue and Ray and my brother Mark, his daughter Leiomi and wife Aalmah for their endless love and encouragement . . . thank you. Thanks again to my friends and sounding boards Tess Cuming, Sean and Amber O'Harrow, Sean and Kiley Hanish, Josh and Christine Friedman, Ben Stoll, Mark Evans, Simon Mirren. Thank you to Mike Baker and Nick Day for intelligence and help beyond the call of decency. Marlovian scholar A.D. Wraight's work inspired some fictionalized elements featuring Marlowe, for which I am very grateful. Thank you to *The Economist* for first informing me of Braudel and the 'wisp' concept. Thanks to Peet's Coffee & Tea on Main Street, Santa Monica for refuelling. Most importantly of all, thank you to my readers.

SPECIAL OFFE

Buy official SPOOKS DVDs and get £15 off RRP!

David Wolstencroft is the creator of SPOOKS, the BAFTA award-winning spy drama, produced by Kudos for BBC ONE. We're giving CONTACT ZERO readers the chance to purchase the official DVD box sets of the first three Complete Series of SPOOKS at a bargain price of £24.99 each – that's a saving of £15 off the RRP.

Alternatively, you can buy all three Complete Series DVDs for £49.99.

To take advantage of this fantastic exclusive offer, telephone the SPOOKS Hotline on 0870 129 5039, and quote ref: **CONTACT ZERO**.

P&P is free with the UK and Eire.
Offer ends 16th July 2006.

TERMS AND CONDITIONS: Offer is open until 16th July 2006, and the promoter is Contender Home Entertainment. The offer is subject to availability. The offer enables applicants to purchase a SPOOKS Complete Series DVD at £24.99 (currently available are SPOOKS Complete Series 1 to 3), or all three SPOOKS Complete Series DVDs for £49.99. Contender Home Entertainment reserves the right to withdraw or change this offer without prior notice. Order line is open Monday to Friday 9am to 5pm. Contender Home Entertainment will endeavour to fulfil all orders within ten working days. Offer open only to residents of the UK & Eire. This offer cannot be used in conjunction with any other offer or promotion. This promotion is only open to CONTACT ZERO readers who can quote the ref.

CONTENDER
HOME ENTERTAINMENT

kudos